SEDUCTIVE TEMPTRESS

He followed her. How could he resist? He wanted to touch her so badly his hands were clenching convulsively. "And here I thought we were getting to be friends," he murmured, fascinated by the soft white skin of her neck.

"Friends?" Something flashed behind the darkness in her eyes as she stopped and looked up into his face. "I would have said friendship was the last thing you wanted from me."

"Oh?" He stood close, near enough to smell her sweet scent, near enough to see the pulse at the base of her throat, near enough to set his own pulse beating like the hooves of a galloping horse. "What did you think I wanted of you, Marina?"

She turned, but her movement brought her up so close, she was almost pressing against him. She tilted her face toward his.

"I thought," she whispered, "perhaps this . . ."

Her hands flattened against his chest and her lips touched his. He didn't stop to ask why. Every instinct in him was dazed by her provocative move, and he welcomed her, then quickly took control, his practiced technique smooth and seductive, honed over years at the royal court, moving and probing with a mastery all his own . . .

FEEL THE FIRE IN CAROL FINCH'S ROMANCES!

BELOVED BETRAYAL   (2346, $3.95)

Sabrina Spencer donned a gray wig and veiled hat before blackmailing rugged Ridge Tanner into guiding her to Fort Canby. But the costume soon became her prison—the beauty had fallen head over heels in love!

LOVE'S HIDDEN TREASURE   (2980, $4.50)

Shandra d'Evereux felt her heart throb beneath the stolen map she'd hidden in her bodice when Nolan Elliot swept her out onto the veranda. It was hard to concentrate on her mission with that wily rogue around!

MONTANA MOONFIRE   (3263, $4.95)

Just as debutante Victoria Flemming-Cassidy was about to marry an oh-so-suitable mate, the towering preacher, Dru Sullivan flung her over his shoulder and headed West! Suddenly, Tori realized she had been given the best present for a bride: a night of passion with a real man!

THUNDER'S TENDER TOUCH   (2809, $4.50)

Refined Piper Malone needed bounty-hunter, Vince Logan to recover her swindled inheritance. She thought she could coolly dismiss him after he did the job, but she never counted on the hot flood of desire she felt whenever he was near!

Helen Conrad

STRANGER'S EMBRACE

ZEBRA BOOKS
KENSINGTON PUBLISHING CORP.

ZEBRA BOOKS

are published by

Kensington Publishing Corp.
475 Park Avenue South
New York, NY 10016

First printing: August, 1992

Printed in the United States of America

Chapter One

Marina Crafts stood at the edge of the crumbling cliff, letting the wind tear at her powder-blue cloak, shading her eyes as she looked out over the storm-maddened sea. There was a ship coming into the crescent harbor below. Its white sails were taut before the driving winds, an arrogant salute raised high. As she watched, the salute was lowered and the sails were pulled away, readying the wooden vessel to ride out the winds.

The ship was still too far out to identify, but she knew it was likely to be the *Prospect,* out of Boston, and lately of these California shores, plying its trade and collecting hides and tallow from the *ranchos* and missions along the coast. If so, Captain Brandene would soon come to call, and that would be pleasant, if unexciting.

Excitement. Was that what she wanted? Was that the nameless thing she longed for? Impatiently, she scuffed her calfskin shoe against the fossiliferous sandstone, heedless of the bits and pieces of history she crushed beneath her heel. A gust of wind jerked her hood back, and she let it fly, enjoying the fierce pull of the storm as it tossed her chestnut hair out in a bright flag behind her.

Another blast from the wind and the sun was suddenly revealed, finding a break through which to pour its dazzling power. Its rays lit the golden highlights in Marina's tumbled mane and warmed the cream-colored skin of her fine-boned face. But her gray eyes still mirrored the surface of the troubled seas, both in color and in the emotion they shared.

Something was wrong. Some vague, persistent worm had slithered in, slyly, surely, corrupting Marina's peace of mind. If only she could grasp it, bring it out to squirm in the bright light of day, then she would be able to deal with it, dispense with it, and go on. But so far it had eluded her searching mind, and she wondered uneasily if she might be going a little mad.

She drew her cloak in about her and began to turn away, looking back out over the sea searching for one last sight of the storm-tossed ship. There was another ship now, joining the *Prospect* in the harbor. As she looked out, the sun broke through the clouds again, and suddenly a golden shaft of sunlight shot down over the ocean, spilling its shimmering light down upon the second ship, lighting it with a heavenly glow that made Marina gasp with wonder.

She stayed where she was, mesmerized, watching as those sails also were lowered and the anchor weighed. The second ship flew Mexican colors. More soldiers for the Presidio, no doubt. They came and went with boring regularity, a dull lot, most of them. But now and then a handsome officer would find his way to this outpost. One could always hope.

A flash of light from on board the second ship caught her attention, and she frowned, wondering what it was. The flash came again, and realization struck her. Someone was looking through a spyglass at the shore. Whenever the sun broke through, the reflection was what she saw. And then realization dawned further. With a strange certainty, she knew the man who was looking—and she had no doubt it was a man—was looking at her.

A thrill shot through her, making her breath come quickly in her throat. He was looking at her, and yet he was much too far away to be of any danger to her. She twisted the large silver ring on her right hand. Shaped like a unicorn's head, it was meant to bring her luck, and she twisted it whenever she needed some, or was about to do something new and uncertain.

Slowly, her chin rose. She let go of her cloak, letting it sail behind her again, standing tall and proud, letting the wind plaster her light skirt against her legs so that her form was well defined. And then she smiled, her eyes laughing, and waved to the mystery man with the glass.

But her saucy spirit lasted only a moment. It was late and she had to get back before she was missed. Turning with a last laugh, she began to run down the path toward town. Her foot slipped and she crashed into a manzanita bush, scratching her shoulder badly, but she hardly felt a thing, and in less than a moment she was up again and running toward home.

Sebastian de la Cruz frowned and took the glass away from his eye. Leaning his tall, elegantly uniformed body out over the rail of the ship, he gazed inland at the cliff near the beach, trying to catch a glimpse of the figure he'd just lost sight of. A shorter, stockier officer joined him.

"What are you looking at, *mi amigo?*"

"A vision." Sebastian sighed. "A goddess." He grimaced. "A mirage, I'm sure. She's disappeared now."

Tomas Bata rubbed his hands together. "Just a harbinger of what we'll find once we get to shore," he opined optimistically, his black eyes sparkling with dreams of orgies to come.

Sebastian looked at his friend and couldn't help but be amused. "I doubt it. This rough backwater will be singularly lacking in feminine grace, of that I can assure you."

Tomas shrugged. "Grace I can live without. Females — well, that's another matter. Do you know how long it's been since we sailed from Mexico?"

"Too long," Sebastian agreed, but his eyes were already glazed over and his mind was not on romantic conquests. "Too long," he repeated softly, staring at the rough coast which would be his home for at least the next year. If he looked back behind the harbor and the town, he could see mountains dried a golden brown, so like those of his native Spain. But this was not Spain. This was Alta California, and he, Sebastian de la Cruz, once a guest at the court of King Carlos of Spain, was condemned to stay here, as much a prisoner as any lost soul in the most hellish pit of a jail this world had to offer.

Bitter anger burned in him, turning his handsome face as hard and cold as stone. Somehow, he vowed silently, and not for the first time, he would find a way to make this pay off for him. He couldn't bear to think this entire year would be wasted. One way or another, he had to come out ahead. No matter who got hurt in the process.

Marina walked steadily down the grassy bank of the stream until she found a place hidden from general view by tall ferns and sycamore trees. Sure that she would be undisturbed there, she sank down near the water and began to remove her leather shoes and cotton stockings. The storm had passed as quickly as she

8

had predicted, and now the afternoon was getting hot and she was tired. She'd accompanied her cousin Carmen, as she often did on Wednesdays, to the mission and then to a visit to Carmen's father.

These visits were always difficult. Juan Ortega was a lost man. Years ago he had been a soldier, handsome and strong, and he'd married Marina's aunt with every expectation of making a good life for the two of them. But Carmen's mother had died a day after giving birth, and Juan had lost the will to live. Carmen had been sent to live with Marina, and Juan had been slowly trying to drink himself to death ever since. He lived among the dregs of San Feliz society, with court-martialed military men and sailors who'd jumped ship and the women who'd made their way here from Mexico to take a coin or two from the soldiers.

Carmen certainly couldn't make the trip here by herself, much as she claimed she could every week. Marina came along to El Camino de Los Osos because she had to. It was a part of town she might never have seen if it weren't for Carmen. As it was, she'd seen it often enough to have grown blasé about the half-dressed women who sold their bodies to make their living, and bleary-eyed men who staggered about the dirty section. Usually she went into the rickety shack with Carmen and endured Carmen's lectures to her father on ways he might reclaim his life, lectures he ignored with casual unconcern, while pouring himself yet another drink. But today she'd balked, unable to face another lecture, wanting to be alone for a few moments.

She sighed with pleasure as her feet touched the cold water of the stream. Pulling back her full skirts to keep them from getting wet, she dangled her legs in as far as she dared, and enjoyed the rush of the silvery water. Her shoulder hurt where the branch had scratched it earlier that day. She grimaced, then had a thought.

9

The water that felt so good on her feet might feel good on the scratch as well.

Without hesitation she began to unbutton her bodice to bare the shoulder. She had a good half hour, she reasoned. A half hour to be all by herself and do whatever pleased her. It was like a gift on a day when her head ached and her spirit seemed to sag. And she meant to make the most of it.

The Spaniard looked around the dusty yard of the Presidio from the vantage aback his lively California pony. Quite a few of the soldiers' families lived within the Presidio walls in small hutlike houses not much bigger than the cell he'd found he was to occupy. The place reminded him of a medieval castle. The scene was depressing.

But it didn't seem to bother Tomas, who rode beside him, rattling on and on with his hopeful dreams.

"I tell you, I have it from the best of sources. California girls are the most beautiful, the most obliging, and the least inhibited in all of Mexico. I swear it must be true. These things are legendary among the men who have served here."

The truth behind the legends remained to be seen, but Sebastian, ever the cynic, held out little hope. Judging from the women he had seen inside the Presidio walls, the outlook was dim for finding the beautiful girls Tomas had been dreaming about since their ship had first weighed anchor at San Blas.

They turned their horses out through the gate and left military territory behind. At first glance, Sebastian had to admit the area had a certain charm. One-story houses dotted the landscape, their roofs made of thatch or covered with red clay tiles. Flowers spilled from windows and over fences, trees pushed their young, straight limbs toward the sky. Everywhere there was color: golden hills, dark green trees, red tile roofs, soft adobe-brown houses, bright scarlet and pink flowers. The colors were vivid, assaulting the senses through an exquisite atmosphere which seemed clear as crystal.

But these visual effects were lost on Tomas. He had seen a group of fair maidens ahead, and his attention had been claimed. Spurring his horse, he came alongside them quickly, then pulled the huge beast to a stop.

"Hola, California beauties," he called, taking off his hat and waving it in a broad salute. "And where are you going this lovely day?"

The objects of his cordiality were three Indian girls in mission uniform. Three pairs of eyes turned toward him in wide surprise. Three hands shot up to cover three grins, three heads were lowered, three pairs of legs went into action, and the girls disappeared, giggling, into the nearest yard.

"My dear friend," Sebastian drawled as he came up to where Tomas was waiting, his dark face furled in a crestfallen frown. "Your technique leaves a lot to be desired. The object is to entice, not to terrify."

Tomas gave an expansive shrug. "I've only just begun. I'm a little out of practice and it may take a few attempts before I reach my peak. Surely I may be allowed a few rehearsals."

Sebastian laughed. "Of course, but I must say, I think your basic premise is all wrong. A woman must be approached with an air of dignity and respect. An added dash of mystery to excite the imagination is also helpful."

Tomas pulled a long face and nodded solemnly. "I can see that I have a lot to learn. You must be an expert on women."

His face cleared. "But wait, I heard the best place to

11

go — El Camino de los Osos, where the cantinas are, where the women are. When we get there, we'll try your method against mine and see who wins the contest. Agreed?"

The street they sought was instantly recognizable. Instead of the neat adobes of the rest of the town, houses were mere shacks, unpainted and dirty. Guitars and singing were heard up and down the way. Here a man lay, drunk and sleeping, on the side of the road. There another leaned against a building, looking sick and unwanted. In one window, women dressed only in corsets or camisoles leaned out and called to the two men.

Tomas called back, grinning. "This is more like it," he said happily.

A woman stepped out into the street and smiled at them. Her lips and eyes were heavily painted and she held her skirts high, pretending to keep them from the mud, but obviously exaggerating the move in order to show off as much as she dared of her legs with their shiny silk stockings.

"Greetings, Lieutenant," she said, reaching out to stop the horse and directing her welcome to Sebastian. Her bodice was cut so low, her breasts nearly spilled out when she bent forward. "My name is Juanita. You must be new in town and in search of a drink."

Sebastian nodded, his eyes narrowed and waiting. She smiled, her eyes glinting with admiration for the figure he cut.

"Come with me, then. I have a private room where you may rest between bouts with the bottle. I promise to take the best of care of you and your friend." She touched his leg suggestively. "Come with me."

Sebastian gazed down into her hard face. The mouth managed to turn down at the corners, despite the smile. A feeling of revulsion shook him.

"No thank you, *Señorita*," he said shortly. "I believe I'll tour the town a bit first."

Tomas gasped, uncomprehending. "Are you crazy?" he hissed, sliding down from his horse. "This is exactly what we've been looking for, and you want to turn her down? Some teacher you are! If this is your method, I think I'll stick to my own."

He grinned at the woman, bowing before her. "Look at her," he cried. "She's a California beauty if ever I saw one. I'd love to accept your kind offer, *Señorita*. Lead the way."

Juanita looked from one man to the other, then shrugged as Sebastian saluted them both and started off. He continued down the street, Tomas's laughter ringing in his ears, and he wondered himself if he were crazy.

"It isn't as though you're only used to lying with ti-tled ladies," he chided himself silently. "You've never been squeamish before."

But this time he was. There were plenty of women on the street, many openly hawking their wares, but not one appealed to him. Perhaps he was sick, he thought uneasily. Perhaps the long sea journey had done permanent damage of some sort.

He slipped down from his horse and tied it to a post beside a likely-looking tavern, then stood, uncharac-teristically uncertain. He could hear the sounds of laughter and shouts of comradeship from inside the little building, but those things didn't seem to draw him either.

And that was when he noticed the flash of a white cotton skirt and chestnut hair disappear into the trees near the stream. Something about the bare glimpses he'd caught reminded him of the vision on the cliff. He hesitated only a moment longer before deciding to in-vestigate.

13

First making sure his horse was secure, he found his way to the slope, then walked down toward the stream. He stepped carefully, silently, and so had a chance to watch Marina for a long moment before she knew he was there. What he saw made him smile, for he had immediate confirmation that there was nothing wrong with his libido after all.

It was the girl from the cliff. Her skirt was hiked up above her knees, showing off her slender legs and shapely feet, the toes pink from the icy stream. Her rich hair tumbled down her back, catching golden highlights from the dappled sunshine that came through the trees. Her pretty face was frowning in concentration as she examined her shoulder. The bodice of her dress was open, exposing a swell of white breast along with a lovely collarbone. She was altogether the most enchanting sight he'd ever seen.

Two factors were at work in what happened next. In the first place, he'd found her just off El Camino de Los Osos, and from all evidence he'd seen, every woman on that street was a whore. Second, he'd been raised as the eldest son of a major landowner in a feudal system and he was used to having the right to pretty much pick and choose among the daughters of his father's serfs whenever the mood took him. So it was with complete confidence and no sense of transgression — and no memory of the good advice he'd given Tomas — that he approached Marina.

"Hello, lovely one," he said softly as he came up beside her.

Her head jerked up and she gazed at him, her mouth open in surprise, almost blinded by the way the sun haloed around him, the way the brass buttons of his uniform glowed in the light. She'd never seen the man before, and he was dazzling, larger and more elegant than anything she'd grown accustomed to in this provincial town. For just a moment, she thought she might be dreaming.

Sebastian dropped on one knee beside her, his mouth turned only slightly into a smile. He was used to making an impression on females.

"If your talents equal your beauty," he said, his voice low and husky as he reached out to touch her, "I must prepare to die of ecstasy tonight."

Marina stared up at him, still stunned. Everyone in town knew who she was. No man had ever dared to approach her this way before. For just a moment, she couldn't move, couldn't speak. This was a situation she'd never experienced, had never expected to experience.

"Lovely one," he murmured again as his large hand pushed back her bodice to reveal her soft white breast, its curve full and inviting, its nipple pink and tugged high and tight in the cool air. His gaze fell on the sight and his fingers tightened on the edge of the bodice. He drew in his breath sharply, as though he'd been hit in the stomach with something hard and heavy, and he reached for the nipple.

"Take me quickly, beauty, right here by the river," he muttered, desire making his voice low and rough, "and I'll pay you double what you usually get." His fingers closed on her nipple, pulling it out, as he bent to take it in his mouth.

Sensations the likes of which she'd never imagined shot through Marina's system, finally bringing her to life.

"Oh!" she cried in outraged anger. Using both hands, she pushed at him with all her might. "You bastard!" she cried. "You . . . you stupid one!"

Sebastian blinked in surprise, grabbing her wrists to hold her there. "Wait," he said, annoyed. "I'll pay you well. Don't worry about the money."

15

"Money!" She yanked at her hands, pulling them free from his grasp and trying to scramble out of his reach. "Don't touch me, you . . . you . . . !"

He took hold of her hair, twisting it around his hand so that she couldn't escape.

"Look," he said, using his free hand to reach for his coin purse. "Look here." With a cock of his wrist, he sent gold coins flying onto the grassy slope. "More than you've ever seen in one place before, I'll wager."

His sneering tone was almost worse than his grip on her. Fury filled her with an energy she'd never known before. Struggling to her feet, she ripped away from him, heedless of the pain where her hair pulled, and she whirled, trying to run.

But he was too fast for her, and she felt him grab her from behind, felt his hand slip in beneath the heavy fabric of her bodice and take hold of her breast, his grip hard, his skin rasping, and she screamed out, "Leave me alone, you filthy bastard son of a dog! I'm not a whore. I'm a virgin!"

And at the same time, she spun in his arms, lashing out at his face with the back of her hand, and she could feel her ring connecting hard, and suddenly he'd released her, his own hand going to his face, and she thought she saw blood, but she was racing for the street, racing out of his clutches, and she wasn't sure.

She clattered up the back steps into the shack where Juan Ortega spent his days, clutching her bodice closed with one hand, holding her skirts with the other. Just before she stepped through the doorway she looked back. There was no one behind her. Still, she rushed the door closed and leaned on it, breathing heavily.

"Dear God, cousin!" Carmen rose from the table where she sat with her father. "What's happened?"

Marina stared at her and the words didn't come. She

16

shared everything with Carmen, always. But this was different. The look in the man's face when he'd reached to touch her . . . it stirred things in her she'd never felt before, and how could she explain what she couldn't understand?

"Nothing," she stammered, in answer to Carmen's concern. She saw her cousin's glance go to her bare feet and she swallowed. "I . . . I was washing in the stream and a sound frightened me," she said weakly. "I thought it might be a bear."

Carmen's face went completely blank, as it did when she was thinking things she didn't want others to read in her expression.

"A bear," she repeated softly, her glance going to the open bodice that Marina was fumbling to button together again. No one had seen bears in this area for fifteen years at least. But no matter. "I'll just run down to the stream and get your shoes and stockings," she offered.

"No!" Marina put up a hand to stop her. "No Carmen, don't go down there."

Carmen frowned. "All right," she said slowly. "We'll send a boy down to get them."

Marina opened her mouth to object again, but then closed it without saying a word. If she put up too much of a fight, people would begin to wonder what was going on. So she nodded instead, and Carmen, after another curious glance at her cousin, called to Chico, a little boy who lived in the house and had a reputation for being the best pickpocket in town, and gave him instructions.

"Come sit down. I'll get you something to drink." Carmen led Marina to the table opposite her father. Juan Ortega nodded at her absently, his dull eyes hardly comprehending anything that was going on, but Marina was used to that.

17

"Good afternoon, Tio," she said politely. "How are you today?"

He smiled at her wistfully. "Alive," he grated out as though he regretted it.

Carmen sank down beside him and took his hand. "He's promised to come for dinner on Sunday. Haven't you, Papa?"

The man nodded, though Marina wasn't sure he knew what his daughter was talking about. Carmen chattered on, but Marina hardly listened. Her mind kept going over what had just happened by the stream. She could hardly believe it could have been real.

The boy was back in no time with her things. She jumped up and met him at the door.

"Here you are, *Señorita,*" he said, putting her shoes and stockings on the floor beside her.

"Thank you, Chico," she replied, wishing she had something to give him for his trouble.

"And here," he added, holding out a clenched fist.

"What is it?" She put her open hand under his little fist, ready to take whatever he had there.

"These." His fingers uncurled and a shower of five round gold coins fell into her hand.

"Oh!" She closed her hand around them quickly and looked up to see if Carmen had noticed, but her cousin was busy talking earnestly to her father and hadn't seen a thing.

Marina's cheeks went scarlet. She pushed her hand quickly into the pocket of her skirt and let the coins slide down inside. Remembering a *dulce* she had wrapped in paper in her other pocket, she reached for it and gave the small piece of candy to the boy. "Here you are, Chico," she said. "Thank you."

His eyes grew round. It was obvious there hadn't been much candy in his life. *"Muchas gracias, Señorita,"* he cried, backing away with his prize.

18

Marina turned back to the others, her heart beating very fast. The gold coins burned like fire against her leg. She wanted nothing so much as to go home and get into her own bed so that she would be alone and free to try to make sense out of what had happened this afternoon.

Turning away from the others, she pressed her hand to her breast, trying to erase the terrifying sensations the officer had left there. To have a man touch her that way — she'd never even imagined such a thing. To feel those feelings — was that what it was like when men and women . . . ? No, she wouldn't think about that. She would clear her mind.

But try as she might, the thoughts wouldn't go away. Every time she tried to think a rational thought, the lieutenant's wild, hungry look filled her mind, and her breath came short again. A part of her wished she'd never seen it, and another part wanted to see it again.

Chapter Two

Marina raised her large gray eyes from her embroidery to steal a glance at Carmen. Just as she'd thought — Carmen hadn't sewn a stitch. Her chin was in one hand while the other played absently with her jet black hair, which hung free about her shoulders.

"Carmen, tell me true," Marina chanted, repeating an old rhyme they'd used since they were children. "What in the world is bothering you?"

Carmen looked up warily, then her irrepressible smile broke through. "It's a secret," she said, unnecessarily, for half of what they told one another could be classified as such. "You've seen the two new lieutenants at the Presidio?"

Marina hesitated, fighting the flush she could feel beginning to fill her cheeks.

"One is jolly, but not much else," Carmen went on. "But the other . . ." Her eyes glazed. "Have you seen him? Sebastian de la Cruz is his name. He's magnificent. His carriage is noble, his uniform exquisite, and his speech . . . have you heard it? He's a Spaniard, and from a wealthy family. I'm sure of it." Carmen tossed her head. "I'm considering falling in love with him."

Marina choked back her first inclination to cry out against any such idea. She smoothed her red satin skirt over her many petticoats and looked back down at the sash she was working. It had been two days since she'd met the man who she was sure was this very same Spanish lieutenant near the stream, and still the memory of his intensity shocked her.

"Don't be ridiculous," she said a bit breathlessly. "He looks arrogant and horrible to me." She looked up at her cousin. "What do you want with him, anyway? You have half the men in town in love with you."

"Yes, and each is poorer than the next."

"But Carmen . . ."

"Don't you see?" Carmen's face was set with conviction. "I swear I will find a path out of this backwater town. The Spaniard might be the way."

Marina stared at her cousin. Carmen was always coming out with the most outrageous things. Usually, Marina just laughed. But today the things Carmen was saying seemed to strike a chord within her as well. Instead of scoffing, she felt interest grow.

The Spaniard was the cause. She still had the gold coins, though she'd tucked them carefully into a handkerchief and placed them in the trunk in her room. Somehow she had to make sure they got back to their owner. She didn't want the filthy things. But how was she to get them back to him without having to face him again? And that she couldn't do—could she?

Carmen thought he might be wealthy. He certainly seemed to throw his money around, by the evidence she'd seen. Still, there were other factors to consider.

"But . . . Carmen, why would a rich Spaniard have remained with the Mexican Army after the Independence unless for some reason he was unable to go home and claim his wealth?"

Carmen frowned. "Yes, there is that. I will have to do some investigating."

Marina went on, her brow creased with thought. "If

21

he is from a wealthy family, he is probably betrothed, or even married. In either case, he couldn't marry you."

Carmen looked up and laughed aloud. "My poor little innocent. There are other ways of using a man besides marrying him."

"Carmen!" Marina's hand went to her throat. There was a pulse beating there that she'd never noticed before. The man's hand had cupped her breast. His fingers had tugged at her nipple. Just thinking about it made her feel hot and strange. No one had ever touched her that way before. The pressure of his fingers, the heat of his palm, seemed to be there all the time now. No matter how she tried, she couldn't erase the feeling.

Carmen went on, not noticing how the conversation was affecting her cousin. "Oh, I know if I were to stay in California, marrying is the only way to get all that I want. But if I can't have that, a ticket to Europe would suit me. I have heard of women in Paris and London who live like queens without husbands."

Marina's fingers were tingling. "And you could be that kind of woman?" she asked breathlessly, more in wonder than in shock.

Carmen sighed. "No, Marina, I only meant to say that there are other things I would rather do with my life than to marry a local *vaquero* and bear him a child every year. There are other ways to live, and I mean to find them. Now." She rose and smoothed her long skirt. "I'm off."

Marina blinked. "Off? Where are you going?"

"To see Father Pedro at the mission. He's such an old gossip, if anyone knows the truth about the Spanish lieutenant, it will be him."

Marina sat very still, listening to Carmen leave. A part of her was tugging, wanting to go out, too. Life was out there. She felt it in a way she'd never done before. The world outside her door was pulsing with action and emotion, and here she was hiding out in this cave of a house. It was safe here. But not very exciting.

So Sebastian de la Cruz was his name. She dropped the embroidery and stared at the whitewashed wall. She wished he'd never come to Alta California. The man was trouble, pure and simple. Carmen had to be headed off. Everyone knew she was a fuse waiting to be lit.

The front door banged and Marina turned quickly, hoping that Carmen had returned, but found instead Tía Josefa, her mother's oldest sister who ran the house. Tía Josefa was red-faced and panting. She threw her ample form down into a chair and lay back her head.

"Marina, Marina, those girls are so stupid. Year after year we make soap and every year it is the same. They can't remember anything from one year to the next. Every year I must show them, every move they make. I have to tell them, 'Yes, do this' and 'No, don't do that' until I am so tired I'm afraid I will drop. Please, *niña,* call the girl to fetch me a cool drink."

Marina did as she was asked, then returned to wave a fan over her aunt's perspiring face.

"Tía, you mustn't get so excited. How can you expect the girls to remember how to make soap when they are usually a new group of girls each year? Except for Jose and Maria, you know we have never been able to keep a servant longer than six months. Being a servant in this house is not nearly so exciting as you think."

"Flighty girls." Josefa snorted. "After all their mission training, you would think they would be glad to work for a decent family. Instead, they run off with the first *vaquero* that winks an eye, or worse, they run back to their heathen tribes in the mountains. What's to be done?"

Marina smiled and patted her aunt affectionately. "The same as we have always done. Treat them well while they are here, and if they leave, find replacements."

Josefa straightened and looked about the room. "Speaking of flighty girls, where is Carmen?"

Marina turned away. "She . . . went to see the priest."

"What? All alone on the street? What am I to do with that girl? Do you know they are talking about her already?"

Marina flopped down into her chair and took up her embroidery. "A lot of gossip. Who listens to those old tattlers?"

"You know as well as I do what happens to girls who are too loose. They start out, like our Carmen, because they're bored and discontented. A little flirting here, a little flirting there, then one day they find they have provoked a man a little too far, and there is no turning back."

Marina laughed at her aunt's woeful expression. "No turning back," she echoed with pretended horror. "Oh Tía, no!"

Josefa took a half-hearted swat at her charge. "You may laugh, *niña,* but it's true. There's a dark side to men you are too innocent to know about."

Marina sobered, suddenly remembering the Spanish lieutenant's green eyes.

Josefa rattled on. "No turning back, I say, and then what is there left? A job in the *cantina,* perhaps. And who knows? The Comandante may decide to enforce the laws as an example to others, and that could mean a firing squad for the two of them."

24

"Oh, Tía."

"Oh yes! There have not been many such of late, but in the early days, before you were born, we often saw sinners executed. It could happen again. The laws are there."

Marina threw down her sash. "Well, the laws may be there, but they will never be applied to Carmen. She is a bit careless, and even a bit restless, but she is not bad, so you and all the talkers needn't worry."

"Worry . . . hah! That's all I ever do. And now . . . have you heard? These two new lieutenants at the Presidio." She threw up her hands. "It's enough to turn your hair gray overnight."

Marina rose and paced to the window. Why did she get that quiver of dread every time he was mentioned? Nervously, she twisted the silver ring on her finger and kept very quiet, hoping Josefa would think of something new to chatter about.

"They've sent every woman in town into a tizzy. They act too bold, talking to young girls right on the street . . . did you know they terrified Antonia Cota's Indian girls the other day? Had them running through yards to get away. And half the women in town seem to be taken with the Spanish one. Gloria Estancia says she's already in love with him."

Marina snorted. "Gloria is in love with anything in pants," she said scathingly. "She can't even know the man yet."

Josefa shrugged. "She claims she'll marry him by summer. You know, they say he's so handsome." She harrumphed. "Well, he might have been handsome once, but with that awful scar on his face, how is one to know?"

Marina's heart went cold within her. "Scar?" She turned to face her aunt. "I . . . what scar?"

Josefa grimaced. "Haven't you seen him? A dueling

wound, so they say. Quite hideous, and it looks very recent. The sword made a long slash right across his cheek."

Marina gasped, her hand to her throat. The memory of what had happened by the stream was vivid once again. She felt the contact of her hand with his face, how he'd recoiled. She'd known her ring had hit him, but she'd had no idea it had done any permanent damage. The thought sickened her.

Josefa frowned at her extreme reaction. "Don't worry about the man," she said gruffly. "I'm sure he deserved whatever he got."

Marina looked down at her ring. Her hands were shaking. Could it possibly be . . . ?

"Hush now," Josefa said quickly as the front door opened again. "Here comes your father. Don't upset him with this business of the new lieutenants. He's already troubled with something, I don't know what."

James Crafts walked in favoring one leg to a degree that slowed his progress considerably. He was a tall man, gray-haired and distinguished, with a vague look befitting a dreamer rather than an activist. Having come to California from Boston years before, he had taken on Mexican citizenship right away. His young wife had died within the year, leaving him with a baby boy, Marina's brother Jonathan. Not long after, he married into a California family. Now he was considered a part of the establishment in the little town of San Feliz. In Californian terms, he was an old-timer.

Marina ran forward to help her father into his chair. He smiled fondly upon her, then changed to a more serious expression. "Where is Carmen?"

"She went to see the priest," Marina answered quickly before Josefa could begin a more extended explanation.

James Crafts frowned. "I should wait to tell you of

this when we are all assembled."

His tone frightened her. "What is it, Papa? What has happened?"

Her father turned toward her with a troubled gaze. "Bad news, I'm afraid. It first arrived with the ship the other day, but I didn't want to worry you with it until I was sure. Now, I've talked to some men lately from Boston, and I am certain."

He hesitated once again. Marina went down on her knees before his chair and grasped his hand in hers. The warmth between the two of them was strong. Marina would do anything he asked if she were sure it would make him happy.

"Papa. Tell me."

He nodded slowly. "Here it is, in a nutshell. All my wise planning for my children's future has come to nothing. Every cent I invested in New England has been swept away. Wiped out."

He shook his head, his puzzled gaze flitting about the adobe walls. "I don't know how it happened. It was all done on the best advice . . . the soundest, I thought."

So that was all it was. Marina could see that he was greatly upset and that worried her, but she couldn't feel any special regret about the money. There had always been enough money to get by, but never an abundance. That some special investment abroad had been lost seemed a remote tragedy to her.

"We still have the land," she reminded him.

He smiled at her sadly, his eyes still haunted by bewilderment. "Yes. There is the land, though it does us little good at present, other than enhancing our status. And there is still a special savings of your mother's, something she set aside as a modest portion for your marriage, Marina. But there is nothing for Carmen or for your brother Jonathan. I'm afraid we are going to

27

have to send for him. I can't afford to keep him at his studies in Boston any longer."

Marina's heart leapt. It would be wonderful to see Jonathan again. But quickly she sobered, knowing it would be a sacrifice for him to give up his law studies.

"If Jonathan returns, we can put the land to better use. In the meantime . . ." His brave smile touched her. "I have thought about this for some time, and I have a plan. I will offer my services to the Comandante or to the Alcalde, as secretary, should either of them require one."

Marina bit her lip. "But Papa, that wouldn't pay much. Besides, it has been so long since the soldiers were paid, everyone says they're on the verge of mutiny. You might never get any money at all."

"I will have to take that chance. What else can I do?"

Tía Josefa had been uncharacteristically quiet during this entire exchange, and now she finally found her tongue. "Worry, worry, worry. You people are the saddest worry warts. Go to the Alcalde, James, and be his secretary. It will at least keep you busy and make you feel you are accomplishing something. I, meanwhile, will make soap. I have preparations made, the lime is ready, it will be easy to obtain more tallow. If I can somehow manage to wring a few days work out of those useless girls, I will have enough to sell for a nice profit. That will keep us alive for a few months at least. And then . . ." She shrugged expansively. "Our cares will be over, anyway."

Father and daughter stared at her. "What do you mean?"

"Tsk." She smiled slyly. "We all know Don Felipe Diaz will soon be asking for Marina's hand. And then we will all be rich."

James stared at her in amazement. "Imagine that," he murmured.

Marina's cheeks flushed scarlet as she remonstrated with her aunt. "Tía, he hasn't asked anything yet."

Josefa threw up her hands. "No, of course not. Don Felipe Diaz is not to be hurried. I am sure he has never done anything quickly, at least not while off his horse. But everyone knows what is in his heart. And . . ." She winked openly, "in yours, *querida*."

"Tía!" Marina was shocked, confused. She knew very well which way the wind was blowing with Felipe. How could she miss it? He'd made it clear enough. And she'd been pleased. But not excited.

She hadn't known until very lately that she even wanted excitement. The concept hadn't entered her mind until it had been put there. And now, instead of beaming and looking forward to Felipe asking for her hand in marriage, she wanted to shut it from her mind. Instead of a foregone conclusion, it was a decision she would no doubt have to make.

Josefa chuckled. "Don't worry, child. I only speak this way here, among our family. Oh, but I've been thinking about it for a long time. It's true we have always lived quite comfortably, but just imagine how it will be once Don Felipe takes this family under his wing."

James looked at his daughter, a frown between his bushy brows. "Well, Marina, I had noticed a marked attention there, but I had no idea . . . Tell me, do you love him? Do you wish to marry him?"

Marina looked from Josefa to her father and back again. It was a time of crisis. They would all have to pitch in. Her father would put aside his pride and go to work for the Alcalde. Jonathan would have to give up his studies and come home to begin ranching. Josefa would make soap. Even Carmen had plans to take the burden of her care off the Crafts family's hands. Marina must do her part. What was she willing to sacrifice for the good of them all? Was it this? Would she marry Don Felipe?

"I . . . I think so," she whispered.

James sighed. "That does set my mind at ease," he admitted. "I know you will be well provided for in the Diaz family. Josefa goes a bit far in saying it will resolve all our difficulties. We must still care for ourselves. But it will certainly be a vast relief. Now I have only Jonathan and Carmen to worry about."

Josefa rose. "No more worrying. Sometimes I think you enjoy it, you do so much of it. So earnest, you two. Come, let's go in to supper. We will see what a mess Maria has made of it without my help."

Marina followed them slowly, her heart beating quickly. Just days ago, seeing Felipe had always seemed a pleasant prospect whenever she had thought of it. Why did it suddenly seem like a trap?

"Come along, Marina," Tía Josefa called to her. "We'll begin without Carmen. As usual."

Marina glanced out the barred window, wondering what Carmen was finding out, wondering where the Spanish lieutenant was right now. Her skin was tingling and her breath was coming just a bit faster than usual. Tonight at the plaza, perhaps she would see for herself this "dueling scar." The thought sent her heart skipping even more quickly.

Chapter Three

The plaza was alive with the sound of guitars and laughter. Groups of young girls circled the dirt walk, talking softly, laughing excitedly, surveying with careful eyes the young men still mounted on their horses. The horsemen called to one another in casual banter.

The two groups, male and female, said not a word to one another. But their eyes spoke volumes, and the songs the young men sang told even more.

Marina felt her own excitement stir as she and Carmen approached the square, Tía Josefa close behind. Spring evenings at the plaza were almost as enjoyable as attending a *baile* or a *fandango*. The time spent at the plaza was much shorter, and contact with the opposite sex much more restricted, but in these restraints lay a large measure of the appeal. The continuous effort to bend the rules to their limits without getting caught was half the fun.

Carmen's head was on a swivel as they walked on, stopping here and there to say a word to people they knew. Marina knew she was looking for the Spanish lieutenant. She found her own gaze straying about the lawn more than once.

"There he is," Tía Josefa cried, squeezing Marina's arm. "Don Felipe — over there, by the oak. Let's walk that way, shall we?"

Felipe Diaz sat tall in the saddle. His broad, handsome face held eyes which always looked slightly sleepy. His ebony hair was pulled into a queue at the back of his head and covered with a black silk handkerchief which bound his head tightly. Over this a low-crowned black hat was cocked at a dashing angle. His short purple velvet jacket was decorated with lovely silver buttons, as were the side seams of his breeches.

In his arms he held a guitar, and as the women approached, he tilted back his head to gaze at Marina. The other men quieted around him and he began to sing, strumming the instrument in his arms softly, a song about a dove who had lost her mate.

Josefa stopped their little group not far away so that they could enjoy the song. Setting her fan to her cheek, she smiled her satisfaction, happily looking around at the other matronly women who she was sure were gazing back in envy. Marina kept her back carefully to where Felipe sat on his horse, but Carmen watched him with unabashed amusement.

"Isn't he wonderful?" she whispered sardonically to Marina. "The best horseman of the entire region, isn't he? And so much besides. Why, the man dances with the grace of a stallion, fights with the courage of a bull, sings with the voice of an angel. Who could ask for anything more?"

"Exactly," Tía Josefa chimed in, completely missing the irony in Carmen's tone. "Oh, he is perfect," she added before turning to greet an old friend.

Marina glared at Carmen. "At least we know where he comes from and who his family is," she hissed at her cousin. "At least he's not some stranger with danger in his eyes."

"Danger in his eyes," Carmen repeated, looking at Marina curiously. "You've seen him, then?"

Marina hesitated, then nodded reluctantly. "Did you find out anything new about him from Father Pedro?"

"No, not really. Only that everyone is suspicious of him, since he is a Spaniard. It's not likely that he will have a very good time here in our town. His Spanish arrogance doesn't sit well."

Felipe had finished his song and Marina turned to acknowledge it with a shy smile in his direction. His hand moved to salute her and he began a loud gypsy song that the others around him joined in with.

"What was that?" Carmen gripped Marina's arm, glancing quickly to make sure Josefa wasn't within earshot. "What are the two of you cooking up?"

Marina gave her a "Wouldn't-you-like-to-know?" smile and turned to her aunt. "Tía, you promised that Carmen and I could circle the plaza with some of our friends. They're waiting for us now."

"Go along, go along," Josefa told them both jovially, turning back to her chat with her own friends.

"Where are we going?" Carmen asked as they began to walk over the dirt path toward the bandstand.

"To walk with Carla and Anita, of course," Marina answered blithely. "What else would we be doing?"

In the guise of a loving pat, Carmen pinched her. "Tell me," she hissed. "Are you going to leap up in front of Don Felipe on his horse and ride off into the hills? Are you going to run away and marry him? Are you going to meet him in the moonlight and make mad, passionate . . ."

"Carmen!" Marina shook her hand off. "Don't let your imagination send you into a frenzy." She lifted her chin. "I'm merely going to meet him by the old sycamore at the center of the square . . ."

"That's good enough." Carmen's black eyes were

33

alight with excitement. She loved anything daring, even if it involved someone she wasn't sure she approved of for her cousin. Meeting in the overgrown area of the huge old sycamore was a tradition. It took daring to attempt it, because to be caught there was to be humiliated before the entire town. But if it worked, a few moments alone, away from prying eyes, were worth the risk.

"I'll help you. What do you want me to do?"

Marina flashed her a quick smile. "Just walk with me. I'll leave you with the others after we pass the benches."

"Of course." Carmen laughed with delight. "Are you going to kiss him?" she asked eagerly.

Marina met her glance with wariness. "He may think so. But I doubt it."

Carmen's face fell. "Then what is the use of going at all? To talk? You can talk anytime."

Carmen was right and Marina knew it. A few days before, she might have told her cousin the kiss was a certainty. But not any longer. Nothing was a certainty to her now.

They met the other girls and began to chat for a few minutes before beginning their walk. Suddenly a pretty girl with bright red curls that bounced as she moved came running up to join them.

"Is he here yet?" she cried, craning her neck to look up and down the plaza. "Just a warning, girls." She managed to glare at Marina and Carmen in the guise of a friendly smile. "I've already claimed the Spanish lieutenant, the tall one, as my own. So don't any of you go trying to flirt with him."

"Heaven forbid we should get in your way, Gloria," Carmen told her sharply.

Gloria tossed her raven curls. "You've done it before. Carmen, you stole that *vaquero* with the gold

34

ring in his ear from me at the Comandante's *baile* last month and you know it."

"I only saved you, Gloria. The man was a pig."

"Well, he was *my* pig, until you hogtied him."

They all burst into laughter at that and Gloria flushed, but laughed along with them. "Just remember, everyone. Sebastian de la Cruz is mine."

They broke into groups and began to walk about along the dirt path, slowly making the turn around the plaza. The others laughed and chattered and cast quick, darting glances toward the men who rode their horses out on the road.

As they reached the benches, Marina glanced at her cousin. "I . . . I've forgotten to tell Tía something," she said lamely to Carmen. "I must go back."

"Go, cousin," Carmen said with a shrug. "We'll meet you later on the other side."

The others hardly noticed. Marina started back, looked about, then made her way quickly to the center of the square.

At the edge of the overgrown area, she looked about once, then slipped in among the plants, making her way toward the foot of the large sycamore tree. Standing very still, she studied her position.

The scent of orange blossoms filled the air, making it seem soft and seductive. She could hear voices in the distance, gentle voices, laughing talk, and a distant guitar, but she couldn't see a thing. As far as she could tell, the bushes hid her from view, except for one tiny, narrow gap.

She put her hand over her heart. It was beating so hard she thought she could hear the cadence echoing among the shrubbery. She'd never done anything this daring before, at least, not with a man involved. To be caught was unthinkable. But to take the chance was thrilling.

Felipe had whispered the plan to her the last few times they had seen one another, and she'd known that one of these balmy Spring nights during the promenade he would give her the signal that she was to put the plan into action and prepare to meet him. They wouldn't have much more than a few stolen moments. But that was more than they usually had.

She stepped forward tentatively, moving toward the tree. A sound came from behind and she paused, breath held, and looked back, peering in among the branches of the bushes. She couldn't see anything at all. Still staring back, she took another two steps and ran into something hard and lean that knocked the breath right out of her.

Two hands grasped her arms before she could fall, and she whipped her head around, staring in paralyzed shock into the green, fathomless gaze of the Spanish lieutenant.

"Oh!" she gasped. Her hands shot out and reached his chest, but her strength faded before she could complete the act of pushing him away. Her eyes wide, she stared at him, frozen to the spot.

"Well, *paloma,* where are you flying to?" he asked her, his voice a low rumble that she felt as well as heard.

"Please . . ." She could barely whisper the word, and before she could finish her plea for release, her gaze took in the angry red slash that marred his face, cutting across the side of his arrogant nose and deep into the swell of his lean cheek. She gasped again, her hands coming back quickly to her face, and this time it was a low, moaning sound of anguish.

Had she done this to the man? He knew what she'd seen, and he touched it delicately with one finger.

"Do you like it?" he asked bitterly, his eyes hard and cold as diamonds glittering in his dark face. "Some say

36

it adds character to my visage, but I'm not so sure it's character I enjoy."

She moaned again and looked from the ugly scar to the unicorn ring on her finger.

His gaze followed hers and he reached out to yank her hand up to where he could see the ring. He stared at it for a long moment, then deftly pulled it from her finger for a closer look.

"So this is the instrument of my mutilation," he commented, turning it in his fingers. "I had wondered how your nails could do so much damage."

"I'm sorry," she whispered, utterly stricken. "I had no idea . . ."

He raised one eyebrow, then slipped the ring onto his own little finger. "None at all? Do you mean to tell me I'm the only man you've ever scarred this way?"

He dropped her hand as though it burned him, but he still stood very close, as though holding her in some sort of spell against him.

"What made you choose me, *querida?*" he asked, his voice soft with menace. "How did I get to be the lucky one?"

She swallowed hard and the entire scene came back to her. As she looked up, fear and doubt clouded her gaze.

"You attacked me," she reminded him, finally getting her voice back. "If you had only left me alone . . ."

She tried to pull away but he reached out too quickly and held her shoulders, his fingers biting hard.

"The gold coins," he said, his mouth twisted into a sneer. "What have you done with them?"

The gold coins. Relief filled her. If that was what he was after, she could take care of it in no time.

"Oh, they're at home. I'll get them to you . . ."

His hard hand went under her chin and tilted her

face up so that she wouldn't be able to misinterpret his angry purpose.

"They're yours, *querida*. But I still haven't received what I paid for."

Her eyes widened. "No . . . it was all a mistake. I'm . . . I'm not one of those girls from El Camino de los Osos."

She stared up into his unconvinced face and finally, humiliatingly, she whispered, "I told you, I'm a virgin."

His wide mouth twisted with bitter humor and his shoulders lifted in a lazy shrug. "I've taken virgins before. The first time can be the sweetest." He laughed shortly. "Though usually not for the virgin."

Fear shivered through her. He was so tall, so overpowering, that she felt suddenly as though it was inevitable that he would get what he wanted from her. Her mouth was dry. She didn't have the strength to pull away. His face was close to hers, shadowed evilly in the dappled light, and she was very afraid there would be a kiss after all.

And then, suddenly, Felipe was there, his eyes blazing his anger, his knife in his hand.

"You're a dead man, Spaniard," he spit out through bared teeth, and the Spanish lieutenant was moving away from Marina, his body reacting like that of a jungle cat trapped by a hunter.

The two men stared at each other, hot hatred blazing from Felipe's eyes, cool contempt from the Spaniard's.

"So this is your protector, *paloma*," Sebastian murmured. "I heard him singing to you before. Does he fight as well as he sings?"

"Don't dare to speak to her, you bastard," Felipe growled. "Speak to me. I am the one who will introduce you to your maker."

"So you do want to fight." The Spaniard's voice was

world-weary. "What a bore."

He gathered himself together, coming to a full military pose and snapping his heels smartly. *"A sus órdenes,"* he spat out with a flourish, his fingers curling about the hilt of his silver sword. "At your convenience."

Watching, Marina was appalled. She could sense the intensity between the two men. Someone was going to get killed if she didn't do something to stop this.

"No," she whispered, then gathered the wherewithal to cry more loudly, "No," springing between them. "No, Felipe, don't do this. It wasn't what you think."

Felipe's rage burned in his eyes. "He touched you, didn't he? He will die for that."

Marina looked at Sebastian and then back at Felipe. "No. I ran into him. I . . . I stumbled. He only helped to keep me from falling."

Felipe waved her explanation away. "What does it matter?" he said angrily. "I knew it would come to this the first time I saw him. If I don't kill him now, I will only have to do it later."

That Felipe meant what he said she never doubted. Matters of honor were all-important to him. But such an act could ruin everything—lives, futures, her own peace of mind. She couldn't let it happen. *"No."*

She thought fast and did the only thing she could think of, falling to her knees before him. "Felipe, please. I could not love a murderer. If you do this thing, I'll . . . I'll go to a convent, I swear I will."

He frowned at her impatiently, then looked again at Sebastian. "Get up, Marina. This no longer concerns you."

And, though she stayed on her knees, she knew what he said was true. The two men had awareness only for each other now and the battle at hand. She was forgotten, irrelevant, a mere bystander.

She looked back and forth at their faces and anger churned where horror had been only seconds before. What a pair of idiots they were. Felipe was standing with legs bent, as though ready to spring, and his knife was held waiting, a flash of silver steel poised in the air.

"Come then, soldier," he said, his hoarse voice low and grating. "Let us see if you fight as proudly as you wear that uniform."

His chuckle was the sound of gravel thrown against a stone. "I thought we got rid of all you cursed Spaniards when Mexico won independence ten years ago. You must have been overlooked. Perhaps I'll be able to do the job now."

He moved menacingly toward his adversary, but the Spaniard stood tall, a contemptuous smile twisting his wide mouth, his hand on the hilt of his sword, but loosely, casually, as though disdain held him back.

"Not here, you fool," he flung at Don Felipe. "Not like a barbarian in front of the women and children." His sneer drew a growl from Felipe, but he went on, heedless. "We'll handle this as it's done in more civilized lands. I'll meet you at dawn. My second will call upon you within the hour to arrange the details. Until then, I take my leave. *Señor.*" He bowed curtly. *"Señorita."*

A sharp turn on his heel and he was striding off through the trees, leaving the other two to stare after him.

Voices were coming closer. Marina threw Felipe a startled look and began to back away.

"Someone is coming," she whispered. "I must go."

He nodded and swore softly. "We shall try again, *querida*. Until next time."

He whirled and began to retreat in the opposite direction.

Marina hurried out of the brush and walked quickly

across the grass toward where she could see Carmen walking with the other girls. She felt as though she were moving in a dream. Her head was full of the things the Spaniard had said, the way he'd looked.

The sense of inevitability was gone, at least. He would never catch her alone like that again. She would be very careful to stay away from situations where he might find her. No, she wouldn't fear that. He would never get a chance to touch her.

But he still had her ring. She cried out softly as she realized it, clutching her hand. He still had the unicorn ring Jonathan had given to her. She had to get it back. That would present a problem. But that was a puzzle for the future. There was a far greater problem right now.

The duel. How was she going to stop it? The nightmare of it stayed with her on the walk back home and into the night as she lay in her bed.

What was she going to do? There was no time. There was no help at hand. Only hours away lay the horror of death. Death that she had caused.

She wasn't sure exactly why this was her fault, but she knew unswervingly that the blame was hers. Somehow, in the space of a few days, her world had been shaken, all the underpinnings knocked out of kilter, and she did not have the slightest idea of how to go about shoring it up again.

In only a few hours, the yellow flame of pistol fire, the sharp flash of a silver sword, the thick clang of a steel knife, could stop a man's life in its tracks. If Felipe was killed, she would never forgive herself. But the Spaniard . . . no, his death would be just as horrible. The duel must be stopped.

The inky black sky was beginning to lighten to a vel-

41

vet purple when Marina, heavy embroidered shawl wrapped tightly about her head and shoulders, slipped out through the heavy front door and ran out into the street. She had no idea where to go, but she knew she couldn't stay at home any longer while lives hung in the balance.

She looked up and down the silent street and tried to think where they might be planning to have their fight. She didn't dare take a horse, for surely that would be heard. But she could run very quickly.

Gathering her skirts around her, she did just that. The mission orchard was her first choice, but it lay quiet, the spring flowers just beginning to break free from their winter sleep. A fog was rolling in off the sea, and wisps of a blue-gray mist floated in about the trees like threadbare rags in a gentle breeze.

Marina ran the length of the garden, then back again and out to check the corrals behind the blacksmith's stables. These were empty, and so was the carpenter's meadow where she ran next. By now the fog was thickening, and though the sky was becoming lighter and lighter, she knew that the fog would soon make her search impossible.

The sea cliff: why hadn't she tried that in the first place? Sobbing with fear and exhaustion, she ran on and on, stumbling as the way became steeper, climbing, climbing, until finally she had reached her goal. But the fog was thick now, a heavy, soggy cloak that shrouded her view, making it impossible to see anything more than a few feet about herself. The edge of the cliff was the end of the world, a stepping-off into nothing but the cold, gray void.

She held her breath, listening for any sound that might give her a clue, but she heard only the eerie, distant crash of the waves, over and over, and nothing to evidence the presence of men.

Drained and hopeless, she sank to the ground, her dark satin skirt in a circle about her, her eyes red but dry, her mind as foggy as the skies. She had failed.

The night was no longer an ebony mystery. The gray mist obscured the landscape, but the light skies heralded the dawn. Whatever had become of the two men, it was over by now.

She rose, weary and heartsick, and made her way back down toward the town, walking first along the children's path, then right out in the road. She didn't care if others saw her. What did that matter now? Dully, she placed one foot in front of the other and kept going.

There was a sound behind her. She lifted her head, not sure at first, but then knowing it must be the clop of a walking horse. She stopped and turned to wait, her heart thumping. The figure of a rider loomed through the haze. Shading her eyes, she tried to see who it was, but the man who loomed into view was unfamiliar to her. He seemed to recognize her, though, pulling his horse to a halt beside her.

"*Señorita*. What are you doing out here in the cold?"

The man was in uniform and she realized he must be the other new lieutenant, the Spaniard's friend. Probably his second. Marina reached toward him beseechingly.

"Have you been with them?" she asked. "Please, quickly, tell me what has happened."

A veil covered his eyes, and his face remained an expressionless mask. "Happened? I don't know what you mean, *Señorita*. Nothing of any consequence has happened."

She grasped the stirrup, impatient with his attempt to cover up. "Did . . . is anyone hurt? Tell me." She yanked on the stirrup. "Tell me the truth. Is . . . are they alive?"

43

He shook his head slowly. *"Señorita,* I think it would be better if you were at your own house. There are things it is better if a woman did not know."

Anger shot through her and she loosened her grip on the stirrup, grasping instead the man's leg, her fingernails biting into the cloth.

"I know about the duel, *hombre,"* she cried in furious frustration. "Now tell me what has happened, or I will scream this street awake around us."

Surprise flickered across his face and he shrugged uneasily. "Duel? I know nothing about any duel." Leaning down close to her tortured face, he whispered fiercely, "It is one thing, *Señorita,* for your champion, Don Felipe Diaz. He is king in these parts and may do as he pleases. But Sebastian de la Cruz must answer to the Comandante, who is well known to be against dueling. He has dealt harshly with participants in the past. So mind your tongue, I warn you."

Straightening, he went on in a normal voice. "A sad thing has occurred. A hunting accident. The fog, you know. It made the whole expedition impossible, but fools that we are, we went after the bear anyway, and now look what has happened."

"What?" Marina rasped out, staring into the lieutenant's face. "What has happened?"

He shrugged again. "A ball in the shoulder. Painful, but not serious if the wound is kept healthy. He is with the Presidio surgeon now."

Marina felt faint. The stirrup was in her hand again, and she held it tightly to keep herself from falling. "Then your friend was hit?"

"Yes, but he has been hit before. Do not worry, *Señorita,* he will survive."

"And . . . and Don Felipe?"

"Untouched, and quite proud of his victory." He

frowned at her pale face. *"Señorita,* if I may assist you . . ."

"No." She gathered all her strength and pulled away from the horse. "No. My home is very near. I need no assistance."

Without another glance at the soldier, she stumbled along the dirt road toward her house. It was over. No one had died. But new emotions had been triggered within her soul, emotions she would not soon forget.

Chapter Four

A gentle rain was falling, as it had been for three days. Steadily, surely, without undue effort or unseemly haste, Nature was providing the overdue moisture to green the golden hills for Spring. The courtyard of the Crafts' house was a miniature lake filled with plants storing up an ecstasy of abundance against a certain scanty future. Inside a cozy group was gathered about the sitting room fireplace.

"This rain certainly is a godsend," James Crafts said with satisfaction as he leaned back in his chair.

"It may be a godsend to you, but it must be called a trial to me," answered Captain Brandene. A stocky man of average height, he had a pleasant face with bushy brows and twinkling blue eyes. "I'll be late meeting my ship, and when I do arrive, I'll find that my men were forced to set out to sea because of the storm, and have left piles of hides on the beach to rot. I'm afraid it will delay my return to Boston by almost a month."

"Then you won't be going until the end of May?" asked Marina. "I don't mind that. It will give me more time to embroider a vest for you to take to Jonathan."

"Oh, Marina." Carmen rolled her eyes. "What in

the world makes you think Jonathan will want more embroidered sashes and vests? I'm sure he'll cringe when he opens the package. He'll probably hide them away so the other fellows can't see them."

The captain threw back his shaggy head of graying hair and laughed. "You're probably right, Carmen. Not many in Boston walk about in such outlandish dress. Jonathan wouldn't want to be conspicuous."

"That shows how little you know of my brother." Marina gave them both a superior smile. "What you are describing is how you would react in his place. Jonathan isn't like you. He's proud of his *vaquero* heritage."

She waved the vest she was working on under their noses.

"I'd make you a wager on it if I didn't know you don't hold with such things," the captain teased.

Marina's eyes flashed. "I don't call it wagering on a sure thing such as this. How much will you bet?"

"Marina." Josefa cried out. "There will be no gambling in this house."

Marina smirked down at her sewing, looked sideways at the captain, and whispered, "We'll set the terms later, if you dare."

He laughed again, and when she met his glance, she almost regretted having teased him. He had that look again, and she didn't want to encourage it. A year before, he had hinted to the family that he was thinking of making Marina an offer. His suggestion had been kindly and tactfully refused, and he hadn't seemed especially crushed. Marina reasoned that he was not a particularly passionate man. He'd liked her and had thought it might be pleasant to settle down, but when she'd rebuked him, he'd shrugged and gone on his way, much to her relief.

47

She liked him well enough. But he was not her idea of a lover.

But who needed a lover, anyway? It had been almost a week since the encounter in the plaza and the duel that followed. Marina had stayed home and carefully avoided going anywhere she might meet either one of the combatants. The more she thought about them and the silly fight they'd had, the more angry and disgusted she became. It would be all the same to her if she never saw either one of them again.

"Now you must tell us the news, Captain," her father was saying. "We've been waiting all this time for a visit from you while you took your sudden trip north upon landing your ship in our harbor. Come, tell us. How was Jonathan when last you saw him?"

The captain hesitated. Looking up, Marina was surprised to note a furtive look on his face.

"He was just fine when I saw him last summer," he began.

"No, no," James Crafts cried. "We've had letters from him since then, though it has been a long time now since we've had word. That is why I was so anxious to hear how he was when you came from Boston last. You did visit him?"

The captain's glance met Marina's and slid away again. "I . . . I tried. I did go to his quarters and ask for him, but he was away at the time and . . . and I never had a chance to go back. So, I'm sorry to say, I have nothing new to report." He finished his statement in a rush, like a schoolboy glad to have his recitation over with.

Marina stared at him curiously as her father talked on about how unfortunate it was that the two men missed one another. Something was wrong; she was sure of it. But she was equally sure it was something the captain didn't want her father to know. She decided to take care to find a moment alone before he left, to quiz him on this strange behavior. If anything had happened to Jonathan . . .

She placed her hand over her heart and closed her eyes for just a moment. Jonathan, her dear brother. What would she do if something was wrong?

The talk around the fire was interrupted by a sudden imperious knock on the huge wooden front door. Carmen jumped up, caught herself, and sat down again. James and Josefa looked at each other.

"Well, who could it be at this time of night, and in such weather?" Josefa asked the group.

"I can't think who," answered James, shaking his head.

"Tío," Carmen ventured. "Don't you remember? The man you met at the Alcalde's this morning while I was with you. The one you invited to visit us this evening."

James's brow cleared. "Of course! A fine fellow." He turned to the captain. "You'll like him, I'm sure."

Jose, the serving man, stepped into the room and James waved him on.

"Well, let him in, let him in. Don't leave him out there in the rain."

They all peered into the hall as Jose went to the door and unbarred it. A sudden gust of wet wind thrust it open with a bang, and there in the lantern light stood Sebastian de la Cruz, the Spanish lieutenant.

Marina held back her gasp, but everyone seemed strangely affected by his appearance. He looked taller than ever, his head held arrogantly, his gaze steady and sure. His boots and uniform had an impeccable look which seemed impossible considering the condition of the weather and the roads. His only concession to the storm was an enormous cape, deep blue and lined with scarlet, which floated about him as though to set him apart from earthly beings. A sigh seemed to pass through the group as they viewed him, and for a moment, no one said a word. Sebastian finally stepped inside and bowed.

"I hope I'm not intruding. Señor Crafts was kind enough to invite me to stop in this evening."

Josefa turned to James with a scowl, but James was smiling warmly.

"Come in, dear fellow, come in. Come sit by the fire. You'll need warming after being out in that rain."

"Thank you, *Señor.*" After relieving himself of his cloak, Sebastian entered the room.

Though he hadn't met Marina's gaze, she could feel his awareness of her. That horrible tingling was starting again. She rubbed her hands against her skirt, trying to rid herself of it.

Of all of them, James seemed the most pleased with their visitor. "Allow me to make introductions," he said happily. "Josefa, may I present Lieutenant Sebastian de la Cruz of His Majesty's . . . oh dear, no, not any longer. Of the Republican Army of Mexico. He has recently been assigned to our Presidio. This is my sister-in-law, Señora Josefa Maria Elena Cepeda. My niece, Carmen, you met with me this morning. Captain Alex Brandene of the trading vessel the *Prospect*. And lastly, my daughter Marina."

Sebastian bowed politely in answer to each introduction. His reception ranged from a stony stare thrown by Josefa to a friendly handshake from the

50

captain. Carmen smiled back at him with warm delight.

Marina met his gaze with a touch of defiance in her huge gray eyes. "Don't imagine this is going to get you anywhere," her look said.

He smiled. It was the first time she'd ever seen him smile, and the effect left her blinking at him — like, she thought in despair later when she went over the scene in her mind, a frightened rabbit.

"I've been looking forward to meeting your lovely daughter," he said smoothly as he smiled at her. *"Señorita,* your reputation, though exalted, hardly does you justice."

Marina swallowed and tried to smile. "Thank you," she managed to murmur. "I . . . thank you."

Feeling like an utter fool, she sank into her chair and took up her embroidery again. Her heart was beating and her face was flushed and she hated him with all her soul.

What was he doing here in her house? Why was he trying to worm his way into the affections of her family? The others sat down around her, beginning to chat with the visitor, and she tried desperately to quiet her racing pulse.

She didn't look at him again, but she could see him seating himself out of the corner of her eye, and the picture of how he'd first looked out there in the storm was engraved on her mind.

The scar was still as fiery as ever, and he held his shoulder stiffly, as though the wound from the duel still hurt him. The man had certainly received his share of physical injuries in the short time he had been among them. She pressed her lips together. It served him right, of course. But what was he doing here?

She glanced at James. The saving grace was that her father would soon see through the Spaniard's facade of gracious manners and know him for the blackguard he was. And then he would no longer be welcome here, and she could breathe more easily.

Yes. A feeling of satisfaction took hold, slowing her heartbeat. Her father was a very good judge of character. He would soon realize the Spanish lieutenant didn't belong here.

But for now, the group seemed fascinated with him, wanting to know all about his background, where he'd been raised, why he'd come to California, when he planned to return to Spain. When he evaded their questions, Carmen jumped to his defense.

"What does it matter why anyone comes to California?" she asked with spirit. "It's how they behave once here that counts." She glanced at Sebastian. "Good breeding is difficult to achieve and impossible to disguise."

Marina's head came up at that. She couldn't let it pass. "If what you mean is that good, kind, polite behavior will be returned in kind," she said to her cousin, "I agree with you. But if 'breeding' means 'birth,' you're dead wrong. They've proved that in the United States, and we're just now doing the same with the new Mexican Independence. At least," she added under her breath about her last statement, "I hope we are."

The captain nodded his support. "That's right. In the States it don't matter who your daddy was, you've got to prove your worth on your own."

"In civilized countries," Sebastian suggested smoothly, "one's worth does not constantly require proving."

The captain's brow darkened and he sat forward.

"Now, listen here. Are you saying the U.S.A. ain't civilized?"

Marina ignored the captain and turned to glare at Sebastian herself. "Lieutenant, surely you don't mean to imply that you find the arbitrary and confining class system, where one has no opportunity to change one's lot in life, preferable to a system based on merit, where any man may aspire to any position?"

He met her glare with equanimity. "I mean exactly that. I like a society where the cream has already risen to the top. In young countries such as yours, the process is only beginning. The families with the best, the leadership qualities, will emerge eventually. But in the meantime, you have chaos. The goal must be to arrive at that settled state so that the nation's energies may be directed in other areas."

Horror was mirrored in Marina's gray eyes. Not only was the man arrogant, he was an elitist — and proud of it.

"Why, that's preposterous," she cried. "Haven't you ever noticed how people at the top in your 'settled' societies become fat, lazy, and useless? How the vitality rests in the people who work for a living? I'm sure you'd find more admirable qualities of thrift, hard work, and piety in the average shoemaker than in ten grandees."

Sebastian found it amazing that it was a woman who was challenging him to this sort of verbal duel. He eyed her warily, not sure if he should even attempt to answer her. But in the end, he couldn't resist. How long had it been since anyone had actually attempted to discuss an idea with him?

Still, he managed to set his face with a bored expression. It wouldn't do to let her know how much he relished this conversation.

"What does the grandee need with thrift and hard work?" he asked lazily. "He's capable of learning and thinking on a level impossible to your shoemaker."

Marina knew they were monopolizing things with their argument. She knew the others were frowning and wishing the two of them would quiet down and turn the talk back to light chatting.

All except for her father. James was chuckling softly as though it did his heart good to see his daughter hold her own this way. She glanced around the room and saw the frowns, but she didn't back down. Instead, she set her shoulders and plowed ahead.

"My shoemaker is just as smart as your grandee. With the right training he would do twice as well, for he would know the meaning of work and concentration." Her eyes flashed as she prepared her final salvo. "It is horrifying to think of these useless drones living off the labor of others, doing nothing all day but laughing, singing, and chasing pleasure."

That set off a buzz of murmuring about the room, and under cover of it, Sebastian turned to Marina, eyelids drooping, and muttered, "Like your friend Don Felipe?"

Marina opened her mouth, but for once she was without a retort.

Carmen made a comment and the talk went on without Marina. Inside, something was crumbling.

Was it true? Did Felipe lead an aimless life? No, of course not. He spent a lot of time riding the borders of his land, searching out straying cattle and watching for Indians.

At least he spent some time at such things. And at

roundup he worked night and day. But did that really make up for the days he spent riding his horse, visiting friends, attending parties? Was she going to end up married to a man who embodied the very qualities she hated most?

The others were laughing over something Sebastian had said, and Marina tried to bring her mind back to the conversation, but it wasn't until Captain Brandene rose to go that she was able to cast off her misgivings about Don Felipe and listen to what was going on around her.

Tía Josefa and her father were accompanying the captain to the door. The three young people had stayed behind in the sitting room and Carmen was using this opportunity to capture the visitor's attention.

"And how is it going with you in our little town, Lieutenant?" she asked him, her head cocked to the side coquettishly. "Have you met many people?"

"Not yet. Mainly the other officers at the Presidio. But they seem a good lot."

Carmen smiled significantly. "And how do you find the ladies?"

An answering smile curled the corners of Sebastian's mouth. "Very beautiful, I'm sure. And also very friendly. There is a young woman who continually puts notes under my door . . ."

"Gloria Estancia," Carmen said, nodding knowledgeably. "She imagines herself in love with you."

He shrugged, his eyes expressionless. "She's a lovely young lady."

Carmen gasped. "Don't tell me you've fallen for her!"

He threw his head back and laughed. "Not yet."

"Well, don't. There are plenty of other women

who want their chance." Carmen gave him a flirtatious grin. "Don't be hasty. You'll break too many hearts."

"I doubt that," he said casually, but his eyes met Marina's, and she thought she read how they mocked her.

"But tell me," Carmen went on. "What do you think of our town? From all reports, you've spent much of your time wandering our streets, so by now you must have formed an opinion."

Sebastian's voice was low and amused. "Are everyone's actions so well reported?"

Carmen smiled at him. "Of course. There are those in this town who do nothing but keep an eye out for others. They consider it a solemn duty to keep the townspeople well informed of everything that happens. After all, towns in civilized countries have their newspapers. We must depend on our gossips."

He laughed.

Marina watched him, still unable to speak, appalled at how attractive he was. And the way Carmen was flirting! What if she were to fall into his traps?

"Civilized towns have their gossips, too," he assured Carmen. "But tell me, how may I become a part of this system? I'd like to hear all there is to know about you."

Marina almost gagged at the way Carmen fluttered her eyelashes over that one. How could her cousin be so demented?

"Oh, never fear," Carmen was saying back to him. "You will hear about me. I have no doubt."

He raised one dark eyebrow. "But only compliments. I will allow no one to speak of you in any other way in my hearing."

Carmen grinned. "Then maybe you won't hear so much about me after all."

Marina's father and aunt were back and the flirting ceased abruptly. Josefa made excuses to retreat into the kitchen, but James sat down and launched into a discussion of literature with Sebastian that left the two young women out entirely.

Marina glanced at her cousin accusingly. Carmen gave her a slight shrug and stuck out her lower lip in a pout. They both turned and pretended to be interested as Sebastian and James argued the relative merits of Art versus Nature.

"For all my talk of the superior charms of Nature," James said at last, "I must confess, I can't get along without my library."

"You have a library?" Sebastian was surprised. "I had heard that libraries were very rare in this region. And that reading was frowned on by the Church here."

"True." James nodded. "But I do have one. If you promise not to give me away at the mission, I'll show it to you."

The two men rose and left the room, remembering to excuse themselves from the ladies only at the last moment.

Marina and Carmen looked at one another. "So much for all your work at enticing him," Marina whispered loudly. "He'd rather see a lot of dusty old books."

"I wasn't enticing him," Carmen protested. "I was merely testing the ground."

"Oh?" Marina tossed her embroidery in her canvas bag. "And how did you find it?"

"I'm not sure," Carmen answered thoughtfully. "I

can't tell for sure how to read him. He's not like the other men around here."

Marina snorted, rising from her chair. "That's certain."

Looking at her cousin she hesitated, wanting to warn her. But for the first time in her life she had a secret she couldn't bring herself to share with Carmen. Biting her lip, she turned away.

"I'm going to bed," she said firmly.

"But you haven't said goodnight."

"You say it for me." She started out of the room, but her father's call stopped her in her tracks.

"Marina, come here please. I can't find that copy of the biography of Lope de Vega that Jonathan sent me last year."

Marina turned slowly and looked at Carmen, who shrugged and pretended to yawn into her hand.

Caught. She would have to face the Spanish lieutenant one more time. Sighing, she went down the hall to the little room her father liked to call his library. Her father was standing in the center of the room, books cascading from his arms. Sebastian was leaning indolently against the desk, thumbing through a thick volume.

She met his gaze only fleetingly, then smiled at her father. "You've lost the biography?"

"Yes. Weren't you reading it just the other day?"

"Yes. I . . . I think it might be in that stack . . ." She nodded toward a pile of books near the shuttered window across the room from where she stood.

James gestured helplessly. "You look for it, dear, would you? I've another volume in my bedroom I want to find for the lieutenant. I won't be but a moment." Dropping the pile he carried, he hurried away.

As he disappeared through the doorway Marina looked up at Sebastian. Amusement lit his green eyes. Tilting his head back, he stared at her.

"So, *querida*," he murmured, "alone again."

Marina swallowed hard, looking at the stack of books she was obliged to search through and looking at the small space he'd left for her to squeeze by in order to get to them.

"Not so alone," she retorted. "My father will be right back."

Catching her breath in her lungs, she started toward the window. He stopped her, just as she'd known he would, with a hand out to bar her way. Gently but firmly he took hold of her upper arm. She stood still, determinedly avoiding his gaze, staring at the window. He spoke softly, so close to her ear she could feel his warm breath on her skin.

"You haven't forgotten our transaction, have you?" he asked her. "I'm still waiting to receive what I paid for."

His touch seemed to burn her arm. She closed her eyes. When he was this close to her she seemed to lose control of her will. But not her determination.

"Give me back my ring," she whispered.

"Your ring?" The fingers of his free hand went into his waistcoat and brought out the silver unicorn. "Do you mean this weapon that you used to maim me?"

Turning quickly, her eyes widened and she lunged for it, but he deftly held it out of her reach.

"No, Marina," he said, laughing softly. "I'm going to keep this." He considered it, holding it up to the lamplight. "It reminds me of you. Beautiful, graceful . . ." He tapped the sharp tip of the unicorn's horn with one finger. "And deadly."

"Give it back. I need it."

He smiled. "Don't you think I deserve it?"

Her mouth was dry. She stared at the ring. For a moment she was tempted to explain to him why it was so important to her. But no, she decided quickly. She wasn't going to explain anything to him. He had no right to keep it, and she would get it back somehow.

"If you don't give it back to me, I . . . I'll have to tell Don Felipe."

His gaze hardened and his fingers curled around the unicorn. "Why don't you do that? Yes. Tell Don Felipe. That will give me the excuse I need to meet him once again. And this time, perhaps I won't fire into the air."

Startled, she gazed fully into his eyes. She hadn't heard he had done that. Was it true? Had he been hit because of his own gentlemanly gesture? Or was he just trying to confuse her, to muddle her judgment?

"Give it to me," she demanded roughly, pulling at his hold on her arm. "It doesn't belong to you."

"Yes it does, Marina," he said softly, balling his fingers around the ring and bringing the closed fist up to touch her cheek. "It belongs to me now. Just as you do."

She gasped and then she couldn't breathe. He was holding her firmly and his face was so close. Much too close. And coming closer.

She couldn't move. Closing her eyes, she felt his touch on her neck. Her knees weakened and she swayed, just barely holding back a sigh, for it was his warm lips that were caressing her, his hot tongue that was drawing exquisite designs upon her sensitive skin. The room seemed to spin about her. No man had ever done this to her before. The sensations he conjured with just these fleeting touches shook her to her foundations. Never before had she felt the shimmering ghost of desire flicker through her soul, but she felt it now.

"No, please no," she moaned, frightened by what she was feeling. But her face was turning toward his, as though her own lips needed to feel the pressure he could bring.

His face hovered so close, the slashing scar, the arrogant mouth. She could feel his heat, could smell the rough mixture of soap and masculine energy casting a spell on her senses. Her lips parted and she swayed toward him.

And then there came the shuffling sound of her father's return. It drew them apart with a jerk that seemed to wake her from a drugged stupor. She reached out to catch her hand against the desk to keep herself from falling. Shocked by what had just been going on, hardly able to believe it could have happened, her face blushed scarlet.

Luckily, her father didn't seem to notice. "Did you find that biography?" he asked as he entered the shadowed room, his eyes blinking in the gloom.

Marina turned guiltily, her heart beating. But there it was, right at the top of the stack. She reached for it and presented it to her father.

"Here you are," she said shakily. "It was right here, where I put it."

"Give it to the lieutenant," he said, gesturing at her absently and frowning as he looked through the new books he'd brought from his bedroom. "I know he will enjoy it."

She turned and looked into Sebastian's eyes again. They weren't quite as arrogant as they had been before. Something cloudy was going on behind his usual bored expression. He took the book from her and his fingers brushed hers.

"Thank you," he said softly. "Did you enjoy it, *Señorita?*"

For a stunned moment she misunderstood, and then she realized he meant the Lope de Vega biography.

"I . . . very much . . ." she stammered, then flushed again, wanting to kill the man. He was tripping her up on purpose. She hated him more than she had ever hated any living soul.

But when she looked up, it was still there, that cloudy something. She stared at him, caught by the mystery in his gaze, then turned and fled from the room, more confused now than she had been when he'd aroused her a few moments earlier. There had been something in those green eyes that had spoken to her in a language she didn't know through words — a language she hadn't realized she knew at all.

"I hate him," she reminded herself fiercely as she ran to her own room. "I hate him, I hate him!"

Her hatred sustained her as she prepared for bed. Plans for revenge swirled through her mind. The man deserved the worst kind of punishment, if only she could think of how to deliver it to him.

It wasn't until she was safe under her covers that she remembered she had forgotten to quiz Captain Brandene before he left about her brother Jonathan. That was something she would have to do soon. Just as soon as she'd come up with a way to get her ring back from Sebastian de la Cruz.

Chapter Five

"The Spaniard's a bit high and mighty, isn't he? I can't say that I care much for the fellow." Alex Brandene sat back in his chair, hands folded across his chest, and frowned at Marina. "What do you think of him?"

Marina hesitated, choosing her words carefully. "My father gets along well with him. He's a guest in our house."

Alex grinned. "You hate him too, don't you?" he said. "I can tell by the way you were looking at him just now."

They were sitting before the fire, just as they had a few nights earlier. Carmen and Tía Josefa had gone to the kitchen to supervise the coming meal. Mr. Crafts and Sebastian had gone to the library. Marina and Alex were alone for the moment.

Marina smiled at the captain, her eyes flashing. With him she could let down her guard a little. "He is a snob, isn't he?" she said in a loud whisper. "I'm surprised he deigns to speak to us."

She thought back to the scene as it had played itself out only moments before. Sebastian had sat across the room leaning back in his chair, his cold eyes half closed, staring at her. The slight bulge in his waistcoat told her where her ring was resting. And as usual when he was around, her nerves had been on edge and her fingers trembling.

She had to get that ring back. Jonathan's ring.

And that reminded her of something else.

"Captain," she said quickly, hurrying to get out her question before the others returned to the room. "The other night you were very evasive when my father was asking you about your attempt to visit my brother in Boston."

"Evasive?" Alex suddenly began to shift nervously in his chair. "I don't know why you would say that." But he wouldn't meet her gaze and seemed to be searching for something to add, but did not come up with what he wanted.

"Alex." She put a hand on his arm and gazed up into his face. "Tell me the truth. What happened when you went to his room in Boston?"

Alex looked down into her infinite gray eyes and swallowed hard. "Don't tell your father," he said at last, his voice husky and reluctant. "Jonathan wasn't there. In fact, the landlady said he had moved out weeks before."

"Moved out?" She stared at him blankly. "Do you mean he moved to another room?"

The captain slowly shook his head. "No, Marina. In fact, he left many of his possessions behind. He took a few things, personal things, and vanished."

"Vanished." She said the word slowly, trying to take in its full meaning. "No." She shook her head, denying the implications that came to mind. "No."

"It's difficult to say what might have happened," the captain told her quickly, patting her shoulder with characteristic awkwardness. "A chance to visit Paris, perhaps. He often spoke of wanting to travel there. An invitation to stay at the home of a friend."

"No." She shook her head again. "He would have written to us. We would have heard by now." Anguish filled her eyes. "Oh, Captain, if something has happened to Jonathan . . ."

"There, there." He patted her again, leaning closer, wondering if he dared pull her head to his shoulder. "I'm sure it's all right."

She hardly heard him. If anything had happened to Jonathan, she wouldn't be able to bear it. She took a deep breath and shook her head as though to clear it.

But wait. She was being much too hasty. Jonathan was young and strong and brave—what could have happened to him that they wouldn't have heard about by now? She put a hand over her heart and steadied herself. He was just off on an adventure. Surely that was the case. She was just about to push Captain Brandene's hand away and tell him so, when Sebastian's voice cut between them like a knife.

"Captain Brandene," he said evenly, his green eyes glittering cynically as he watched the captain and Marina spring apart and rise from their seats to face where he was entering from the hall. "Excuse me for interrupting this tender scene, but Señor Crafts has found an old sea log he wishes to show you."

Spots of color appeared in Marina's cheeks, but she hardly paid any attention to that. She knew she was about to be alone with the Spaniard again. She could see that from the look in his eyes. And that would give her one more opportunity to get her ring back.

Captain Brandene disappeared into the hall and she turned to face Sebastian. He stood where he was, waiting, the scar a slash of angry pain in the lamplight, his shoulder held stiffly where Felipe's shot had hit him. Rather than weakening him, those wounds made him strangely more dangerous. But she couldn't think about that and do all the things that needed doing.

"The ring," she demanded, glancing down at where she was sure it was hiding. She put out her hand. "Quickly, I must have it."

His smile was slow and lazy, and he reached out to take her hand in his own. "You'll get your ring back when you have fulfilled our bargain," he said softly. "And not before."

Her gaze flew up to meet the hard determination in his eyes and she jerked her hand from his, itching to slap him across the face.

But that was how this had all begun, and she didn't want to make matters worse, so she forced herself to remain calm.

Slipping her hand into her pocket, she came up with the handkerchief tied around the five gold coins.

"Here you are," she said, holding out his money. "Here are your coins. You see, we made no bargain at all."

She plunked them into his hand. He looked at them, amusement in his face.

"What is this?" he asked. "Are you trying to bribe me?"

She frowned. "No, you know what that is. The money you threw at me that day. You have it back now. I don't owe you anything at all."

He laughed softly and dropped the coins in a chair. "I don't want to be paid in gold, *querida,*" he said softly. "I have something else in mind."

He was hateful, but she wasn't going to lose her temper. There had to be a better way to deal with this. Was he not an officer and a gentleman? Surely she would be able to appeal to his better nature if she handled this right. If she were clear and logical, set the facts out before him in a simple, declarative manner, wouldn't he have to see the light? Wouldn't he have to admit that it wasn't right to hold out on her this way?

She walked toward the fireplace with measured steps, preparing herself as she went, controlling her temper and her intellect at the same time. Turning, she stood before the fire and gave Sebastian a cool smile.

"You've never met my brother Jonathan, have you, Lieutenant?" She didn't wait for an answer. "Let me tell you about him."

Sebastian walked slowly across the room until he was in front of the fireplace as well. "I've heard a lot about him already," he told her. "I know that he is in Boston reading for the law. And that he is your father's pride and joy."

"Yes." Her smile was more genuine now. She was right about him. He wasn't really a monster. This was going to work.

"Well, Jonathan is a few years older than Carmen and me, but growing up, he was always our best friend. He was a bright, happy boy and always treated us much more kindly than older brothers usually do. We would play any game that he set up, trudging behind him, carrying his slingshots, pretending to be damsels in distress so that he could rescue us from dragons. But when he was about thirteen or fourteen, of course, he began to draw away from us. It was time for him to become a man, and he left us to go off with the other men and learn all there was to know about riding and roping and shooting a gun."

She laughed softly, remembering. "We missed him so much. He was always off riding with the men, staying away for days at a time. And we were left behind, kicking our shoes in the dust and wishing he would come back and brighten our lives."

She looked into his eyes, hoping to see the warmth of some sort of response by now, but there was nothing there, not anger, not friendliness, nothing. She paused, a bit taken aback, but looking away, she went on with her story.

"His journeys began ranging further and further, and once he was gone for over a week, lost in the land of the tall mountains covered with snow, the Sierras. We didn't know what had happened to him, and Carmen and I cried and cried. He missed my confirmation, and I went through the entire ceremony with tears in my eyes." She shook her head, remembering.

"But finally he returned, and after everyone had welcomed him home, he came to me secretly and kissed me and told me I was his princess, and that a princess should have a unicorn ring." She smiled. "That was when he gave the ring to me. He'd found it in one of the snow caves he'd taken shelter in while he was lost. He swore a sorcerer must have left it there for him to find, and that it had magic qualities. He gave it to me as a sign of the bond between us, a bond that would be there always." Her voice broke before she could complete the last sentence, and she had to stop for a moment to regain control.

Looking up into his eyes, she made her plea. "When you keep the ring from me, Lieutenant, it's as though the bond were broken, and I feel the loss of it as though a lifeline had been cut off. I need that ring back. I need it desperately."

She waited, watching his eyes, wishing she could read what was there, but finding nothing she could put her finger on. He stared back for a long moment, then gave her another one of his smiles that didn't reach his eyes, and leaned back against the mantel.

"A touching story, *Señorita*. A very good tale. But I'll tell you one of my own."

She folded her arms, feeling suddenly cold. He hadn't been moved at all. Was the man inhuman?

"It's all about a man who comes to live in a new land," he began, holding her gaze with his own. "And, looking to make himself at home in the neighborhood, comes upon a woman who seems to be offering herself up to the next taker."

His eyes were very cold now, cold as ice caverns, cold as an Arctic storm.

"She's beautiful and tempting, and he reaches for what she offers, but instead of getting what his heart desires . . ." His eyes glittered with meaning. "He is slashed in the face, scarred forever, for the

69

sin of wanting what was being so blatantly offered. The man has paid dearly, but the strange thing is, he never actually got what he paid for. And it is time justice was done."

"That's not justice," she replied as calmly as she could manage. "It's not even truth. It's a fairy tale."

His smile was lethal. She didn't understand his need for revenge. But that was only natural. He'd been damaged beyond repair and his Spanish pride demanded repayment. "But it's my fairy tale, and I will supply my own happy ending."

"That's impossible," she said firmly. "I don't like this game you're playing, Lieutenant. You know very well when we first . . . met . . ." She remembered what had happened beside the stream and her cheeks flared anew. "You know very well you misunderstood why I was there."

He shrugged, his eyes hardening. She called it a game, and she was right. It was an amusement now, something to while away the time in this exceedingly boring land. "That may be. But you were quick enough to inform me." He touched the scar on his face with the tip of one finger. "I'll carry this reminder for the rest of my life, *querida*."

The sight of the scar made her slightly sick. She wanted to tell him how sorry she was that she had maimed him, but he made it completely impossible with his grating arrogance. So instead she defended her actions, glaring at him.

"I had to stop you somehow. You were attacking me like a . . . an animal."

"An animal." His teeth flashed in the firelight. "Is that how it appeared to you?" He reached out

70

and touched her cheek with a quick stroke from his index finger. "Come to my quarters tonight, Marina, and I'll show you I am not an animal. I'll show you how a gentleman makes love to a lady."

Without waiting for a response, he turned on his heel and returned to the library, leaving Marina to sputter uselessly.

"Come to his quarters, indeed!" she muttered, clenching her hands into fists. "Is he insane? I would rather impale myself on a sharp stick than . . ."

"Ooooh, sounds ugly," Carmen commented as she came swishing into the room. Her eyes narrowed with interest as she looked her cousin up and down. "What did Alex do to make you so angry?"

Marina turned quickly and tried to smile. "Nothing. Really. I was just . . . just . . ."

Not one good excuse came to mind and she dropped the pretense, grabbing hold of Carmen's arm. "I can't stand that Spanish lieutenant," she hissed, clutching her. "He's hideous and hateful and . . . and . . ."

"And far too good-looking for your peace of mind, obviously," Carmen retorted.

"Oh!" Marina pulled away from her cousin in anger. "You don't understand at all," she cried, and flew from the room.

Carmen looked after her, her dark eyes huge and knowing. "Marina, my dear cousin," she whispered softly to herself. "I fear you do protest too much."

Alone in her dark room, Marina lay on her bed and stared into the black corners. It was evident that Sebastian de la Cruz planned to torment her for as long as possible. She was going to have to do something soon to thwart his intentions. The time for polite requests was over. The stage was set for drastic action.

"Hold your fingers like so, *señorita*." Chico's dark little face was screwed up in concentration. "Then slip in your hand like this, moving quickly."

He demonstrated his light-fingered technique. "You slide in swiftly, like a snake, and curl your fingers around whatever is there. Then you slide out again, smooth and quick. Don't stop to look and see if they felt anything. You just move on, walking quickly, getting yourself out of reach, just in case."

Marina nodded, biting her lip. "Like this?" She flattened her hand against his chest and aimed at his pocket, but her fingers got caught on the laces of his shirt.

"No, *señorita*." Chico laughed, putting a hand over his mouth, his black eyes snapping with delight that the lovely young lady could be so clumsy at something he was so good at. "No, that is not the way. Look. I will show you again."

His hand moved with swift grace, snatching the bag of sand from the waistcoat they had set up against the fence. Marina had accompanied Carmen to visit her father again, but this time she had pulled the boy, Chico, aside and made a strange request that had made his mouth drop with astonishment.

"Will you teach me to pick pockets?" she'd asked. "I will give you a whole bag of *dulces*."

He'd been happy to comply, but after almost

half an hour, he was beginning to worry that his bag of candy was in jeopardy if the young lady didn't make some major improvements in her style.

"The most important thing to remember," he told her earnestly, "the most important thing is to draw their eyes away from what you are doing. You bump them like so . . ." He demonstrated. "Or you make a loud noise, or you have a friend call to them, or you use your other hand to capture their eyes. Like this." He made moves a magician would have been proud of, doing exactly what he'd hoped to achieve.

She smiled. He was so good at it. "I'll never be able to do it like that," she lamented.

He shrugged. "You must practice, *señorita*. That is the only way."

She practiced for another half hour, and then for the next few days, alone in her room. She wanted to be ready. The next time the Spaniard came to call, he was going to find out she wasn't quite the pushover he thought her to be.

That thought pleased her, making her smile. She'd never had this kind of purpose in her life before. It was a new experience to begin every day with such determination. She was going to beat the man, and to that end, she practiced even more diligently, until she thought she was actually getting pretty good at the pickpocket game.

"Just you wait, Sebastian de la Cruz," she whispered, looking out her window toward the Presidio. "We'll see who has the upper hand after all."

"There's Don Felipe." Carmen chuckled. "I

73

wouldn't wander too far from the crowd if I were you. He has the look of a man ready to throw you across the front of his palomino and ride off with you."

Marina glanced over at where Felipe, atop his horse, sat with the other young men. "He would never do such a thing, and you know it," she protested, but absently. It was the Spaniard she was watching out for. Did Spanish lieutenants come to market?

Every other Tuesday, the *padres* ran a farmers' *mercado* in the side yard at the mission. Food and goods were laid out everywhere—produce from the mission lands and the farms nearby, leather goods made by the mission Indians, silverwork made by *vaqueros,* saddles, bridles, bolts of cloth. And this Tuesday, Josefa had sent Carmen and Marina to do the shopping, as she was laid low with a bad cold.

Everyone came to the farmers' market, the women to shop and gossip, the men to sit on their horses nearby, chatting idly and strumming guitars. But something seemed different today. Marina frowned and looked toward the mountains. Was there something different about the light? Was there a breeze blowing from the east? It was as though a change was coming over her beloved land, and she didn't like it.

"Look, sailors from Alex's ship," Carmen hissed near her ear, directing her gaze toward a rough, unattractive bunch of men laughing and jostling one another near the cart selling homemade wine. "Alex usually doesn't allow them to come ashore in a bunch like this, does he? And I can see why."

Marina hardly wasted a glance on the sailors.

She looked about her at the familiar scene and thought how her life had changed in the last few weeks. For years she had followed her comfortable existence — lessons with the *padre,* light chores at home, an evening at the plaza, a day at the *mercado,* quiet visits with friends, an occasional *fandango,* the yearly rodeo — with very little to ruffle the pleasant calm of her life . . . until Sebastian de la Cruz had come crashing into things. With one fell swoop he'd cut away all her assumptions and thrown her life into turmoil. Now she was uncertain. She looked at everything about her with new eyes.

"Hello, girls." Delores Delgado met them over the display of crockery, smiling knowingly. "I haven't seen you in a long time. You don't come to the plaza anymore."

"We've been busy," Carmen said quickly, glancing at Marina and noting that she was frowning off into the distance, not paying any attention at all.

"So I've heard." Delores giggled and swished her full skirts. "My, Marina, it must be exciting to have men fighting over you." She waited, her dark eyes huge, to see what the two women would answer to that.

Carmen stared at her for a moment, then elbowed Marina, who was still oblivious. "Wake up, cousin. Delores says you've got men fighting over you."

Marina blinked at them. "What?"

"A duel," Delores whispered behind her hand. "So exciting."

Carmen's fingers gripped Marina's arm. "Surely

this is someone's fantasy," she said softly, her words meant more for her cousin than for her friend.

"Oh no, Carmen. Didn't Marina tell you?" Delores leaned closer and whispered, "I hear Don Felipe fought the Spaniard for Marina's honor."

Both young women stared at her open mouthed.

Marina was the first to recover. "That's ridiculous," she said tartly. "For my honor?"

Delores gave an elaborate shrug. "Yes. They say the Spaniard was too familiar with you and Don Felipe called him out to atone for it." Her dark eyes glittered and her voice lowered. "They say Don Felipe had the Spaniard on his knees, begging for mercy before the sun was fully up that day."

Marina looked toward where Felipe was laughing on the back of his horse, his hat cocked to the side, his shoulders set with pride. Noticing her gaze, he saluted her with a hand over his heart, and she turned away quickly. So Felipe had been spreading that version, had he? She was afraid that was not exactly how the scene had been played out, and he knew that very well. But if that was the story he wanted to tell about town, there was nothing much she could do about it.

"If Felipe fought a duel, it certainly wasn't for my honor," she snapped. "His own pride is much more important to him."

She regretted her nasty words before she'd finished uttering them, and her gaze flew to Delores's face to see how she had taken them. But Delores was looking toward the mission, and so was Carmen.

"He's here," Delores said.

Marina turned. Sebastian and Tomas were strolling unconcernedly through the marketplace, looking at the goods, their horses left behind at the post. The morning sun glinted on their polished boots, their shiny gold epaulets, their bright scarlet coats. A sigh went through the crowd. They were indeed cut from different cloth than this far-flung outpost was accustomed to seeing.

"Look at that," Felipe stated baldly, in a voice loud enough to be heard by half the area, including Marina. "On his feet like a common peasant."

A murmur swept through the crowd, but she couldn't tell if it was critical, like Felipe's comment, or interested, as Delores surely was.

"If it weren't for that sickening scar, I would say he was the most handsome man in the district," Delores said flatly.

Marina looked back at him curiously. In a way, he was she supposed. She'd never really thought about it. But the scar—that was her fault, to a degree, and it gave her a twinge of regret.

"I suppose it's another dueling wound, wouldn't you think?" Delores said, shivering deliciously. "The man is definitely dangerous."

Dangerous was the word for him. Marina watched him pause to look at a mirror for sale along with other household items, and most of the crowd seemed to be watching him as well. He spoke to his companion, but seemed casually unaware of the interest the town held in them both.

Still, there were others who noticed. Suddenly Don Felipe laughed loudly, tossed off a jest to one of his companions, and spurred his horse into action, dashing between the carts laden with produce. The animal seemed to dance, controlled superbly by his practiced touch. A wild *vaquero* yell guaranteed that attention was fully drawn away from the lieutenants, and then Felipe was gone, riding off toward some other gathering in some other place. A murmur arose among the other *vaqueros,* and many turned their horses and followed him.

"So dashing," Delores sighed, looking in the direction the audacious horseman had disappeared. "You're so lucky, Marina."

Lucky was not what Marina felt; desperate was more like it. There were emotions being kindled that threatened the peaceful life she loved. Turning to Carmen, she grimaced. "Let's get our shopping done and get back home," she said firmly.

"What's your hurry, cousin?" Carmen was still watching the two lieutenants, her face set in a speculative expression.

Marina threw her a glare and started off. "There's a bad wind coming, Carmen," she said back over her shoulder. "We'd better get home before it hits."

Carmen laughed, taking the warning for the metaphorical threat it was, and Marina left her behind, hurrying to buy the eggs her aunt had asked for, the dried beef, the spices, and a little sugar. That ought to do it for the day. Satisfied, she turned and looked for her cousin. What she saw sent a stinging pain like an arrow to lodge itself in her chest.

Carmen was flirting with the Spaniard. There was no other way to describe the brazen way she was looking up into his face and laughing, tossing back her hair, fluttering her eyelashes, as the Spaniard leaned toward her, laughing back. Anger poured through her. She'd never felt so betrayed. It was as though Carmen had defected to the enemy. Her oldest friend had turned traitor on her.

Moving with the angry grace of a stalking cat, she approached the two of them.

"I have everything," she announced, glaring at Carmen, avoiding Sebastian's eyes. "I'm going home."

Carmen smiled. "Don't let me stop you," she purred.

Marina could hardly believe what she'd heard. She hesitated a moment, sure that Carmen would come to her senses. But Carmen leaned close to the Spaniard and said something soft and quick, and Sebastian laughed aloud.

Marina turned, her cheeks blazing with fury, and hurried away. She was furious with her cousin, furious with the Spaniard, and completely determined to let neither one of them know how much she had been hurt by their behavior.

Things were getting worse and worse. Now he was coming between her and members of her family. First her father had been charmed by the man, and now Carmen. If she could only get her ring back, somehow she knew it would break the tie that seemed to bind him to her and her family. She had to do it, and she had to do it soon, so that she could put her mind at rest again.

Chapter Six

The very next day she had her chance. She was halfway to the chapel with Josefa and Carmen when she claimed a headache and returned to the house. Her father had mentioned, out of earshot of the others, that he'd told Sebastian that no one was to be at home and he was free to enjoy the library on his own for as long as he liked. She was never going to have a better opportunity than this.

So, her heart beating wildly, she turned back and made her way quickly to the house. Sebastian's huge black stallion was tied outside, just as she had hoped. She took a deep breath and tried to think clearly. It was now or never.

Sebastian looked about the cozy little library with pleasure. He loved books. Though this room was small and the collection limited, the look of the dusty shelves, the smell of the leather bindings, took him back to the extensive library his father had kept in their manor house in Catalan. As he ran his hand over a well-tooled cover, he remembered the golden light from the window in his father's house, the little desk that had been his alone, the table where he had sat with the priest, working on his lessons. Life had been so simple then. Filling his head with learning and running his father's vast estates had been all he had foreseen for his future.

Instead he found himself exiled to this barbarian country, living in squalid quarters, wearing a uniform he hated, drilling ragtag soldiers every day, preparing to defend the worthless land against Russian invaders who were very unlikely to venture down this far.

But at least there was this library to provide a respite. He appreciated James's eclectic interest. There was everything here from Shakespeare to sketchbooks. Rummaging through some old volumes, he'd found a cache of papers detailing some of the early experiences of settlers here. Those would be interesting to look over. But right now, he had other thoughts.

Idly he picked up a slender volume of love poems and traced the gold embossing with his finger. It was very much like another book he remembered, a journal filled with similar poems written by his sister Angelique, so long ago. He smiled as he remembered how he'd found her love sonnets and read them back to her, teasing her unmercifully, until she'd chased him through the house, shrieking plans for revenge. If he closed his eyes, he could almost be back in that house, in that time . . .

A sound at the door spun him around. He looked up and for just a second there she was, Angelique, her hair soft around her face, her eyes lit up with laughter.

It took him a moment to focus, a moment to breathe again, and then he realized that the vision he saw was not Angelique at all. It was Marina, standing in the doorway, her white bonnet in her hands, the pink ribbons fluttering toward the floor.

"Hello," she said, looking at him searchingly, as though she wasn't quite sure how he would greet her.

"Señorita." He frowned, still reeling from the trick his eyes and mind had played on him. He'd thought he would be alone today. James had promised him a solitary afternoon perusing the library on his own, and he'd been looking forward to it.

"No one will be at home but the maids," James had promised. "You may browse at leisure."

"I didn't hear you arrive," he said to her now. Somehow he couldn't get the feeling of Angelique out of his mind. And because of that, he found himself losing the frown and slowly smiling at her, enjoying her fresh prettiness. "Won't you come in?"

She hesitated. "You won't mind if I join you for a few minutes?" she asked lightly.

He was surprised that she hadn't refused. She usually tried to run from him. There was usually anger in her eyes. Instead of the usual termagant, he saw before him a soft, pretty young woman.

"No, of course not. Please, come in."

She entered slowly, looking sweet and vulnerable, her pretty dress swishing against the stacks of books. He swallowed and tried to steady himself, stop the way he could feel himself softening toward her. This wasn't Angelique, damn it, this was Marina, the girl who had scarred him. He had to keep that in mind.

She glanced at him and then away, moving slowly through the room until she'd made the circuit and had ended up where he was standing once again.

"What's that you have found?" She took a few steps closer to peer curiously at the book and the papers he'd spread out on the desk.

"Nothing. Just some old documents." He quickly picked up the book of poems and stuck it back onto a shelf.

She watched him do it but didn't comment. Instead, she smiled again. "Would you like something to eat?" she asked softly. "I can have one of the girls make some tea . . ."

"No," he said hastily. "No, thank you."

She turned, her hair drifting after her, and her scent hit him like a slap in the face, knocking his head back. Spicy, sweet, like roses in Spring, it overwhelmed him for a moment, and he couldn't speak.

This was insane. Just yesterday they had been glowering at one another with open animosity. And now she was smiling, embodying every attribute of femininity he appreciated most, and his resistance was crumbling faster than a fresh adobe wall in a hailstorm.

He couldn't take his gaze off her. What just hours before had seemed hard, sharp, and hateful now seemed soft, compelling, and very tantalizing. She moved a little closer, examining the stack of books he'd taken down.

"Do you read in English?" she asked, turning to look into his face.

"A little." He could hardly get the words out. He stared into her huge, liquid gray eyes uncertainly. She was so close he could almost feel her, and for some reason that was turning his legs to rubber. He blinked, unsure for a moment if he might not be coming down with something strange. This had never happened to him before. It must be the heat, the stuffiness of the room . . .

And then she was moving away again, wandering

along the highest bookshelf, looking for an old favorite of her own.

"I know it's in here somewhere," she was saying. "It's a book of poetry, but each poem is a puzzle that is answered by the next poem . . ."

He leaned against the desk, steadying himself. What was the matter with him? He'd never swooned over a woman before in his life, and he'd had plenty of opportunity to do so. He had to get hold of himself.

"Do you like poetry?" he asked, his voice strained.

She looked back with a smile. "I like stories where goodness is rewarded and evildoers get their just desserts," she said quietly, and for just a moment he frowned, wondering if she'd meant to mock him. But she was going on, looking for the volume of poetry she wanted, and he dismissed the thought.

"Ah, you like fairy tales, then," he commented, stepping out from beside the desk to follow her progress along the bookshelf.

She glanced up. "You don't think the world really works that way?" she asked.

He shook his head, his mouth twisting cynically. "I know it doesn't. I've seen the world firsthand. There is no justice."

She stopped, staring at him, searching his gaze as though wondering at his bitter tone. "Why do you say that?" she asked softly.

Her face was so open, so trusting, he found himself telling her things he had told no one, not even Tomas.

"In Spain, I was involved in a power struggle of sorts." A picture of Don Hernando Hidalgo de Coronado flashed in his mind. The thought of him and his family of stunted gnomes inhabiting the beautiful

84

house that had been in Sebastian's family for centuries cut like a mortal wound, and he winced. "I was the one with less power, and consequently, I was the one who lost everything."

"Oh, no. I'm so sorry."

For just a moment he thought she was going to reach out to him. She actually looked as though her sympathy was sincere. "Is that why you're in the Mexican Army?"

"Yes." He turned away, unwilling to go into it any longer.

"Oh, well." She sighed, and laughed softly. "How disappointing."

He turned back, puzzled, but enchanted by the picture she made with the light coming in behind her from the high window, filling her soft hair with glints like fireflies.

"How so?" he asked.

She laughed. "I was sure your story had to be much more romantic. I thought perhaps you had been caught in the bedroom of a duke's wife or trifling with some nobleman's daughter."

She was smiling, but her words carried a sting. He frowned, wondering if he was reading her right after all. "You have a high opinion of me, I can see that," he said evenly.

She turned and shook out her hair, sending her scent sailing toward him in waves.

"You forget, Lieutenant," she said as she moved away. "I've seen you in action."

He followed her. How could he resist? He wanted to touch her so badly his hands were clenching convulsively. "And here I thought we were getting to be friends," he murmured, fascinated by the soft white skin of her neck, the tiny satin hairs that curled at her hairline, the curve of her ear.

"Friends?" Something flashed behind the darkness in her eyes as she stopped and looked up into his face, but he couldn't be sure he understood what it was. "I would have said friendship was the last thing you wanted from me."

"Oh?" He stood close, near enough to smell her scent again, near enough to see the pulse at the base of her throat, near enough to set his own pulse beating like the hooves of a galloping horse. "What did you think I wanted of you, Marina?"

She turned imperceptibly, but her movement brought her up so close that she was almost pressing against him. Only the width of a piece of paper still lay between them. She tilted her face toward his, her eyes on the sharp, cruel cut of his lips.

"I thought," she said, her voice barely above a whisper, and trembling slightly, "perhaps, this . . ."

She went up on her toes to reach him, her hands flattening against his chest as her lips touched his. There was no time for him to be surprised. She was there, and he wanted her.

Her lips parted alluringly, their coolness giving way to the sweet, hot excitement of her mouth. He didn't stop to ask himself why. Every instinct in him was dazed by her provocative move, and he welcomed her, then quickly took control, his practiced technique smooth and seductive, honed over years at the royal court, moving and probing with a mastery all his own.

But somehow this wasn't what he was used to. She was offering her lips and the mystery of her mouth, but he could sense right away she was withholding everything else, including her heart. She tasted clean as water from a mountain spring, fresh, completely innocent. And though there was apprehension, there was no real fear. But neither was there passion.

She didn't really want to kiss him. That surprised him. But instead of repulsing him and making him wonder, it only challenged his arrogant pride.

He tried harder. He moved more seductively, taking her face between his hands, caressing her with his fingertips as he caressed her with his tongue. He was going to show her how desirable he was, make her want him as much as he wanted her, let her understand what sort of man she was dealing with.

But suddenly he realized something: her hands were no longer flattened against his chest. One hand had moved, sliding surreptitiously into the pocket of his waistcoat, and was sliding out again, fingers curled around the unicorn ring.

He jerked back and caught the hand before it had time to escape, his hold tightening about her wrist until she cried out, dropping the silver piece of jewelry, which he deftly caught. He had it again.

Still holding her, he stared appalled into her wide, defiant eyes. She'd tricked him. She'd used his stubborn pride to make him think she was attracted to him, then tried to use that to cover up her theft. And he'd fallen for it like a country fool.

"So," he sneered, fury turning his tone to ice. "You thought you could deceive me with a kiss, did you, *querida?*"

She blinked, not giving an inch. "All I want is what belongs to me."

He held the ring in his fist, inches from her face. "I told you what you would have to do to get it," he said softly, his eyes deep with anger. "Don't you remember my terms?"

"Yes, I remember your ridiculous terms." Her

eyes flashed. "You think I would come to your quarters like a common tramp?"

"No," he growled back, "I think you should come to my quarters like an honest woman who keeps her side of a bargain."

She struggled to free her hand. "I made no bargain with you and you know it."

"Ah, but you did, *querida.*" He released her hand, but held the unicorn ring up high where she could plainly see it. "I'll be waiting to complete our transaction." Slipping it into his pocket once again, he caught hold of her chin before she could get away, holding her close and staring hard down into her face.

"By the time you come, I hope you will learn to show a little more passion. Your kiss was as cool as a winter rain. If you can't dredge up more heat than that, you'll hardly be worth my time."

She ripped herself away from his touch and stormed out through the doorway, but his laughter seemed to echo throughout the house, and she covered her ears as she ran to her room, hating him more than ever, more than she had ever hated anyone or anything before.

Marina sat on the wooden bench at the edge of the patio and looked about herself with discontent. Why did things have to change? She hated change. Nothing was the same as it had been.

The scene was a familiar one to her, the family with a few friends sitting on the patio on a warm evening, watching the sun go down while they waited for their dinner. Josefa was talking a mile a minute, Carmen was laughing at her aunt, Alex was there, along with neighbors Jorge Dimas and his wife

María, and Manuel Guerrero, another bookworm who was a close friend of her father's.

It was who wasn't present that was bothering Marina. James Crafts had been detained at his new duties with the Alcalde. These days, when the Alcalde called, her father had to go. She hated to see him in this position. Perhaps once she was married to Felipe . . .

And there was a puzzle. Everyone was beginning to whisper about Felipe, and she knew it. They were all beginning to wonder why he was taking such a time to ask for her hand. She was even beginning to wonder herself, though she was in no hurry. Marrying Don Felipe seemed, in a way, to be what she had been born to do. Yet that too would bring changes. Was it all just part of coming into maturity? Was the safe, protected time of childhood now completely gone? Was it going to be like this from now on?

Something stirred in her, something deep and disturbing, and she didn't like it.

"Marina, can I get you something to drink?"

She looked up and smiled at Captain Brandene. "No, thank you, Alex. I'm just sitting here enjoying the sunset."

He hesitated, and she could tell he wanted to sit beside her.

"I think Tía Josefa needs help carrying that pitcher," she said quickly to distract him, then sighed with relief as he hurried off.

Alex was acting strangely lately. For some reason he seemed to want to touch her knee all the time, and it disconcerted her. She found herself edging away when he came near, wondering whether it wasn't about time his ship set sail for Yerba Buena.

On the whole, she realized suddenly, men were

annoying her in almost every phase of life. Her father, Don Felipe, Alex — and worst of all, Sebastian de la Cruz.

She'd certainly made a mess of that. She'd come so close to getting the ring back. Well, pickpocketing was out of the question now. All that practicing for nothing. From now on, he would be on his guard every time she came near. The one good thing was, there was no reason to try to kiss him again.

She pressed her hand to her mouth when she thought of it. She hated to think the man frightened her, but she found her nerves quivering every time she thought of him. She had to make herself stronger where he was concerned. And she had to find a new way to get the ring back.

Wracking her brain for another scheme, she had thought of something, but it was so dreadful, so immoral, so utterly shameless, she didn't dare let it come to full realization in her mind. Only if she was absolutely desperate would she sink to that level.

In the meantime, there was the puzzle of her cousin. Carmen, her closest female friend and confidante for most of her life, her "sister," her companion. She hated the fact that there seemed to be a rift growing between them. It was only because of Sebastian, of course. Ever since he'd arrived in town, Carmen had been intrigued with him. It seemed that just having him around made her more and more dissatisfied with her everyday life in ways that Marina couldn't understand at all. Carmen seemed to crave change, the very thing Marina dreaded.

But as she watched the growing colors in the evening sky, she realized that what was really bothering her most was Jonathan's disappearance. Behind everything else she did or thought or said, that mystery was lurking. Where had he gone? What was he doing? Was he actually back by now, living in his room in Boston again, going to classes? It could very well be. It did take so long to get news. Perhaps they were all worrying for nothing.

"What is it, cousin, that has you frowning so?"

Marina looked up at Carmen with a start. "Oh. I . . . I was just thinking of Jonathan."

"Jonathan?" Carmen sank down onto the seat beside her. "What about Jonathan?"

"It's so puzzling what might have happened to him, why he wasn't in his rooms when Alex came to call."

She'd told Carmen what Alex had told her about the matter a few days before, and it seemed to her that Carmen had been coldly quiet about the dilemma.

Carmen nodded now, staring off toward the horizon. "If he was coming home, he should have made it back by now," she said softly.

Marina frowned her impatience. "Yes, but why would he be coming home? He had another year at least to go in his studies, and he would have said something, written to us."

Carmen gave her a look, then shook her head, avoiding Marina's gaze.

"I told him to come home," she said, her voice strained and muffled as she turned away. "I . . . I told him that . . . that he was needed here, and if he didn't come back quickly, things were going to . . . get worse. In the last letter I got, he said he understood, and . . ."

"What?" Marina grabbed Carmen's arm. She couldn't believe her ears. "When did you tell him this? When did he write to you?" She stared at her cousin. "He writes to the entire family, all at once, in one letter."

Carmen's cheeks were unusually rosy and her dark eyes slid away from direct confrontation with her cousin. "I know that, Marina. But I wrote to him about some . . . private things. And he wrote back a few times."

"A few times." Marina was stunned, her heart sinking. "Only to you?"

Here was another example of how things were changing. Jonathan was *her* brother, *her* best friend. If he had something private to say, he would have said it to her, not to Carmen. He and Carmen had always been friends, but after all, they weren't even related by blood.

She pulled her hand back and looked away from Carmen, resentment filling her with pain. Closing her eyes for a moment, she fought it back. After all, the point here was the worry about Jonathan, not about whom he wrote to.

"What did he say?" she asked in a choked voice. "Did he say he was coming back?"

Carmen shook her head slowly. "No, he never said that. But I made it very clear that he should."

Marina stared at her, not sure what her cousin was talking about. Who was she to order Jonathan home? And why?

One of the kitchen girls came out to call the group in to dinner, and the conversation between them was over for the time being. But Marina was more than ever convinced she had stepped off the stable ground of her normal life and was tiptoeing across quicksand these days. Nothing was any longer what it had seemed.

Chapter Seven

Moonlight hitting the bars on her window made an odd pattern against her bedroom wall.

"Like a prison," she whispered to herself, staring out onto the street drenched silver in the full moon.

A prison. She shook herself. Now she was beginning to sound like Carmen. Was this restlessness in her soul like what her cousin was feeling?

She heard hoofbeats and quickly closed the shutters, waiting in the darkness. There was no way she was going to let Felipe think she was anticipating him with baited breath.

The hoofbeats slowed and then there came the muffled sound of a horse being walked to her window. A moment later, knuckles rapped softly.

She waited, counting to ten, then undid the shutters and yawned in his face. "You are very late," she whispered.

His hat was back on his head and his eyes were bleary. *"Preciosa,* I'm truly sorry, but I was riding by the Delgado *rancho* and they had such a *baile* going, and they called me in. What could I do? I couldn't be rude." He laughed softly. "And I couldn't tell them where I was going."

She stared out at him. She had only dared let him come to her window this way twice before, and both times she had met him with her heart in her throat, terrified of being caught, excited at seeing him this way. Tonight what she mostly felt was cross at being kept up so late.

"Well, what is it that you had to tell me?" She'd received a message earlier that evening that Felipe had something very important to say to her, and to be ready. She'd known he'd meant he would visit her in the night. For some reason, she had done no speculating at all as to what he might have to say that required this clandestine meeting. Her mind had been on other things.

He laughed and she could smell the liquor on his breath as he leaned close to the bars. "First, a kiss, beloved one," he urged.

She stared at him. Perhaps it was the late hour, or her general state of annoyance, but the thought of kissing this man left her absolutely cold tonight.

"You're dreaming, Felipe," she snapped. "You dance and sing with other women all evening, then come to me for a kiss?"

"Ah, Marina, don't doubt my love. You know I love no one but you in all the world." His smile had a hint of his usual attractiveness. "I may dance with other girls from time to time, how can I help it? They are all so insistent, and I do love to dance. But you know I will always come back to find you when the fun is all over."

Marina almost laughed aloud. "When the fun is all over?" she hissed instead. "When you come back to find me, *hombre,* you will find me gone."

She reached out to close the shutters, but his hand shot in through the bars, stopping her.

"Marina, Marina, you're only angry because I'm late and you missed me," he cajoled. "When we are betrothed, you'll forget this sort of nonsense."

"Betrothed?" She froze, wondering why that word had the power to terrify her so.

For the first time that evening, she really looked at the man, and what she saw surprised her. He was dressed in an unfamiliar *serape*. She glanced quickly at his horse, tied nearby, and saw that it carried his leather shield with the old Spanish crest still painted on it, and his carbine as well. Looking back, she read the truth in his eyes.

"You're off on campaign?" she whispered, suddenly cold. "What has happened?"

His eyes widened with excitement. "Indians. They came down out of the mountains and hit the Lopez *rancho*. Drove off all his horses, butchered his cattle, and killed his *mayordomo*. We're off to teach them a lesson."

A wave of guilt washed over her. Here she was being churlish and the man was about to go off and risk his life for them all.

"Will it be dangerous?" she asked quickly. "Will you be safe?"

He gave her a swashbuckling smile. "I've been on campaign before. I know what to do to stay alive. I've taken their arrows and everything else they've got to throw at us. I'm a survivor, *preciosa*." He held out his hand for hers. "I must come back for you after all."

She took his hand and held it tightly, her eyes wide and full of apprehension. "Are . . . are any of the soldiers from the Presidio going with you?"

He frowned, his hand loosening on hers. "Like the Spanish lieutenant, you mean?" Turning, he spat into the dirt. "Not likely. The officers say this is not a big enough battle for their star performers, so they're sending a few of the dragoons along, and that's all." He laughed harshly, not noticing the odd look on Marina's face. "The truth is, they're afraid. But we have enough men from the *ranchos* and the *pueblo*. We'll have a glorious time."

"But . . . how long will you be gone?" A thought suddenly occurred to her. "Will you miss the Alcalde's *baile?*" It threatened to be the social event of the season. Everyone had been talking about it for weeks.

"The Alcalde's *baile.*" He sneered. "We've no time for such frivolities. We'll be gone at least a week." He squeezed her hand, gazing at her soulfully. "You'll have to dance alone, my darling." His face changed. "But I didn't come just to say good-bye. I wanted to warn you."

"Warn me?" She went still, intuition already telling her who this warning was going to be about. "Warn me about what?"

"The Spanish lieutenant. The arrogant one. The one I humiliated the other day. Sebastian de la Cruz."

She hardly felt she needed a warning about that one. She already knew his dark side better than anyone else in town, even Felipe. But she couldn't tell him that.

"I have as little to do with the man as possible," she told him quickly instead. "I don't like him at all."

"But he's received in your house almost daily," Felipe said, his voice revealing his surprise at that turn of events. "Your father acts as though he's an old friend."

"They both love books and take pleasure in discussing them."

"Books." Felipe snorted his derision. "Yes, you see what comes of too much reading of books. I haven't read a book since I was a boy and I hope I never have to."

Marina stared. "That's hardly something to brag about. There's more to the world than cattle and horses."

"*Sí*, there are blackguards like this Spaniard. It is not only your father who seems to like the scoundrel. Carmen is seen flirting with him in public." His eyes narrowed. "Even you are said to favor him."

"I?" She pulled her hand away in shock. "Who says this?"

He took hold of the bars on the window with both hands. "I say it, Marina. I have eyes in my head."

How could he be so wrong?

"I hate the man!"

He laughed shortly. "I've no time for that now. Hear me out. Sebastian de la Cruz has been seen riding that old piece of land the governor gave your father ten years ago."

Marina had to think for a moment to know which piece he was talking about. "That patch of weeds by the dry river?"

He nodded. "It's not insignificant, Marina. Most of the land around here has been parcelled out by now, that which the *padres* haven't claimed for themselves, and even lots like that given to your father are becoming dear. It's certainly good enough to maintain a small *rancho,* if your father ever has a mind to try ranching. Part of it runs alongside my family's land, you know. We've been letting cattle graze on it for years. I would hate to see the man gain any sort

97

of control over it."

"How on earth would he gain control of it?" She was genuinely puzzled as to what he was concerned about.

"I don't know, *preciosa*. I only know he was seen surveying it and writing figures into a book. Warn your father. And take care."

He moved restlessly, looking over his shoulder. "It's getting late. The others are waiting for me. I must go." He sighed and looked at her with love. "Give me some remembrance to take with me into battle, beloved."

She hesitated, then went to her chest. Lifting the lid, she let her hand rest on her best scarf, a long, blue silk with initials worked into one corner in gold thread. She had been saving it for a special occasion. It would be perfect.

But somehow she couldn't force herself to take it up and hand it to him. Instead, she plucked up a small sachet bag decorated with embroidered roses and went to the window. Solemnly, she kissed it and handed it through the bars to him.

"Vaya con Dios, Felipe," she said softly.

He pressed it to his heart. "Now I know that nothing can harm me, for I have your love to protect me," he declared. But from the look in his eyes, the battle to come was beginning to take precedence over love. "Marina, I'll bring you back a trophy. What would you like? An Indian pony, or maybe a little boy to serve at your table?"

She drew back, repelled, staring at the excitement in his face. The reality of what was about to happen suddenly became clear to her. Felipe was on his way to administer the brutal justice of the frontier.

"Felipe . . ." She clung to the bars herself. "Felipe,

why do you have to go? Why not let the Indians get away this time?"

He shook his head, giving her the pitying look men give women who just don't understand. "They have to be taught a lesson or they'll just come down and destroy more and more of the herds. If they're not stopped, if they're allowed to get away with it, they'll be out here soon, raiding the coastal ranchos. We have no choice."

A shout came from up the road and he turned to look in that direction. "I must go." He stepped back to the window. "But first, Marina," he whispered, his eyes burning, "one kiss."

Her heart began to beat very fast. She knew she couldn't refuse. Leaning forward, she met his lips between the bars, her eyes closed, her breath held.

It was over quickly. As he drew away and swung onto his horse, she watched him go, her fingertips pressed softly to her lips. His kiss had done nothing to stir the embers she was beginning to realize lived in the depths of her soul. When Sebastian so much as looked at her, small flames flared that ate into her sense of serenity. But Felipe's kiss left her cold. It was hardly fair.

Felipe pulled his horse up into one last salute, then, joined by two other horsemen, galloped off into the night.

Marina remained at her window, looking out into the moonlight. Far in the distance a wild shout raised yet another campaigner as the men gathered for the long ride. The black shadows of the pepper trees hid the road from her view, but in her imagination she could see them and feel their excitement.

Perhaps it was meant to be this way, meant that men should crave this sort of adventure. Otherwise, who would ride out to protect the families and settlements?

The hills surrounding San Feliz looked very black against the purple sky. Looking out at them, Marina felt a flood of warmth for her home, for California and its stark, hard beauty. For all his faults, Felipe was a part of the land that she loved, and in marrying him, she would wed herself forever to the sun-baked soil and its pastoral way of life. That thought brought her contentment and smothered back the doubts which had been pricking at her mind lately. She was California-born and -bred. It was to California that she belonged, and here lay her destiny.

She sighed and closed the shutters, slumping wearily into her bed. Whatever happened, she would pray for Felipe's safe return and welcome him when he came back. That was to be her role if she was to be his wife.

One thing bothered her, though. While she felt anxious for Felipe's safety, the only moment of real fear she had experienced when he'd told her about the trip had been when she'd thought the soldiers from the Presidio might be going, too. She refused to admit, even to herself, why that had been. But along with her prayers for Felipe, she was going to pray for her own deliverance — from this obsession with the hateful Spaniard.

Chapter Eight

Marina pulled the bright blue sash tightly around her waist and expertly tied it at her side, letting the ends fall almost to the floor. She then pulled a long necklace of white pearls over her head and looked into her mirror. Slowly she shook her head, took off the pearls, and took up a large gold brooch which she pinned to the low neckline of her pale blue bodice. Her cream-colored linen skirt had four deep flounces, each of them beautifully embroidered with red, blue, green, and even gold thread. As she tied on her blue satin heelless shoes, she heard the door of her room open.

"Well, your best dress, and Don Felipe is not even planning to attend." Carmen stared at her without her usual sisterly affection. "Whose heart are you planning to steal tonight?"

Marina couldn't keep the color from flooding her cheeks, but she did her best to turn away to hide it. "You're the one the *caballeros* all flock around, Carmen." She glanced at her reflection in the mirror one more time. "Besides, Felipe went campaigning on his own accord. I can't help it if he's not here for the Alcalde's *baile*."

Carmen flounced down onto her bed and positioned herself to watch Marina's reactions. "Have you two had a quarrel?" she asked. "You'd best be careful, Marina. Offend the man and he just might disappear from your life. He'd never have the energy to make the effort to patch up an argument. The only things he has energy for are lovemaking and riding. And, I guess, fighting Indians."

Marina gave her an icy glare. "Will you please be polite enough to keep from criticizing Felipe to my face?" she asked evenly. "He's from the finest family in San Feliz, you know, a family which has treated us with nothing but kindness."

Carmen sighed, her shoulders sagging. "I'm sorry, Marina, I really am. I just . . ." She bit her lip, looking her cousin over with narrowed eyes. "It surprised me to find you dressing so carefully, that's all. Tonight I'm planning my main attack upon Sebastian's defenses and I don't relish the thought of any distractions cluttering up his line of vision."

Her words hit Marina like a thunderbolt. She swung around to face her cousin. "You're *what?*" she said breathlessly, paling.

"Going after the Spaniard," Carmen replied with utter candor. "I've decided I want him."

"Want him?" Marina felt faint. "What are you talking about? You can't just 'want' him, like a new pair of shoes or a ripe fruit."

Carmen grinned wickedly. "Why not?"

"Because . . ."

The words wouldn't come. Emotions seemed to be getting in the way. She looked critically at Carmen's scarlet lace dress, from her daringly low neckline to her shockingly high hemline. Her jet-black hair was pulled back with combs and then allowed to fall in long, swaying ringlets. A cream-white camellia was pinned behind her right ear, echoing the creamy white exposure of her breast. She looked enchantingly playful and lovely. What man could resist a come-on like this?

Marina swallowed hard and looked into her cousin's eyes with dread. "Do you love him?" she asked in a choked voice.

Carmen shrugged, her own eyes glazing over. "What do I care about love?" she answered quickly. "It's not love I'm looking for. I'll do anything to escape this place."

Marina took a deep breath. Relief flooded her. If there was no love involved, there was still time.

"Oh, Carmen, leave Sebastian alone. There are other ways to get what you want."

"Are there?" Carmen's lip came out petulantly and her tone became sarcastic. "How shall I go about it, Marina? Shall I go off to Boston to study, like Jonathan? Shall I ask Alex to give me a job on his ship so that I can work my way to New England? Shall I stow away with the next shipment of hides to South America? Which course of action would you suggest?"

Marina shook her head. "Carmen . . ."

"The only way a woman can get what she wants is through a man," Carmen said resentfully. "Sebastian hates it here. I know he has asked for a transfer back to Mexico City. He hopes to get back to Spain eventually. As his wife, I could go with him . . ."

Marina threw out her palms in exasperation. "But what makes you think he would ever marry you?"

She shrugged with more bravado than she actually felt. "As his mistress, I might at least go along for the ride."

"Carmen!" Marina wanted to shake her. "You've

103

got to stop this. I've written to Jonathan about your crazy plans . . ."

"You've *what?*" Carmen jumped up from the bed, a look of horror on her pretty face. "He's not even there. You can't write to him."

Marina shrugged. If Carmen could write to him on her own, so could she. "He's somewhere, and sometime he'll come back to his rooms, I'm sure. So I'm writing to him . . ."

"No!" Carmen turned distracted. "No, you can't, Marina. You mustn't. Not until it's all over."

"What?" Marina frowned, not understanding at all. "Until what's all over? Carmen, what are you talking about?"

"Marina, don't you understand?" Carmen stood before her cousin with tears trembling in her eyes. Her mouth opened and she began to say something, but Josefa's voice interfered.

"Girls, are we ready?" Josefa was calling from the hallway. "It is time to go."

Carmen shook her head, blinking back the tears. "Oh, never mind!" she cried, running from the room.

Marina stared after her in confusion. She and Carmen didn't seem to be able to communicate anymore the way they always had before. What was more, they didn't seem to be able to sense things about one another, either. They were becoming strangers in the same house, and Marina didn't like it at all.

Sebastian stopped at the doorway of the brightly lit room and looked it over like an actor counting the house. His trousers were sky blue, his waistcoat a deep purple velvet with gold buttons. His coat was vivid scarlet, impeccably cut and heavily embroidered with gold braid. The hat he carried in his hand was black and trimmed with more gold braid and an elegant white plume, and the sword at his side glittered silver.

Confident and dignified, he entered knowing that all eyes were turning to look him over, the older ones with apprehension, the younger female ones with anticipation. But he hardly seemed to notice at all. He stood with his back ramrod straight, his head high and haughty, his green eyes on the distant corner. A slight sneer curled his lips, and every girl in the room knew he held the room and its occupants in a sort of jaded contempt. This didn't bother them, though. Far from being insulting, his scorn only added to his fascinating qualities and made each woman wonder if she could be the one to prove herself worthy of his regard.

He knew all this, but hardly cared. He wasn't here to impress the ladies. He was here to fulfill a promise he had made to himself. Revenge was never completely satisfying, but it did serve to pass the time and to give purpose to life. All he had to do was catch sight of the scar on his face in a pane of glass and the need for revenge burned bright in him again.

A commotion at the entry attracted his attention, along with that of everyone else present. Señor Crafts entered, escorting Tía Josefa in black and gold, Carmen in a blaze of scarlet, and Marina, softly cool in blue and cream, to sighs and exclamations on all sides.

Yes, it was abundantly clear that the Crafts family was held in high esteem here, the daughters beloved. He couldn't have picked more compelling subjects for his plan. The only fly in the ointment was James

Crafts, and watching him, Sebastian frowned. The man was a genuinely decent fellow. It was going to be a shame to hurt him. But things of value never came easily. There was always a price to be paid, even in the best of situations.

As he met the family, bowing to each member in turn, he made a quick judgment on how things stood. It was obvious that James candidly liked him, and Josefa was beginning to treat him with a grudging friendliness. Carmen had a plan of her own. From the flash of her eyes, he could see she was primed to put it into action tonight. But Marina still looked at him with dread and loathing. He was going to have to change that if he was to get what he was after.

He turned to James. "The dancing has already begun. May I have the honor of leading out your daughter, *Señor?*"

"Certainly," James responded without so much as glancing at Marina to check for her consent, and ignoring at the same time the jabs his ribs were enduring from Josefa's fan. "Go right ahead."

"Not a waltz, James," Josefa hissed. "Stop him!"

But Sebastian was already placing his arm around Marina's back and pulling her out of the protection of her family and into the spell of the music. It was too late.

She hadn't expected to be assaulted by his presence quite so soon into the evening. Remembering the last time they had been this close, she colored and glanced quickly at his waistcoat to see if it was sporting the familiar bulge that would tell her where her unicorn ring was hiding. But there was no telltale lump, and she felt a sense of relief. Perhaps tonight she could get through the evening without having to

106

think about the ring. If only she could survive one dance with the odious man, she would make sure he wasn't able to get near her again.

She followed him now because she didn't seem to see any alternative to doing so without making a scene. Holding herself stiffly, she glanced nervously out at the onlookers. A dance was so public, there was no way anyone could object to her being here with him this way. So why was it that she felt so furtive about it?

Sebastian led superbly and expected her to melt into his arms as she got into the step, but that didn't happen. He waited for her to look up, but very soon he realized she had no intention of meeting his gaze, and he chuckled.

"You can relax," he told her as they swayed together to the rather stately waltz. "I'm not going to do anything to embarrass you."

That brought her gray eyes up for a flashing moment. "Just forcing me to dance with you is embarrassment enough," she said evenly.

He had to smile to himself. At least she wasn't a mousy little thing. She had a way about her that was making the entire operation much more interesting than it might have been.

"You don't like waltzing?" he said, pretending not to know exactly what she was talking about.

"Oh no, it's not that." She flushed. For some reason she felt she had to explain. "I love it. Only it's not often danced here. The mission *padre* doesn't approve of it, and many people won't allow it in their homes."

She glanced up, expecting to see disdain in his face for their provincial ways, but instead his green eyes were calm and unreadable.

"There are always people who are afraid of anything new," he told her quietly. "Are you one of those?"

Was she? She supposed, if she were honest, she might have to answer yes. But she couldn't bear to have him laugh at her.

"Of course not," she said quickly. "I told you I love the waltz. But . . . it makes me a little nervous to look out there and see disapproving faces."

"I see," he murmured, his eyes hooded. "You like to play the part of the good girl, don't you, *querida?*"

Her mouth set as she gazed at him. "I *am* a good girl, Lieutenant. I don't have to play a part."

He smiled at her indignation, looking almost guileless. "Then it must be your partner the others disapprove of, Marina. Could that be it?"

She almost smiled back, surprising herself. "Perhaps," she said. "You are a sophisticate. Some people may feel threatened by that."

He raised one eyebrow. "But not you," he stated as fact.

Now she really was smiling. "Never," she agreed, her eyes sparkling.

He laughed and she almost joined him. He saw the urge to do so in her eyes, and suddenly he realized something he hadn't really allowed himself to think about before. Marina was by far the most attractive woman in the room. She had a spark he liked, and yet a soft femininity that made him want to hold her close and . . . well, it was best not to think about that right now.

"But you are a man of the world," she was saying, still trying to explain her town and its people. "Most of us have never been any further than Santa Barbara, and you've lived at the court in Spain."

He grimaced. "That shouldn't impress anyone. The Spanish court is not necessarily an attractive place, believe me."

Marina reacted from pure intuition. "Oh, I can't believe that." Her mind conjured up pictures of storybook castles and princesses at high windows and her eyes shone. "It must have been wonderful."

He smiled at her enthusiasm. "Not really. In fact, it was more a penance than anything else. You see, when living at court, one is never free to do as one wishes. Everyone attending must follow the whim of the monarch of the moment. If he happens to be pious, all the courtiers must spend every waking moment poring over the Bible. If he is dull, no one is allowed to read at all. If he is a frivolous man, all his time will be spent at amusements, and every courtier must plot and intrigue against every other or lose his place, if not his life."

Marina stared up at him, fascinated. Suddenly she understood the appeal this man had to Carmen. He'd lived things she could only dream of.

"The women at court . . . are they beautiful?"

He smiled and nodded, then moved closer. His voice was soft when he answered, soft and so close, she could feel his breath against her ear, warm and caressing. "The women at court are stunning. But I've never seen one I have wanted the way I have wanted you, Marina."

She blinked, not sure if she had heard correctly. The words weren't said in the mocking, menacing way he had said every other comment he had ever made about her. And they weren't said in the ritualistic way every compliment that came out of Felipe's mouth sounded, as though he had said them a thousand times and was almost bored with the repetition. He'd spoken with calm sincerity, a sense of genuine candor she could hardly believe had come from him. And yet he had spoken with the kind of familiarity men could be killed for. And if he really meant what he had said . . .

There was a tingling in her body, a ringing in her ears, and she could hardly breathe.

The music was slowing to a stop, and to her shock, she found she didn't want this dance to end. His arm was strong and hard against her back, his shoulders wide as the sky before her, and when she looked into his face, she saw the clean-cut jawline, the white teeth, the glittering emerald eyes, and hardly noticed the fiery scar at all.

She felt dizzy for a moment and had to fight the urge to lean against him, let herself flow into his arms and be held there. Her eyes met his and caught as something wordless blazed between them. But the dance was over, and he was depositing her with her aunt.

"Thank you, Marina," he said softly. "I hope you'll allow me the pleasure of your company again a bit later this evening."

She couldn't speak, and she turned away quickly, appalled at how she was reacting.

Behind her, Sebastian smiled, and as he turned to go across the room, began to whistle tunelessly. All in all, things were going quite well.

But Marina moved in a haze, like a swimmer trying to fight to get her head above water. She had to think clearly. The man had done something to fog her mind. For just a moment, she trembled all over.

"Marina, what's wrong? Are you coming down with something?" Josefa fussed over her, making her sit down in a chair.

Marina sat and looked about her. The music was playing. Another waltz. And there, out on the floor, was Sebastian, dancing with Carmen.

It hit her like a thunderbolt, jolting her from within. Candor? Genuine feeling? Sincerity? Was she really such a fool?

The man was treacherous. He was also a liar and a philanderer, and she had better not forget it. She took a deep breath and her mind cleared. That had been close. She had gone through a moment or two of insanity, but it was over now. Thank heavens she hadn't said anything while under his spell. She would be more careful the next time.

Fully restored and fortified by anger, she stood and smiled as Jose Delgado came up to ask for the dance. Of course she would dance with him, and with any other man who asked. She was bound and determined to have a wonderful time, and to show that crafty Spaniard that she was not taken in by him at all.

She danced to every tune the next hour brought with it, though never with Sebastian.

"Don't let him come near me," she'd warned Josefa.

Her aunt, eyes snapping, had been glad to oblige. "I always thought he was a bad egg," she muttered as she flapped about her charge like a giant crow. "I warned James about him again and again . . ."

Sebastian saw the way the wind was blowing right away and didn't press the issue. He did, however, dance with Carmen more and more, a fact Marina didn't miss. He also danced with Gloria Estancia, who clung to his arm, simpering, until a bright-eyed *vaquero* with a gold earring came and took her away.

111

Half an hour later three of her six brothers came by, looking for her with pistols in their belts and murder in their eyes, but Sebastian was quickly exonerated and they went on to look for their errant sister elsewhere.

Marina watched it all from afar. Carmen's behavior was agony to witness. It was all very well to save herself from the man, but what about her cousin? Shouldn't she at least warn her?

One look at Carmen's flushed face and she knew it would be of no use. Carmen would just accuse her of wanting the man for herself. She was going to have to think of some other way to protect her.

Warm and wilting, she joined some of the other girls at the punchbowl and turned just in time to see Carmen handing Sebastian a note, which he read, then quickly stuffed into his back pocket, before sending Carmen a significant nod across the room.

Marina's heart began to beat very quickly. An assignation. Carmen was out of her mind, but what was she going to do to stop her? Jorge Martinez asked Josefa if he might lead Marina out to dance and when he presented himself before her, she smiled, though she hardly knew who he was at the moment. Her mind was going like the wind down an *arroyo*.

She wasn't going to stand back and watch Carmen ruin her life without at least trying to do something about it. Once again, she had a plan. And if that didn't work, she would make another. She was committed to stopping Sebastian de la Cruz and making Carmen see him as he really was.

When the call came for a *jota,* she joined the line on the women's side, singing out the verses with zest as she danced the steps. Sebastian didn't seem to

112

have any trouble learning the pattern, but when they passed one another and he smiled at her, she managed to look right through him and call out a greeting to Ricardo Cruz, just behind him in the line.

Sebastian turned and watched her go back to the protection of her aunt, his expression speculative. What had looked so promising was fast slipping through his fingers. Josefa was guarding her charge like a hawk and it was obvious the vigilance was meant to keep him as far as possible from his goal. It was time for drastic action.

Chapter Nine

Turning, Sebastian found his friend Tomas on the sidelines.

"Are you having a good time?" he asked.

Tomas shrugged. "Not as good as you are, I can tell you that. Every time I see you dancing with the gypsy in the red dress in your arms . . ."

But Sebastian wasn't really listening. *"Mi amigo,* I need your help. Can you bewitch a woman to the point of forgetting her family and her responsibilities?"

Tomas stared for a moment, then clasped his hand dramatically over his heart and sighed happily. "Try me, friend. That is exactly where my talents lie."

Sebastian nodded, his face serious. "You must keep her occupied so that I can get to Marina."

"Ah, is that the problem? Too many fish to fry, eh?" Tomas smiled broadly. "I'll have her eating out of my hand. I've been admiring her from afar all evening."

Sebastian's head twisted around and he stared. "You have?"

Tomas was consumed with rapture. "That raven hair. That noble brow. The way she moves . . ."

Sebastian scowled. "This surprises me, *hombre*. I hardly thought she was your type." He grimaced. "Don't you find her . . . a little old?"

"Old? You call that old? Well, she may have been on the shelf a few years longer than most of the girls I usually romance, but *amigo,* think of how much she has learned in her time."

Sebastian turned and looked at Josefa with narrowed eyes, trying to see what on earth Tomas could be talking about. Josefa's hatchet-faced glare made him shiver.

"You don't find her . . . just a bit severe?" he tried again.

"Severe?" Tomas laughed. "Let her lecture me if she will." He rubbed his hands together in anticipation. "When do I start?"

"Right away. There she is, by the fireplace."

Tomas frowned. "No, friend, she's by the punchbowl talking to the captain."

Sebastian looked and laughed. "Not Carmen, you fool. Josefa!"

Tomas's face fell and he looked aghast, backing away. *"Hombre,* you know I would lay down my life for you in an instant, but I've been thinking . . . my back has been bothering me and it is getting late . . ."

"Tomas, don't desert me. It won't be for long. Go over and keep her occupied. Show off some of your sparkling wit, shower her with compliments, dance with her. As soon as I have Marina on the dance floor, you can go nurse your back."

Tomas shook his head resignedly. The joy seemed to have drained out of his evening. "I sometimes wonder if friendship is worth the effort," he muttered as he started off after the older lady.

Sebastian stayed in the shadows, watching his progress, then struck when the opportune moment presented itself, brushing off the young man who seemed to be Marina's current ardent suitor with a glare that stopped him in his tracks.

"I claim the next dance by virtue of my own cleverness," he murmured to Marina, directing her gaze to where Josefa and Tomas were laughing merrily together. "Will you have me?"

His eyes issued the challenge, and her chin came up in response. She wasn't afraid of him and he mustn't be allowed to think it. She was fortified now. She knew what she was getting into.

"Of course," she said coolly, rising to take his hand. "Lead the way."

His face was still as handsome and his body was still as strong and lean, but she was prepared this time. When he leaned close enough to tickle her ear with his warm breath, she brushed the area as though she'd just been bothered by a fly. And when he told her she was the most beautiful woman in the room, she laughed and said, "And what did you tell Carmen, that she was the second most beautiful?"

That actually rendered him speechless for a good ten seconds, but then he laughed and looked down at her with new respect.

"What I don't understand," he told her softly, "is how a clever girl like you can imagine herself in love with a clod like Don Felipe Diaz."

She couldn't allow him to say such things. Rearing back, she glared at him. "Felipe is not a clod. He's out defending our territory right now, while you and your fellow officers enjoy the music and the women and generally behave like craven cowards."

His face didn't change, but something moved deep

in the emerald mist of his eyes. "I'm not a craven coward, *querida*."

No, she knew he was not. But neither was Felipe a clod. Still, at the moment, she didn't think she could stand either one of them. That didn't mean she wanted to see the two of them facing off against each other again. She just wished them both somewhere she was not.

But Sebastian wasn't going to go away very soon, at least not until the dance was over. As it was, he was holding her rather too closely. She knew the older women were talking about them behind their fans. But she also knew if she said something to the man, he would laugh at her. So she endured his hard arm, endured his sweet-smelling breath, and tried to calm her own nerves while she made her own plans.

Sebastian leaned close and said softly, very near her ear, "And when Felipe returns with his trophies of war, will you love him more, Marina?"

She could smell his scent. It was musky, like a trunk from the Orient, not like the colognes other men used. Something in it seemed exotic, dangerous, stirring her senses, but she couldn't have said it was unpleasant.

Turning her head, she answered him firmly. "I don't fall in love with compliments and presents, Lieutenant," she said, managing to maintain her serenity with effort. "Battles and ribbons are no way for a woman to measure a man."

"Then it's just as well I didn't go," he said, amusement glittering in his green eyes. "What would be the use of heroics if they mean nothing to you?"

She wished his gaze weren't quite so direct. Sometimes she had the feeling he could see right into her soul. "There are more important qualities in a man

117

than heroism," she said, stubbornly keeping up the conversation, though her response to his physical presence was growing.

"Oh? How interesting it would be to understand the workings of your mind . . . and your heart." His fingers tightened around hers. "Would you care to list a few examples of the things you admire most in a man?"

"Certainly." She cleared her throat and thought fast, avoiding his eyes. "Strength of character, purity of heart, sincerity, a well-educated mind." She looked up at him, pleased with her answer, but disconcerted to see that laughter still loomed in his eyes.

"Using those criteria, the leading candidates for your affections should be the mission *padre,* Captain Brandene, and your own father." His white teeth flashed at the absurdity of that, and then his voice lowered. "But none of those men make you tremble when they touch you, do they, Marina? Tell me the truth. What is it that really makes your heart beat faster?"

She was terrified he would see the answer in her eyes, so she avoided looking at him. Instead, she took a deep breath and kept her voice light.

"You would like to hear me say 'looks, style and breeding,' I'm sure, but I'll never say it."

His laugh was soft and low in his throat. "You mean you'll never admit it."

She had to meet his green eyes. If she didn't, he would know she was afraid to. Steeling herself, she looked up, blinking rapidly. "Believe me, sir, it is not you," she claimed with spirit she had to conjure from the depths of her courage.

His grin was wide now. "You do admit I have

118

those features to my credit."

She was working hard at steady breathing: in, out, in, out. "Of course. How could I deny it?"

"Well, that's a relief. I was afraid perhaps life in this ditchwater town had dulled my luster."

She licked her lips and tried to smile. The dance was coming to a close, she could hear it in the music. Relief was at hand. She was going to make it through this dance without making a fool of herself after all.

"Never fear." She managed a pert smile as she turned out of his arms. "You shine brightly. And you know it only too well." She took two steps away from him before she added the clincher. "And that is just what I dislike about you."

To her annoyance, he threw back his head and laughed.

"I see." He bowed, his eyes dancing. "Thank you for the dance, *señorita*. I'll never forget it."

"Good-bye, Lieutenant."

He laughed again as he watched her walk away. He hadn't had such a lively conversation with a woman since he'd left Mexico City. It was a shame that the very woman he had sworn to bring to her knees was the one he liked the best of anyone in town. It was enough to give a fellow second thoughts.

But there was still the rendezvous with Carmen to take care of. He reached into his back pocket and found it empty. Strange. The note she'd written him seemed to be gone. But he remembered very well what she'd asked, and it hardly mattered.

Turning slowly, he smiled again. Yes, Marina was proving a very interesting subject. It was a shame it would all have to end badly.

Marina smiled secretively as she walked across the crowded room. So pickpocketing had come in handy after all. Finding a relatively lonely corner, she took the note from her glove and pressed it out onto the palm of her hand near a lantern.

"Meet me on the rose path at the stroke of midnight," it said. *"I have something to tell you that can't wait."*

"Oh, Carmen," she whispered, tearing the note up and dropping the pieces into the closest fireplace. "My cousin, my sister, am I going to have to save you from yourself?"

The time was almost here. She saw Sebastian slip away, and Carmen beginning to cast furtive glances toward the back of the house. Avoiding Josefa, who was still roaring over the jokes Tomas was telling her, she slipped out toward the back door, walking down the hallway in the shadows, finding an empty bedroom with a key in the lock, opening the door and positioning herself across the hall, out of sight. Carmen would have to come this way to get to the rose path.

The music was loud. The musicians had been drinking and their play was getting more and more raucous, along with the shouts and laughter of the dancers. No one would hear Carmen's cries, if her plan worked, and if she was lucky.

It wasn't long before Carmen came along the same way, humming as she came. Marina waited until she was just outside the door to the back bedroom. Then she spun out of the shadows and gave her cousin a firm shove. Carmen cried out as she stumbled into the bedroom, but Marina had the advantage of surprise and she slammed the door shut before her cousin could **do a thing**, turning the key quickly in the lock and hurrying out as Carmen's cries of outrage melted into the general sounds of merriment.

Gravel crunched beneath her satin shoes as she ran toward the rose path. He was already there. She could see the moonlight glinting on the hilt of his sword. Slowing as she neared him, she put a hand over her racing heart.

"Carmen?" He turned, his smile freezing on his face, his eyes widening, as he realized who it was.

"No, not Carmen." She stepped forward boldly and confronted him. "Carmen has been detained and won't be able to meet with you after all."

Sebastian took in the situation at a glance and his mouth twisted. "Don't worry, Marina," he said coolly, reaching out and snagging her arm with his hand. "You'll make a fine substitute for what I have in mind."

His eyes were dark in the moonlight, his fingers strong, and she thought the pounding of her heart would drown out the sound of his voice.

"Take your hand off me, Lieutenant," she managed to order calmly. "I didn't come for this, and I find your familiarity insulting."

For a moment she thought he was going to refuse. She couldn't tell a thing from the expression in his face. But then his grip loosened and his fingers slipped away.

"I'm sorry, Marina," he said softly. "I meant no disrespect."

She steadied herself, breathing quickly and praying that her knees wouldn't buckle beneath her. She had to say her piece quickly and get back before she was missed.

"I came to ask for a favor," she told him, noting

how he turned and seemed surprised at her words. "I . . . I want you to stay away from Carmen."

He froze for a long moment before replying. "Is that not Carmen's decision to make?" he said at last.

"No. Not in this case. Carmen is going through a . . . a period of weakness. I'm not sure why. Something in the air, perhaps. Something in her background. But she is very susceptible to your charms right now, in ways she wouldn't be if she were stronger."

She couldn't tell if he were really listening as attentively as he seemed to be. In the dark it was hard to tell. She could see the planes of his face, long and distant in the moonlight. Was she getting through to him? She could only hope.

Impulsively, she reached out and touched his sleeve. "Please stay away from her. Let her get her strength back."

He stared at her for a moment, then covered the hand on his sleeve with his own free hand. "Wait until she's strong, like you are, Marina?" he asked in a voice barely above a whisper.

Strong? Right now she felt as weak as a kitten, but if he couldn't tell, she was still ahead.

"Yes."

His eyes glittered, the crescent moon reflected in their depths. "You have no trouble at all resisting me?"

Her breath caught in her throat. "Of course not."

His hand curled around hers. "What if I were to say I don't believe you?"

She tried to pull her hand away but he wouldn't let it go. "I don't give a pumpkin seed what you believe," she protested, beginning to feel desperate. "It means nothing to anyone."

He tugged her closer, staring down into her eyes. "Prove it to me."

She stammered, startled by the silky smooth seduction of his voice. "Wh . . . wh . . . what?"

He pulled her closer still, until she was close enough to sense the heat of his body, close enough to feel the electricity in the air between them.

"Prove to me how strong you are, Marina," he whispered, his face very near hers, his hand sinking into her hair.

She was not going to waver. She wasn't under his power at all, and it was about time he realized his cause was completely lost. But somehow she couldn't pull away. Something stronger than his arms, stronger than her will, was holding her there.

She wasn't at all sure what it was until his mouth came down on hers and his fingers dug into her hair and her body came in against his and she knew this was what she had been longing for ever since the last time they had met alone this way.

She wanted to yell, kick, fight him off, but it was so much easier to stay in his embrace and let the sensations he created wash over her like a wave, crashing against her resistance, setting in motion a rhythm as old as time itself.

His mouth was hot and irresistible, moving on hers with a tantalizing hunger she could only open to. His hands caressed her, leaving a trail of fire in their wake. She let herself sink into his passion like a leaf into a hot desert wind, tossing and turning, being carried along, only trying to keep from being crushed by the forces set in motion by something beyond her control.

Beyond her control—that was the way it seemed. And yet, those were her hands sliding beneath his

123

shirt to feel more of his heat, that was her mouth greedily urging his deeper. She could feel him in a way she'd never felt a man before, as though she were a part of his body, as though she knew his mouth, knew his iron-hard flesh, knew the muscles of his arms, the strength in his legs, could feel them flex, could feel them course with power, a quick, potent male power that she suddenly knew she needed as she needed air to breathe.

His heart beat against her, pounding as loud as her own, heightening the sense of fusion, and without thinking, she raised her arms and let her hands run along the planes of his face, as though she were memorizing his features, as though she were ready to hold him to her should he try to escape.

But he wasn't going anywhere. His hands were spread across her back, holding her where he could get to her mouth, holding her where he could feel her breasts. If he'd thought he wanted her before, it was nothing like the ache that was beginning inside him now, an ache that had nothing to do with revenge and everything to do with insatiable hunger to possess, to know, to feel—even to love.

The passion he'd missed the last time he'd kissed her was present now, overwhelming the natural distance between them, tearing down walls and building a fire. He couldn't get her close enough, he couldn't kiss her hard enough, he couldn't get enough of her into his hands.

And she felt the same way. Her blood was like a liquid flame racing in her veins, clouding her mind. When he dragged his mouth away from hers, she made a sound deep in her throat, a sound of need, a sound of desire, that hit him in the pit of his stomach.

She was innocent. He could tell that, even if he hadn't already suspected as much. She'd been telling the truth when she'd told him she was a virgin. These feelings were new to her and she didn't know how to deal with them. It would be easy to take her right there, pull her away from the path, find a grassy slope, and initiate her into the ways of men and women in one quick lesson. His body was ready and eager to do just that. Her body was ready to learn. Why not?

He looked down into her glazed eyes as she moaned, reaching for more of him, and he hesitated. She wanted him. Left to develop naturally, the moment was here. He could have her body, possess her soul, and at the same time, exact his revenge. He could make love with her now and pay her back at the same time he ruined Don Felipe's dreams. Two birds with one stone. So simple. So clean. So apropos.

But he pulled away. He knew he couldn't do it. Not here, not now. It was just too easy. And at the same time, it was just a little too wrong.

"Marina," he whispered, stroking her cheek. "Marina, listen to me."

She raised her head and looked at him, groggy for a few seconds, then slow realization began to dawn on her face. She dropped her arms and began to back away, hands covering her mouth, eyes wide with horror at what she had been doing, what she was still feeling.

"Marina, wait."

But he wasn't sure what he could say to her. She was right to feel abhorrence. That was what he'd wanted, wasn't it?

And yet, something in him wanted to reach out

and comfort her, protect her, tell her it was all right, that she hadn't been wrong or bad to have responded to his kisses.

But he watched her run away and didn't say another word. And all the time, his mind was replaying the scene he had so recently lived when he had been dancing with her for the first time tonight. "I've never wanted another woman the way I want you." He'd said something very like those words to her, and at the time he'd said them, he'd thought they were a lie. Now, as he watched her disappear into the house, as he took air deep into his lungs and tried to calm his body, he wasn't so sure any longer.

Chapter Ten

"I'll hate you until the sun dries up the sea."

"I did it for your own good."

"I'll hate you until every grain of sand blows away from the beaches."

Carmen threw a pillow across the room and turned on the bed, pulling up the covers so that all Marina could see were pillows and blankets and a few strands of black hair.

"If I hadn't done it, just think what might have happened," Marina replied sensibly, filling a glass with water for her ailing cousin and setting it on her bedside table.

Carmen's muffled voice emanated from the crumpled covers. "I'll hate you until you're on your deathbed begging for my forgiveness. And even then I'll hate you."

Marina sighed and sank down into a chair. This was getting to be a very stale song. Carmen was working hard at making her pay for what she'd done.

When she'd hurried back into the house the night before, Carmen had still been pounding on the locked bedroom door, unheard by the partygoers in the ballroom. Marina had fumbled with the key, her hands

127

trembling from what she'd just been through with Sebastian, and finally she'd worked the lock and released her cousin. Carmen had burst from the room like a scalded cat and she'd been in a fury ever since.

All things considered, she had every right to her anger. What Marina had done was reprehensible, high-handed, and, according to Carmen, possibly illegal, but Marina was getting tired of hearing about it.

"Leave it be, Carmen. I've heard your complaints. I know you have a grievance against me. And I don't really care."

Carmen swung back so that she could glare at her cousin. "I'm sick because of you, too. The doctor said I'm so full of rage against you, it brought on this fever."

Marina raised an eyebrow. "You told Doctor Cortez about how I locked you up at the Alcalde's *baile?*" she asked.

"No, of course not." Carmen sat up, punching pillows until the feathers flew in an effort to try to make herself comfortable. "I haven't told anyone about that."

Marina sighed. "Good. Because if you tell anyone what I did, I'll have to explain to them why I did it."

Carmen made a face at her cousin. "You did it because you were jealous."

"I did it to save you from Sebastian's clutches."

Carmen snorted. "You saved me from Sebastian, did you? I'll tell you what you saved. You saved him for yourself."

Marina had to turn away at that, so that Carmen couldn't see the truth in her eyes.

"I did no such thing," she said stoutly, feeling like a liar. "I made sure you didn't throw away your life on a scoundrel, that's all. And that fever is just what you get for plotting evil." She nodded toward the many

128

glasses awaiting Carmen's pleasure on the side table. "Now take your medicine and settle down. You need rest to throw off this illness."

Carmen continued to grumble, but she did as Marina suggested. Watching her, Marina wondered if she knew how close her accusations came to being the truth. Every time she let herself think about what she had done on the rose path the night before, she felt a slight gasp in her chest, as though she still couldn't believe it.

But she had to believe it. That wanton hussy kissing the Spaniard last night had been her. And she had enjoyed every second of it.

She'd already been to confession and done penance, but she knew it wasn't enough. Because deep inside, she wasn't really sorry. And that was her greatest shame of all.

It was all because of the ring and the hold the man had over her while he kept it. It was as though he'd cast a spell over her, making her do and feel things she'd never imagined possible. Once she had her ring back, maybe life could go back to the way it used to be. The key to everything was the unicorn ring Sebastian de la Cruz had possession of. She had to get it back.

"Sleep now," she told Carmen, rising from the chair where she'd been sitting. "I'll come and check on you in an hour or so."

"Where are you going?" Carmen asked petulantly. She was still very angry and determined to make Marina sorry she had ever meddled in her life.

"I'm going to my room to read for a while," Marina said, avoiding Carmen's eyes again, sure that her cousin could see when she wasn't telling the truth. They had known each other so well for so long.

But Carmen was completely centered on herself at the moment, and she didn't notice a thing.

"All right. I'll try to sleep. But I'm going to need chicken soup."

"I'll make sure you get some this evening, I promise. Sleep well."

Once out the door, she ran quickly in the opposite direction from her room, grabbing a cloak and slipping out through the courtyard, out the iron gate, into the back, and around through the alleyway. Josefa would be back from market in little more than an hour. She had to move fast before her absence was discovered.

Pulling the hood of the cloak up around her face, she walked toward Camino de los Osos as fast as her feet would take her and prayed that no one she knew would see her go.

One half hour later, the deed was done. The unthinkable plan was in the works, and she could hardly believe she had sunk to this level. But what could she do? She had to have that ring back, and she didn't dare confront Sebastian herself. He'd already shown her how vulnerable she was to his methods of persuasion and she knew she couldn't risk going through that again. No, the ring had to return to where it belonged.

It was to this end she had paid a visit to Chico, the pickpocket and general know-it-all of El Camino de los Osos. She'd explained the situation to him in as sketchy terms as she could, merely saying Sebastian had taken her ring and refused to give it back. It had been difficult to get out the details of what she planned to do about it, but her scandalous scheme didn't seem to faze him, and he'd immediately promised to help her find a likely woman for the job.

Now the only thing she had to do was wait for him to signal her that a woman had been hired. Then they would name the time and place to meet, and it would all be over — if it worked.

She walked quickly down the street, staying in the shadow of the adobe wall, stepping around the potholes. This was not the way she usually came with Carmen, but it was a less crowded area and there was less likelihood of being seen.

"Marina!"

She spun, eyes wide with shock, and her heart sank when she saw her father approaching on horseback.

"Marina, what on earth are you doing in this part of town?" he demanded sternly as he reined his horse in near her.

Not an easy question to answer, and she hadn't thought up a good cover story yet.

"Oh, Father," she stuttered out lamely. "Where are you going?"

"That is hardly the point, young lady." James rarely raised his voice to his daughter, but she could see by the agitation in his face that finding her here had truly upset him. "And all alone, too? What are you thinking of?"

She had to think of some excuse. If he found out what she was really doing here, she would never be able to face him again. What would he think if he knew she'd been hiring a prostitute to lure a man into doing what she wanted him to do? Her father was so decent, so fair, so honorable. It would kill him to know his daughter was none of those things.

What could she say? That she'd gotten lost? Lost her mind was more like it. He'd more likely believe that.

"I . . . I . . . uh . . . I . . ."

"What is it?" he demanded impatiently.

She swallowed hard and lied to the father she loved and respected. "I went to try to find Carmen's father. I

131

. . . I thought he should know she was sick. But I couldn't find him and . . ."

"Is she really that ill?" James's brow was furled with concern.

"No. Oh, no, Father, not really." Yes, this was an unpersuasive excuse, but she was stuck with it now, though deep inside she was already in agony over what she was forced to do. "But I thought he might worry."

James stared down at her for a long moment that left her mouth dry, but finally he shook his head and gave her the beginnings of a wry smile.

"Always thinking of others, aren't you, my dear?" he said lovingly. "Well, come along. Let me swing you up here in front of me. I'll give you a ride back home where you belong."

For a moment Marina couldn't move. She was paralyzed, frozen where she stood. She had just done a terrible thing in plotting to hire a prostitute, and then done an even worse thing in lying to her father. She should be struck down by lightning, or at least hit by a fever like Carmen. Instead, her father praised her compassion.

She didn't deserve this. She should be brave and come clean right now. She should tell him the truth and take whatever punishment was coming to her. If she was an honorable daughter, that is what she would do.

"Well, come along. Here, give me your hand."

She should tell him. But she wouldn't. And she reached out her hand and let him help her up onto the horse and rode all the way home with tears streaming down her face, tears she managed to wipe away before he could see them.

Laughter from the open windows at the Crafts'

house rang out and was heard all up and down the dusty evening street. Mouth-watering aromas followed at a more leisurely pace. Together they combined to give a picture of the friendship and entertainment to be found within.

Inside the thick adobe walls, a table was laden with the remains of a sumptuous meal. Roast beef lay beside piles of steaming *tortillas, enchiladas,* and *tamales* rested on beds of red *frijoles,* dishes of potatoes, squash, and greens remained half eaten, and bowls of oranges and shortcakes were being set out with the wine.

The diners sat back in their chairs looking happy and satisfied. Don Felipe had returned from a successful Indian campaign, and he and his frail elderly uncle, robust mother, and two young sisters had been invited to a celebration in his honor.

Felipe was the returning hero who had met adversity and faced it down. Everyone wanted to look at him, touch him, hear his stories again and again. He was definitely the star of the hour, and he was enjoying it to the hilt, his dark, handsome face relaxed and lively, his black eyes sparkling.

A few close friends had been asked to join the party. And for some reason inexplicable to everyone but James Crafts, Sebastian had been invited, too.

"What?" Josefa had cried when she'd heard. "Is James blind? Doesn't he know that de la Cruz and Don Felipe hate each other?"

"He doesn't see what he doesn't want to see," Marina had agreed, but didn't worry too much about it. It would be crazy for the two men to be together in this house. After all that had passed between them, the Spaniard would know better than to show up. Why would he want to come and listen to Felipe being touted as the next savior of the universe? Surely

133

Sebastian would find some excuse to stay away.

The shock of finding him at the door after all had been covered over by politeness and the fact that Don Felipe's family had no idea he was an enemy of their heros and they welcomed him with enthusiastic curiosity, which, in the sisters' case, bordered on relish. They giggled and poked one another and ogled him across the table. And he ignored them.

At least he'd been quiet. Marina knew he couldn't be enjoying the bragging and the gushing over Felipe and his escapades. But there wasn't a sneer to be found on his noble face. He listened and said nothing, and despite all the turmoil in her heart over him, she blessed him for it. The last thing they needed was an argument between the two men.

Marina looked down the table at where he sat, watching him from under lowered lashes. The main meal was over and he was sitting back, turning the stem of his wineglass in his long, tapered fingers, staring into the depths of his drink with stony eyes.

As she watched, he glanced up and found Carmen's eyes measuring him. He smiled at her, and his face changed so dramatically, Marina felt the breath stop in her throat, leaving her to gape at him as he suddenly turned and caught her at it.

He didn't smile at her. Instead, he stared at her without expression, and gave just the merest salute with a movement of one eyebrow. Cursing herself and her contrary emotions, she dragged her glance away, her heart beating so loudly she was afraid the others would notice.

But there was hardly any risk of that. At the moment, they were loudly going over Felipe's exploits yet again.

"And they say he saved Don Pedro Carillo's life," Rosita, one of Felipe's sisters, was chirping.

"How? What happened?"

"Don Pedro was hit with an arrow and an Indian jumped him and Felipe jumped the Indian just in time. You should hear Don Pedro singing his praises."

"And well he might," put in Felipe's uncle Jose, waving his wineglass in the air. "Well he might."

"Tell us again, Felipe. How exactly did it happen?" Josefa leaned forward and smiled at him. It was evident he had ascended even higher in her regard. "We've had it all in bits and pieces and my head is spinning. Tell it once from start to finish, so I can get it straight."

Felipe smiled and shrugged with extravagant modesty. "Again?" He looked at Marina, just to check that she was taking in all this adulation, since she was being annoyingly quiet herself. She smiled at him quickly and he was satisfied.

"Again?" he repeated, laughing.

"Yes," the others called, laughing as well. "Again!"

He sighed. "All right. It was Wednesday night when we got the news of what had happened to the Lopez *rancho*. The Indians have not been very troublesome in this area for a long time, so we were a little surprised to hear about it. I went right out to the Presidio to see what they wanted to do about it, but the Comandante was not interested. According to him, he and his officers had more important business here."

He sent a sidelong glance Sebastian's way and made a face that caused his sisters to giggle, but the Spaniard continued to stare into his wine and pretended not to notice.

"Well, they sent along three dragoons and that made nine of us, plus three Indians from my *rancho*. We headed out by midnight and reached the Lopez *rancho,* where we waited until dawn. We slept a little and gathered our equipment, and prepared ourselves and our horses. At dawn we took off for the mountains, but it was late evening before we picked up their trail. We made camp at the foothills and got ourselves ready for battle."

"Where were you?" James asked. "Near the Ortega River?"

"No." Felipe shook his head. "It was closer to the foothills of Las Montañas de Plata, near where the limestone caverns have been found."

"Ah, yes." James nodded. "I once rode there as a young man. Beautiful country. Very wild, as I remember."

"The next morning," Felipe went on, "we woke before the sun and started up in the first light. It was rough country, slow going. We didn't catch sight of the Indians until late afternoon. They had the Lopez horses with them, all right, the lousy horse-eaters." He shook his head in disgust. "We sent two of our Indians in to tell them to give up the herd and we would leave peaceably."

He stopped and took a sip of wine, shaking his head. "That wasn't my idea. I firmly believe that justice must be served. You have to teach those Indians what it means to steal another man's property. You have to kill off a few of their best men, make them suffer. But Don Pedro was all for showing mercy. He's a saint, that man. He felt that taking away their food supply by taking back the horses was enough punishment. Everyone agreed it was the Christian thing to do."

"And the safe thing, too," Sebastian murmured, his eyes still on his glass.

Felipe blinked in his direction, but the comment didn't really register. Marina glared at him. His sour grapes were unnecessary. This was Felipe's moment, and she wasn't going to let Sebastian sully it for him. One more comment like that and

136

she would make a few of her own.

"So we sent the Indians in," he went on. "But they came back with no deal. They wanted to fight. That made us mad. The rest were all for riding straight into the enemy forces and shooting it out, but I knew we would be sure to suffer from many arrow wounds if we did that. They'd be lying along the sides as we came up the canyon. We'd be massacred. We needed a plan. I told the others I would make one."

He paused and looked smugly about the room, obviously proud of his plan-making abilities. His sisters oohed and aahed, his uncle nodded wisely, and his mother clucked her appreciation of his prowess. But when he looked at Marina for a little praise, he hardly found what he wanted to see. She was staring off into space with a vacant look on her face, as though she wasn't even listening. He frowned and cleared his throat, bringing Marina's attention back with a start. Smiling, he went on.

"I made our Indians gather their extra horses and herd them up the canyon, pretending it was our whole force. Meanwhile, half of us went up and around on the left, and the other half on the right, so as to come up behind and trap them between us."

"Sounds like a real good plan," James said. "And I guess it worked."

"Not at first," Felipe snorted. "We had our share of problems. I went up on the left with Don Pedro, the trapper Smith, and Juan Ortega . . ."

"What?" Carmen exclaimed. "I didn't know my father went with you."

"He did indeed, and a very brave fighter he was."

Carmen turned her wide, incredulous eyes toward him. "Are you sure it was him?" she murmured.

But Felipe was going on with his story. "We went up slowly and carefully, because to surprise them was very important. It worked on the right side, and they were successful right away. The Indians were busy raining arrows on our Indians and horses and our men got the drop on them. But on our side of the canyon, Señor Ortega was on a horse which tripped and fell to its knees, and the shouting that commenced from that mishap would have waked the dead. It also alerted the Indians to our presence."

"Ah, yes." Carmen nodded wisely. "Then it *was* my father."

"Señor Ortega was busy tending to his horse, and the trapper Smith disappeared over the ridge, so Don Pedro and I were left to fight alone." He shook his head, remembering. "Arrows were spraying all around us so thickly we could hardly see, but we were holding our own. Then Don Pedro was hit by an arrow which passed right through his *cuero,* and the next thing I knew, an Indian was on top of him with a knife in his hand."

He paused modestly as the others murmured their horror. "It was lucky that my knife was quicker, and Don Pedro was able to rise and fight again, though he was wounded. Trapper Smith came back, Señor Ortega left his horse, and together we were able to overpower our enemy. We rounded up the Lopez horses and brought them back down the mountain. And that is all."

"Isn't that wonderful?" bubbled Rosita. "And not one of them seriously hurt."

Marina was surprised. "I thought one of your Indians was killed and another badly wounded."

Felipe shrugged and nodded. "Yes, we lost two good workers, but I brought back more than enough prisoners to make up for it."

It might have been the look on Sebastian's face that did it, and the thought of how he must see them as an outsider, or maybe the fact that all the change happening lately was making her look at her life and everything in it from a fresh perspective. Marina had been hearing about campaigns and the taking of Indian prisoners for as long as she could remember. It had never bothered her before. But suddenly an uneasy feeling was beginning to nag at her.

"What a shame that people have to die for horses," she said softly, to no one in particular.

"Of course people have to die," Felipe said sternly. "The Indians steal. They have to be punished. They stole horses from us and we had to pay them back."

"And who will pay you back for stealing the land from the Indians?" It was Sebastian's voice, spouting heresy, that stopped them all dead in their tracks.

Felipe stared and his neck began to turn red. "We didn't steal anything," he protested. "There was plenty of land for everyone."

"Is that why you have to drive the Indians up into the hills?" Sebastian asked quietly.

Felipe could hardly believe what he was hearing, and there was murmuring from the others around the table. It didn't do to challenge the orthodoxy. "We don't drive them up there. They like it. That's where they go to be free."

"That's where they go to be away from you."

"Listen, *hombre.*" Felipe began to rise from his chair and was only prevented by James's hand on his shoulder.

"Don't misunderstand me," Sebastian said coolly, not looking in the least perturbed by the threat implied in Felipe's voice. "I think you have a wonderful system here. In fact, I'm beginning to toy with the idea of applying for some land of my own. I may just stay here and ranch."

"What?" cried Carmen, her face showing genuine

distress. "How could you possibly lock yourself away in this godforsaken place?"

Sebastian's smile was thin. "It was only a passing thought. But *Señorita,* perhaps you are too close to this land to see it clearly. Life here has much to recommend it."

James smiled broadly, glad the situation seemed to have been defused. "I'm sure we would all welcome you as a neighbor. I haven't gotten into the ranching business myself, but those who have seem to have profited by it. Of course, you'll have to marry an *'hija del país,'* daughter of the land, to help you out. That's what we all do."

"Yes," Josefa chimed in. "A man can't make it here without a wife to help him run a *rancho.*" She threw a significant glance at Felipe, a glance everyone saw.

Laughter flew about the table and Felipe's mother called out, "Some young men think they can rely on their mothers to do it all, but some young men had better prepare for the future, for some morning that mother might decide she has earned her rest."

She and Josefa chortled together, and Felipe grinned. He tried to catch Marina's eye, but she was peeling an orange and didn't look up. A feeling of impending doom was coming over her, as though a huge storm lurked off the coast. Would anything ever be the same again?

Chapter Eleven

The table rang with jokes and laughter, until Carmen stood up. "Let's have some music," she said, reaching for a nearby guitar and testing the strings. "If none of you men will play, I'll do it myself."

She began to play a lively folk song, singing in a strong soprano, and the company was soon clapping and laughing along. Felipe leapt up and began searching for his guitar to accompany her.

The party moved outside into the courtyard where lanterns had been set up to lighten the darkening shadows. The company spread out on the wooden benches and all joined in singing. Carmen and Felipe played well together and James soon joined them on his violin. They played and sang Spanish love songs, Mexican folk songs, Californio ballads, and even a few New England ditties James remembered from his boyhood.

Marina sang along, but her heart wasn't in it. Mostly she watched Sebastian, trying not to be too conspicuous about it, curious as to why he was here, and how he was reacting to the way Californios entertained themselves. This must seem tame fare to one used to the elaborate diversions at the Spanish court.

He stood alone, his dark head held high, the gold

141

braid on his perfect white coat gleaming in the light of the lanterns. Every time she saw him she found him more handsome, but at the same time, she knew that was only bait for his trap. He still had her ring. And he still posed a threat to Carmen. She hated him. At least, she ought to.

It had been three days since she'd given Chico the assignment to hire someone, and he still hadn't come back to her with news of success. Surely there was some woman on the Camino de los Osos who was young enough, pretty enough, seductive enough, to tempt Sebastian and make him forget himself long enough to get hold of the ring. How could it take so long to find her?

Sebastian turned and met her gaze and she nodded quickly so as not to be impolite. But his hard, cold eyes didn't soften, and he didn't nod back. She turned away, her heart fluttering, and wished the ground would open and swallow the arrogant man.

She'd noticed there was no bulge in his waistcoat pocket and she wondered where he kept the ring now. It would help to know. What if the woman she hired got into his room and did her best to distract him and then couldn't find the ring? Somehow her plan was beginning to look more and more tenuous.

The music went on, and one of the sisters coaxed the uncle into dancing with her. By now, sounds of their revelry had filled the neighborhood and little by little, most of their neighbors wandered in to pay their respects and join in the fun. Soon the courtyard was full of people.

Marina played the onlooker, standing back away from the knots of laughing people, watching what was going on. She saw Carmen smile at Sebastian, saw him respond, and it worried her. She wasn't sure how seri-

142

ously to take Carmen's talk about running off with the man. On the one hand, she was sure it must be idle chatter; on the other, she'd seen the desolation in Carmen's face at times lately. She was vulnerable, and Marina wished she knew what she could do to protect her from her own wild emotions.

Suddenly, Carmen was calling to Sebastian, gesturing for him to join the musicians, and others called out his name. He straightened, smiling slightly, and reluctantly began to walk to the center of the courtyard. Marina's fingers knotted together as she watched. What was he going to do? Surely he wouldn't stand alongside Felipe and harmonize?

No, seeing him coming, Felipe was abandoning his guitar in disgust, walking away. Sebastian picked up the instrument, his fingers moving experimentally on the strings. He tuned one or two of them and tested it again. While the others joked around him, he seemed serenely unconcerned, as though he were in another world.

Marina couldn't take her eyes off him. Something about him, the way he stood out in a crowd, the way he didn't care if he was different, made her wary, watching for him to make some sort of disastrous mistake, her heart in her throat. But when he started to play, she realized immediately that she'd been worried for nothing.

His long fingers moved on the strings as though he'd had a lot of practice, and the sound that came out of the guitar caused a hush in the crowd, now entranced by the haunting grace of the eerily beautiful *flamenco soleares* he played. Everyone froze as though enchanted by his playing. Marina thought she'd never heard anything so beautiful in her life.

Suddenly, Carmen was stepping forward, putting

down her own guitar, and she began to improvise a dance to go with the haunting tunes. As though possessed by the sound Sebastian was drawing from the instrument, she began to stamp and whirl like a gypsy born to the music. The onlookers clapped and shouted encouragement, then stood and cheered when the two of them finished.

Carmen turned to Sebastian, her face radiant with excitement, and his smile took her in and caressed her in a way that made Marina turn away, a gasp choking in her chest. She stepped back into the shadows so the others wouldn't see her face and read her emotions.

This was insane. Carmen was going to throw herself away on the Spaniard if Marina didn't do something about it. But what could she do?

A sound, a movement, and Felipe was by her side in the dark.

"Marina," he said softly, his voice rich and melodic. "How I missed you when I was out there in the mountains. Every night, looking at the stars, I dreamed of you."

She turned and tried to smile, glad for the darkness that hid the nuances of emotion in her face. She was certainly happy that he had returned unharmed, a hero. But somehow she was incapable of the sort of joy she knew she should be feeling. She tried, but it wouldn't come.

Perhaps it was because she was so worried about things—the ring, Carmen, what had happened to Jonathan, and also, her father.

The money crisis seemed to be getting worse and worse. Even this party today—well, it had to be done, of course, but there had been no money for it. All the food, all the drink would have to be paid for soon. And where was the money to come from? Earlier that

144

day she'd seen her father's head bowed in worry over it. And everyone knew all she had to do was to marry Felipe to change all that.

"We all missed you, Felipe," she said quickly. "Especially at the *baile* last Saturday. It was dismal without you. They played a lot of waltzes. They say the Alcalde is wild for them."

"I wish I'd been there to waltz with you." He came nearer and she moved backward, nervously, avoiding his touch.

"Well," she said hurriedly, her hands convulsively pulling at the royal blue velvet of her skirt. "How have things progressed at the *rancho* with you away? Are you ready for the Spring roundup?"

If he noticed her retreat, he didn't mention it. His attention was caught by her mention of the gathering that was held at his *rancho* every year.

"Of course," he said. "We're preparing a feast like nothing this valley has ever seen before. We're even having a special musician come down from Santa Barbara to help provide the music for the dancing." He leaned toward her. "Maybe that would be a good time for me to ask your father. We could make the announcement of our engagement at the dance. What do you think?"

Instead of answering, she looked out at the crowd in the circle of light in the middle of the courtyard.

"We should go back to the others," she said nervously. "Someone will notice us here."

He took her hand in his, laughing. "Don't be so timid, *querida*. Everyone knows we are as good as betrothed. They're happy to see us together."

Marina turned to get away from him and the first thing that met her gaze was the vision of Carmen and Sebastian in the shadows on the opposite side of the

145

courtyard. He was tilting her chin up with one hand and laughing down into her face. Marina stood transfixed and let Felipe put her hand to his lips without even noticing what he was doing.

Her lack of attention wasn't lost on Felipe, though. He looked across the courtyard as well, scowling when he saw what had caught her interest.

"That man shouldn't be allowed in your father's house, Marina. And look at Carmen. How can she be so shameless?"

"She's . . . she's fascinated by him. It's gone to her head."

"He's a scoundrel. No decent family should receive him."

"My father considers him a friend," she said faintly, still staring.

"A friend? Did you tell him what I told you about how he rode your father's land, measuring and planning?"

She shook her head, looking back at Felipe. "No. I haven't told him yet."

"Well, then I shall have to. James must be on his guard."

She supposed that was true. So why was it that she felt annoyed with Felipe for bringing it up?

"Don Felipe!"

It was her father's voice calling and they broke apart immediately.

"There you are," said James, coming up to where they stood. "Come. Marina will excuse you. I must have your company for a brief discussion. Will you share a drink with me in the library?"

Felipe bowed. "At your service, *Señor.*" He winked at Marina as he turned to go. "You see," he whispered with an affectionate smile. "Perhaps it is time."

Marina watched him walk away with her father across the tiled patio and shivered. Why did everything in her scream out to stop him?

"Change," she said softly. Yes, she was so reluctant to accept change. That had to be it.

And yet, it really was time. It had to happen. And the sooner it happened, the sooner her father would have peace of mind.

But she had other things to worry about right now — mainly, a cousin who was acting as though she had lost her mind, as well as her sense of propriety. Threading her way through the crowded courtyard, she found Carmen, who was at last alone.

"Where is your champion?" she asked, pinning her cousin with a glare.

"Gone to get me a drink of water. Why do you ask?"

Carmen's face was hardly any friendlier. The two women stared at one another like wary strangers.

"What do you think you're doing?" Marina asked her.

"What am I doing?" Carmen replied, tossing her head and smoothing her full velvet skirt. "I'm having a good time." She glared at Marina. "And this time there is no handy room to lock me away in."

Marina made a sound of disgust deep in her throat. "I only wish there were," she said vehemently, while trying to keep her voice low enough so that others nearby couldn't hear. "You're acting very strangely. Perhaps you still have a fever. You look for all intents and purposes as though you were preparing to elope with the Spanish lieutenant tonight." She looked into Carmen's eyes, not wanting to miss her reaction to the charge. "Maybe you should go directly to your bed before you do something crazy."

Carmen's grin was smug, her eyes sparkling with

excitement. "Why? Because I can make Sebastian smile at me?"

"Yes," Marina snapped back. "Only someone touched by madness would want to."

Carmen's face became serious and she spoke softly. "That's where you're wrong, cousin. I *do* want him to smile at me." She clutched Marina's arm and leaned close to her ear. "I want him to take me with him when he goes."

This was just what Marina was most afraid of. Couldn't Carmen see how risky this was? She seemed ready to gamble everything she had on a very shaky proposition. Reaching out, she grabbed her cousin's arm and shook it.

"What makes you think he will go at all?" she asked, looking into Carmen's eyes and trying to get through to her. "At dinner he was talking about staying here and getting a piece of land."

"I heard him," Carmen replied calmly. "And I want to get him out of here before he begins to think that way seriously."

Marina shook her head, incredulous. Could Carmen really be living in such a dream world? Had she lost all touch with reality?

"But he can't leave. He's been assigned here. What do you expect him to do, desert his post?"

Carmen's mouth twitched and she shrugged lightly. "He hates it, you know. I'm trying to convince him that he doesn't need to stay in the Mexican Army. We could go to Paris . . ."

Marina threw up her hands. Was there no way to breach this wall of smug determination?

"Carmen, you're insane. What if he does take you? How long will he keep you? A man like that . . . he'll use you and discard you when the mood strikes him.

He doesn't love you."

Carmen's face was stone cold. "I don't care about love."

Marina knew that was a lie, but she didn't know how to get her to admit it. She shook her head in despair.

"Well, you should care about it. A man who could transfer affections as easily as the Spaniard will leave you penniless and heartbroken on some distant shore."

Carmen shrugged. "I'll have to risk it."

Marina shook her head in despair. "You think it's a remote possibility right now, don't you? You think you've put him under your spell. You think you've got him wrapped around your finger." She felt like crying. "Well, you're wrong, Carmen. You're fooling yourself and you're headed for disaster."

Carmen had a strange look on her face, as though she were actually plumbing the depths of her feelings and about to reveal them to Marina. She turned, leading Marina further from the others, back into the shadows under the spreading bougainvillea, so they could talk more openly. Once there, she gripped Marina's arm again and spoke forcefully.

"What I am doing, cousin, is living. I'm reaching out to grab what I want instead of waiting, hoping it will by some miracle fall into my lap. I did that once before, and what I wanted packed up and went sailing out of my life without a backward glance."

Sebastian appeared behind Marina with a cup of water in his hand during Carmen's last speech, and she gave him a fleeting smile. Marina glanced back and saw him, but she hardly cared. She was bound and determined to talk Carmen out of this right here and now, even if she had to do it right in front of him. The main thing she wanted to do was to convince her cousin it was folly to put her trust in the lieutenant.

"I understand that you have dreams, Carmen," she said forcefully. "But how can you think you're going to get what you want by running off with a . . . a scoundrel, a debauched outcast who tries to seduce every woman he meets?"

The Spaniard raised one eyebrow in surprise. "A seductive, debauched outcast," he murmured. "What could be worse?"

He handed a glass of water to Carmen, but neither woman seemed to notice him at all. They were both too caught up in their anger.

"Is this the way you repay us, then?" Marina had decided to go for the guilt attack. "By shaming us in front of the whole neighborhood, chasing the man like a floozy?"

"Well, you see, you said it," Carmen returned icily, her eyes glittering dangerously. "It's *your* family, not mine."

Marina's head went back, reacting to the offensiveness of Carmen's last remark.

"We have certainly tried hard enough to include you over the years. I guess that was our crime. We tried too hard. And now you want to repay us by chasing after this . . . this . . ."

"Debauched outcast," Sebastian supplied helpfully.

She threw him a furious glance and went on. "I think you would gladly destroy yourself just to spite us."

"And why not?" Carmen was just as angry. "What do I owe you? I didn't ask to be brought into your house. I'm not your sort. If I had stayed with my father, I would never have learned to read and to know what else there was in the world. I would have been satisfied with my days. I would have seen you and . . . and your brother Jonathan only from a distance, and I would have laughed at your stuffy way of life."

Carmen's words hurt, and Marina acted accordingly. "If that's what you want, why not do it? Go back to your father. Maybe you could get a nice job as a barmaid in some lowdown den of iniquity. Then you wouldn't have to bother with our stuffy ways."

Carmen glanced at Sebastian and shook her head. "Just leave me alone, Marina," she said with controlled anger. "Before you ruin everything once again."

But that was exactly what Marina wanted to do. Carmen was hurtling down a steep slope toward disaster. Was there any way left she could stop it?

Glancing at Sebastian, she had a thought, but it seemed almost as crazy as Carmen's plans. Still, she had to do something. Carmen had to see how little she could trust Sebastian.

"I . . . I'm going to have to prove it to you, aren't I?" She stared at her cousin, the plan crystallizing. Could she do it?

Yes. Yes, she would have to. There was nothing else that had the potential to make Carmen sit up and take notice.

Her pulse was pounding at the incredible idiocy of what she was about to do. But she couldn't stop herself now. Sebastian was standing beside Carmen and Carmen was smiling up at him, trying to ignore Marina. But Marina was not about to give up and go away. Instead, she steeled herself for what she had to do.

"Don't think," she told herself silently. "Just do it."

She made herself smile at Sebastian, and even reach out and touch his sleeve. There was no expression on his face and his eyes looked black as coal. Turning, he waited, one eyebrow raised, to see what she had in mind.

"Well, Lieutenant," she said silkily, fluttering her

151

eyelashes in a flirtatious manner that under ordinary circumstances would have made her gag. "Will you squander all your favors upon my lucky cousin? Or do you have some time left for me?"

She heard Carmen's sharply indrawn breath, but she didn't look at her. All her attention was centered on the Spaniard. She stared into his eyes, willing him to respond, willing him to help her prove her point to Carmen.

He stared back, his eyes shimmering in the lamplight. She could tell that he knew exactly what she was doing, and tiny beads of perspiration began to form along her hairline. But she managed to keep her smile frozen on her face.

Would he, or wouldn't he? Time seemed to be suspended for much too long.

Sebastian glanced at Carmen, and looked back at Marina. Finally, his voice slow and measured, he spoke. "I am your servant, *Señorita*. How may I serve you?"

Marina swallowed and prayed that her mouth wouldn't be too dry to let her speak clearly.

"Carmen has had quite enough of your company. Now it is my turn. I claim you as my partner for the *fandango*."

Carmen was saying something, but Marina paid no attention. Her eyes were held by the green ones above her. She knew by the smoldering light she saw there that he would accept her challenge.

Deliberately, he held out his hand for hers. Deliberately, she took it. The two of them walked to the middle of the dancing area.

"A *fandango*," she called out to the musicians, tossing her hair back.

"A *fandango!*" came the answer, and the men took

152

their places and began to tune up while the crowd cleared a space for them.

"*Aaiiiyee,*" came the cry from one or two *caballeros* in the crowd.

Sebastian's hand was hot as fire, hers as cold as ice. He seemed tall, his shoulders broad, standing beside her as they waited for the music to begin. She didn't dare look at him directly. It was as though she were about to dance the *fandango* with the devil himself.

"You're trembling, *querida,*" he said to her softly. "Are you sure you want to do this?"

"Yes," she replied, staring straight ahead. "I have to do this."

His laugh was low and husky. "You know what they say about the *fandango, querida.* Only those who are already lovers can dance it with the passion it deserves."

She flashed a quick look at him. "Then we will have to pretend, won't we?" she snapped back.

Color blazed in her cheeks. He was right about the significance some placed in the dance. She'd never done this so alone, so openly before, in front of such an audience. But she was going to do it now. She was going to dance as though her life depended on it. Looking up at Sebastian, she threw him as saucy a smile as she was capable of, and saw an immediate response in his face.

The violins and guitars began to play, and from somewhere, someone handed her a pair of castanets. The dance began.

At first the tempo was slow. Too slow. She wished she didn't have time to think. Thinking only made things worse. She tried smiling out at the audience, but then she noticed the shocked looks, the whispering behind fans, interspersed along with the faces bright

153

with eager anticipation, and she resolved not to look out there again. The looks meant her strategy was succeeding, but it wasn't pleasant to know the position she was putting herself in.

But enough of that. This was the *fandango*. She was supposed to concentrate completely on her partner. So be it.

She lifted her arms high, clicking the castanets in time to the music, in time to the steps, and began to let the form take over. Her partner danced like a dream and she had no problem following along with his moves. It was going well. If she only lived through it.

The pace began to quicken. Looking up, her gaze caught his and held as though there was no choice. His eyes were burning. The special trance of the *fandango* was taking over. Every sway, every turn, locked them together in the spell, aware only of the music and of the pull between them.

She felt it then. They both did. It was a warm, vibrant thing with a will of its own, and as long as she fit the movements of her body to the sinuous movements of his, as long as she held his dark green eyes with her own, as long as they let it, it lived between them.

The dance seemed to go on and on, a whirlpool of sound and motion. All she saw were his eyes and the whirling flash of lights as she turned; all she heard were the guitars, the violins, the castanets, the wild yells from the crowd. She was lost in the ecstasy of the dance and feeling an excitement she'd never felt before. This was true enchantment, as though she were flying, high above them all, with only this strong, exciting man to hold her. They were soaring together as though they'd been made to do this. For just this moment, they belonged together, locked in a magnetic field, tied to one another, living and breathing as one. Her heart sang, her blood raced. She didn't want it ever to end.

When the music suddenly stopped and someone yelled, "Bomba!" it took a moment for her to get her bearings and remember that she was supposed to sing a verse before they went on. She looked at Sebastian uncertainly, but his eyes were smoky with something dangerous and she looked away quickly, singing the first thing that came into her head, breathless.

Someone came up and put his hat on her head, a sign that he had found her dancing especially fine, and there was a buzz all around them. The music started again and she filled the form automatically, suddenly drained of energy, careful not to look into his eyes this time.

She had done what she'd set out to do. How could Carmen go with Sebastian now that he'd shown how easily he could transfer his attention? If she still trusted this man, perhaps she deserved him.

Finally it was over. Everyone was clapping and calling out, but it was all a blur to her. She turned, seeking to blend into the shadows again, but Sebastian wouldn't release her. As they walked out of the limelight, his arm was still curled around her and when she looked up questioningly, his eyes were blazing.

"I don't know what you've been trying to prove, Marina," he said softly, very close to her ear. "But I learned one thing."

He stopped, turning her with his hands on her shoulders, making her look up into his hard face. "You have more passion in you than you have ever allowed anyone to see before."

His mouth twisted in a dangerous smile. "You may be about to marry Don Felipe," he whispered, "but I'll have you in my bed before you present yourself in his." Releasing her, he stood back and held her with his

155

gaze, his voice rich and husky with meaning. "That I swear."

Her heart stopped and she stared up at him, eyes wide, lips parted. She believed him. It seemed all but inevitable. It was meant to be.

And then he was gone, and she had to try to catch her breath.

She didn't have much time for that before Carmen had pounced on her, eyes flaring with anger.

"Why would a girl who is about to marry Don Felipe Diaz want to dance the *fandango* like that with another man?" she hissed, linking arms with her cousin and pretending to take her on a friendly walk about the perimeter, while all the time her eyes and her tongue were spitting venom.

"Why, Felipe and your father are in the library right now, and they are probably talking about your marriage plans. And here you are, behaving shamelessly with a man who everyone knows is a scoundrel."

"Exactly my point, cousin," Marina shot back. "If he is a scoundrel when I dance with him, he is also a scoundrel when you talk about running away with him."

Carmen took a deep breath to calm herself. "What are you trying to do, Marina? Are you really so jealous of anything I might do to gain a little happiness that you have to destroy it for me?"

Marina couldn't answer. She knew it was a terrible thing she'd done to Felipe, but she couldn't think about that. This was not about Felipe. It was about Carmen, and Sebastian . . . and about Marina herself.

She found the man who had put his hat on her head and returned it, shaking Carmen away as soon as she could. She seemed to be moving in a fog, hardly knowing what she was doing.

Felipe came out and heard about what had happened while he was gone from the courtyard, but he didn't seem able to assimilate it fully. He stared at Marina with puzzled eyes and she had to turn away. What could she tell him? How could she explain why she had danced the *fandango* with another man when Felipe was only steps away?

So she didn't try. Sebastian's threat was still echoing in her ears as she excused herself from the assembly and ran to her bedroom. His threat was very real, and she knew it. There was something about the man that held her in thrall.

She had to fight it, of course. This was all she could stand. Chico had to come through, and right away. She couldn't go on like this. It was time to put her scheme into action. Where was Chico with that prostitute?

Chapter Twelve

A good night's sleep didn't help at all. The first thing she thought of when she awoke was Sebastian's burning gaze and his words. There was such a feeling of inevitability about his prophecy, it left her feeling chilly despite the sunny day.

Getting up, she busied herself with housework, hoping to drive the experience from her mind, but between Josefa's sniping about how embarrassing it was to have a niece with no sense of shame and Carmen's black looks, there was no way to forget it.

Carmen truly hated her now, but she had to expect that. What she had done was guaranteed to build more walls between them. It had to go against the grain with Carmen. But at the same time, it was meant to save her.

She couldn't tell if Carmen had changed her mind about trusting Sebastian. At this point, there wasn't much more she could do for her cousin. But she was bound and determined to save herself. And to that end, she needed Chico.

As if he'd sensed her desperation, there he was an hour later, scratching on the gate to the courtyard. She ran to it. No one else was within earshot, and she slipped out to find Chico had a girl with him.

"Her name is Teresa," he told her, grinning. "She'll be perfect for the job."

Marina looked her over, nodding thoughtfully. She was very pretty, even though her eyes did look too old for her face.

"Go on," she told Chico, giving him a handful of silver coins. "I need to talk to her alone."

He left them, whistling and jingling the money in his pocket. Marina turned to the girl. She had half a mind to offer her clothes and shelter instead of a job. But from the hard mouth and jaded eyes, she could tell her offer wouldn't be appreciated nearly as much as cold, hard cash. Teresa might be young in years, but she was old in experience.

She detailed what she needed quickly. She'd researched the Presidio and knew exactly where Sebastian's room was. She also described the ring and gave a few suggestions as to where it might be hidden. The girl was bright and she seemed to understand.

"I know the man you speak of," she said. "The Spaniard with the scar. Am I right? I'll get into his room. No problem."

Marina noted her casual confidence and shuddered. Another handful of silver was exchanged, and a promise of more if the job succeeded. "You understand that I'm not paying you to . . . to . . ."

"You don't really want me to sleep with him. I understand. You just want me to throw him off guard so that I can take the ring and bring it back to you."

"Exactly."

She shrugged. "I'll do what I can." Suddenly she grinned. "But he's a very handsome man, you know. What will be, will be." She laughed, flouncing her full, brightly colored skirts. "I'll do it tonight. See you at midnight."

Marina stared after her, wondering what she was doing. There was no guarantee this would work. What if she only made matters worse?

But Marina had to try it. Sitting still and waiting for the next time he had a mind to mock her was more than she could bear.

The rest of the day passed at a snail's pace. She helped Carmen with her mending and put up with her complaining and helped Josefa with dinner. But all the time her mind was on Teresa and the plan. The woman had claimed to know exactly who Sebastian was, but what if she was lying? What if she went to the wrong room at the Presidio? What if Sebastian saw through her seduction? What if he turned her away?

On the other hand, what if they were making love right now? The thought flashed through her like the thrust of a knife and she gasped aloud, making Josefa worry that she was coming down with something herself.

At least that gave her a good excuse to leave the others and go to her room. Once alone she was free to writhe and moan and wish she were dead. She'd sent a woman to seduce a man she wished she could be with herself. That was the size of it. It was time she admitted it.

And once she'd done that, all she had to do was close her eyes and remember how it felt to be kissed by him, to have him touch her, to feel his breath on her cheek. She still hated him. But he fascinated and tantalized her like no other man ever had. That was her curse. But it was also her pleasure.

At least, until she thought of the pretty Teresa in his room again. And that was pure torture. Even if her plan succeeded, would she ever get over the horror of it all?

160

The night grew quieter. Everyone had gone to bed. Marina lay in her dark room with her eyes wide open, waiting for midnight, waiting for Teresa to come. At midnight, either it would all be over, or she would be in bigger trouble than ever.

The moon was a silver slit in the sky when she pulled her cloak over her nightdress and stole out into the courtyard. She'd told Teresa she would let her in by the back gate. A visit to her window would be too risky. It was too visible from the main road and the other houses on her street. After the other night when Felipe had met her there, half the town had complained to Josefa the next morning, and Josefa had been livid.

She waited in the courtyard, her heart beating like a drum. Time was dragging again. It seemed to take forever. Maybe Teresa had failed. Maybe Sebastian had realized what she was doing. Or maybe he just hadn't fallen for the trap.

Finally, there it was, a tapping on the gate. Marina's heart flew into her throat. It had to be Teresa. That must mean the mission had been successful.

She ran to the gate and went to work on the heavy bar that held it.

"Just a minute," she whispered. "I'll have it open in no time."

The bar stuck and she needed all her strength to move it. Grunting softly, she pushed it aside and threw open the gate, waiting for Teresa to enter.

But Teresa didn't enter. Instead, into the courtyard strode Sebastian, his blue and scarlet cloak swirling around him.

Marina recoiled in horror, her hands to her mouth, her gray eyes huge. He turned and stared at her, his mouth grim, the scar a slash of pain on his hard face.

"Is this what you are waiting for, Marina?" he asked.

161

He held the ring in his hand. The sharp point of the unicorn seemed to glisten in the moonlight. "Is this what you so want to have back?"

She stared at it, knowing that there was no use in lunging for it. He would only snatch it away. Her plan had fallen through. But worse than that, Sebastian was going to make her pay somehow, of that she was certain.

"Your little friend found it," he went on evenly, "but I told her not to bother — I would see that you got it." He held it closer to her, letting her see it but not letting her touch it.

"Marina, Marina," he said softly. "You disappoint me. Why would you hire someone to do something you could do so much better yourself?"

His voice was hard, cruel, and she could suddenly imagine him capable of almost anything.

"What did you do to her?" she asked, searching his stone-cold eyes, afraid of what she might have let the woman in for.

He looked surprised that she would care. "I didn't hurt her, don't worry. In fact, I paid her off instead of beating her, believe me. I find it's a more productive way to handle things like this."

"You paid her off? But I paid her . . ." She flushed.

He chuckled. "Ah, but you forget. Those who can be bought will always go to the highest bidder. It didn't take much to get her to tell me everything."

She looked up at him, refusing to plead her case. "I just want my ring back," she said as firmly as she could manage. "Please give it to me now."

"You shall have your ring back, Marina." But he slipped it into his pocket. "Of course. Why would you worry? You shall have your ring back . . . just as soon as I have you."

162

It was her turn to sneer, and she did it with a toss of her head, her hair flying about her shoulders. Her chin jutted out as she challenged him. "Never!"

He shrugged, his mouth turned down in disdain, his voice just a little too loud. "Then that's my answer also."

His words seemed to reverberate through the courtyard, echoing from wall to wall.

"Lower your voice," she told him quickly. "They'll hear you."

"Will they?" he said at normal volume. "What does it matter? Who are you hiding from?"

She didn't bother to answer that one. "Just be more quiet," she whispered. "My father is a light sleeper."

He laughed. "A woman who sends a whore to do her work for her surely has nerve enough to face her own father."

Before she could answer, her father made any further explanations unnecessary.

"Marina." The call came from inside the house, and she went weak with panic, clutching at Sebastian's arm to hold herself up. She would die rather than let her father find her here with this man. "What's going on out there?"

She glanced up at Sebastian, determined he wouldn't see how afraid she was of being discovered this way. To have her father look at her with hurt disappointment would be more than she could bear.

"Nothing, Father," she called. "I'm just getting some air."

She tried to push Sebastian into the shadows, but he wouldn't budge. Seemingly, he preferred center stage in the middle of the courtyard. There he stood, as big as life.

"Please, they'll see you," she whispered fiercely, tugging at him as her father's answer came from inside.

"Well, Marina dear, if you must parade about in the middle of the night, do it a bit more quietly," he called to her. "I can't sleep with you making all that noise."

"Please," she begged him, pulling on his cloak, the word sounding more like an order than a plea. "Please . . ."

But she knew he didn't care, at this point, who knew he was here. He was angry with her. She could hardly blame him. Still, it was inconvenient.

There was only one thing she could think of to get him out of sight and out of earshot.

"My bedroom," she whispered, and that was all she had to say.

"All right," he replied, turning right away, his eyes deep as the sea. "Lead the way."

Quickly she pulled him along the corridor and into her own room, closing the door and locking it, then leaning against it with a tremulous sigh.

Turning, she looked up at him with anger. "Have you no pity whatsoever?"

He looked down at her, his anger beginning to dissipate. He was enchanted by the picture she made with her shiny chestnut hair flowing about her shoulders. The cloak was hanging open, showing her soft white nightdress beneath, the opening exposing the swell of her snowy breasts.

He could already feel them melting in his hand, feel her slender body beneath his, feel her strong young legs wrapping around his hips. He'd waited a long time for this. His blood was a burning liquid in his veins. Tonight, he wasn't going to be turned away.

"I'm an honorable man, *querida,*" he said softly. "I'll keep my part of our bargain. You paid for a whore to sleep with me." Reaching out, he touched her hair, his eyes on her red lips. "But I don't want her. I want you."

"I didn't pay for her to sleep with you," she protested, reaching up to push his hand away, but finding that her fingers automatically curled around his instead, holding him to her. "I . . . I only paid for her to steal from you."

He smiled. "Good," he murmured, touching her cheek with the flat of his hand. "Because, Marina . . . right now you're the only woman I want."

She stared up at him, at the blaze in his eyes, the light of passion behind them.

"I want you, Marina." He was whispering now, and his hand curled around her chin and drew her closer. "And you want me, too." Leaning down, he dropped a slow, delicious kiss on her neck, a kiss that made her tremble. "You know it. I could feel it at the *baile,* and last night. And you could feel it, too."

She shivered, closing her eyes, unable to deny what he was saying, but unwilling to help him in any way.

"All we need is one night together and the ring is yours," he said softly. "I'll never touch it again."

His face was pressed against her neck, his warmth flooding her with an odd sensation she couldn't resist.

"You'll forgive what I did to you?" she asked breathlessly.

He was startled for a moment. He'd almost forgotten that part of the bargain. "Yes," he said quickly. "I'll forgive what you did to me."

He would forgive anything right now, do anything, say anything. The need for her was quickening in him and he ached to have her. His hand slid into her hair, reveling in the warm softness, and before he knew what he was doing, he'd pulled her toward him and was burying his face in it, pulling her scent deep into his lungs, his eyes half closed, his heart pounding.

165

"Marina." He said her name like a prayer. She said something but he wasn't sure what it was. His face was sliding against hers, until his mouth found her mouth, and he took possession of her soul, his tongue exploring, moving and thrusting again and again in a near-frenzy of desire.

As she responded to his kisses, there was no hope for her, and she knew it. There was something new driving her. Hesitantly, she put out her hand and pressed it to where his shirt was open. She could hardly breathe, but she needed to feel that he was real and not a dream, that he had a heartbeat, that he had flesh and blood and substance, that he wasn't just a fantasy she'd built in her head. This was too sweet, too fine, to be real, and suddenly she couldn't understand what she had been so afraid of.

He lifted his head groggily, glancing at the bed, and in a moment he had her up in his arms and was laying her down there, her hair spread out around her like a wake in the water. Her cloak was gone and it was a simple matter to push aside the cotton cloth of her nightdress and reveal her rounded breasts, their pink tips soft as rose petals, wide as buttercups. She moaned a soft protest, but she didn't do anything to stop him, and he lowered himself above her, touching one nipple with the tip of his tongue, drawing it up into his mouth and tugging it hard and erect,until she cried out, her hips churning with a new sense of raw hunger she'd never known before.

She could hardly breathe, and when she did draw air into her lungs, it was full of him, the smell of him, the sense of him, the heat of him, and she wanted to drown in everything about him. His hands explored her, slipping under the gown, finding her breasts, her navel, and finally tracing a line of tingling fire toward the place between her legs where she was beginning to realize she wanted him most of all.

All restraint was slipping away. She wanted him hard and naked and now. Her hands plunged beneath his shirt, tugging and pulling until she had his chest under her palms, ripping until she could see his flesh, press her cheek against his heartbeat, drag her mouth across his cool skin.

She was gone, lost, spiraling through a cloud of sensation such as she had never dreamed possible. His body was all there was in her world. His heart was all she wanted. And she was his for the taking, with no remorse.

But suddenly, something intruded on her frenzy, something harsh and hideous. She stopped, drawing back her head and listening, her face confused, her eyes unseeing. There was something going on in the house. Someone was screaming . . .

An agony of quick fear for her family drove the desire out of her in one quick rush. Someone was screaming and crying aloud. It sounded like . . .

Carmen. And then she heard Josefa. Scrambling now, she pushed herself off the bed and began to rearrange her clothing, reaching for her cloak.

"Stay here," she ordered the man who had just been in the process of changing her life forever. "I'll see what it is."

Sebastian rose more slowly, watching her disappear through her doorway in a swirl of cloth. He'd heard the shouts as well, but they hardly penetrated his state of mind. He was staggered by what he'd just been going through, and not sure why.

He'd had his share of amorous adventures. Over the years, he'd known a lot of women, from titled ladies to parlormaids to barroom dancers. But he'd never been

167

with a woman like Marina. There was something about her basic innocence, something about the honesty of her passion when she finally released it, that took his breath away.

But something was going on in the house and he'd best be prepared. Rising, he straightened his clothing, rebuttoned his shirt, and waited, listening intently. Someone was crying. What on earth could have happened?

Footsteps sounded down the corridor and he put his hand on the hilt of his sword, but when the door came open, it was Marina who hurried inside. She closed the door again and turned to face him, her features drawn, her complexion ashen.

"It's my brother Jonathan," she said, her voice shaking. "A rider has just come from San Diego . . . they say he's dead."

"Dead!" Sebastian moved forward and took her shoulders in his hands. "How? What happened?"

She looked at him with blank eyes, as though she didn't know for sure who he was. "I . . . he was coming home. They say the ship he was traveling on was attacked by pirates and sank somewhere in the Caribbean. There were no survivors." She touched his chest with her hand and stared at where it lay. "He was coming home," she repeated without inflection, then looked into his eyes, searching for some sort of answer. "Home."

He wanted to draw her into his arms, but he couldn't do that. Somehow he felt he didn't have the right, and he dropped his hands from her shoulders, turning away.

He'd come to her as a protagonist, an enemy, challenging her rules, challenging her virginity, demanding access to things he really had no right to desire. And just as he really had no right to her body, he had no right to her pain. She needed someone close to comfort her. He would have to go.

He looked back at where she stood, her face wooden, her body stiff, her eyes dry, as though she were still in shock, still unable to take in what had happened.

"I'll go," he said softly.

She nodded, not looking at him.

He swung his cloak about his shoulders and turned toward the door, but he hesitated. She looked so sad, he could hardly bear to leave her like this. Hesitantly, he reached out toward her, wanting to give her some sort of solace, if only he could think of something he could do that could possibly lessen her agony.

He almost touched her, but then he let his hand drop and stood staring at her for a moment. She didn't move, didn't say a word.

"Here." Quickly, he reached into his pocket and pulled out the unicorn ring. Taking her hand, he pressed it to her palm and curled her fingers around it. "Take it," he said, his voice husky. "You need it now."

Turning, he opened the door and disappeared into the night.

She stood where she was and looked at the ring. It hardly registered. Jonathan was dead. Her best friend in the world was gone. It couldn't be. She couldn't accept it. Her mind shied away, trying to protect itself. There had to be a mistake, a way out, a reason not to believe it.

But no matter which way she turned or what she tried to think of, the truth wouldn't be denied. There it was, a terrible, heavy black thing that was going to crush her if she let it. The horror was still fresh and raw. She was afraid of it, afraid of what it could do.

She needed help to bear this burden.

Sliding the ring onto her finger, she gathered her cloak about her and hurried back out to be with her family. It was a time when they all should be together, for they all needed each other. The comfort of her family — that was what she needed now.

The messenger was gone. Josefa sat in a chair before the fireplace, crying softly into a handkerchief. James was pacing the floor, following a pattern in the Persian rug, muttering to himself, his eyes red, his face suddenly old and gaunt. Carmen was nowhere to be seen.

"Father." Marina went to him, holding out her arms. "Oh, Father!"

He looked up sternly, holding a hand up to fend her off. "Stop that now," he ordered her. "There will be no mourning here. They've made a mistake, that's all. Jonathan wasn't on that ship. Why would he be? He's in Boston, reading for the law. It's all a mistake, and we should all go back to bed and get a good night's sleep."

Marina stared, letting her arms drop. There was desperation in her father's eyes. He couldn't face what had happened and he had to cling to hope. Was it wise to let him? She could tell him what Alex had said about Jonathan being missing from his room. But could he stand to know the truth? Was it better to let him grasp at straws of faith?

"Tía." She turned and looked at her aunt. Josefa ignored her, crying a bit louder and waving her away with her free hand. Her own grief was too deep to allow her to let anyone else in.

Marina whirled as she heard her cousin coming back into the room.

"Carmen."

She stepped toward her, knowing she would be as

170

wounded by this as she was, hoping to share the pain. And at first glance, she could see how Carmen was suffering. Her face was twisted and wet with tears. Surely this tragedy would bring the two of them back together again.

But Carmen was waving papers at James, ignoring Marina. "Look, Uncle," she cried in a broken voice. "Look at this. You see? This proves it."

James turned his head away stubbornly. "I won't believe he was in the Caribbean. I won't believe it at all."

Carmen lifted the paper and read from the letter, her voice trembling but strong.

Do you remember, Carmen, when you and Marina and I were children and we would play at being pirates? I've always had a pipe dream of being a pirate. Think of it — on the deck of a burning ship with a colorful rag on my head and a knife between my teeth, swinging from the sails, leaping aboard another vessel and plundering the gold and jewels it carries. Not to mention, the carrying off of the beautiful women. Excuse me for including that, but I must be honest with you, Carmen, if with no one else. When I sailed to Boston we didn't see one pirate on the whole trip. Things will be different when I return. I mean to take the southern route through the Caribbean, and I shall look for pirates everywhere. And if I find a merry group of pirates in a fast sailing ship — who knows? Maybe I'll join them. What would you think of that? Would you welcome me home with a knife between my teeth?

She stopped and looked about the room. The others were all staring at her in shock.

171

"Jonathan wrote like that to you?" Marina whispered.

Josefa shook her head. "I don't believe it. You ungrateful girl, you've made it up."

Carmen came toward her with the paper. "See, look here, it's his handwriting." She waved the letter under Josefa's nose, but when the woman reached to take it, she snatched it back. "No, there are private things in here that you mustn't see."

"Private things?" James said like a man coming out of a dream. "Private things from my son to you? What are you talking about, Carmen?"

"Nothing." She folded the letter quickly and slipped it into the pocket of her dress. "I just wanted to show you that it could be true. That Jonathan did want to find pirates in the Caribbean."

"You were writing to him behind our backs?" The raw emotion of fury began to suffuse James's face. "How could you do such a thing, Carmen? Why didn't you tell us?"

Carmen's face was bright red and stained with tears. "I couldn't tell you, Uncle. It was private, between me and Jonathan."

"How could anything be private between the two of you? Are we not a family? How could you keep secrets from us like this?"

"Because she's a viper," Josefa shrieked. "We've harbored a viper among us . . ."

Marina backed away from the ugly fighting. She could hardly stand the thought that Jonathan had been closer to Carmen than he was to her. She had no secret letters to show. How could this be? How could he have done this to her? Jonathan was hers. She wanted to hear from his own lips how he felt about Carmen, and now it was too late. Now she would never really know. The things Carmen claimed would live on, no matter whether they were true or not.

Turning, she went quickly to her room. But, pacing and wringing her hands, she found no peace there, either. And for some reason, though her throat ached with the lump there, she couldn't cry.

Carmen could cry. She envied her the tears. Carmen had letters from Jonathan. Marina had nothing. Nothing but the unicorn ring, and a house full of family who were at each other's throats.

She had to go away. She couldn't stay here. This seemed a madhouse to her. There was no comfort here, no shelter. She had to go somewhere else, find someone who would listen to her and understand . . . and let her cry. Where could she go?

After Jonathan, Carmen was her best friend. But that was lost to her now. Her other friends were not close enough, not dear to her in the right way. The mission *padre* would hardly want to be awakened for this sort of thing. He was a gruff man under the best of circumstances. Felipe . . . she couldn't imagine going to him. How would he receive her? What would he say? He would be uncomfortable, and he would probably give her over to his mother to handle. No, she couldn't go there.

And suddenly she knew the only place she could go. The only place she wanted to go. The only person who could give her what she needed right now.

Closing her eyes, she said a quick prayer, asking for forgiveness and a little understanding. She was going to need a full share of both those things if she went through with what she was thinking of right now.

Chapter Thirteen

Moving quickly, she took a candle and slipped out of her room and into Jonathan's, across the hall. She knew she couldn't go out alone at this time of night as the young lady that she was. A boy, however, would do just fine.

She went directly to a chest set up against the wall. Inside she found piles of men's clothing from which she extracted a white cotton shirt, corduroy breeches and jacket, and a stained, moth-eaten *serape*. She stepped out of her nightdress and put on the clothes, topping off with a hat she found hanging on a peg on the wall. She left the room and went back to her own, where she pulled on her riding boots, then gave herself a good look in the mirror.

She made a funny-looking boy, but there were a lot of those. Everything she wore was masculine. On impulse, she went into her own chest and pulled out her blue scarf, tying it around her neck and stuffing the ends into her shirt. She had to have something to remind her she was female.

Going into the hall, she listened. They were still arguing in the main room of the house. Maybe that was the only way they could deal with this hideous, crushing grief, but it was not her way. Silently, she slipped from the house.

She led the horse out of the stable, not taking the time to saddle it. As a child she'd lived on horseback and seldom used a saddle, and she had no doubt she could do the same now. She walked the horse to the road, jumped up on its back, and was off toward the Presidio.

The sound of hooves was eerie in the cold, dark night, and she huddled down close to the horse's neck. She felt as though she were riding into hell. And maybe she was.

The Presidio loomed ahead and she slowed her pony, then stopped it and slid off. She tied the animal to a tree a little distance off the road and walked toward the entrance gate, keeping well back within the shadows, and stopping to look things over when the sentry post was in view.

She'd been prepared to have to talk her way inside the walls, but now she saw that it might not be necessary. The sentry was out of his box, sitting in the dust alongside the road, and from the sound of it, he wasn't alone. Triumphant laughter, muffled oaths, and the clinking of coins signaled that he had company, and that an absorbing game of chance was in progress.

None of the gamblers was seated directly facing the entrance. Marina crept up to the corner and stopped for a last glance in their direction. Squaring her shoulders she stepped out into the lantern light as though she had a right to, walking gingerly, but with an air of bravado so as not to arouse suspicion should one of the men look up and notice. Ten steps, twelve, another three, and then she turned the corner and flattened herself against the wall, holding her breath and waiting for a shout or the sound of running feet coming to stop her.

Nothing. All she heard was the game and the players, still intent on their gambling.

Looking around the yard, she found no sign of life abroad in the night. Here and there a window was still lit, but there was no one wandering about outside. She breathed a sigh of relief and stepped out into the common. Now to find Sebastian's room.

She'd seen it in daylight, had it pointed out to her, but things looked different in the late-night shadows, and there was a spooky feeling in the air that made her doubt her own perceptions. Her heart beat a little faster as she surveyed the two windows lit in that general area. One of them should be his. She would only know by looking in the windows. Taking a deep breath, she started out toward them.

A cold breeze blew in from the sea and she wrapped the *serape* more tightly around herself. Her steps sounded startlingly loud on the packed dirt, scaring her for a moment before she realized she was making the noise herself. She tried to set down each foot slowly, without a sound, and almost managed it. But doing so required concentration, and while she was concentrating on that, she didn't notice that another pair of feet had joined her own in stepping quietly along the sideway, each step matching hers, though the shadowy figure had longer legs and came closer and closer as they moved.

The first lit window was just ahead. She was going to have to look inside like a prying thief. She didn't like the thought, but there was no other way, so she steeled herself and reached for the sill.

Just before her fingers touched it, a hand clapped

down over her mouth, and then another hand grabbed at her, and she found herself being dragged back against the building, despite her struggles.

Her first inclination was to scream, but she stifled that in time. Still, she fought wildly, trying to break the grasp of her attacker, make him hesitate, anything to give her a chance at escape. But the man was too strong, and he gave her a rough shake that stunned her for a moment. His breath whistled in her ear and she recoiled in disgust from the smell of *aguardiente*.

"So," he breathed, holding her fast, his grip painful. "It is as I thought: you're not a boy at all. I knew it from the way you walked. And what are you doing out all alone, lovely one?"

She twisted her head around and looked into his bleary eyes. He'd been drinking all right, and she didn't recognize him, but she wasn't sure if that was good or bad. The man was huge and very strong. She knew her only chance to get out of this fix was going to come from talking her way out, but as long as he held a hand over her mouth, there wasn't much she could do.

"So, little bird, you are caught," he chortled, leering in the moonlight. "I'd better put you in my cage for safekeeping. Come along quietly, now."

He began to drag her along the walkway, one shuffling step at a time, his hand still over her mouth. The thought of being held in this man's room was enough to turn her stomach, and she knew she was going to have to do something fast to keep it from happening.

She tried going limp, hoping to slow his progress, but he was strong and didn't seem to notice at all. As they came abreast of the doorway of the first room she'd planned to try, she sprang into action, surprising him enough that she was able to pull out of his grasp

177

and throw herself at the doorway.

"Please . . ." she managed to cry softly before he had her again, his hand over her mouth, dragging her away. She looked back desperately, but no one opened the door. She was going to have to think of something else.

"Ah, little bird," the man said in his drunken voice. "Don't try to fly away again, or I will have to punish you. Such a naughty little bird."

The second door opened, and there, silhouetted against the light from the room, stood Sebastian, looking out at where the man was dragging her off. She made a muffled noise, trying to call to him, but the man's hand tightened around her mouth painfully, and she realized that all Sebastian saw was a drunk dragging off a dirty street urchin. Here she was right in front of him, and he would very likely let her go.

She struggled harder, determined to break free, but at the same time, she heard Sebastian call out to the man.

"Hey, you—what are you doing to that boy?"

The hand slipped from her face as the man turned to see who had called to him, and Marina managed to cry out before he turned back to her again.

"Sebastian!" she called, and he took in the situation immediately.

The next moment or two passed in a blur. The man who held her was suddenly releasing her, and she felt herself sinking to the ground, flailing for support, but then Sebastian had her in his arms before she landed, and was putting her back on her feet.

"What in God's name?" He swore softly, standing back and looking at her with a mixture of amusement and exasperation.

"What are you doing in this ridiculous outfit?" he asked her, laughing softly as he dusted her off. "Is there a masked ball in the neighborhood? You'll have to excuse your escort. I'm afraid he's not used to keeping such late hours. He seems to have dropped off to sleep."

Looking down dazedly, she noticed that her assailant was lying unconscious in the dirt, and she swayed toward Sebastian, whose arms came around her once again, but this time he didn't let go.

Doors were opening around the yard.

"Come with me," he said quickly, leading her, wrapping her in protection that filled her with warmth. "I think we'll be more comfortable with a little privacy."

He took her into his room and closed the door. She was alone with Sebastian. She closed her eyes for a moment, taking in the enormity of that situation. He'd saved her from the soldier, but she knew he couldn't rescue her from her pain. Still, wasn't that why she'd come?

Opening her eyes, she began to look about her. She stood in the middle of the floor and turned slowly, looking at his bed, his chest, the spindly bookcase he had made to hold the books he had borrowed from her father.

He stood back, not wanting to scare her, letting her get her bearings before he said a word, and as he waited, he watched her turn, watched her eyes, saw the incredible sadness, and suddenly his heart was in his throat.

What was he going to do with her? Why had she come? He knew how to deal with flirts and madams and curious virgins, but he had no idea what to do with a grieving woman. It was a position he had never

179

really been in before.

"What are you doing here, Marina?" he asked her.

She turned her huge gray eyes his way. "I came because . . . I had no place else to go."

Why did that make his pulse race? "But your family . . ."

She shook her head, looking away. "They're crazy. Jonathan's death . . ." She swallowed hard after forcing the words out. "It's thrown them into such turmoil, they're attacking each other. I couldn't stay there and listen to that."

He sighed, turning away. He couldn't have her here. It wasn't safe. He wouldn't be able to keep his hands off her. And if he took advantage of her now, he would hate himself.

"Marina, you shouldn't be here," he said in a strangled voice. "You've got to go."

She shook her head again, then pulled off the hat and shook her hair out, letting the cinnamon halo fly out about her head. "I can't go," she said simply. "Please let me stay."

She looked young and appealing in the boy's clothes, her breasts straining beneath the white shirt. He stared at her, his conscience fighting a hard battle for his soul. After all the baiting and goading he'd done to her, now he found himself in the role of her protector. It was a powerful position to be in, and he could use it to his own advantage in whatever way seemed useful.

"I feel as though there's a vise on my heart," she was saying, looking at him as though he would know the answer. "It's so tight, I can barely breathe."

He stared hard at her and he knew this was the crucial moment. He could walk away and sit on the bed

180

and try polite conversation, or he could open the door and walk out into the dark and never come back. But he wasn't going to do either of those things. Instead, he was going to take her in his arms and comfort her. Because he didn't really know what else to do.

He was used to taking women into his arms. He was an old hand at it, practiced and smooth. But this was different. This time he didn't want to seduce, he only wanted to offer solace to ease pain, and he felt awkward and new at it.

She felt like heaven as his arms came around her. He thought his heart would stop when she put her cheek against his chest and sighed. His hand patted her back rather clumsily and he tried to keep his breathing even.

"From the moment I heard the news about Jonathan," she said softly, her voice muffled by his shirt, "I've been dead inside. I can't wake up. I can't . . . cry."

"Marina," he said softly, just to say her name.

She looked up at him, her eyes ancient as the hills, and to him they looked full of wisdom. "You gave me back the ring," she said, her voice clear and quiet. "That's important to me. I needed it so badly."

What was it she had called him the other day? A debauched outcast. A scoundrel. That was exactly what he felt like. A bastard of the first order. And for the first time ever, he regretted it.

He touched her face with his hand. Her skin was cool. His hand felt hot against it. She was still looking up at him, searching his eyes, and he was sure she could read everything he was thinking.

"You need sleep," he said simply. "Come. You can sleep in my bed. I won't . . . hurt you."

Her fingers locked with his. "You'll come too?" she

181

asked softly, her eyes as deep as a mountain lake.

For a moment he wasn't sure what she was talking about. Could she really want him in the bed with her? But then he realized she needed the comfort of another warm body nearby. The night was a frightening thing to her, and sleep meant dreams.

"Of course," he told her. "I'll be right beside you."

He meant to turn away while she pulled off the shirt and trousers, leaving her in her thin chemise, but once she'd begun revealing her silvery skin, he couldn't stop staring at her. His heart was beating very loudly, and desire was stirring with a fierce flame that was going to be very hard to keep contained.

He pulled back the covers and she climbed in, shivering against the cool blankets. He set the candle near the head of the bed and turned to pull off his boots and then his shirt. He left his trousers on as cheap insurance, and she noticed, but she had the good sense not to question him about it. She pulled back the covers and he came into the narrow bed beside her, trying very hard to keep from touching her in any way.

"Better?" he asked her.

She looked into his eyes and nodded, but she was lying. There was nothing getting better. She needed some sort of catharsis to clear her spirit and let her mourn.

Rising on his elbow, he looked down at her. "Now tell me about Jonathan," he said softly. "Tell me everything—why you loved him, when you were angry with him, why you care."

She blinked at him. She'd hardly expected this. But maybe he was right. Maybe it would help.

She started to talk, hesitantly at first, but as she remembered more and more, the memories came rolling back, flowing out of her. She recalled the time when

182

they were little and he'd tried to make her eat a snail, the time he broke his arm, the time he made her be Sancho Panza to his Don Quixote. She remembered how bravely he'd fought his first bull, how solemnly he'd learned his Latin phrases, how he would chase her with a potato bug. As they got older, he grew very handsome and merry and the girls loved him with his laughing eyes and bold, dashing ways. She thought of the time he and she and Carmen had gone to the beach, playing hide-and-go-seek, and she hadn't been able to find them for so long, she thought for a while that they'd gone off and left her. But then they'd come out from a clump of trees, and Carmen's cheeks had been so red . . .

Her eyes stared at the ceiling, and suddenly other memories came pouring out, how Jonathan had always danced more with Carmen, telling Marina it was because she had more suitors and he didn't want Carmen to feel bad, an excuse she should have known was false. How they would pull apart when she came into a room where they had been alone for a while. How many times had they all three meant to meet, and when she'd arrived, she'd found they'd gone on without her?

How could she have been so blind? Why hadn't she read the signs that dangled right in front of her nose? It was obvious now as she looked back. But at the time, she'd never thought such a thing possible. They were brother and sisters, the three of them. She tended to forget that Carmen wasn't related to Jonathan by blood.

She'd been blind, an idiot, but somehow she felt that Carmen had stolen something from her. She was in love with Jonathan. That was obvious now. But that didn't mean she had a right to him, or his memory.

She looked up and found Sebastian still watching her. Suddenly she was aware of him as a man, his naked chest so near, his warmth filling the bed that had seemed so cool at first. She still felt dead inside and she was desperate for some sort of emotion. Anything. If she made love with him, maybe she could lose this crushed feeling. Maybe it would break the dam that held her emotions tightly inside. She could hardly stand it any longer.

She lifted her hand and touched his face, her eyes full of the possibilities. He grabbed her wrist and wrenched her hand away.

"Don't do that, Marina," he said roughly. "You're on thin ice as it is."

She thought she knew what he meant, and she wondered for a moment what he would say if she asked him to make love to her. But that would be very wrong, wouldn't it? She only wanted him to help free her from pain, and he only wanted her to get back at Felipe. It would be better to go to sleep.

She settled, feeling protected in a way. To her surprise, sleep came quickly, and soon she was drowsing, her eyes closed, her breathing even.

He watched her sleep, her breath stirring the hair on his arm. The unicorn ring was on her finger, the ring that had maimed him on the hand that had wielded it. That fateful encounter had set the tone for the rest of their relationship, and he was beginning to wonder if he regretted it.

He should sleep too, but he knew he couldn't. He couldn't stop watching her, taking in her soft, guileless beauty, the sweet, honest face, the lovely curve of her shoulder. He wanted her with a need that was a painful throbbing, but there was more here. Stronger than the

184

physical need to have her was the emotional need to protect her. Where that had come from, he didn't know. He'd never felt like this before. At least, not since he was young. Not since Angelique.

But that was far away and long ago. Swearing softly, he pulled back and rose to pace the floor of his tiny room, remembering how Angelique had betrayed him. His love for his sister had been very like Marina's love for her brother. But Angelique had betrayed him, and Jonathan had died. What did love ever do for you, anyway? It was just another way to kick you in the teeth. He looked back at where she slept. He was a fool not to take her tonight when he had her here this way. Tomorrow would be a different story. She would be herself again. The vulnerability would fade.

She sighed and turned in her sleep, and he thought she said a name. It was probably Jonathan's. Perhaps in dreams she would learn to deal with his death. She moved restlessly, and he leaned close in case she spoke again.

"Sebastian," she murmured. "Oh, don't . . . I need . . ."

She was dreaming about him. He stared down at her, spellbound, and as he watched, her body arched up as though to accept a lover, and her lips parted.

This was too much to resist. As though in a trance, he leaned down and kissed her mouth, hard and hungry and angry for what he was going through, with all the pent-up longing he held inside for her. He kissed her with fierce aching fire, and whispered her name against her lips.

Her eyes were open now and she was staring at him, fully awake, her eyes like deep, dark caverns. "Yes," she whispered, reaching for him. "Yes, please . . ."

He drew back, hesitating, knowing this was wrong, wondering where his control had gone, and she reached up and ran her hand across his naked chest, staring at how it looked there, savoring the feel of his hot flesh, so smooth, so hard, so tight. He said something soft and rough that she couldn't understand and threw back his head, his eyes closed, and she brought her other hand up to explore him, smoothing and stroking, running her hands down his sides until she reached his trousers, and her fingers curled inside the belt.

His head jerked back and he pulled air into his lungs in a painful lurch, trying to hold back the craving that threatened to overwhelm him. She stared up into his eyes, wondering if he realized that he was trembling. There, beneath her hands, the arrogant seducer was trembling as he tried to control his desire for her. Maybe she really was dreaming, after all.

Sighing, she slid her hands up to link around his neck and tugged to get him back down where she could taste him again. As she watched, his face twisted in agony, and then he returned, kissing her again, as though he couldn't get enough of her, as though he were starving for something only she could provide him. His mouth was fused to hers, drawing out everything she could give, and his hands found her breasts, rubbing with an urgency that made her cry out with the torment of pleasure.

Her body arched again, wanting him, needing him, and she heard him utter an oath as he began to drag himself away from her.

"Where are you going?" she whispered, reaching to hold him to her.

He let his hands claw into the covers around her to

186

keep from clawing into her, but he couldn't answer with words. Pulling away, he vaulted free of her, off the bed, cursing as he went.

He couldn't do this now. Didn't she understand that? He made love to willing women. He didn't rape, he didn't trick, he didn't force his way into anybody's bed, the unicorn ring ploy notwithstanding. And he certainly wasn't going to take advantage of her grief just to have her. He might be a scoundrel, but he wasn't the devil himself, and he refused to play the part.

"Go to sleep," he said harshly, and he grabbed a jacket and slammed out of the room.

She lay very quiet, trying to understand what had just happened. She'd never offered herself to a man before and she really didn't know how it worked, but she was pretty sure this wasn't usually the way it ended if the man had any real desire for the woman. He didn't really want her; that had to be the problem. He only wanted to fight with Felipe. She didn't matter to him at all.

Did she matter to anyone? She'd lost Jonathan, and in the process she'd lost Carmen as well. And when she'd turned to the man who had been letting her know that he couldn't go on without her lovemaking, he turned away from her too. She felt very much alone in an alien world.

The candle sputtered and she blinked in the gloom, wondering what Jonathan would say if he could see her now.

"Life is like a love song, Marina," he'd told her once. "If you can get through the sad part, you know you'll get to laugh in the end."

Tears began to prickle her eyelids, and then the sobs began. Her shoulders shook and she buried her face in

187

the pillow, crying for her pain, crying for Jonathan, who hadn't made it through the sad part, crying for all they had lost. She sobbed long and hard, and didn't notice when Sebastian slipped back into the room, sat on the chair and watched her until she finally cried herself to sleep.

She awoke as the first streaks of purple began to appear in the sky. It took a moment to orient herself. Sebastian was lying beside her, fully clothed and on top of the covers. Trying not to wake him, she slipped out of the bed and reached for the boy's clothes she'd worn the night before.

"What are you doing?"

She jumped at the sound of his voice, but she didn't stop dressing.

"I'm going home."

She glanced down at where he lay back, looking at her. How strange to see a man so early in the morning, so intimately.

"Thank you very much for your hospitality, and . . ." She hesitated, not sure how to characterize what else he had done for her.

"And my bed."

"And your bed."

The thought of how much more she had wanted from him filled her with an odd, trembling panic. "I want to get home before I'm missed," she said quickly, sitting down to pull on her boots.

He watched her for another moment, amazed that he could still want her as badly now as he had the night before. Would this hunger never ease in him? It seemed not. And he knew that he had missed his

188

chance at getting what he most wanted. The moment had passed. He might never have another.

"You can't go alone." He pulled himself up and swung his legs over the side of the bed.

"Yes I can. I'm perfectly capable of taking care of myself."

He yawned and stretched and she tried to avoid noticing how good his body looked beneath the flimsy cotton shirt, the body she had felt beneath her hands the night before.

"Just as you took care of yourself coming here," he drawled. "I had to pry you out of the clutches of a drunken soldier in the middle of the Presidio yard."

She pulled her hair back and tied it behind her head. "I would have gotten away without your help, given a little more time."

He stood, towering over her. "You didn't have the time and you know it. He would have had you for dinner. And breakfast, and lunch as well, if I hadn't helped out."

She turned and faced him. "But he didn't, did he? And now I'm going home."

He reached out and stopped her with a hand on her arm. "Are you sure you're all right?"

She looked at him and nodded. She felt drained, spent. The heavy weight of Jonathan's death was still hovering over her, but she had hope that she would eventually learn to deal with it now.

Despite her protests, he insisted on accompanying her home. They took his horse. He put her before him in the saddle, holding her with his arm of iron.

She still quivered to his touch. Did he know? Could he feel it? She wanted him so badly, hungered for him in a deep, primitive way she had only imagined before he had arrived in their town. But he only wanted her so he could get back at Felipe.

They picked up her horse where she had tied it and he dropped her near enough to the back of her property that she could make the rest of the trip on her own. He waited, watching her as she led the horse to the stable, but she didn't look back. As far as she was concerned, it was time to get Sebastian de la Cruz out of her system once and for all.

Chapter Fourteen

Once inside, she found Carmen waiting in her bedroom, looking as though she hadn't slept at all.

"Where have you been?" Carmen asked, her eyes red from crying.

"Out," said Marina, pulling off the hat and shaking out her hair.

Carmen nodded. "You were with the Spaniard. I know."

She stared at her cousin. There was such a wall between them now, nothing could bridge it.

"We both lead separate lives now, don't we?" she said evenly. "It was only I who didn't realize how soon you started doing so."

Carmen flashed her a resentful glance and looked away again, "I don't know what you're talking about," she said dully.

"You and Jonathan. Why didn't I know?"

Tears trembled in Carmen's eyes. "There was nothing to know, believe me. I meant nothing to him."

She flopped down beside her on the bed. "Carmen, how can you say that? The way he wrote to you . . ."

"That was just the way he was. You know that. He was friendly to anyone who was friendly to him. He was more fun than any other man I've ever known." Her voice broke, but she forced herself to finish. "There will never be another like him."

Marina wanted to take her cousin in her arms. She wanted to cry with her, hold her, comfort her. But Carmen was like an animal with spines to keep off intruders. Her every look, her every gesture, said, "Don't tread on me," and Marina didn't know how to tear down that barricade.

"Carmen, what will you do?" she asked at last, reaching out and touching her cousin's sleeve.

"What will I do?" She wiped the tears from her eyes and her laugh was hollow. "Throw my life away, just like you warned me. Why not?"

"With Sebastian?" she asked, drawing her hand back.

"With the next man who looks interesting."

Carmen turned and looked at Marina. For just a moment, there seemed to be a crack, a tiny opening that the two of them might be able to use to find a way back to each other. But just as quickly it was gone.

"I want to get out of here, Marina," Carmen said, "and soon you will, too." She waved her hand. "Your father is acting like a crazy man. He says we're not allowed to think of Jonathan as dead. He's still alive, until we see a body. So we aren't to wear black. We aren't to acknowledge words of sympathy from our friends. We're to go on as if nothing had happened."

Marina sat for a long moment in silence, and when she finally raised her head, she looked Carmen in the eye.

"What if he's right?" she said softly. "What if Jonathan isn't dead?"

Carmen stared back, then made a rude sound. "Don't be ridiculous. That's just clinging to false hope.

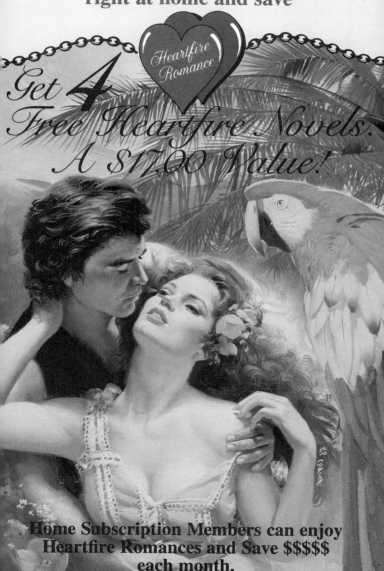

TO GET YOUR
4 FREE BOOKS
MAIL THE COUPON BELOW.

FREE BOOK CERTIFICATE

Heartfire Romance

GET 4 FREE BOOKS

Yes! I want to subscribe to Zebra's HEARTFIRE HOME SUBSCRIPTION SERVICE. Please send me my 4 FREE books. Then each month I'll receive the four newest Heartfire Romances as soon as they are published Free for ten days. If I decide to keep them I'll pay the special discounted price of just $3.50 each; a total of $14.00. This is a savings of $3.00 off the regular publishers price. There are no shipping, handling or other hidden charges. There is no minimum number of books to buy and I may cancel this subscription at any time. In any case the 4 FREE Books are mine to keep regardless.

NAME _____

ADDRESS _____

CITY _____ STATE _____ ZIP _____

TELEPHONE _____

SIGNATURE _____

(If under 18 parent or guardian must sign)
Terms and prices subject to change.
Orders subject to acceptance.

HF 104

GET 4 FREE BOOKS

HEARTFIRE HOME SUBSCRIPTION
SERVICE
P.O. BOX 5214
120 BRIGHTON ROAD
CLIFTON, NEW JERSEY 07015

You've got to face the truth now, Marina, or it will only hurt worse in the end."

"Maybe." She shrugged. "Maybe."

At first, there was great consternation in the neighborhood when it was realized that James Crafts refused to act as though his son were dead. People muttered among themselves and shuffled their feet and didn't know what to do about it. The mission priest came to visit, and when his advice was ignored, came again, bringing with him the priest from the Presidio chapel for backup.

James didn't budge.

"Show me a body," he said to anyone who wanted to listen. "Until I see the proof with my own eyes, I won't believe it."

And then he smiled and told a joke or asked a question to change the subject, and the other person in the conversation got red in the face and found an excuse to go somewhere else where people weren't so contrary and followed the usual guidelines for normal behavior.

But James won. Before the week was out, most people had just about forgotten that Jonathan was supposed to be dead. Life went back to normal.

Sebastian watched this from afar. He'd decided to stay away from the Crafts family until he could think straight about Marina. She disturbed his days, she disturbed his sleep, and he wanted to rid himself of this obsessive behavior. The best way to do that, he reasoned, was to stay away from her and her cousin Carmen. And that was what he was doing.

That meant he also deprived himself of the company of James Crafts, however, and he hadn't realized how much he had begun to count on their talks for intellectual stimulation. So when James stopped in to visit him one day about a week after the party for Felipe's return, he was glad to welcome him inside.

"I was passing by," James said as he took a seat at Sebastian's small table, "and thought I would stop in and see if you had delved into that volume on John Locke I left here last time. What did you think of it?"

"I haven't finished it, but what I have read I found fascinating. The concept of man's inherent rights, which he is born with and which no government has the right to tamper with without his consent, was a revelation to me. Of course, I had heard of this philosophy before. It clearly underlies much of the thinking behind the American Revolution. But I had never seen it thoroughly discussed before. It is certainly going to force me to rethink some of my basic assumptions."

James nodded happily. "Of course it will. That's the whole point, isn't it? When you have finished, I will give you some papers by Addison which explore another aspect."

"I would appreciate that."

"Don't mention it. It's a real treat to have someone to discuss these things with. Ever since Jonathan left for Boston, I've been hard pressed to find anyone interested in any sort of reading and philosophy."

Sebastian glanced at James's face when he mentioned his son, but his expression was bland without a trace of sorrow, and Sebastian mentally shrugged. If the man wanted to skip the mourning, who was he to hand him sackcloth and ashes?

"The previous Comandante was a great reader," James was going on. "We got along famously. But when he was recalled to Mexico City, they sent us this present fellow, and I doubt if he could read a grocery list."

Sebastian laughed. "Your daughter is a reader, too, isn't she?"

"Marina, yes. She's as smart as Jonathan ever was. If she were a boy, she'd be in Boston with him right now. And beating him at recitation, too, and you'd better believe it."

Sebastian smiled, enjoying the picture of Marina in a studious mode. "Perhaps we could invite her to join our next discussion session," he said before he could think.

James looked surprised, and well he might, Sebastian thought, cursing himself for a fool. He really had to get over this obsession with the girl.

"That might be a very good idea," James said. "She's a sharp one, my Marina. She'll change your mind on a thing or two, I'd wager."

"She already has," he thought silently, but he smiled and nodded as James began to gather himself to leave.

His age was affecting him more and more, and it took him a moment to collect the strength to rise. Then he dropped his hat and bent to retrieve it. Suddenly his eyes sharpened and his brows came together in a mild frown. He seemed to have detected something under Sebastian's bed. Sebastian saw his look and he glanced down, but at first he couldn't see what James had discovered until the man reached down and pulled it out, and then a feeling of dread crept over him.

As James straightened, he held in his hand a long blue silk scarf with the initials, "M.C." embroidered into one corner in gold thread. He stared at it for a long moment, then turned back to Sebastian, his face pale. Suddenly he seemed to be unable to meet the younger man's gaze.

"I'm afraid you must have dropped this," he said quietly, handing the piece of flimsy fabric to him.

195

Then he turned and walked stiffly to the door.

Sebastian stood rooted to the spot. He didn't remember ever having seen this scarf before in his life, but who would believe him? Every excuse, every protestation that rose half-formed to his lips, sounded false and hollow, even to himself. Silence was better than pleading for trust. But silence left James to walk away in misery. And Sebastian couldn't think of any way to prevent it.

The scarf felt impossibly light in his hand. If he didn't look, he could almost believe it had disappeared, vanished, never been there at all. But that was wishful thinking. It was there all right, with the initials blazing its ownership to anyone who cared to look. Slowly, he raised it to his lips. The scent it gave was sweet and natural as the woman herself. The silk was cool and smooth as her skin. Her image came to him with a startling clarity, her gray eyes gazing levelly into his, full of a puzzled innocence mixed with a sure intelligence.

And her father now knew she'd been here to visit him. Sebastian's lips curled in a mirthless appreciation of the irony of fate. When he had wanted to compromise her before the whole town, he hadn't succeeded, but now, through a careless quirk, he had compromised her to the one person in town he would have spared the pain.

The door still stood open as James had left it. The Presidio yard wasn't crowded, but there was a general air of busyness developing as horses and men passed through in growing numbers. He stared out idly for a few minutes, the scarf still in his hand, his mind absorbed by disturbing questions. And then his eyes focused on a familiar-looking pair hurrying by. Marina and Josefa were on their way to the Presidio chapel.

On impulse, he stuffed the scarf into his jacket and left his room to follow them, staying discreetly behind. Entering the dimly lit chapel, he slipped into a niche to the side and stood behind a large statue while he surveyed the territory.

Josefa had gone on to the altar and was seeking counsel with the Presidio priest, leaving Marina behind in the pews. She was on her knees not far from where he stood, her head bowed over her hands, her eyes tightly closed, oblivious to all around her.

He watched her, moved by the devout picture she made. She was so beautiful. The dim light seemed to illuminate her, giving a translucent glow to the smooth skin of her cheek, the soft line of the hair over her forehead, the curl of her small ear against the side of her head. She was almost sublime, in the realm of the angels. He frowned, startled by the effect this vision was having on him.

It was sacrilege, the way her piety made him want her even more. He seemed less and less in control of himself where she was concerned. To see her this way was pure torture. Not to see her at all would be even worse.

But he'd come to give her back the scarf she must have dropped the other night, and it was time to get on with it. Softly, he called her name.

Her eyes flew open and she looked around quickly, and then she saw him. She half rose, looking toward where her aunt had gone, then slipped quietly out of the pew and came toward him.

"Sebastian . . ." she began, but he put his finger to his lips, grabbed her wrist, and pulled her firmly into his hiding place.

There wasn't much room. They were pressed together, and his arms circled around her to protect her

197

from the rough walls. He looked down into her face and for some reason he couldn't remember why he'd called her here.

He couldn't say a word, and neither could she. Their eyes met and held, and they didn't need words. He was looking straight down into her defenseless soul. He reached for her hand, his fingers curling around it, slowly lifting it to his chest, slipping inside his jacket, inside his shirt, so that her palm flattened against his bare skin, right over his heart.

She couldn't speak, could barely breathe. She had his heart in the palm of her hand, and her existence had suddenly narrowed to encompass only the growing passion she could glimpse in his eyes, the pounding of his pulse beneath her hand. It was as though she held his life in her power. All else faded, fell away, mattered not at all. She could stay here forever and be content.

"Marina . . ." His face was close, too close. His free hand came up to cup her cheek. "Oh God, Marina . . ."

She closed her eyes and gave a small, strangled cry. This couldn't be. Not here, not now. It would be like tearing her heart out to leave him, but she had to do it, do it quickly, before Josefa came back and saw her. Summoning all the strength she possessed, she broke away from heaven.

Closing her eyes so she wouldn't have to see his face, she pushed her way blindly from the niche, then fled the chapel, racing through the dusty courtyard as though pursued by demons.

Sebastian took two stumbling steps after her, then stopped and leaned against the chapel doorway, staring out at her disappearing form.

Josefa pushed her way past him roughly, uttering a

rude insult as she passed. She dashed after her niece as quickly as her portly form would carry her, but Sebastian didn't notice her at all. His mind was numb and struggling with a truth he would have to face. Nothing could be the same again.

He pulled the scarf from his jacket and raised it to his lips, breathing in the fragrance. Now he knew he would never give it back.

Marina turned the corner to the sentry box and slowly regained control, slowing her steps and focusing her flurried mind on only one thing — getting home and into her own room without thinking about what had just happened.

Josefa was calling from behind. Reluctantly, she lingered so that her aunt could catch up.

"Marina, you go so quickly! Let me catch my breath. My heart is beating so fast, I may have an attack right here, and then how will you get me home?"

She clutched her niece's arm, forcing her to wait while she got back her breath and her composure.

"What happened? What did he do to you? What did he say?"

Marina shook her head, refusing to meet her aunt's eyes. "I don't know what you mean. I was praying and suddenly . . . a sort of faintness came over me and I thought I'd better hurry home before I became ill."

Josefa snorted. "Do you think I'll believe such a tale? Come now. I saw you running from him. And I saw him looking after you like a stricken sheep. If he did nothing to you, you certainly must have done something to him. Where . . . ?"

Marina pulled away sharply and began to walk as fast as she could toward home. *"Basta!* I don't have to tell you everything, Tía. I won't be grist for your gossiping tongue."

Josefa's shock rendered her speechless. Never before had Marina spoken to her this way. The two of them made the rest of the trip home in silence, Marina leading at a steady clip. When they reached the house, Marina went on in without acknowledging Josefa's presence in any way, and Josefa went off to the kitchen, her face a study in puzzled surprise.

Marina swept through the parlor and started into her room, but before she had made good her escape, she heard her father's voice coming from the library.

"Marina? Is that you?"

She closed her eyes for a moment, steadying herself against the wall, pushing down the thoughts and feelings she was going to have to deal with when she had the time, and entered the book-lined room.

"Why, Papa," she said brightly, "I thought you would be at the Alcalde's."

He turned toward her and she gasped. His face was gray and slack. He seemed to have aged ten years since morning. Lurching toward him, she sank to her knees at his side.

"Papa, what is it? Are you ill? Shall I send for the doctor?"

He smiled at her quietly, shaking his head and motioning for her to rise and be seated.

"No, my darling," he said in a low, sad voice. "I am only a bit anxious. It has come to me suddenly what a careless father I have been."

He raised his hand to still her protests. "No, my dear, it's quite true. I've never directed your life, I've only allowed you to drift. I've taken for granted that the morals and values your mother and I believed in would somehow be automatically implanted in you,

200

but I've never taken the time or effort to learn if this was true, or to do anything to remedy false notions you might have acquired." He looked at his hands, folded upon his desk, and murmured, "I just hope it's not too late."

Marina shook her head in bewilderment. She had never seen her father so distraught, not even when Jonathan had been reported killed in the Caribbean. Of course, he still refused to believe it. Something must have happened that he didn't feel he could deny. But what?

"Papa, what is it? Have I done something?"

He smiled at her with all the love he had for her shining in his eyes. "No, darling. It's not your fault. It's mine alone."

He lifted his shoulders and raised his head, replacing his melancholy aspect with one of resolution. "But I shall now make some belated attempt to mend my ways. It's time we ended this aimless drifting and organized our lives. Tell me — how are matters coming with Felipe? Why hasn't he asked as yet for your hand? I've certainly given him every opportunity."

Marina looked away, feeling suddenly trapped. "I . . . I suppose he is too busy with the rodeo . . ."

James frowned thoughtfully. "I would have thought the rodeo the perfect time for an announcement," he said, looking at her for agreement, and seeing only a blank look in her eyes. "Perhaps you would prefer the celebration to be more strictly your own affair. Very well, I shall instruct Josefa to plan a gathering of our dearest friends the Saturday following the rodeo. See that Felipe speaks to me before that day. It's time we settled this matter."

She studied him seriously, surprised by this newly acquired firmness and worried by it as well. Something ominous must have happened to set him off this way. He was obviously very worried. His financial situation must be worsening and he wished to have her safely provided for as quickly as possible.

So the matter of her engagement was here and had to be made final immediately. But how could she marry Felipe when all she could think about was the Spaniard? Her fingers went to the unicorn ring and she twisted it, wishing it really did have the magic Jonathan had promised.

Chapter Fifteen

Carmen looked up briefly from her sewing as Marina entered the room a few days later.

"So, you're finally back from chapel. Alex is here."

Just what she needed, some relief from this endless anxiety. "Wonderful. Where is he?"

"Out in the courtyard with Tía."

Marina flew from the room, her heart lighter than it had been for days. She and Carmen were barely speaking, her father walked around like a ghost, and Josefa, even after she'd apologized for the way she'd spoken to her at the Presidio, was watching her like a hawk, certain she was up to something.

And here she was, up to nothing at all, trying to juggle the responsibilities she felt toward her family with the fascination she was caught up in over Sebastian de la Cruz.

She hadn't seen him since that day at the chapel, and it was just as well, because if she had tried to talk to him, Josefa would have been at his throat like a mad dog. She had seen Felipe at a friend's house, but his formal manner had been a clear indication that he was still annoyed with her over the way she had danced the *fandango* with the man he hated most in the world. Secretly, she was relieved. She knew the time was coming

203

when he would ask for her hand, but she still didn't know what she was going to do when that happened.

The more she contemplated life with Felipe, the less she liked the look of it. Even though she had been raised in town, she had to some extent been born and bred to the *rancho* existence. However, when she came to analyze the parts of her life that gave her true joy, Felipe promised to share very few of them. He was handsome and brave, admired and exciting, and there had been a time when she had dearly loved to dance, ride and flirt with him, but was he the right husband for her?

As her doubts grew, so did the pressure on her to go ahead and marry him. Tía talked about nothing but how her marriage to Felipe would solve all their problems, catapulting them into a veritable land of milk and honey. Carmen made acid comments, but she obviously thought marrying Felipe was the thing to do, as soon as possible. James had made it quite clear it would be a relief to him that she should be safely out from under his wing. What would they all say if they could see what was in her mind?

But now here was the captain. Hopefully his visit would cheer them all up a little.

"Captain." She stepped out into the courtyard and hurried toward him.

"My dear Marina." He took both her hands in his own and looked at her affectionately. "You see, I've come for the roundup, as I promised."

"I'm so glad. We've been so dull around here lately. We can't even seem to get up much enthusiasm for the rodeo, and it starts tomorrow. But now that you're here, we'll surely perk up." She laughed along with him. "How long will you stay?"

"Only two days. I must leave the day after tomorrow, if the weather agrees, and we'll stop in San Pedro for a day before heading for home."

"Well, two days is better than none. Where is Tía?"

"She had to see about some bread baking, out in the yard." He paused and looked at her more seriously. "Marina, what is this I hear about Jonathan?"

Paling, she took his hand in hers. "Alex, a messenger came to say that Jonathan was lost when his ship went down in the Caribbean. We don't know what to believe. Papa refuses to admit anything might be wrong."

"So Josefa was telling me." He squeezed her hand. "And you know? I think he's right. These reports often err. What is the use of thinking the worst until you're forced to?"

She searched his eyes for hope. Did he really believe that, or was he just trying to make her feel better?

"So, tell me," Alex went on. "How is your father doing? Financially, I mean. Is the work for the Alcalde going well?"

"Oh yes, he loves it. He goes whenever he can and works all day. The trouble is, there has been no talk of a salary yet, and we haven't seen one *centavo.*"

"I was afraid of that." Alex shook his head ominously. "They say the soldiers at some *presidios* up the coast haven't been paid for over a year. Mexico had better start paying some attention to California, or she may just wake up some day and find that California has turned to greener pastures. But about you and your father, Marina . . . I tried talking to Josefa about it, and she just laughed and said that salvation was just around the corner. Then she hinted that you were about to marry Don Felipe Diaz. Is that true?"

Marina turned away from him, not wanting him to see her face as she answered, even though, with Carmen so cold toward her, he was probably her best friend at the moment. "I don't know. They all think so here. But I'm not sure yet."

Alex frowned and moved restlessly. "Do you love him?" he asked bluntly.

She hesitated, then turned to look him in the face. "That really isn't the point, is it? You can love someone and still be miserable living with him. The point is, do I want to be married to him, for ever and always, sharing his way of life, his values, his family. And I'm not sure that I do."

There, she'd finally said it. She looked at him expectantly, waiting to see his reaction, expecting to be roundly chastised for being so pragmatic about a subject that tradition held should be based on romance.

But Alex was smiling broadly. Her placement of logic over passion appealed to him. "You're a right smart girl," he told her.

She smiled and shook her head. "Not smart, confused. Oh Alex, I don't know what to do. I hope you don't mind if I talk to you about this. I really have no one I can go to for advice."

Alex shifted his weight uncomfortably. "Well, sure, I'd be glad to help, but wouldn't Carmen be better?" He coughed. "After all, this is a pretty important decision. I mean, you're deciding the future for a lot of people here. Don't forget, if you marry Felipe, you'll be the . . . uh . . . mother of his . . . you know . . ."

"Children." She stopped, aghast. "I hadn't thought that far." Squinting her eyes she could see five little boys who looked exactly like Felipe, each on horseback, grinning with mindless gaiety. She shook her head to rid herself of the vision. "No, I can't think about that. I have to make my choices with what is real."

Alex smiled and looked furtively toward the house, hoping for a rescue. But there was none forthcoming. It appeared he was going to be forced to listen to Marina's train of thought, whether he wanted to or not.

She sighed, not noticing his dilemma, and began to pace as she talked. "As I see it, I have two choices. Either I marry Felipe and make everyone happy, or I refuse him and watch my family's fortunes crumble in the dust."

Alex spoke hesitantly. "There's another choice, you know."

She stopped and looked at him expectantly. "Such as? Maybe run away to China?"

"Yes, in a sense." His smile was bashful. "You could marry me."

She stared at him, dumbfounded, and wishing she had remembered how he had once spoken to her father about her.

A radiance was spreading across his face as he thought more about it. "That would solve all your problems. I would be glad to work something out with your father, if he were my father-in-law. I could hire him as my California agent at a decent salary. And you could live aboard ship with me for a few years, traveling and seeing the sights, until we were ready to settle down."

He grabbed her hand, getting truly excited by his idea. "Marina, I know you don't love me, but I don't think we need that. We could be happy without it. And who knows? Eventually, perhaps it would come of its own accord."

She was touched and embarrassed at the same time. He really was a dear. And he deserved to have his suggestion considered seriously. After all, he was a good man and she had always been very fond of him. He wouldn't be hard to live with, wouldn't treat her badly.

"You're right," she said aloud. "I have the highest regard for you, Alex, but I don't love you, not as a girl thinks of the man she will marry. Surely you deserve to marry someone who feels that kind of love for you."

He smiled ruefully. "Well, Marina, I've lived a good bit of my allotted time already and I can't say I have ever found that yet. But I do care for you." His face reddened. "I think I care for you more than any woman I've ever known. I know it would make me happy to have you for a wife. If you think you could put up with me, I'd be proud to have you."

Marina felt a warm rush of affection for this dear man. "Alex," she said, her hand over her heart. "You've quite stunned me. You'll have to give me some time to catch my breath over this one."

Raising his hand to her lips, she kissed it. "But whatever I decide, I want you to know how deeply honored I feel. You, sir, are a true gentleman."

He smiled back at her, then dropped her hand in relief when he heard Josefa returning. One half of him was elated at his bold stroke, the other half was outraged at his impetuous gamble. He needed a moment to get his bearings and decide whether he had made a move of genius or a terrible mistake.

"Ah, Marina." Josefa was back, bustling in from the yard. "I'm glad you finally got home to help welcome the captain. Isn't it nice? He'll be staying with us for two nights for the Spring rodeo." She threw up her hands in dismay. "There is still so much to do. Marina, get Carmen and come help me in the yard. I promised Felipe's mother ten baskets of sweet breads, but the girls are complaining and we have baked only enough to fill five. We must get it done now, or we'll never get off in the morning."

Marina laughed and went in to get Carmen. The two of them went back out to the yard where the well, bake oven, and open pit were to be found. Josefa was just sending away the servant girls to rest and she motioned Carmen and Marina to come to her.

"Here, pat this dough. And mind you, do a better job than those wretched girls."

She stood back and watched them critically for a moment, then hurried away. Carmen looked across at Marina as soon as she was out of earshot.

"Well, cousin, we haven't talked much lately. Tell me, has Felipe spoken to my uncle yet?"

Marina turned her solemn gray eyes to stare at Carmen, then said calmly, "We're going to need more candied fruit for this batch."

"I see." Carmen gave her dough a vicious punch. "There's nothing new to tell."

Marina went back to shaping loaves. "And what about you, Carmen? Are you still courting danger?"

"Not danger, cousin. Life."

Marina looked up. "With Sebastian?" she asked, and immediately wished she hadn't.

Carmen smiled. "What about Sebastian? You can't have them both, you know. If you're going to marry Felipe, you'll have to give up chasing the Spaniard."

Marina flushed. "I never chased him."

The sparks in Carmen's eyes ignited the air between them. "Oh no? What do you call that *fandango,* then? What about the night you slept with him?"

She choked. "I . . ." What was the use of denying? Carmen would only laugh in her face. "I just wanted to prove to you that he was a rake. He'll never be true to you. He'll always go after others."

" 'Others'?" Carmen spat out the word. "You mean

yourself. Don't tell me you still haven't figured out why he would be so attentive to you."

Marina was sure she didn't want to know what Carmen's theory was, but she couldn't help herself. "What do you mean?"

"He does it only to infuriate Felipe, of course. His only motive is revenge."

Marina felt sick. That was exactly what she was afraid of herself. "Then you have nothing to worry about, do you, Carmen? But tell me, are you making any progress? Is he prepared to carry you off to Paris?"

Carmen sank back on her heels and sighed, looking suddenly pensive. "No, I must admit I haven't been making the progress I would like to be making in that direction. But there is always hope." She hesitated, her bright black eyes staring at her cousin. "In fact, I'm meeting him in the mission orchard tonight. And we will see what comes of that."

Marina heart was frozen in her chest, but she kept moving, working the dough, folding the loaves. She remembered Sebastian's kiss, his touch, the hunger in his eyes, and for just a moment she hated Carmen. The mission orchard . . . she wanted to burn it down.

But Carmen was going on, chattering as she worked. "I suppose I should work on a backup plan in case my hopes for the lieutenant fall through," she mused. "What do you think of this, Marina? Do you suppose Alex would like some company around the Horn?"

Rising, she started back toward the house, humming a tuneless ditty, and leaving Marina behind staring after her, her fists clenched in fury.

Chapter Sixteen

The day dawned warm. The wind off the inland desert had blown every hint of a cloud out to sea. The air was so clear, Marina imagined she could almost see the features on the faces of people traveling a mile away.

The oxcarts loaded with piles of food had begun to creak their way toward the Diaz *rancho*. Around them danced the horses of males of all ages, and some women, too. From every side festive white dresses dazzled the eye. From every hat, waist, saddle, and oxcart, a brightly colored streamer heralded the coming festivities. Everyone in the area was on his way to the same place.

By the time the first wagons began to arrive at the Diaz *hacienda,* the quality of the air in their lovely valley had changed dramatically. From the first light *vaqueros* had been herding in the cattle, and the dust from the many thousands of hooves began to fill the valley with a brown haze.

But the merrymakers didn't seem to mind. As they alighted from their horses or their carts, each face was alive with expectation and shouts of greeting filled the fields.

Sebastian sat easily in the saddle, picking his way

211

carefully among the heedless crowd. The exuberance of the Californios was infectious and he felt a vital sense of pleasure at being a part of the happy scene. He had ridden out with Tomas, who had now deserted him to search for more excitement, but Sebastian was happy to ride lazily around the grounds, watching the people arrive.

A voice hailed him from behind and he turned.

"Ah, Lieutenant, I thought I recognized you." It was Alex Brandene riding up behind him. "Is this your first rodeo?"

"The first in this country."

"You'll have a great time, don't doubt it. Come along with me and I'll show you where they're doing the branding."

Sebastian followed a bit reluctantly. He didn't relish being tied to Alex for the day. He'd been hoping to see the Crafts cart arrive and he hadn't seen a sign of it yet.

Alex led him through the crowds to a large corral filled with horses, men and cows. All along the perimeter, platforms had been erected, and they were filled with spectators.

"You see," Alex explained. "Everyone just lets their cattle run free, so every now and then they've got to pull them all in and sort them out. See that fellow in the red *serape?* That's the *juez del campo.* He judges the cutting, makes sure there's no cheating on deciding which cow goes where. The ones that belong on other *ranchos* are either herded home at the end of the day or worked here in a separate corral. The Diaz cows they go ahead and brand, as you can see, and the calves are being castrated over there." He pointed out a neighboring enclosure.

"If you watch how they work their animals, you'll

see some real evidence of how expert these local *vaqueros* are. Here, look at that lasso work."

The lasso work was indeed spectacular, but the Crafts had arrived along the cart path and Sebastian turned to greet them, his gaze immediately singling out Marina. Carmen was sitting beside her, and he remembered himself in time to nod to her. But just as he was about to speak, a call came from a passing wagon.

"Oh, Lieutenant! Yoohoo! Here I am."

He turned to catch sight of Gloria Estancia's red curls bouncing past as she waved at him frantically. At the same time, her brother's fierce, dark face was turned toward him with a fearsome glare.

The girls giggled and Sebastian flushed. He saluted Josefa and James, but his attention was still drawn to the gray eyes that watched him from the backseat of the cart, and Josefa's sharp stare caught on right away.

"So nice to see you, Lieutenant," she said without conviction. "Have you seen Felipe? He promised to escort Marina for the morning." She came down off the cart like an ostrich settling on an egg. "Meanwhile, I could use your help with the baskets, if you would be so kind."

She glared at him, daring him to refuse to help her, and he had to award her the upper hand for this round.

Alex was still bubbling, happy to see the Crafts and even happier to be at the rodeo.

"I'm so glad we got together so soon," he told Marina and James. "In this crowd, you never know. I've just been explaining to the lieutenant how these things work. It's his first rodeo, you know. But now that we have you good people with us, he'll get some more expert descriptions. Say . . ." He turned to Sebastian. "If you're going to be helping to take the baskets to the

213

kitchen, Josefa should show you the open pit where the food will be cooked. It's really something."

Nodding coolly, Josefa led the way. The cooking area was a beehive of activity as they were getting ready for the afternoon meal. Huge bins of sweet breads and tortillas were being placed out. Baskets overflowing with fruit and nuts were being set on tables where children were already gathering to get a good spot. Bowls of frijoles and preserved fruits were being prepared, along with huge platters of enchiladas. The open pit fire smoldered from the fuel of huge logs, barbecuing whole sides of beef that were being turned above them. Smaller spits were threaded with whole chickens. The smells were mouthwatering, and even Josefa began to loosen up as she caught the enthusiasm, laughing and joking with Alex.

Sebastian took the opportunity to slip away and go back toward the *carreta,* hoping to steal a moment or two with Marina. But when he got back to the cart, he found Carmen sitting on a barrel with a parasol in her hands, and Marina riding off on horseback with Felipe on one side and James on the other.

"Too late," Carmen observed. "You'll have to make do with my company."

He hesitated, looking after the disappearing horses, then smiled graciously. "And lovely company it is," he told her, swinging down from his horse and dusting off a seat beside her. "It's always a pleasure, *Señorita.*"

Carmen rolled her eyes and gave him a cynical look, but before they could have a private talk, Delores Delgado stopped by to say hello and gossip about who was flirting with whom and who would be competing in the roping events.

"Have you heard?" she chortled just before she left.

214

"Gloria Estancia's brother finally shot that *vaquero* who was after her." She pretended to fire, then blow off the end of the barrel of a gun. "Pow. Right through the heart."

Sebastian was startled. "He killed him?"

"Oh, yes. Those Estancia boys take protecting Gloria very seriously."

"They have to," Carmen chimed in with a grin. "It's a full-time job."

Delores laughed and gave Sebastian a sly look, then took her leave. Carmen turned back to him with a sigh.

"Well, Lieutenant, I missed you last night. I wandered in the mission orchards for quite a while before I realized you didn't mean to show up."

He frowned. "I sent a boy to your house in the afternoon with a note explaining that I would be unable to meet you. Didn't you receive it?"

She smiled. "Yes, I got it," she confessed. "Something about being detained by pressing business. I only wondered why you didn't attempt to name another day."

She paused but he didn't answer, and when she looked into his eyes, she could see he was still looking out in hopes of catching sight of Marina. Her eyes darkened and she looked him full in the face.

"It's my cousin, isn't it? You're infatuated with Marina."

Her voice was low, but it had an edge like a razor.

"Take care, Spaniard. Marina doesn't understand these things like I do. If you do anything to hurt or dishonor her, she won't be able to shrug it off as I might. Besides, Felipe will kill you."

Sebastian looked at her and curled his lip in disbelief. "I would never do anything to hurt Marina. But as for Felipe . . ." He made a sound of disgust. "I don't believe he could kill anyone in a fair fight."

"Then you misjudge him. But you'll see the evidence of his talents for yourself before this day is over. I only hope, for your sake, that you heed my warning."

Josefa and Alex returned, chattering excitedly, and pulled the party together to travel to the banks of a sparkling stream where they were going to make their camp. The sides of the *arroyo* were covered with lush green grass and dotted with young sycamores. All up and down the stream, people had already gathered, spreading their possessions and children out on cloths or *serapes* on the ground. Groups of men sat in shady areas with their guitars and violins, and the air was full of music.

The captain and Sebastian were sent back to the *carreta* for ground cloths which they spread out on the grass. Josefa and Carmen sat and received visitors while Alex and Sebastian lolled on the grass beside them. The day was fine, the music happy. Neighbors stopped by to gossip. And Sebastian felt as though his head were on a swivel, he turned it so often, watching for Marina's return.

When James came back alone, his eyes hardened. He wanted to accuse the man of neglecting his own daughter's safety, but he knew he had no right to say any such thing. So he waited, and when he heard James say to Josefa, "I left her with a group of young people by the lake; Felipe will take care she gets back safely," he swung onto his horse and rode off in the direction James had indicated without saying a word to the others. He wasn't about to leave her fate in Felipe's hands.

He found the small lake but saw no sign of Marina. Getting off his horse, he tied it securely and began to make his way through the crowd. He wandered for a few minutes without seeing a familiar face. Suddenly a boy appeared, grabbed his hand, and pulled.

"Señor, Señor," he whispered. "Come quickly. She waits."

"Who waits?" he asked, but the boy pulled away and ran toward a large thicket of laurel bushes that obscured one end of the lake.

It had to be Marina. She'd sent this boy to find him. Perhaps she was in trouble. Sebastian followed him, threading his way between groups of picnicking people and horsemen and carts, keeping the fast-moving boy in his sights.

He caught up with the boy just before reaching the thicket.

"Who is it?" he asked him again.

The boy merely pointed toward the bushes. *"Señor,* she waits in there. Go through that space. Go quickly."

Sebastian frowned as the boy turned and ran off into the crowd. The whole thing seemed a little fishy. But what if Marina *was* waiting for him in there? What if she needed him? He couldn't take the chance.

Stepping warily, he approached the thicket, heading for the gap in the middle. The branches were thick and intertwined. Though he couldn't see through the foliage, he thought he heard voices. There seemed to be a group of people waiting there.

He had to bend to get through the gap in the bushes, and as he came out on the other side, straightening, he literally ran into Gloria Estancia. Before he could react, she'd thrown her arms around his neck and kissed him full on the mouth.

"Lieutenant!" she cried, her red hair as glorious as ever. "You came."

All around them young men and a few women were laughing heartily at the trick that had been played on him. Felipe was laughing loudest of all, and as Sebastian looked around and took in the full import of what had happened, he thought he knew who had engineered his humiliation.

"I knew he'd fall for it," Felipe crowed, slapping his leg. "He thought it was going to be you, didn't he?"

Sebastian's gaze shifted and took in Marina astride the horse that stood beside Felipe's. Her face was pale, and she wasn't laughing.

Rage burned in him, but he knew he had to repress it. He wanted nothing so much as to run Felipe through right here and now, but that would look even worse than what had already struck a blow to his dignity. He couldn't even call the man out for the following morning. He would look like a poor sport indeed if he couldn't take such a harmless joke on himself.

But the fact was, he couldn't. Somehow he would make Felipe pay for this.

He forced himself to smile. "Who do I thank for setting up this lovely surprise for me?" he asked. Turning, he very deliberately took Gloria in his arms and bent her backward. "I'll have to thank him. But first . . ."

She was completely willing, even though he kissed her with passion that came more from fury than from passion. Still, the others had no way of knowing that, and they gasped and cheered at his ardor. He swung Gloria back upright and bowed to her.

"Thank you, lovely lady." Turning, he bowed to the others. "And thank you, Don Felipe," he said, his smile unable to warm the ice in his eyes.

"Think nothing of it," Felipe retorted, still grinning. "I'd do as much for any *caballero*."

The party began to move on, those on horseback riding off. Gloria was clinging like a leech, and by the time Sebastian rid himself of her, Felipe and Marina were nowhere in sight. His hatred of Marina's suitor was growing by leaps and bounds.

"I should have shot him dead when I had the chance," he muttered to himself as he mounted his horse and turned it back toward the streambank, where the Crafts had settled. There would come an opportunity to make Felipe eat dirt, he had no doubt of that. He just had to be patient.

When he got back he found that Marina had returned and was sitting with Carmen on the ground cloth. She avoided his gaze and chattered animatedly with her cousin, but before he could join them, Josefa commandeered him to help carry food back from the *hacienda* for the midday meal.

The feast was a sumptuous one and everyone ate too much and lay back groaning when it was over. The men smoked *cigarrillos* and talked sleepily while the women lay under the trees, napping and resting drowsily.

Sebastian noted that James was treating him politely but without the ease and familiarity he had once enjoyed. He wished he could do something to allay his fears, but anything he said would be pretty much a lie anyway. So it was probably best that he keep his silence.

Finally the siesta was over and the party was packing up the food and linen in preparation for a return to the main business of the rodeo. Alex and Sebastian carried the supplies back to the *carreta* and then made their way to the corrals to watch the show.

The platform around the corrals had become crowded with spectators, everyone pushing and shoving to get a better view. Sebastian found seats for James and Josefa on the platform, but he and Alex and the two girls were forced to stand behind the enclosure fence in order to watch.

The main corral was very large and several hundred head of cattle had been driven into it. Into the center of the ring rode the *mayordomo* of the Diaz rancho, ringmaster of this event. At the entrance, fifteen or twenty *vaqueros* mounted on beautifully groomed horses waited to be called out.

The *mayordomo* studied the bullocks milling about him, decided upon a perfect selection, and signaled for the next pair of *vaqueros* to enter, pointing out the animal he had chosen for them. The cowboys rode in, whirling lassos. The first fell deftly over the bullock's horns, while the second scooped up around his hind leg, dropping him neatly to the ground. The Indians whose job it was to act as butchers then rushed in and did their work. The poor beast was dragged off to the slaughterhouse and another pair of riders entered to down the next victim.

The *vaqueros* and their horses worked with great dexterity and skill, and especially good teams were rewarded by the cheers of the crowd, but the whole business was beginning to seem a bit monotonous to Sebastian, when suddenly a bull broke away and made a bid for freedom.

He was a large animal, exceptionally fleet and muscular, and as he loped off in his desperate escape, the crowd cried for his capture. The *vaqueros* dashed after him, jockeying for position, each anxious to be the one to bring him down. One rider quickly pulled ahead of

220

the rest, and it soon became apparent that he would be the winner. As he neared the beast, he began to swing his lasso over his head. With effortless grace, he flicked it to settle about the animal's neck, checked his horse at precisely the proper moment, and flipped the steer onto his side on the ground. Soon he was galloping back, the fierce bull trotting docilely at the end of his rope.

The crowd went wild. Cheers grew even more fervent as they began to realize what they had suspected all along—the champion was Don Felipe himself.

Testimony to Felipe's certain skill and bravery was suddenly on everyone's lips. Anecdotes of his adventures dating back as far as infanthood were passed back and forth, and many nudges and significant glances were cast Marina's way. Her cheeks reddened, but she stared straight ahead, pretending not to notice.

"He's very good," Sebastian admitted when Alex made his own comments. "I'll have to give him that." Much as he hated to. But facts were facts.

Soon the slaughter was over and the rejected cattle were herded back out onto the range. The crowd was now dispersing as some wished to attend the horseracing taking place in a distant field, and others wished to watch the drawing of the cock, which was being staged along the side of the Diaz entry road.

"He's never seen a drawing of the cock," Alex noted about Sebastian. "He's got to see that. How about we head for that one?"

"But Don Felipe is riding in the horserace," Josefa argued. "Marina should be there."

Marina sent her aunt a look and shook her head. "Let's show the lieutenant the drawing of the cock," she said, smiling at Alex. "I agree with the captain."

"Oh, you'll enjoy it," Alex told him as they started off. "It's pure poetry to watch these Californios ride."

Up and down the sideyard, men had gathered to watch and shout encouragement to their particular favorites. As each horseman came forward to make his run, whistles and catcalls mingled with cheers, the proportion of each dictated by the skill and popularity of the rider.

Wagers flashed up and down the line, then the crowd hushed and the drama began.

Each participant sat on his horse at the end of the road. At a signal, each spurred his horse into a gallop, attempting to reach top speed before approaching the target.

The target was a live cock, buried up to its neck in the middle of the road. The object of the competition was to pull the cock up and out of the ground by its head as one passed at great speed.

"Isn't this something?" Alex poked Sebastian in the ribs, trying to get some enthusiasm from him. "You'll never believe this."

As each rider came within about ten yards of the cock, he leaned down over the side of the horse, keeping hold of the horse's mane with one hand, reaching for the cock with the other. If he succeeded in drawing the cock, he claimed it as his prize. If he reached too far, he risked losing his grip and being trampled by his own horse. The feat took strength, agility, and a certain bravado, and it looked spectacular.

"Isn't this great?" Alex said, applauding as rider after rider went away with a new rooster to call his own.

"Interesting," Sebastian allowed reluctantly. "I think they should try it with porcupines. It would be a more even match that way."

Alex stared at him for a moment, then laughed uproariously. The others had already begun to walk toward the field where the horseracing was scheduled, and Sebastian started after them.

"Wait for me," Alex called as he caught up with Sebastian. "You'll like the races, too. You can bet on it." He grinned and Sebastian gave him a smile.

The captain was a strange one. All his former animosity seemed to have evaporated. In fact, his mood was almost brotherly as he threw his arms wide and took the valley air deep into his lungs.

"This is wonderful, isn't it?" he said exuberantly. "I tell you, I love the sea, but owning land like this and living on it—that has to be the ultimate aspiration. And in country like this, all you need is a few thousand acres, a few head of cattle, and you're on your way."

"You sound like a man tempted to try it yourself."

Alex looked around with a contented smile. "Maybe. Maybe. One of these days. 'Course, it really helps to have a good woman to help you. Especially an *hija del país* who understands the land and the people and can help you get along."

Sebastian had an idea he might know who the captain had his eye on for that job. "Did you have someone in mind?"

Alex smirked. "Could be. It just could be."

They arrived at the racetrack to find the main events had already taken place.

"Don Felipe won everything he entered, of course," a young man who knew the Crafts told them. "He's gone on over to get ready for the bullfighting."

So the Crafts party went in that direction, too. As they walked along, they called to others they knew, and

223

goodnatured jokes were tossed back and forth. Felipe's name was bandied about as well, until Sebastian began to feel a gnawing irritation building inside. The man could do no wrong. It wasn't going to be easy to compete with the local hero on the day of his triumph.

This time they were all able to get seats right along the front row of the platform, at the edge of the corral. The two girls sat between Josefa and James, with Alex and Sebastian completing the row.

At last the bullfight began.

Having grown up in Spain and lived in Mexico for a number of years, Sebastian had certain expectations when it came to bullfighting. To his surprise, very few of them were met.

One bull, with horns sawed off, was put in the ring, which soon filled with twenty men on horseback. Each man carried a blanket or poncho which he held over one arm as he competed with the others for the attention of the bull. When the bull noticed one rider and made a charge, the rider took his horse in as close as he could get and maneuvered cleverly until he could throw the blanket or poncho over the bull's eyes to blind him. When the bull was finally exhausted, he was let out of the corral and another was let in to take his place.

When the riders were finally as tired as the bulls, they all left the ring and the excitement of the audience began to mount as they prepared for the special spectacle they had been promised. Their special hometown star was about to appear.

Chapter Seventeen

Into the center of the ring rode Don Felipe upon a magnificent white stallion. The silver buttons on his velveteen breeches shone, newly polished, as did the silver trappings on his mount.

The crowd stood and cheered him lustily, waving *sombreros* and scarves as their hero swept off his hat and bowed to them. Pricking the flanks of his mount, he trotted around the circle until he came to a stop before the Crafts party. He gave Sebastian a proud, sullen stare, a look as full of challenge as it was of hatred. Then his expression changed and he bowed to Marina, and turned to her father.

"Señor," he cried. "I request the honor of dedicating this fight to your lovely daughter."

With a flourish, he pulled up his horse and raced back to the center of the ring. The gate was opened and in rushed a large, fierce-looking bull whose horns were still intact and very long. The animal pawed the ground and snorted as Felipe prepared his approach. Closer and closer he came, his eyes on the bull, his knees guiding his horse, his voice softly encouraging it. The bull sprang, and in the same instant, almost as though part of the same movement, Felipe and his horse leapt sideways, just out of reach.

Turning, they approached the bull again, this time coming even closer, until the bull again attacked, and Felipe again escaped atop the nimble-footed horse.

The maneuver was beautiful; horse and rider seemed a part of one whole, directed instantaneously by the same brain, in perfect harmony and of one purpose. Again and again they approached the bull, again and again they deftly avoided his horns.

The crowd was on its feet, breathless. They were used to superior horse skill, but this was something exceptional. No one was cheering, they were all too stunned by the show of expertise. The cheers would come later. But at each pass, the crowd sighed as though with one voice. And as each attempt went nearer and was more dangerous, the sighs grew deeper.

Finally, Felipe judged the time to be right, and instead of edging slowly in, he gathered himself and his horse into an arc of energy and thrust in at a dash. Before the bull could react, he reached its hindquarters and with a quick slap, started the bull running. Riding alongside, he reached out and grasped the tail of the huge animal, placing it under his right knee. With one quick movement, he pricked his horse to the left and flipped the mighty bull, tossing it into the air.

The stands went wild. Throwing a bull was common enough, but seldom had they seen it done with such finesse, and to such a large bull.

Don Felipe's star, already the highest in the

district, had risen higher still.

Don Felipe rode slowly around the ring, acknowledging the ovation with a solemn dignity. He stopped once again before the Crafts and studied Marina's face for her reaction, all his male pride in his face.

She smiled at him, but her attention was caught by something else. "Oh, look, you're bleeding," she cried.

His hand had been cut badly, but he'd hardly noticed. Shrugging, he smiled. "It's nothing. Ignore it."

"Ignore it and you may bleed to death," she said firmly, pulling out a pink handkerchief from her bodice and thrusting it at him. "Here, wrap it tightly."

He took her offering and raised it to his lips, his eyes alight with triumph. His glance flickered to Sebastian, then returned to fix on Marina. Though his eyes never left hers, he spoke to her father, and loudly enough for most of the others nearby to hear.

"Señor Crafts, I have a particular matter to discuss with you. I hope you will find time to accommodate me this afternoon. I need your counsel, your permission. I have an announcement I would like to make tomorrow night at the *baile*." He smiled and gave the crowd a big wave. "I hope you'll all be there to congratulate me," he called up to them.

Amid the cheers, James stood and shook Felipe's uninjured hand. "Anytime, my son, anytime. I will be happy to discuss this with you."

227

Sebastian glanced at Marina. Her eyes were wide but unreadable. All about them, people were laughing, and the phrase "It's about time" flew everywhere. Meanwhile, everything inside him was rebelling against the mood of the crowd. The thought of Marina and Felipe together sent excitement singing through his veins. He had to do something to stop this. But short of challenging Felipe to another duel, what could he do?

Right now the man was at his zenith, master of all he surveyed. Flushed with victorious, arrogant pride, he turned his horse to stop in front of Sebastian, his smile superior and patronizing.

"And you, Lieutenant," he called loudly, the slightest suggestion of a sneer in his tone. "We haven't seen a sample of your skills. Don't they ride horses in the old country?"

Sebastian managed to maintain an icy dignity, though hatred blazed behind his eyes.

"We do ride horses in Spain," he said. "Though we don't live on them, as you do here. As everyone who visits this land admits, there are no better horsemen in the world than those of California."

"I'm sure that's true," Felipe said, his eyes gleaming with malice. "But I would think an officer with the Mexican Army would be able to show us something. Come on, now. I have a fine cow pony you could borrow. Try yourself with a bull."

Sebastian hesitated. He was certainly no novice at horsemanship, or even at handling cattle, but his basic, functional ability was nothing compared to the expertise of the Californios, who were placed on horses before they could walk and hardly ever got off again except to go to sleep at night. Attempting to duplicate Felipe's success would only make him look ridiculous. At the same time, refusing a challenge would make him a coward, and that was unthinkable. There was really very little choice.

"If it's a show of skill you want, I'm afraid you'll be disappointed. However, I won't shrink from attempting to learn something of your methods."

The few scattered cheers gave him some encouragement, and the horse Felipe brought forward looked agile and competent. He began to think this might not be such a disaster after all. If the horse knew its business, perhaps he could get by, letting it do all the work.

He rode the animal easily around the ring, getting a feel for its rhythm and testing its reaction to his guidance. The horse was quick and intelligent. At least Felipe hadn't stacked the deck. He signaled his satisfaction and the bull was let into the corral.

Here again, Felipe had been thoughtful. The bull wasn't the massive monster he had tackled, but a smaller variety, leaner and younger. Sebastian rode about him a few times, studying his reactions, and noted that he was not even unduly quick.

Drawing his horse back a few paces, he set him, and then began to approach the bull as Felipe had done. Slowly, they stepped closer and closer. Twice his horse whinnied softly and shook its head. Probably he was feeling uncertain under this lack of specific and familiar direction, but Sebastian couldn't see any alternative. He went on.

Suddenly the bull charged. The horse jumped quickly to the left, but Sebastian had been prepared to cast to the right, and in the next instant he found himself set down hard, alone in the dust.

Getting up quickly, he made his way to the fence amid the whistles and laughter of the crowd, heading straight for Felipe, blood in his eye. The man was laughing—laughing at him. He wanted to kill him, but he restrained himself with great difficulty.

"I'm afraid this isn't going to work out," he said through clenched teeth. "The Californio way of handling a bull is completely alien to me. However, I have had some experience with the Spanish style of bullfighting. Perhaps you would like to see an example of that."

Felipe frowned. It was obvious he would not like to see that at all. But everyone else who had heard Sebastian's suggestion thought it sounded interesting, and as word passed through the crowd, excitement grew. Most had never seen a man challenge a bull on foot. The prospect was thrilling.

Felipe looked up and heard the buzz. Pursing his lips, he nodded curtly. "Go ahead," he said.

"I will need my cape," Sebastian replied, his gaze steely. "I'll send Tomas Bata back to town to get my things, and then I will be happy to accommodate you."

Felipe shrugged. "We won't have time for that today. We'll watch your bullfight tomorrow." He flashed a grin at the crowd. "Good, that will give us some entertainment while waiting for the *baile* to begin tomorrow night." He waved to the audience, a true showman. "See you all there!"

Felipe sprang onto his horse and made him rear up. The crowd loved it and he sent them a slashing

230

grin before dashing out across the countryside.

Sebastian turned to leave. He couldn't make himself look Marina in the eye. Today hadn't been one of his better days. It might be best if it were ended quickly.

As he walked away, he went over his options. It had been a long, long time since he'd flashed a cape at a bull. But he did know bulls, and he did know Spanish bullfighting. Raising bulls for *la corrida* had been one of his father's prime hobbies when he was a boy, and he'd been filled with the ambition to be a *torero*. Yes, he knew a lot about it—enough to know that what he was preparing to do was very dangerous.

But it had to be done. The ignominious failure he had experienced had to be canceled out, and there was no more glorious way to do it—if it worked.

He was about to swing up onto his horse when Carmen stopped him.

"So, Lieutenant, you're going to display your bravery by challenging a bull on foot. I only hope you're better at that than you are on horseback."

Sebastian gave her an icy stare. "You'll have a chance to see for yourself tomorrow."

She shook her head. "Whatever possessed you to accept Felipe's challenge? I would have thought you'd have more sense. Or is your infatuation with Marina blinding you to reality?"

Sebastian gathered the reins in his hand and mounted. "Marina has nothing to do with this. A man's sense of honor must be maintained, Carmen. If he is nothing before other men, he'll soon be nothing to himself."

"So you're willing to risk your life to show you're as brave as Felipe." She bit her lip and looked at him critically. "I might understand if the results would benefit you in any way. But what do you care what a bunch of paltry frontier peasants think? As soon as you can, you'll be leaving all of us in your dust. So why risk your life to impress them?"

"It's not for them, or because of them, or in spite of them. It's for myself. If I backed down now, I might as well put a pistol to my head."

"Well, then, I hope you're successful. But don't think success will win you Marina, *hombre*. You heard Don Felipe. You saw my uncle's reaction. Everyone is anxious for their marriage. A union between them will benefit all involved. Marina is a good girl. She'll do her duty . . ." She made a face and added softly, "No matter where her heart lies."

Stepping back, she gave his horse a sharp slap on the rump, and he started off toward the grassy area where he and Tomas had agreed to pitch their tent. He knew she was right. Carmen was a sensible girl who looked at things realistically. But he didn't like reality much right now. Reality meant that he was a Spaniard who would soon be going home, and Marina was an *hija del país* who would be staying here and doing what was expected of her. But somewhere in between those two scenes of the future lay the passion that he knew lived between them. What kind of reality encompassed that fact? Only time would tell.

* * *

"Maybe we could run away together, you and I. Disguise ourselves as boys, and . . ."

"Get pressed into sea duty on some trading ship. That would certainly be fun." Carmen made a face at her cousin. "Especially after the other seamen realized we were really girls. That should cause a sensation we wouldn't soon forget."

"You're such a pessimist," Marina grumbled, throwing herself down on the narrow bed in the room she was sharing with Carmen in the Diaz *hacienda*.

"I'm such a realist," Carmen retorted. "You and Sebastian, what a pair. Neither one of you can look truth in the face. I can just see the two of you if you get together, galloping off into some rosy sunset, gazing in each other's eyes — and riding right off the first available cliff."

Marina sat up and looked at her cousin with wary eyes. "What are you talking about? I'm not in love with . . . with the Spaniard."

"Aren't you?" Carmen sighed and shook her head. "You could have fooled me. And he's just as bad."

Marina blushed, her cheeks as red as apples. "That's crazy, Carmen," she said, but somehow she couldn't quite catch her breath. "I . . . I don't know why you're saying these things."

"I'm saying them because they're true. And you wanting to run off to sea disguised as a boy rather than face up to marrying Don Felipe just proves it."

That stopped the words in her throat. Carmen was right. She was having a hard time dealing with the impending engagement, now that it was almost a fact of life. If only she could get Sebastian out of her head, she might be able to accept the thought of being Felipe's wife. But with Sebastian in there, it was just too crowded.

The deal had been struck just an hour before. Her father had talked to Don Felipe. He had offered her dowry, which Felipe accepted graciously, although it was paltry compared to his wealth. In turn, Felipe had offered her father a gift of a pair of matching horses which could probably be sold in Santa Barbara for enough money to keep the Crafts household going for a year.

Felipe was a generous man. Once she was married to him, she was sure he would continue to be generous to her family. Their financial troubles would be a thing of the past. All she had to do was walk down the aisle with a man she now knew she didn't love.

She moaned and closed her eyes. She was going to have to marry him. She'd given her word. Everyone expected her to do it. She was trapped. There really was no way out.

Carmen had been watching her agonize. She hated agonizing. If you had a problem, the best thing to do was to meet it head on. She wasn't about to hang around and listen to Marina whimper.

"Well, I'm going out to the campfire. They're singing old songs and having a wonderful time." Carmen hesitated. "Why don't you come with me?"

Marina was pleasantly surprised. During the last few hours, she'd sensed an opening up on her cousin's part, a warming. It would be nice if their relationship could get back to normal. She smiled at Carmen, but shook her head.

"I've got to think," she said.

Carmen laughed. "If you think of a way out of this one, Cousin, you're smarter than I am."

Marina's smile faded as Carmen left the room. She was right. There was no way out, because no matter how hard she thought, there was no solution. She was going to marry Don Felipe, because there was really no choice.

Groaning, she buried her face in her pillow.

Chapter Eighteen

Sebastian was dreaming. He was in a huge pile of feathers. He could hardly breathe. They were tickling his ears, tickling his nose. He turned, swatting, trying to get away from them, and he heard a giggle that snapped his eyes open wide, the dream coming to a screeching halt in no time at all.

Tomas was his tentmate. But Tomas didn't giggle, at least not like that.

"Good morning, Lieutenant."

He turned, dread like a taste in his mouth, and there were the red, bouncing curls he'd been afraid he would see.

"I came to surprise you," Gloria said, giggling again.

Groaning, he closed his eyes. "Please make this still be a dream," he muttered.

"It's no dream, my darling." Leaning over, she kissed his cheek with damp enthusiasm. "I've been watching for a chance to get away and be with you, and my time finally came this morning when my brothers all went off to practice shooting in the hills. So here I am."

Sebastian opened one eye and looked at her, and

the first thing that met his horrified gaze was one bare shoulder. The woman had stripped down to her lacy chemise before climbing into his bed.

He leapt backward out of his bedroll like a cat out of water.

"What are you doing?" he demanded irritably, rummaging through the covers for his clothes.

"I came to be with you, my darling. Just as we've dreamed of since the first."

"Dreamed? I never dream," he protested, his voice higher than usual. He glanced at her, then quickly looked away. "Believe me, I sleep like a log."

He searched desperately for his trousers. Where the hell were they? How could something like that get lost in such a small tent? And where the hell was Tomas? What kind of friend would leave him vulnerable to something like this?

"Don't worry, my darling," Gloria was purring, reaching for him. "Your friend left to go up to the *hacienda,* and my brothers won't be back for hours, and my father . . . ."

"Your father!" His voice was even higher now. "Don't even bring up all the men in your family, Gloria. I know all about them." He found a shirt, which he quickly shrugged into, but still no trousers. Leaning down, he tried to look under where she was lying.

She pouted. "Do they frighten you, darling?" she asked before reaching out to feel his biceps as he rolled her away so as to look beneath her.

He looked at her hopelessly. Frighten him? How could he explain? If Marina had brothers like that, he'd fight them all at once just to get to her. But he was hardly willing to risk death to be with a woman he really couldn't stand.

"I can't find my trousers," he muttered, turning about and looking desperately.

"Never mind your trousers, dear." She giggled again. "Come back under the covers and you won't need them, I promise you."

There was a sound outside. His head snapped up and he listened. Hoofbeats.

"Lieutenant, please, just give me a chance to show you . . ."

"Quiet!" He put a hand over her mouth. "Listen. Someone is coming."

She went very still as well. The horses were coming directly toward their camp.

He uttered an ugly curse and looked around again. Where the hell were his pants?

"Here," Gloria said helpfully. "Wrap this blanket around you. They'll never notice you have no trousers."

He whipped about to tell her just how stupid he thought that idea was when his trousers fell out of the blanket she was holding. Gasping with relief, he grabbed them and pulled them on as quickly as he could.

The horses had come to a stop outside and female voices were murmuring. More women. Was he living under some sort of curse?

"You stay here and be very quiet," he ordered Gloria, fastening his belt and reaching for his boots.

She bundled down into the covers as though set for a long siege. "Don't worry, my darling. I won't make a peep."

He glared down at her. "If this is your brother . . ."

"No, it can't be. They don't know where I've gone."

He took a deep breath and slid out through the flap opening. There, mounted on a pair of dancing geldings from the Diaz herd, were Carmen and Marina. His mouth went dry. There was far more terror in his heart right now than there had been the day before in the ring with the bull.

"Good morning, Lieutenant." Marina smiled down at him, her eyes sparkling. He looked so appealing with his hair still mussed from sleep and his shirt open halfway down his chest.

He noticed her looking and made a half-hearted attempt to button it further. "I . . . I was just dressing."

Carmen snorted, her eyes brimming with amusement. "So we see."

He stared at them without a clue as to what he might do to avoid the sure disaster he could sense breathing down his neck. He wanted them gone, very soon and very far away. But he couldn't just tell them to get out of here. And how long could he count on Gloria being quiet?

"Well, Sebastian," Carmen said at last, growing weary of waiting while he stared at them. "Have you made your morning chocolate yet?" She gestured toward the small campfire Tomas had left burning. "May we come and have a cup with you?"

"No." He blinked and tried to take back the vehemence. "I mean, actually, I can't make chocolate because I . . . I came away without a pot. I thought I would go up to the *hacienda* to get chocolate this morning."

Good ploy. Maybe they could all go together and

239

leave Gloria to her own devices here in the camp.

But before that could happen, there was a faintly clanking sound in the direction of the tent. Out of the corner of his eye he saw his pot being pushed out through the tent flap and his dry mouth became a desert.

Dear Gloria. Such a helpful girl.

Carmen noticed it right away. "There's your pot, right there," she said, pointing it out.

He turned and glared at it. "Oh, so it is."

"Well."

He turned and gave them a wavering smile. "Well, what?"

"Can we join you for chocolate?"

Before he had a chance to make up a new excuse, the hand inside the tent moved again, pushing out a jar of chocolate to join the pot. This time Marina and Carmen both saw the hand at work.

Marina stared, dumbfounded, but Carmen's voice wasn't lost.

"I see you already have company, Lieutenant," she said crisply, reining back her horse. "I'm sorry we bothered you."

"No." Sebastian felt like a condemned man. No matter what he did or said, he was dead. "Don't go." He reached for Marina's reins and held them. "This isn't what you think."

Gloria's bright red curls appeared through the tent flap. "Darling, are they gone yet?" she called.

Sebastian turned, dropping the reins. There was no way to salvage this and he knew it.

Marina shrank from him, her eyes huge and hurt, and in a moment they were both gone, spurring their horses over the ridge.

Sebastian turned back to the tent, fury cold and hard within him. Opening the flap, he looked in at where Gloria lay back, obviously pleased with herself.

"Why did you do that?" he asked quietly.

She blinked and smiled at him. "I wanted them to know. I got here first."

He nodded, and reached down and yanked up the Persian rug used to floor the structure and laid it down outside. "Come here, Gloria," he said, his voice a hoarse monotone. And when she joined him outside he pointed at the carpet. "Lie down here in the center."

She looked at him doubtfully. "What for?"

He took a deep breath and lied. "So that I can ravish you here in the sunlight, you gorgeous woman," he said woodenly.

"Oh, *querida,*" she cried, bouncing down to lie where he'd suggested. "Like this?"

He nodded. "Hands to your sides," he told her. "Lie very straight."

She giggled. "Like this?"

"Yes. Exactly like this."

And he began to roll the carpet as quickly as he could, ignoring her shrieks. When he had her in a nice neat bundle, he stuffed her clothes into the end near her feet, and threw her up in front of his saddle, then mounted and began to ride toward the area where he was sure Josefa would be setting up the Crafts picnic cloths. He knew Josefa didn't like him, and this wasn't going to endear him to her. But he trusted the woman. And he had nowhere else to turn.

He rode up to find her alone, putting out baskets

241

of fruit at the corners of the cloths. The *carreta* had been pulled close by to provide shelter from the breeze, and Josefa had tied a cloth from the *carreta* to a nearby tree in an impromptu tent.

She looked up as he approached, and he reined in his horse, saluting her.

"*Señora, por favor,* I have a great favor to ask of you."

Josefa stood with her hands on her hips, staring curiously at the rug Sebastian carried before him.

"Inside this rug I have a young woman who came to visit me early this morning. I won't tell you her name, because I'm sure when she thinks over what she's done, she'll wish to erase it from her memory, and I would like to do the same."

Josefa squinted, still in the dark. "There's a person in there?"

Gloria's squeal put that question to rest.

"Yes. This young woman needs clothing. She needs an older woman to give her advice on how not to approach a man. And Señora, I need your trust and your support." He put a hand over his heart. "I didn't touch this woman, I swear to you on my mother's good name."

Josefa stared at him for another long moment, then came toward him gingerly, peeking into the roll and nodding. "All right, Lieutenant. I will take care of her for you." She helped him lower the still rolled up rug to the ground. "And now you had better leave. I will handle this by myself."

Sebastian left reluctantly. What if Gloria lied about what had happened? But there wasn't much he could do about that now. He'd done the only thing he could think of. Either it would work, or he would have a bullet through his heart by evening.

"I don't know why you're so upset. This is exactly what you've always said about him. So—you were right."

Carmen frowned at where Marina lay, poking her with her foot.

Marina slapped at Carmen's leg and sat up on the ground cloth, her hair in disarray and dotted with bits of dry grass.

"You're right," she said dully. "Of course, you're right. It's just that . . ." She couldn't go on.

They had ridden back from finding Sebastian with Gloria Estancia and neither one of them had said a word. As if of one accord, they had stopped their horses by a stream and gone down to sit in the grass, and then they had begun to complain, hesitantly at first, and now with full passion. Why were men so perfidious?

"It's just that you're infatuated with him and you thought he felt the same way about you, so why would he need to sleep with Gloria Estancia. Am I right?"

Marina nodded miserably.

"Well, too bad. The man disappointed me too, you know." She looked at her cousin and smiled sadly. It was nice to be able to talk again. The Spanish lieutenant had been between them for too long.

"Come on now. It was just a crazy flirtation. Your last fling before settling down to marry Felipe. Once you and Felipe are together, you'll forget all about those green eyes."

Her own eyes sharpened when Marina didn't answer her back. "Well, is it signed, sealed and delivered? Has your father made the bargain with Don Felipe? Are you betrothed?"

"It seems so." Marina looked out at the horizon and sighed. "The announcement will be made tonight at midnight."

Carmen winced and laughed softly. "What a good little wife you'll make. I can see it now."

"Can you?" Marina turned and pinned her with a stare. "Can you really? Because, I can't. The whole thing turns my stomach."

Carmen waved a dismissive hand. "Bridal jitters. Don't worry. They go away."

"I wish *I* could go away," Marina muttered, turning to face the hills again.

"What did you say?"

"Nothing." Marina didn't answer, but she did begin combing her hair and pinning it back.

"What are you doing?" Carmen asked. "Where are you going?"

"I'm going to go watch the faithless Spaniard fight the bull," she said, looking up at her cousin defiantly.

Carmen looked back, shaking her head. Marina had changed a lot in the last few weeks. She hadn't been a young girl in a long time, but now, finally, she had matured enough emotionally to match her chronological age. That was welcome. Something was lost, but a great deal was achieved as well.

"Good. I'll go too." Carmen stood and smoothed her skirt. "Maybe we'll be lucky and get to see him gored."

"Not gored," Marina said, paling. The thought of him being hurt was agony to her, despite everything.

Carmen nodded. "You're right. Nothing too bloody. Just a little trampling, perhaps. Or a nice concussion."

Marina groaned, but the two of them hurried off in the direction of the corral. Neither wanted to miss the biggest event of the afternoon.

Sebastian stood in the center of the ring, his heart beating wildly, but his hand steady. He had no suit of lights, but his white trousers fit snugly, strapped under the instep, and his white coatee was heavily embroidered with gold braid and buttons. His cape was very near right, a red flash of color against the brown dirt. Any moment the bull would come charging in and he would know if this wild scheme had a chance in the world of succeeding.

The danger was more real and threatening now than it had seemed the night before. Had he been mad to suggest this? He was in an unfamiliar ring, without most of the proper clothing or equipment, without *banderilleros,* without *picadors,* without any help or backup whatsoever. He was about to face a bull that hadn't been specifically bred for this and would be impossibly unpredictable.

Beside all this, he had his own lack of practice to worry about. There had been a time in his youth when he had spent every free moment in the testing ring working with the trainers and true *matadors.* Sebastion had become so good that one old master had urged him to make bullfighting his career, claiming with tears in his eyes that the art would benefit from his natural genius. But that had been long ago and very far away. He had no idea if any of his old

245

skill was still left to him.

A roar went up. The bull entered the ring in a rush. He stopped and looked around him, dazed for a moment, but soon alert to Sebastian's presence. His red eyes seemed to burn into the air and his breath looked hot and humid.

Felipe had chosen carefully. This bull was tremendously powerful, with razor-sharp horns jutting ominously far from his head. He stared at Sebastian, then lowered his head, snorted, and pawed the ground. There would be no problem encouraging this beast to fight.

Sebastian crossed himself and said a prayer. He was going to need all the help he could get. Closing his eyes for just a moment, he put himself against the golden hills of Catalan, in one of his father's rings. He would fight just the same today as he had when trying out bulls in Spain. He would have to.

It was time. Feeling like a condemned man, he stepped forward holding his body proudly erect, the cape at a graceful angle to his right. The crowd seemed to be holding its breath. Slowly, deliberately, he shook the cape, calling softly to the bull.

The animal didn't waste any time. The charge was immediate, those razor-sharp horns speeding toward him with heart-stopping speed. He spun with it, turning quickly to lead the bull back through a series of short passes so as to study his timing and style, but his moves were clumsy and he was letting the bull come a little too close. Another pass like that and he would be wearing the bull's tributes in blood. He was going to have to do better than this if he was going to walk away from this place.

The crowd, not realizing this was merely a

warmup, already seemed impressed. Cheers and calls of encouragement resounded through the valley.

Again the bull charged, and again he made the passes, only this time they worked pretty decently. Another, then another. It was coming back to him. He hadn't lost the knack after all.

He collapsed his cape for a moment as he studied the motionless bull. His heart wasn't beating so loudly any longer, and a new, wild exhilaration was filling him. Things were not quite as hopeless as he had feared. There was a chance. He just might do it.

And if not, perishing in the attempt was as good a way to die as any he could think of. Whatever the outcome, he had stepped out to mold his own destiny, and he was glad he had.

Extending the cape in one hand, he led the bull again, turning as he passed so that the bull followed the palm of his hand and he ended up in position to lead him back again. Three, four times, now he was ready to go to more difficult feats.

A *veronica,* with the cape held in both hands in front, then one hand dropped as the bull passed, the cape sweeping gracefully aside. The first one was a bit awkward, but on the second try, he could feel his body slant forward toward the bull at just the right angle, and he knew the picture he made at that moment was one of artful beauty.

Four more *veronicas,* then a rest. Now he held the cape behind him, and as the bull passed, he leaned into the charge with the grace of a dancer. Twice more, and not a person in the crowd was left seated.

A *rebolera*—with Sebastian spinning as the bull passed so that his cape flared about him like a dancer's skirt—brought a wave of bravos from the

247

stands. Two more *veronicas* and he knew it was time to set up for the grand finale.

This bull wouldn't serve his passes forever. Without the *picadors* to weaken him with sword thrusts, the bull could stand this pace much longer than the bullfighter, and even the most stupid bull would eventually grow weary of charging ghosts and begin to look for a target he could get his horns into.

This was it, and Sebastion intended to make it spectacular. As the bull turned and pawed the ground in preparation for his next charge, Sebastian dropped to his knees, spreading the cape out full on the ground before him. As the bull came toward him he whipped the cape to the side and over his head in a wide swirl so that the bull passed with hooves flashing just inches from his ears.

Instinctively he knew that this was enough. The bull couldn't take any more without losing his grip. Not even glancing the bull's way, he rose from the dust, folded the cape over his arm, and walked with slow dignity to the fence. All the while, his ears were strained for the sound of hoofbeats behind him and he was ready to make a run for it, but his face didn't betray a tremor.

Marina watched him coming their way, her hand on Carmen's arm in a death grip. "He's magnificent," she breathed, unable to take her eyes off him.

"The crowd loves him," Carmen commented after a glance around. She gave a grimace of pain and began prying Marina's fingers from their clutch on her arm. "Felipe is still their native son, the champion of their hearts, but Sebastian's going to be right up behind him, I'd say."

People were streaming from the stands, massing

248

around Sebastian, praising his bravery, touching the cape, reveling in the sphere of another hero.

"He's looking for you," Carmen said, but one glance at Marina showed that she already knew that.

Sebastian came closer, standing directly beneath where they were seated, looking up at Marina.

"I'm going to do it," Marina said tersely, reaching for the gardenia in her hair.

"Marina, no!" Carmen reached out to stop her but she was too late.

Marina's smile was full of exactly how she felt about him. No one looking at her could miss it. Her face glowing, she tossed the pure white flower down into Sebastian's waiting hand. His green eyes shone as he saluted her, kissing it, and then the crowd swallowed him again.

"I'd better go," Marina said, suddenly panicked.

"That's the truest thing you've said yet," Carmen complained, getting her things together too. "If Don Felipe got a look at that flower-tossing incident, you're in big trouble, my little innocent."

Marina already knew that. She shouldn't have done it. But she'd had to do it. He'd risked his life. He'd faced death and won. He was splendid and she wanted him to know she realized that.

Chapter Nineteen

"*Señora,* I came to check on the task I left for you this morning." Sebastian swung down off his horse and nodded to Josefa, who was cleaning up remnants of the afternoon meal.

Josefa turned and gazed at him as he came toward her, her eyes wary but not unfriendly.

"It is taken care of, Lieutenant. There is not a thing to worry about."

That was good to hear, but not likely true, knowing Gloria and her brothers. He smiled his skepticism. "I can hardly believe that."

Josefa waved away his doubts, smiling as well. "I clothed her and I talked to her, once I got her to calm down. I made it very clear that she was destroying her reputation for no good reason."

She shrugged. "Too many years without a mother, that one. I think she truly didn't understand what she was doing. She's used to competing with her brothers for everything and she thinks she has to act that way out in the world, too. I fixed her up and sent her on her way."

Sebastian was pleasantly surprised. Josefa was a miracle-maker. And for some reason she seemed much friendlier to him than she ever had in the past, despite what had happened.

"I want you to understand, *Señora,* that I in no way encouraged the woman. She came into my tent while I was sleeping . . ."

Josefa shook her head. "I know the woman, Lieutenant. And she told me herself how it was, once she had calmed down. Don't worry. Your secret is safe with me."

He sighed. "I thank you, *Señora,* more than I can say. Now I'll just have to wait and see if one of her brothers wants to put a bullet in my heart, like he did last week to the *vaquero* who was courting her."

Josefa laughed and shook her head. "I don't think you'll have to worry about it. I told her quite plainly what would happen if she complained to her brothers." Josefa smirked. "Besides, her mind is already on something else."

"Oh? What?"

"Pues . . ." She winked. "Your friend Tomas Bata happened by when I was finishing up with her, and I assigned him the duty of escorting her back to where her brothers are camped." She chuckled. "They talked. They looked at one another. And somehow I had the feeling that she was quickly forgetting you, Lieutenant. I hope that doesn't hurt your feelings."

Sebastian reached out and took her hand, kissing it in the continental manner and making her blush. "I am vastly in your debt. Please let me know how I may repay you."

She sobered, her smiling face now wreathed with a frown. "You can repay me, Lieutenant, by staying away from my niece. Marina is betrothed to Don Felipe now. The more you come near her, the more you will hurt her."

Unfortunately, that was the one thing he couldn't

251

promise. He left Josefa, knowing it was good advice, but knowing also that it would be impossible to implement. As he moved about the valley, enjoying the praise and greetings of everyone he met, his gaze was constantly searching for her.

It was evening before he found her. She was with her father near the corrals, but James was caught up in a conversation with a group of other men and Marina was alone, leaning against the corral fence, watching the horses.

"Are you picking the mount to use for your wedding ride?" he asked as he settled next to her.

She barely glanced at him out of the corners of her eyes. She'd known he was coming, had sensed it, had longed for it. But now that he was here, she wasn't sure what they could possibly say to one another that would do any good at all.

"No, *matador*. To tell you the truth, I was just reliving your beautiful performance." Turning, she looked him full in the face, her eyes shining. "Where did you learn to do that? It was the most beautiful thing I've ever seen."

He wanted to take her hand, to kiss her. Pride swelled inside him. He'd done it for her, all for her. And she'd liked it. What more could he ask for?

"My father raised bulls for *la corrida* in Spain," he told her. "I trained with the best when I was young. But that was long ago."

La corrida . . . there was something very romantic about his Spanish past.

"You were stunning," she said softly. "I've never seen anything like it. But . . . I had always heard that Spanish bullfights were very bloody. That you kill the bull slowly, one stab wound at a time."

He nodded. "In a real bullfight it would be that way, to some extent. The bull must be weakened. I couldn't do that because there are no men here skilled in the form."

She made a face, shuddering. "I like the way you did it," she said. She turned back to watch the horses. "Beautiful, aren't they?" she murmured. "The Diaz *rancho* has the best of everything."

"They have the money to gather what they need to complete their collections," he responded, his voice bitter. "Horses, cattle, musicians, food." He moved closer to her. "And now, a wife for Felipe."

She stared away studiously. What he said was true, but what could she do? "Every man needs a wife."

"True. And Felipe wants the best."

She glanced at him. "I would hardly say I was the best," she protested.

He watched the breeze tease the hair at the back of her neck. "I would say it," he said softly. "You're too good for him."

Her hands clutched the top bar of the fence, knuckles whitening. Good or not, what did it matter? Besides, who was he to criticize what she was doing when he was rolling around in tents with people like Gloria Estancia? The thought of him with that woman sent ice through her veins. She knew what kind of man he was, surely, but she didn't like having her nose rubbed in it.

When she finally turned to look at him, her eyes were hard with anger. "And what would you know about it?" she asked icily. "You choose women like Gloria Estancia to warm your bed. How 'good' is she?"

His shoulders sagged. He'd known they would

have to get to this at some point, and he also knew there was almost nothing he could do to convince her of the truth about Gloria. He would have to rely on complete sincerity and hope that she could see it for what it was.

"I don't know how good she is, Marina. And actually, I don't care. But I do know I didn't invite her into my bed. In fact, I didn't stay in my bed once she got there. When you and Carmen arrived, I was in the process of trying to get her out of there."

Something flickered in the depths of her gray eyes. Was it trust? Was it understanding? But why should it be? He'd done nothing to deserve her faith.

"You didn't seem to be succeeding very rapidly," she said, wishing she could believe him.

He shook his head. "Ask Josefa about it," he said in frustration. "She knows everything."

Marina's eyes opened wide in surprise. "Josefa?"

He nodded. "Just ask her when you see her again. And now, let's be done with this subject. I hope I never see Gloria again, and I wish I had never met her." He gazed soulfully into her eyes. "Do you believe me?"

She held his gaze for a moment, then looked down at her hands. "Why should you care what I believe?"

His hand covered hers. "Marina," he said huskily, "I care more than I can say."

She stared at his hand for a long moment, then pulled away from it, raising her chin defiantly. "Well, you mustn't care. Not ever again."

He felt cold. "Is it done?" he asked harshly. "Are you betrothed?"

She nodded. He swore crudely, and she turned away.

254

He wanted to take her, to shake her, to make love to her until she realized that she couldn't do this. "Do you love him?"

She stared straight ahead, refusing to answer.

"No," he said firmly, his eyes steely. "I know you don't love him." His hands gripped the top rung of the fence as though he would rip it out of its sockets. "You can't marry the man."

She sighed and shook her head, her face filled with sadness and anger. Her hand went to the unicorn ring and twisted it.

"I must marry him. It's already been decided."

"No." He moved restlessly, wanting to fight something. "You don't love him. You can't consign yourself to a loveless marriage just because they tell you to."

"What do you want me to do?" She pinned him with her direct stare. It was time for him to lay his cards on the table. "Run away in the night? Where would I go? How would I live?"

He stared at her. There really was no answer to this, was there? She was as good as asking his intentions. What could he promise her? Nothing much. He wasn't ready to get married. He didn't want to get tied down. And he certainly didn't want to get stuck out here in California, locked away from Spain.

"You know that I'm going back to Spain as soon as I can," he told her bluntly. "I've told you from the first that return is my goal."

Her heart fell, but still she stared into his eyes, searching for answers. "Why?" she asked softly. "Why do you have to go back to Spain? What's waiting for you there?"

255

His eyes lit up. "I've had news. Things may be changing."

He hesitated. Should he tell her his background, tell her things he had never told anyone? She was the only person he had ever been tempted to tell. Somehow it just seemed right.

"I was forced to leave Spain when my family's enemy took over my father's debts, Marina. We lost everything. My father killed himself. My sister . . ." He swallowed. He hadn't realized the emotions would still come to the surface just talking about it. "My sister married the monster."

Despite everything, Marina felt every emotion he expressed as though it were her own. "How could she do that?"

He shook his head, his eyes haunted by that very question, a question he had wrestled with for years now. "I don't know. I was never able to talk to her about it, because he had me deported, sold into service with the Army in Mexico, to help pay my father's debts."

It sounded horrible. She could understand a bit better why he was so bitter. Still, that was long ago. Why couldn't he shed the past and think about settling in a new place?

"And what has changed that makes you think there is hope?"

"There are rumors that he is ill. Besides, politics changes like the shifting of the wind. Friends who had to go into hiding during the bad times are beginning to come back into favor." He looked toward the hills, remembering. "I once had powerful friends. With them back in control, I would be able to return and do something about Don Coronado."

256

To her horror, Marina realized her eyes were burning, a sure sign tears were on the way. She turned her
head to make sure he didn't see, and clenched her
hands into fists, forcing them back. What did she
care if he only wanted to return to Spain? Let him
go.

"I would give anything to be able to restore my
father's estates to their rightful owners," he said, his
mind still far away.

Marina was losing the battle with the tears. She
would have to go before he saw them. Anger swirled
in her. He was full of solutions for himself, but he
had none for her.

As though he'd heard her thoughts, he came back
to the subject of her betrothal.

"You must get out of this bargain, *querida*. You
must speak to your father. I can't stand to think of
you forcing yourself to pretend . . ."

That was just about all she could bear. Whirling,
she gathered her skirts in her hands and cried back
over her shoulder, "Why do you trifle with me this
way when you have no intention of doing anything
to help me?" before she flew off toward where her
father was talking.

James broke away quickly and met her and they
began to walk off together, but not before he had
thrown a look back that told Sebastian he wasn't
welcome to join them.

Sebastian stood where he was, wondering what
had made her so angry. He'd only spoken the truth.
She couldn't marry Felipe. It was unthinkable.
Something would have to be done to stop it.

But her words echoed in his ears. "Why do you trifle with me if you have no intention of doing any-

thing to help me?"

What could he do? Marry her himself? Impossible.

Still, her words disturbed him, and as he walked away, he let them play over and over again in his mind.

"Stay away from that man, Marina," James advised his daughter as they made their way back to the *hacienda* so that Marina could begin preparing for the *baile*.

She attempted an air of innocence. "What do you mean, Papa?"

"You're betrothed to Felipe now," he said rather more sternly than he usually talked to her. "Your days of talking to the Lieutenant are over."

Marina swallowed. She knew she should bow her head and take his advice to heart, but some rebellious streak in her wouldn't let it lie. "He's a friend, a friend of the family, like Alex. Must I stop talking to Alex as well?"

"Marina, don't try to fool your old father. I know he is much more to you than Alex could ever be. But he's a dangerous man."

Marina knew that only too well, but she couldn't stop herself from speaking defensively. "Who says he's a dangerous man?"

"You said so yourself, many times."

True again, but she wouldn't admit it. "That was before I knew him."

"Well, you were right and I was wrong. I took him in and befriended him, and now, from what Felipe tells me, he is plotting to take my land from me."

Marina shook her head as though to shake away a pesky fly. "I don't know what you're talking about. How could he possibly take your land?"

"He's been seen more than once riding the length of it, marking down information in a journal he carries. There seems to be no doubt of his intentions."

That was Felipe's story. She hadn't asked Sebastian and she had no idea what it was all about. She knew in her heart, though, that this accusation had no merit. "But how could he get the land?"

Her father looked into her eyes, his own serious with worry. "Through you, Marina. His thinking seems to be that if he could marry you . . ."

The thought sent her pulse thundering through her veins. If only it were true. She would gladly risk her father's land . . . well, no she wouldn't. But the point was, if Sebastian had given her the slightest hint that he might marry her someday, she would be the happiest woman in the valley. He was a dangerous man, yes. He was a Spaniard. He was harsh and cruel and a philanderer as well. But he was the only man who had ever made her pulse sing in her veins, or who had made her willing to throw aside every rule she'd ever lived by. He made her feel alive.

"Sebastian de la Cruz does not want to marry me," she snapped. "And he doesn't want your land. He wants to go back to Spain to claim his heritage. What would he want with those dusty acres?" She started walking faster, kicking her skirts aside. "I think you should stop listening to Felipe's crazy theories and get back to reality."

"Ah, Marina, you are so young and so naive."

Suddenly her father stumbled and she grabbed his arm. "Papa, what is it? Are you all right?"

He tried to laugh it off. "It's nothing. I'm just a little short of breath." He patted her hand and began to walk again. She hovered near him, not at all reassured. He looked very gray and she was worried.

"Let's get back to the hacienda. I'm sure they'll give you a room for the night. I won't have you sleeping out under the stars again."

"But that's what I love to do," he protested, though rather weakly. "It's half of what *rodeo* is all about."

She didn't listen to a word. Felipe's mother was happy to find a room for her father, kicking out two distant cousins who had ridden in from Yerba Buena, and between the two of them they settled him into bed for a rest.

"I'll come back and check on you before the dance," Marina assured him. "If you're still feeling like this, I want you to keep to your bed. You need rest." She leaned over and kissed his cheek.

He smiled up at her. "It's really nothing, Marina. I'm just a little worried. I want to get things settled, get you married to Felipe, then I'll be able to relax."

She hugged him. "Please rest assured, Papa—I'm marrying Felipe. You have no reason to worry any longer."

She turned and left quickly before he could see the trapped look in her eyes.

"So you gave a token to the Spaniard after his triumph in the ring." Felipe's arms were stiff around her, and his face was hard as iron.

The waltz was beautiful and couples were swaying all around them like flowers in a shifting breeze. The brass fixtures were polished until they looked like gold and the glow of lanterns lit the room like daylight. This was their first dance of the evening. Everyone knew they were going to announce their betrothal. And yet, from the first moment Marina had seen Felipe tonight, she'd known he was angry with her and she had been pretty sure she had some idea why that might be.

"What are you talking about?" she asked him, playing for time.

"I have friends everywhere, Marina. They tell me everything." He glared at her, his black eyes hard as diamonds. "I also know that you were talking to him at the corral this evening."

There wasn't much point in denying it. "I was just talking to him."

He grimaced. "You won't be talking to him any more. Not ever. You're now betrothed to me and you'll do what I say."

The words were guaranteed to get her back up. She tried not to feel angry; it would serve no useful purpose. But how could she help it when he talked such nonsense—as though he were some sort of small town dictator who could dictate her every move.

"As far as I know a betrothal is not quite a contract for slavery," she responded tartly. "It doesn't give you the right to manage my life in all its aspects."

His hand tightened on her. "I don't need anything to give me rights, Marina. I take the rights I need. You would do well to remember that."

"Felipe, you're hurting me."

His hand loosened, but he didn't apologize. "Believe me, Marina, I will make you very sorry if you break my rules. My wife must be beyond reproach. You've lived a fairly lax life. Well, it's understandable, your father is not really one of us. But those days of childlike freedom are over, *querida*. And you will look at no other man but me."

The dance came to an end and he led her off the floor and deposited her before Josefa. But he didn't smile or greet the woman, nor did he say anything pleasant to Marina. Clicking his heels together, he took his leave with a face as hard as the blade of a hatchet.

Luckily, Josefa was engaged in a sprightly conversation with an old friend and had paid no attention to Felipe and Marina. The music started up again, but Marina walked away, avoiding a young man who was obviously bent on asking her to dance. She looked about the room in confusion. The music was too loud, the atmosphere stifling, the whirling colors unsettling. Her head was throbbing and she had to have some relief.

A quick glance around the room found no stares watching her every move, so she took a chance and went out onto the patio. Just outside, five or six *vaqueros* sat easily on their horses, talking, laughing and passing *aguardiente* in an earthen jug. Slipping out the back of the patio, she avoided them and got away from the house without anyone noticing.

Chapter Twenty

Once away from the light of the house, she was on her own. The music and excitement of the dance had drawn everyone in to the *hacienda* as a flame draws moths. She was pretty sure she wasn't going to run into anyone out here in the dark. There was no one left.

There was just enough moon for her to find her way without stumbling. She headed for an area she knew well, walking through the pepper trees and down a steep embankment, and into a small canyon that cradled a small, sparkling stream. The water fed the oaks and sycamores which lined it and wild rose which tangled from every side along the banks. Frogs and crickets after pausing a moment to judge her intent, gave a cheerful serenade.

Sinking down on a grassy ledge, she closed her eyes and hugged her arms tightly around herself, feeling with welcome relief the night breezes cooling her burning cheeks, while the soothing natural sounds of the area coaxed away her headache and comforted her soul. With an almost physical effort, she forced her mind to go blank, rejecting the constant questions and accusations that churned in torment just below the surface.

Soon she would have to sort out her feelings and her

responsibilities, her moral obligations, and when she did, she would have to set aside everything she loved and held dear and do what was best for everyone. That was her lot in life, so they said. So why did she feel this potent streak of rebellion? It was growing stronger every minute.

She didn't want to marry Don Felipe. But what on earth could she do about it?

Suddenly something had changed. Coming quickly alert, she realized that the frogs and crickets had stilled again. But what had disturbed them? She listened intently, but the noise of the stream masked any clues. Every muscle in her body tensed as she strained to identify the cause of the animals' quiet.

But when Sebastian suddenly appeared beside her, she wasn't really surprised. In fact, she felt more relief than anything. She needed him right now. Only him. This was inevitable in a way she couldn't explain and she was glad the step was being taken.

He didn't touch her. Leaning one arm against the tree, he looked down at her. After one quick glance in his direction, she gazed steadily into the stream, waiting for him to speak.

"They say there is much gold and silver to be found along these stream beds, enough to make one very wealthy." He paused. "But then, that wouldn't interest you. When you're married to Don Felipe, you'll be the wealthiest woman in the district. Will that please you?"

Marina didn't answer, but she drew her arms more tightly in, as though she'd suddenly found a chill in the air.

He went on, speaking so softly that she could barely hear him above the babble of the brook.

"You'll be able to import jewelry from Mexico,

gowns from Paris, furniture from England. You may spend your evenings doing nothing but dancing and your days counting your possessions. Who wouldn't be tempted by such a life?" He looked down. "But tell me, *querida,* how will you fare in a household where reading is thought to be close to sin, where ideas are examined only if relevant to a new festivity, where a woman who professes to have thoughts of her own will be quickly brought to heel? Have you considered?"

She had. She'd done nothing *but* consider for days now. But she didn't appreciate him bringing these things up as though he was opening new vistas for her.

"All this sounds strange," she said, "coming from a *caballero* with such traditional views on the position people should take in society. I should think you would deem it a good lesson for me."

He smiled fleetingly. "*Querida,* I don't think you know me as well as you think you do. I may have strong opinions, but I also have a mind trained to think, and therefore those opinions are free to change as new evidence presents itself."

"And have you changed your opinions?"

He dropped down to sit beside her in the grass. "My opinions are constantly changing."

She gazed at him. His green eyes were a shiny black in the dark. "Then your opinions must be a lot like your affections, *hombre,*" she said evenly.

He stared at her. "What makes you think my affections are so changeable?" he asked.

She shrugged, pretending indifference. "Your reputation, Lieutenant. And something about that glint in your eye."

His laugh was low and incredulous. "Glint? What does a glint say?"

She turned back, trying to see his expression. "It

says that you like women, like the chase, enjoy celebrating your victories and then moving on."

His hand flashed out and captured her chin before she had a chance to draw back. "Then my glint is a liar," he said softly, insinuatingly, his thumb stroking her jawline. "Marina . . ."

His voice seemed to break and he stopped, dropping his hand and looking away.

"What?" She had to know. She could hear emotion in his voice and wasn't sure why or for what. She needed more—more words, more feelings, more sense of what he wanted. She twisted the unicorn ring on her finger and waited anxiously.

But he was shaking his head. "Nothing."

"Tell me."

He hesitated, then shook his head again, his gaze burning into hers. "Marina, don't you understand? Don't you know that I haven't looked at another woman since I first saw you?"

He was lying. He had to be lying. "But . . . but you've been with other women . . ." She couldn't accuse him of Gloria. Josefa had told her not to believe that for a moment. But surely there were others. There had to be.

"No, Marina. Not one. Not since I arrived and found you by the stream."

"Me?" She wanted to believe him. "But you hated me at first."

He shook his head, smiling ruefully. "I hated what you did to me. I hated that you wouldn't give me your body right there, after you had raised my expectations so very high." He laughed softly, his fingers tangling with her curls. "You called me a pig, and you were right. I acted like an animal. I should have known . . ."

266

His voice trailed off again. She turned toward him, desperately needing to hear it all.

"What? *What* should you have known?"

His eyes deepened and his fingertips trailed across her cheek. "That you were an angel," he said, his voice so low and soft it might have been a part of the babbling brook. "That I had no right to touch you."

She stared at him, startled beyond belief. He couldn't mean it. She must be dreaming. But his words were so wonderful, more precious than any other gift he could have given her. She could pretend it was true, couldn't she? Pretend — and hope.

Still, despite her doubts, the things he said rang true in a way the words of other men, including Felipe, never did. She could feel sincere emotion in him. And he was certainly saying things she wanted to hear.

She touched him, her palm to his cheek, and suddenly his face twisted in a painful grimace and he threw his head back. Swearing softly, he pulled away from her.

She swayed toward him, not wanting him to leave. "What is it?" she asked him. "What's the matter?"

He stared back at her. "It's just as I said. I have no right to touch you."

Did he mean the betrothal? She didn't want to think about that. She didn't want to think about anything but him. He filled her world right now. She reached for him. No matter what, she couldn't lose him.

"You can touch me, Sebastian," she said softly, urgently, her fingers curling about the edge of his jacket. "I . . . I want you to touch me."

He shook his head as though to clear it, his eyes haunted. "Marina, you don't know what you're asking . . ."

The funny thing was that he was wrong. Some

267

strange wisdom of the ages seemed to have descended on her. She knew. She knew it all. "I know what I'm asking, Sebastian. I know."

She reached out and tugged at his hand, pulling him back close again.

He looked as though he were actually in physical pain. "Marina, don't. You can't understand . . ."

"Sebastian," she whispered, raising her face to his.

He groaned as he lowered to cover her mouth with his, and his kiss was rough, demanding. He wanted to scare her. He wanted to give her a taste of what she was asking for. She was a virgin and had no idea of the wild forces she was gambling with.

"You're not safe with me, Marina," he whispered, rubbing his face against the side of her head. "You don't know what you're risking."

"I think I know, Spaniard," she said, raising her arms to him. There was a glow building inside her. She might not know what to do with her life, but she knew what to do with this moment. "I'll take my chances."

"You're betrothed . . ."

She tried to read his eyes. "Don't you want me?"

He was shocked, his hands taking her face between them. "All I do anymore is want you," he said intensely. "I lie awake at night, wanting you. I spend my days looking for you, longing to see you, to touch you, to kiss that red mouth." He pulled back. "But Marina, we can't. I couldn't do that to you."

She was suddenly very sure of herself. "But Sebastian . . . I want you to."

"You don't know what it means."

"I know. Do it now, Sebastian. Quickly."

He half thought she had an ulterior motive for this, some agenda he hadn't noticed, but it was too late for rational thinking, and he gave up the idea. His mind was in a fog. But his heart was beating very fast, sending his pulse racing.

He kissed her hard again, plunging into her mouth like an invader, taking control of it like a conqueror. She cried out and he tried to pull back, but her arms came around his neck, holding him tightly.

"Don't let go," she whispered wildly. "Don't leave me."

He pushed her back onto the grass. His need was urgent, overwhelming, and his breath was coming very short and hard, rasping in his throat. Her dress came away in his hands, and he cupped her breast, pulling it out of the corset, covering the nipple with his mouth, tugging and teasing until she cried out, her hands digging convulsively into his hair.

Marina was afraid. She was terrified. But not of him. She was afraid of disappointing him somehow, of losing him when this was over. But never of him. He was all she lived for.

He looked down at her—her white skin, her soft brown hair, the full swell of her lovely breasts, the high, dark nipples, the flat stomach—and his equilibrium fell away. He needed her, he wanted her, he had to have her now. Now.

He wanted to be careful, was determined not to hurt her, but it was so hard to hold himself back. His loins ached with physical pain, and he had to fight every inch of the way to keep himself leashed.

He pushed aside her cotton leggings and found the area that made him throb with unbearable desire. He stroked her again and again, softly, impudently, like a sculptor with his clay, taking her to the peak she would need to accept him.

She was trembling, her need as great as his own. She didn't understand it, but instinctively she knew what was needed. There was a swelling heat inside her, growing, building, like the waves, like a storm, and she knew she could never resist it now. She was part of it, riding with the surf, high in the wind, reaching for heaven.

"Please," she whispered, and then her voice deepened, lowered, and came out a demanding rasp. "Please, oh, please!"

He entered as slowly and gently as he could, his breath sounding harsh and painful as he held himself back. She cried out for a moment, her eyes wide open and gazing at him questioningly.

"It's all right, *querida*," he comforted, caressing her, kissing her, wishing he could spare her any pain. "I'll go slow."

But it only took a moment for her to regain momentum. And once she did, she didn't want slow at all. She wanted fast and hard and right now. Her hips ground against him and a low animal sound came from her throat. He could hold back no longer.

"Oh God," he cried out as he came inside her.

Her voice uttered sounds, but formed no recognizable words. She would have devoured him if she could, driving, enveloping, caressing, giving and taking in equal measure. He was hers. This was a dance of possession as well as love. She was branding him with her sense of ownership. He was hers. She was in love.

They lay back in the grass, exhausted. For a long moment, neither of them spoke. Paradise was here, and they drifted in it. Honey oozed through their veins. Their skin sparkled. Their breath was the perfume of roses in bloom.

Finally, Marina raised herself on one elbow and looked at him, dazed. How long had she known that she loved him? And what did it matter? He was the one man she could never have.

But she would always have this—this night, this lovemaking. When she was with Felipe, perhaps she would be able to close her eyes and . . .

No, this was insane. She hadn't even married the man yet, and already she had cheated on him. A wash of guilt came over her, and she reached for her clothes.

Sebastian's strong hand stopped her. "Where are you going?" he whispered, his eyes luminous.

"I have to get back to the dance," she said, trying to avoid his gaze. "I'll be missed."

His fingers tightened, ringing her arm. "Stay with me. I can't lose you so quickly."

Her heart broke inside her. She wanted more than anything to stay with him. Forever. But that was impossible. "Don Felipe . . ." she began.

He yanked her back against his chest. "I don't care about Felipe," he said harshly. "You're not going to marry Felipe. I'll kill him before I let him touch you."

She raised her head and stared at him. She felt as though she were being pulled to pieces. She loved him. The obvious solution would be to marry him. But he didn't want that. So she was going to be forced to marry Felipe. Wasn't she? "But what can I do?"

"Stay with me." He stroked her hair. "We'll think of something."

Lying against his chest was rapture, and for a moment she tried to pretend everything would be all right if she just stayed this way. But deep inside, she knew it couldn't last.

"Sebastian, I have to go back. My father . . ."

"Your father," he said decisively. "That's the key right there."

She sat up and looked at him, pulling her clothes together. "What do you mean?"

"Your father loves you, Marina. And he's a man of conscience. He would never do anything to hurt you."

"Of course. What you say is true. But . . ."

"You'll go to him. Tell him the truth."

"About this?" she asked horrified. "Never!"

He laughed softly, cradling her in his arms. "Not about this. This is ours. No one else will ever know about this."

He kissed her and she turned in to the kiss, wanting to savor every bit of him.

"Listen, *querida*," he said softly between small kisses. "Tell your father that you don't love Felipe — that you don't want to marry him."

"But he's counting on settling me so that he doesn't have to worry about me any longer."

"Marina, believe me, if you tell him how unhappy you'll be, he'll be the first one to tell you to break this betrothal. He wouldn't want you to be miserable. Trust me. Your father wants nothing but your happiness."

Of course he was right. Her heart sang.

"I'll go right away," she said, scrambling to her feet and fastening her dress. "Is my hair a mess? Oh, I think you're right, Sebastian — my father does love me. He'll listen to me."

"Yes." He stood and took her in his arms again as though he couldn't bear to stop touching her. "Talk to your father, *querida*. Then come back to me."

"I'll come back to you." She pressed her palm to his cheek and looked at him with all her love in her eyes. "Wait for me."

One more lingering look and she was gone, dashing through the trees and up out of the canyon, her heart lighter than it had been in days. Sebastian was right. If she just told her father the truth, all would be well.

She had barely come within sight of the house when

she heard her name being called.

"Marina! Thank God I've found you. Come quickly. It's your father."

Carmen came running to meet her, hands outstretched.

"Papa?" Marina's eyes opened wide, startled. "What is it? What's happened?"

Carmen grabbed her arm and began to lead her quickly through the yard. "He's had some kind of attack. The doctor is with him right now."

"Marina."

Another voice was calling her. Marina strained to see into the shadows. It was Felipe, his eyes hard as stones.

"Marina, where have you been?" he asked, but his eyes were already accusing her.

She shook off his reproachful look. She had no time for that now. Anguish was beginning to fill her chest. Turning away, she hurried after Carmen without a word to her fiancé.

Her father was lying back against pillows, very still, his eyes closed, his face almost green. Alex and the doctor were just coming out, and the doctor motioned for them to step back and not enter the room. Marina took a quick look, said a soft prayer, and retreated, turning immediately to demand information.

"It's his heart, I'm afraid," the doctor said, shaking his head. "He's not a young man, you know. Hearts do give out."

"Give out?" Marina seized him by the lapels of his coat, frantic. "What do you mean? Is he dying?"

"Marina, my dear, James would want you to remain strong, I know . . ."

"Marina." Alex pried her fingers loose from the doctor's coat and took her in his arms. "Marina, stay

273

calm. You won't do your father any good by flying off the handle, now, will you?"

She relaxed in her old friend's arms. "Alex, is it true? Is he dying?"

"I'm afraid we must be prepared for the worst, my dear."

Marina pulled out of his arms, whirled, and stared into Carmen's dark eyes. Her cousin took her hand and tried to hold back tears. "I'm sorry, Marina," she whispered, shaking her head. "I'm so sorry."

Marina was trembling, but she kept her head. "I must go in and see him."

"Now, Marina, he needs rest . . ."

She glared at the doctor, eyes blazing. "If he's dying, what good will *rest* do? I have to talk to him. You can't stop me."

She turned, a picture of eternal determination, and the doctor didn't even try to stop her. She opened the door softly and crept into the room, going on her knees at his bedside and taking his hand in hers and kissing it.

"Papa," she whispered, tears streaming down her face. "Papa, please . . ."

There was no indication that he heard her at all. His hand was cold, his features looked as though they had been carved in wax. She dropped his hand and stood staring down at him. Was there nothing she could do but sit here and wait for him to die? She couldn't stand that. She couldn't stand it at all.

"Oh, Papa," she whispered. "I love you so."

Her father, who had raised her all those years alone — he was the truest, kindest, most honorable man she had ever known. It wasn't fair that he should be the one to have his heart fail. There were so many others less deserving.

And she . . . what did she deserve? She had been outside making love with the Spaniard when her father needed her.

A horrible thought occurred to her. Could that be why this had happened? Was this her retribution for the sin she had committed? Was her father going to have to pay the price?

She had promised him that she would marry Don Felipe. That was what he wanted, what he was holding on for. Her heart dropped when she realized what this meant. In order to save her father, she was going to have to marry Felipe after all.

But that didn't matter. Nothing mattered any longer, nothing but her father being well again.

"I'm going to marry Felipe, Papa," she whispered, bending close to his ear. "Don't worry. Everything will be all right."

Backing out of the room, she turned toward the ballroom, rushing to find Felipe. But she didn't have far to go. He was waiting in the entryway of the house, leaning against a wall, watching for her. Motioning her to come outdoors, he met her on the veranda.

"Your papa?" he asked.

She shrugged, troubled, hardly seeing him. "They say he is dying," she answered, her voice hoarse, the tears still on her face. "Felipe, can you do me a favor?"

There was a long pause before he answered, and that should have been a clue. But she was too distracted to notice.

"A favor, Felipe," she repeated impatiently.

"What is it?" he said at last.

"I want to get married right now, in my father's room. It doesn't have to be a legal ceremony, just something to make him think it's real, this wedding of ours. We could do it properly later. But for now, if we

275

just go before the priest in front of my father, I think that may help. To lessen his worries, I mean. What do you say? Do you think we can do it?"

"You and me? Before the priest?"

"Yes." She nodded quickly, hope in her eyes. "Could we do it right away? The sooner the better."

His mouth twisted cynically, his eyes cold as ice. "And what would you promise, *querida?* To love, honor, and obey?"

It was finally getting through to her that he wasn't his usual self. She looked at him warily. "Of course. Those are part of the vows."

"You knew that, then?" he asked, his black eyes glittering. His hand shot out and grabbed her wrist, his fingers painfully rough. "And what about the part where you promise to have no other, Marina? Had you heard about that part of the wedding vows?"

She stared at him blankly, not sure what he could be talking about. "Felipe, you're frightening me," she said softly. "What's happened?"

"What's happened?" He twisted her arm painfully. "I'll tell you what's happened, Marina. The woman I thought I would marry has been out rolling in the grass with another man. That's what's happened."

"I . . ." Marina blanched. "No, Felipe, I . . ."

"Do you think I don't know that look, Marina? Did you think I wouldn't notice the grass in your hair?" As he spoke, his free hand plucked little grasses and burrs from her dress. "You've been with him." He spit on the ground. "If I cared enough about you any more, I'd kill him. But as far as I'm concerned, you have ceased to exist."

He dropped her hand and stepped back. She rubbed her wrist and stared at him. "But Felipe," she said, not bothering to try to deny his charges. "Couldn't we pre-

276

tend, just for my father's sake? He'll die . . ."

Felipe shrugged. "Let him die," he sneered, shaking a fist at her. "Maybe it would be better. If he lived, he would have to face what a slut his daughter has become."

She'd hurt him and she'd never meant to. But there was no time to think about it. Her father was dying. She flung herself at Felipe, imploring him.

"Felipe, please, I swear I will do anything you ask, only please, please do this for me. He was so anxious that we marry. If I could show him . . ."

"Stay away from me, woman." Felipe pushed her away. "You've done enough damage. I just want you out of my house."

She hesitated, bewildered, not sure what to do or whom to turn to.

"What's going on out here?"

Whirling, she found Alex coming out onto the veranda to join them.

"Alex," she cried in relief. "Tell him he must help me. If I don't do something to relieve Papa's mind, he will surely die. If Felipe would just marry me . . ."

"I'll never marry you, Marina," he growled at her. "No decent man will ever marry you now. Go live on El Camino de Los Osos, where you belong."

Marina put her hand up to her face as though she'd been slapped. As Felipe stormed back into the house, she stood very still. It was finally getting through to her just how terrible was this thing that she had done. There was no one in all the world who could defend her for it — no one.

"Marina." Alex was still there, his hand stretched out to her in kindness. "What on earth is going on between you and Felipe?"

"He doesn't want to marry me," she said, her eyes

glazed. "What am I going to do?"

"There, there, dear—I'm sure he'll come around." He patted her arm. "My, you sure do have yourself a pack of trouble tonight, don't you? I feel so bad that I'm going to have to go and leave you to take care of things on your own."

She looked at him, feeling as though she was losing the only floating log in a swirling river. "Don't, Alex. Why must you go?"

He shook his head. "I've already stayed a day too long as it is. I'll have to ride all night to make the sailing for San Pedro in the morning. It wouldn't do for the men to set sail without the captain, now, would it?"

"You're leaving for New England?"

"That's our eventual destination. It should take us some time to get there. We're going to be stopping in San Blas, don't you know. Then, down through the cold country and up and around South America. We'll probably stop somewhere in the Caribbean before we head back up the coast to Boston."

The Caribbean. Jonathan was in the Caribbean, looking for pirates. If she could find Jonathan, that would surely bring her father around. What if he were to think she was out looking for Jonathan? What if he thought there was a chance . . . ?

Alex was a good man. Her father liked Alex. Maybe . . .

"Captain." Marina felt like a sleepwalker, going through the motions. "Alex, does your offer to take me with you still hold?"

His head swung around and he looked at her sharply, as though unable to believe his ears. "Well, sure, but Don Felipe . . ."

"Don Felipe will never take me back. And I don't really want him to. May I come with you?"

"Well, certainly, but . . ."

"Good. I must visit my father once more, and then I will have a horse saddled in no time and meet you at the main road." She looked at him, her gray eyes serious. "One thing, though. Please don't tell anyone. Promise?"

Alex looked as though a stiff wind had blown by and changed reality and he still hadn't made the adjustment. He shook his head, completely baffled.

"Uh, yes, sure, I won't tell anyone. But Marina, shouldn't you stay, with your father so sick and all?"

She smiled at him sadly. "Going is the only way I can hope to make him well," she said. "Thank you, Alex. Thank you so much." With one quick glance toward the ballroom, where music was still playing, she hurried back into the house.

Captain Brandene stood staring after her, shaking his head, not sure whether to be elated or chagrined. He'd always liked her. That was for sure. And now she said she was coming with him. That must mean she was ready to marry him. Well, that would suit him fine, come to think of it. He grinned. Yes, that would suit him fine.

Chapter Twenty-one

The next morning of the rodeo proved to be as fair as the first. The men who had camped in the surrounding areas for the night were late rising, as their celebrating had gone on far into the night, so the *carretas* of the families who had gone home were beginning to return before many of the campers had begun to stir.

Sebastian wasn't one of the lazy ones. He'd been up since dawn, tromping through the gardens and gazing up at the *hacienda,* wondering behind which barred and shuttered window Marina slept.

He was beginning to feel uneasy. She'd never come back the night before. He'd spent an hour or so throwing rocks into the stream, and finally he'd gone back up to the house to look for her.

The ballroom was still crowded with dancers, but Marina wasn't there. Neither was anyone else in the Crafts party. Sebastian made his way around the room, stopping often to talk to well-wishers and others who wanted to compliment him on his exhibition of the afternoon in the bull ring.

Felipe was, as usual, the center of most of the attention, dancing with every pretty woman he could get his hands on. When he saw Sebastian, his lip curled and fire lit his eyes, and in that moment Sebastian knew Marina must have told him something. He had the distinct impression that it was only his current popularity that kept Felipe from lunging at his throat.

Finally he had given up and gone back to his tent to get some sleep, assuming Marina was doing the same. But now he was ready to see her again, and her continual absence was beginning to trouble him.

Restless, he rode out across the Diaz *rancho* to see for himself how Californio spreads were managed. The lands were vast and beautiful, and it was almost noon when he returned. He walked up to the cooking area of the *hacienda* to get some food, but still saw no one he knew.

After eating, he spent some time strolling around the gardens again, looking for some member of the Crafts family. Finally he went to the corral to look through that crowd. The audience today was smaller. Most of the exhibitions were being performed by boys, but the cheers and groans were none the less enthusiastic. However, there was still no one there of whom he could inquire after Marina.

Just as he turned to leave, he found Tomas approaching him. His large, liquid eyes were bright with excitement.

"So there you are, finally. I've been searching everywhere for you. Have you heard the news?"

A sense of foreboding washed over Sebastian. "What news?" he asked, frowning.

"About Marina. Come, let us go where we won't be overheard."

They walked in some distance from the crowd. A pulse was beginning to beat at Sebastian's temple. Finally, he deemed they were far enough away from anyone who could possibly hear and he swung around, stopping Tomas.

"What is your news?" he demanded impatiently.

"She's gone."

He blinked. "Gone? What do you mean, gone?"

"She's disappeared. The family is in an uproar. The Diaz people are frantic."

Sebastian shook his head. There was something here that just didn't make any sense. "But where did she go?" A thought occurred to him. "Perhaps she just went home to sleep in her own bed."

Felipe shook his head. "No. The town has been searched, along with the house, and the *hacienda* as well. She is nowhere to be found."

An icy dagger of dread pierced Sebastian's heart as he remembered where he had seen her last. The stream. She couldn't possibly have lost her footing and . . .

He grabbed Tomas by the shoulders. "Where was she last seen?" he demanded.

"The last person seems to have been Carmen, late last night."

Of course. Relief swept through him. He released his friend.

"Well, what does Carmen say?"

"Nothing; that's the strange part. The lady refuses to talk. Everyone is furious with her, of course, and they seem to have her locked up somewhere, trying to wring the truth out of her, but so far, no luck."

"And James? Can't he get through to her?"

"The papa? Haven't you heard?" Tomas looked at him strangely. "Where have you been hiding to be so out of touch? James Crafts became ill last night. His heart, they say. He is near onto death."

"Death." Sebastian's mouth went dry. "Oh no."

That would have something to do with Marina's absence. He was sure of it. She was at her father's bedside, surely. What was the big mystery in that?

"Where is he?"

"In a bedroom at the *hacienda,* I suppose. They say it will be any time now."

"Well, that must be where Marina is."

"No." Tomas shook his head. "That is what makes it all so strange. No one can figure it out. A devoted daughter like Marina wouldn't go off when her father is dying. It isn't like her."

He was right. Something was very wrong. Turning, Sebastian grabbed him again, his eyes fiercely intense. "I have to get into the *hacienda.* Do you know anyone?"

"In the Diaz household? You must be joking." His face changed. "Well, I do know a kitchen maid."

Sebastian grunted. "I thought you might. She'll have to get me in."

Tomas frowned in puzzlement. "But why would you want to get in there? What good will it do?"

Sebastian smashed his fist into the palm of his other hand, staring off at the mountains. "I've got to get to Carmen. She knows where Marina is — I'm sure of it."

Tomas was still puzzled. "But why would she tell you if she will tell no one else?"

Sebastian mouth twisted. "She'll tell me," he said grimly, "as long as I can get in to her."

Tomas gave him an expansive shrug. "Then let's go, *amigo,* and see if we can smuggle you in."

* * *

283

The kitchen maid giggled when Tomas called her out, but when she heard what they wanted, she drew back in horror.

"Oh, no, Lieutenant. If you're caught, what would they do to me? They're too upset already. Everyone is screaming at everyone else and running around trying to fix the blame on someone. We are all in danger of being whipped as it is."

Sebastian took her hand in his and smiled down at her with his confident sense of reassurance. "Do you think I would let you be whipped? I don't want to jeopardize your position, but only to find Carmen. Just tell me where they are keeping her and how to get there. I'll do the rest."

The kitchen maid blushed and stammered and did as he asked. Soon he was moving down the central corridor of the Diaz *hacienda,* on his way to the bedroom where Carmen was being held. He had taken off his spurs, knife, and pistol outside, leaving them with Tomas, and his progress was virtually soundless. So far, fortune favored him and he had met no one in the halls. If the kitchen maid was right, Carmen was in the room around the corner, at the end of the right corridor that branched off the main one just a few steps away.

So near and yet so far . . . he'd barely taken another step when a voice sounded around the corner and he had to duck into a doorway. Quickly he turned the key, yanking it out and pocketing it just in case, and went inside, closing the door behind him as quietly as he could. Then he leaned against the door and listened as the voices came down the hall.

"With Felipe in such a black mood, I don't know if there will be another *baile* tonight." He recognized the voice of Felipe's mother. "If only we knew where Marina had gone."

"I wish I knew." It was Josefa walking with her. "But I must confess, I don't understand Felipe's attitude. He doesn't seem to care that Marina is missing."

They stopped in front of the door he was leaning against and Felipe's mother knocked with a heavy set of knuckles, making him jump back in alarm.

"Conchita, baby, are you awake? I just want to check on you." There was a scratching sound. "What has happened to your key, Conchita? Oh, well, the door is unlocked."

The door was going to open and reveal his hiding place. But even worse, he had suddenly realized that there was someone else in the room. He'd been too preoccupied to notice at first. But now he saw the bright eyes of Felipe's little sister watching him from the bed. For a moment they stared at one another. Then he winked and put a finger to his lips, before slipping behind the door and flattening himself as it opened against him.

"Mama's little angel," the woman cooed, looking in. "Are you through with your nap? Or should I leave you alone for another half hour?"

The girl stared at Sebastian. Sebastian held his breath.

"Mama," she began, raising her hand as if to begin to point out the presence of a stranger in her room.

Sebastian groaned inside, but shook his head, looking at her hopefully.

Conchita's shoulders drooped. "Nothing, Mama," she said softly.

"Still sleepy, eh?" her mother said. "All right, darling. You sleep a little more. I know you'll be up late tonight, watching the dancing."

The door closed and Sebastian let out his breath in a rush. He looked at the girl in the bed. She was still staring at him. Smiling gratefully, he blew her a kiss, and then went to the door himself, easing it open and stepping back outside, into the corridor. The voices had receded toward the kitchen. Hurrying, he went to the corner and turned it, breathing more easily when he found the way clear. In a moment he was outside the temporary jail cell that held Carmen.

The key was waiting in the lock. In this house, all the young women were obviously locked in at night. Listening at the door for a moment to make sure she didn't have company, he snapped over the key and entered the room with it in his hand.

Carmen sat alone by the window. She looked up as he came in, as though she'd been expecting him. Smiling knowingly, she motioned for him to sit.

"It would be nice to think you had come to rescue me, but I guess I'm too much of a realist to believe that," she said, smiling at him. "I'm sure you're here for the same reason everybody else comes. Am I right?"

Sebastian made an impatient gesture. "Where is she?"

She laughed softly. "What, no small talk? No polite conversation to make me think I might be important in the scheme of things as well?"

"Damn it, Carmen, where is she?"

She sighed. "My dear Lieutenant, you are the last person I could tell."

He went down on one knee beside her chair and took her hand in his. "You'll tell me, Carmen. You know you must." There was no doubt in his mind.

She looked at him mockingly. "Must I?" she murmured.

He didn't bother to reiterate. "Tell me, did you see her last night?"

"After the two of you met?" She smiled at his frown. "Yes, I saw her just before midnight."

"What was her mood?"

She raised her eyebrows. "Well, she was very upset, of course. Her father . . ."

Was dying . . . he had almost forgotten. "Yes, how is James?"

Carmen shook her head, her dark eyes suddenly sad. "Barely clinging to life. He's been unconscious since last evening."

He nodded. They were both silent for a moment in unspoken regret. "So she saw him," he said quietly at last.

"Oh, yes. She talked to him for a long time."

"But I thought you said he was unconscious."

"He *was*. But she talked anyway."

"I see." This was going too slowly. Carmen was a stubborn one, but he couldn't help but admire her. Still, she had to tell him what he wanted to know. If she wouldn't do it willingly, he was going to have to resort to stronger measures. "And then?"

"She came to talk to me. And then . . ." She shrugged. "She left."

He squeezed her hand impatiently. "Left? Left how? On foot? On horseback?"

With a grimace, she pulled her hand away from his. "She had a horse ready."

Now they were getting somewhere. He stood again, as though ready to run in whatever direction she indicated. "Was she alone? Who was with her?"

Carmen merely stared at him.

He frowned, trying to puzzle out her signals. "So she was not alone." His face hardened. "Who was it? Tell me." He barely restrained himself from shaking her and his voice took on a dangerous edge. "Tell me now, Carmen."

Her chin rose and she stared right back. "Don't threaten me, Lieutenant. I've had enough threats for one day."

They glared at one another. Carmen knew he was going to do anything he had to do to gain his end. Her own pride precluded too quick a capitulation, but she had a few tricks up her sleeve as well. Her dark eyes narrowed.

"Here's an idea, Lieutenant. Why not try bribery? The others haven't thought of that yet."

He stared at her, relieved but still annoyed. She was going to tell him what he wanted to know. She just hadn't tortured him enough yet. "What would you like to be bribed with?" he asked softly.

She was silent for a moment, thinking. "When I tell you where she is, what will you do?"

"Go after her, of course."

Her eyes were dark and mysterious as she smiled. "Even if it is very far?"

He threw out his arms in a grand gesture. "To the ends of the earth."

She cocked her head, watching his reactions. "Even if there's a chance you might not catch her?"

He shook his head grimly. "I'll catch her."

Carmen hesitated, then said softly. "Even if she is with another man?"

His mouth turned down in a rejection of that idea. "She can't be with another man. Not, at any rate, in

288

the way you imply by your tone."

Carmen raised an eyebrow. "Why not?"

He looked at her icily. "Because . . ." He hesitated. A quick memory of what they had shared beside the stream swept over him and he had to swallow before he could speak again. "She wouldn't, that's all."

Carmen's smile was just this side of malicious. "But she did. And on their journey they'll be together for a long, long time."

His eyes burned. "I thought she didn't tell you where she was going."

"She didn't. But I saw whom she left with and I know her plan. He's someone who has held her in high esteem for a long time and he will treat her well."

His mouth curved cruelly. "He won't have time to treat her any way at all. I'll bring her back. Quickly, tell me who and where."

Carmen's grin was impudent. "You haven't bribed me yet."

He moved impatiently, stifling the urge to wring her neck. "Anything you want. Quickly."

She stood. "Take me with you."

That went beyond anything he had imagined. "What?"

"Take me with you. Help me escape from this prison, from this barbarian town." She began to move about the room, gathering a few small items which she put into her pockets, taking up her shawl.

Not in a million years would he take her with him. Was she crazy? What would he be able to accomplish with a woman holding him back?

"But you said yourself that I might not be in time to catch her. With you along, the risk would be even greater."

She looked up at him, indignation blazing in her eyes. "I may be a woman, *hombre,* but I am also a Californian. And from the evidence I've seen of your riding skill, I think I can hold my own." Her chin came up defiantly. "You'll take me or you won't go."

He hesitated. Had there ever been a more maddening woman on the face of the earth? But there wasn't much he could do about her now. He didn't have the time. That was the key. Time. He had to race after Marina and catch her before she got hurt or did something stupid . . . or both.

Giving in, he nodded curtly. "Tell me."

Carmen let out a sigh, moved in close, and spoke quietly. "She left last night with Captain Brandene. They would have made it to his ship in a few hours and probably sailed for San Pedro this morning."

Sebastian blinked at her for a moment. "Alex?" he asked, incredulously.

Carmen nodded.

He didn't waste any more time on that. "How much time do they usually spend in San Pedro?"

"It depends on whether they are taking on any cargo. If the winds are right, they should make San Pedro tonight, spend tomorrow loading, and leave the next morning. If that is the case, we have plenty of time. If they don't take on a cargo, they might leave tomorrow."

"Could we make it?"

"Perhaps. If not, we could ride on to San Diego and hope to catch them there."

There was no question about what to do next. "Let's go."

He started for the door, but Carmen stopped him by grabbing his arm. "Wait. We can't just storm through

290

the house."

"Why not? I can take care of anyone who tries to stop us."

"Because they'll know we're going after her and they will follow us."

The woman actually made sense. "You're right. We don't need a lot of company on the road. You wait here while I check the corridor."

He opened the door silently and looked furtively out into the house. Voices were coming from a distant area but there was no sign of any activity nearby. An open door to the left disclosed a portion of the courtyard where Josefa was walking with Felipe's mother, but otherwise, the way looked clear.

Sebastian stepped across the corridor and softly pulled the door to the courtyard closed. Turning back, he found Carmen waiting behind him. He motioned her forward and they crept silently through the house.

At the door of the kitchen, they hesitated. The kitchen maid had been joined by the cook and a dusty *vaquero*. But there was no other way out. Exchanging a glance and squaring their shoulders, they walked through the area as though there was nothing odd in their presence, nodding to the others and making it out the back door with nothing more than a pair of startled looks to hinder them.

Outside, Sebastian caught sight of Tomas holding two horses behind the shed. "That way," he told Carmen. "We'll ride back into town, and from there . . ."

"You're going nowhere, soldier. When I get through with you, you won't be able to walk, much less ride."

Sebastian knew it was Don Felipe before he'd turned, but he turned anyway and stared back at the menacing glare. He'd known a confrontation between the two of them had been inevitable for a long time. He only wished it didn't have to be now, when time was of the essence.

"Go on," he told Carmen softly. "Wait for me with the horses."

"Felipe, not now," Carmen hissed at the man. "For God's sake, my uncle lies dying and Marina is missing . . ."

"We met once before," Felipe said, completely ignoring Carmen. "I was the better man on that day. I think you'll find things haven't changed."

"Go, Carmen," Sebastian said, pushing her with his hand, his eyes all the while holding those of the man who was challenging him. "I need you out of here."

She hesitated, said some uncomplimentary things about the male ego under her breath, and did as he'd ordered. The two men were left alone at the side of the yard, with no one to hinder them.

"I knew you were trouble from the first time I saw you, Spaniard. Your imperial ways are not wanted here in California. Perhaps at last I can convince you to go away and leave us alone."

Sebastian's smile was cold. "The trouble with a smalltown toothless lion like you, Felipe, is that he begins to believe in his own roar."

"I think you felt my teeth when we met before, Spaniard. I tried to teach you a lesson. I tried to convince you to stay away from my Marina. But you didn't listen, did you? And now you will have to pay again."

The flash of something glinting caught Sebastian's eye. Felipe had pulled out a knife. And Sebastian's own blade was with his pistol and spurs, where Tomas stood with the horses.

He looked back into Felipe's cold eyes. He could call

for his knife from Tomas, but he didn't want to do that. He would have to take his chances without it.

"Marina was never yours," he said quietly. "It was her choice to marry you or not."

"No longer, Spaniard," Felipe growled, brandishing the knife so that it flashed in the afternoon sun. "I know what happened last night. I could see it in her eyes when she came in from the dark. You had her, didn't you? You took her right out there in the dirt." He spat on the ground, a gesture of complete disgust and anger. "I wouldn't touch her now. She's no better than a common whore."

Sebastian's lunge was calculated, but Felipe's words gave him the excuse he needed. With one hand he hit Felipe in the mouth while with his other he grabbed the wrist that held the knife and the two of them went down, rolling in the dirt, fighting for control of the blade.

Felipe was strong, and he was angry, and the two elements together made him a formidable foe. Sebastian felt Felipe's forearm come across his windpipe and begin to exert pressure, and he began to doubt the wisdom of his tactic. He should have called for his own knife. If Felipe bested him this time . . .

He used all his might to force Felipe back and then he focused all his effort on the wrist, trying to break his hold on the knife, and so he wasn't prepared when Felipe's knee came up hard in his crotch, knocking his breath away. Somehow he hung on, despite the pain, despite the desperate need to recover from the blow. And when his sight had cleared again, he went after the wrist even harder, grunting with the effort.

Finally, Felipe's fingers wrenched open and the knife fell free. They both threw themselves at it, but Sebastian was just a fraction quicker, and when they came up, he had it in his hand.

One quick move and he had Felipe on his back, the knife at his throat.

"I think you know how things stand now, you bastard," he got out, breathing hard. "If you ever touch Marina again, or insult her, I'll come back and finish this job. But for now . . ." He pressed the knife along his neck, drawing a thin line of blood, six inches long. "That's a reminder."

Rising, he looked down at where Felipe lay panting. "Thanks for the knife," he said, pocketing it. "And thanks very much for the party. I've had a wonderful time."

Turning, he sauntered out of the yard, breaking into a run when he got around the corner, and leaping onto the horse without a wasted movement.

"Let's go," he snarled at Carmen. "We've wasted too much time as it is."

"But what about me?" Tomas asked, watching Carmen take the horse he had brought for himself to use.

"We're going to be gone for days, *mi amigo,*" Sebastian called back. "Tell the Comandante I will return as soon as I can."

And they were off with barely a wave at Tomas, leaving behind the Felipe *hacienda*. They circled the corral and went across a field to get back on the road, branching off toward the south before they reached San Feliz, and before long they were far from people and houses, off into the lonely hill country.

They were chasing after Marina, and Sebastian wasn't even sure what it all meant. He was lost in thought for about an hour, going over everything that had led him to this point, wishing he knew why, wishing he had a more clear picture of what he was going to do. But his emotions were still too raw. It was hopeless.

Now and then he roused himself enough to remember Carmen was with him, and when he did, he frowned. He didn't want her along. Still, she did know where she was going. And he really didn't. So it might be for the best.

But he hadn't had time to integrate everything yet, to understand what was going on. He only knew his time with Marina the night before had been a magic thing, something he never would have believed possible. He was connected to her in ways he hadn't realized. He felt about her as he had never felt about any other woman.

What did that mean? He didn't know. But he knew he couldn't let her run out of his life like this. And he especially knew he didn't want any other man to touch her. That was like a fire in his gut, something he didn't know how to extinguish. He would kill to keep someone else away from her. And that was why he was racing down the coast to catch her.

Chapter Twenty-two

They rode on and on through the hills. As the afternoon sun sank lower in the west, the shadows played on the green and golden slopes, creating a divine spectacle through which they rode, tiny moving specks within a grander scene.

The road began to climb and then dropped away before them, presenting a panoramic view of the blue-gray ocean and the mist-shrouded islands that surfaced in it. The air was much cooler now as they galloped along the sand beaches, scattering the vast flocks of gulls, catching sight of busy sea otters floating on their backs in clouds of kelp, breaking mollusk shells upon the rocks they carried on their chests. As the road turned back inland, the sun disappeared across the water and darkness threatened to overtake them.

"Only about one hour more," Carmen called out. "And we'll come to a *rancho* where we can spend the night."

"Spend the night? We don't have time for that."

"We might as well. We won't be able to make San Pedro in time for a dawn sailing anyway. It would be better to get some sleep and fresh horses."

Sebastian had to admit to the logic of this, so he didn't argue when she led him back from the main road to the *rancho* of the Hernandez family. Two Indian *vaqueros* took over their horses and the Hernandez family itself soon spilled out into the yard to welcome them.

"Carmen," they cried, falling all over her with obvious warmth and affection. "But where is Marina? Where is your uncle?"

The glances they cast Sebastian's way suggested worry. They seemed to be awaiting a good explanation of his presence.

Once inside, Carmen tried to explain. Marina had left just a day before on a trip to visit relatives in New England. Last night James had fallen ill. So Carmen and Sebastian were rushing to stop Marina and bring her back to her father's bedside.

They accepted her story with sympathy, but they still weren't sure about Sebastian. Every time they looked at that handsome face, their worried skepticism would surface. However, they really didn't have much choice but to take what Carmen said at face value.

After a simple but delicious meal, Carmen pleaded exhaustion and the two of them were allowed to retire. Carmen was given a bed in the room with their oldest girl, a pretty thirteen-year-old who had spent most of the evening staring openmouthed at Sebastian and was thrilled to share her room with such an exotic woman of the world as Carmen seemed to her to be.

Sebastian was provided a bed which was only wide enough for one grown man, but already contained two young boys, so his sleep was somewhat long in coming. Every time he shifted position, he opened his eyes to find a pair of dark ones gazing at him. The two boys were endlessly fascinated by every move he made.

Finally he could stand it no longer.

"What do you want?" he asked the oldest. "Why can't you sleep?"

"We want to know what it is like in battle," the young boy whispered shyly. "We want to see the sword you use to kill enemies."

"Did you ever run a man through?" asked the younger one, bouncing up. "Did you get medals for bravery? Did you ever hear a cannon go off?"

"That scar on your face, did you get it in a duel? Did you kill the other man?"

Sebastian sighed, but he had to laugh. For the next hour he found himself telling war stories, most of them apocryphal, until the young eyes began to droop and he could lie still again.

But even then he couldn't sleep. He spent an hour staring into the darkness, and in the quiet, he had to face up to what exactly he was doing here.

He was going to get Marina back. That much was sure. He would get her back, or die trying.

Did that mean he was in love with the woman? Perhaps. But if so, he would never admit it.

They left at daybreak on fresh horses supplied by their hosts. The territory was hidden by the low morning clouds, but as they made their way inland, the sun began to burn back the mists, exposing the rolling hills covered sparsely by scrubby oaks. By midmorning they passed near the San Fernando mis-

298

sion and entered the flatlands between the mountains. The high, round peaks to their left formed an imposing wall holding them toward the coast. Snow could still be seen on a distant summit.

As they approached the Pueblo de los Angeles, farms began to appear on all sides. The dusty green vineyards seemed to stretch for miles, intersected here and there by tumbling streams and smaller plots of newly planted corn and other vegetables.

It was past noon as they rode down the main Los Angeles street. Tired and hungry, they had agreed to stop at a house where Carmen was known, to have a quick meal and see about fresh horses. After that, a few more hours of riding would put them in San Pedro.

Carmen pointed out a bedraggled *cantina* and Sebastian stared at her.

"You can't go into such a place," he told her firmly.

She looked at him and laughed. "Not in by the front door, maybe, but in the back. Don't look so outraged, my fine friend. My cousin Rita is married to the owner. She's a goodhearted woman. She used to live in San Feliz. She served as a nurse to the three of us children as we were growing up. Come along. We don't have much choice in this town."

Sebastian still hesitated. He wanted to get on with it. "What story are you going to tell here?" he asked.

Carmen shrugged. "A good one. Rita likes fantasy. I'll think of something."

Rita was a large, blowzy woman whose bellowing laugh could be heard for some distance. She came out the back door of the crumbling building at a thundering run and swooped Carmen up into her arms.

"Baby, my precious, how I've longed to see you. And at such a time. Did you know? We were just talking about you. Oh, wait until . . ."

Suddenly she caught sight of Sebastian and her flow of words came to a shuddering stop.

"Who is this?" she demanded, eyes huge, finger pointing at him accusingly.

Carmen gave him a sly smile. "This, my dear cousin, is my lover. He has abducted me from my uncle's house and is carrying me off to South America. We are hurrying to San Pedro to make the boat. Will you help us?"

Rita's frown was ferocious. "Do you mean you want to go with him?"

Carmen sighed dramatically. "He's a bully and a brute, but what else do I have to live for? Besides, if I escape him now, he'll just capture me again." She moved closer and whispered, loudly, "He's mad for me, can't you see it?"

Rita didn't seem any more pleased to hear this story than Sebastian did. She glared at him as she held Carmen protectively in one massive arm.

"Pues, I will see if I can find a place to put you."

She disappeared into the building and Sebastian turned angrily to Carmen.

"Quite an amusing tale, Carmen, but hardly the sort of thing either one of us wants passed about, is it?"

Carmen shrugged. "I don't care what they say about me when I'm gone," she said, then she frowned thoughtfully. "Actually, I thought it would amuse her more than it did. She always used to like romantic intrigues. Oh well, as long as she feeds us."

Rita returned, throwing Sebastian dark looks, and motioned for them to enter. She led them to a small, dark room which contained one table and three chairs. Without another word, she left them.

Carmen frowned. "I don't understand why my old nurse is acting so cold," she mused. "I don't like this, Sebastian. Maybe we ought to think about going somewhere else."

He gestured impatiently. "We don't have time to go somewhere else. And I don't need food. Just ask her for the horses and let's get out of here."

Carmen sighed and rose, walking over to a shelf where a pitcher of water stood balancing precariously. Dipping her handkerchief in the water, she began to refresh her face.

Meanwhile, Sebastian began to pace.

"Calm down," Carmen recommended. "If they haven't sailed, you'll be with her in a few hours."

He stopped and looked at her levelly. "And what will you do once we've found her? Surely you can't go back."

Carmen smiled. "Exactly. I'll never go back, with any luck at all. I plan to take Marina's place with the captain."

"What? Just like that? How do you know he'll take you?"

"He'll have to. Perhaps not as a wife, as I'm sure he means to take Marina, but he'll take me."

Sebastian looked thunderstruck. "A wife. You think he means to marry her?"

"Of course, you fool. What did you think? Surely

you know the good captain well enough to realize he wouldn't do anything to dishonor her. He's not like you," she said glaring at him, then added softly, "or me."

Sebastian swore and turned angrily from her. "Why are we wasting time in this dirty place? They could be before a priest at this very moment. Come on, forget about the food. Let's go."

Carmen sighed. "All right. I'll ask Rita to loan us some horses and we'll be off. Here, get the back of my neck with this wet cloth first, then I'll go find her."

Sebastian took the handkerchief impatiently and bent over her to reach her neck, wiping quickly, hardly thinking about what he was doing. He wanted to get to Marina. Ten more seconds of this and he would leave without Carmen.

But before he could say that threat aloud, a sudden voice at his back froze his movement.

"Get your hands off her and turn around slowly. I want to see your face before I kill you."

Sebastian swore softly. This was all he needed, another man itching for a fight. But the voice wasn't familiar. Maybe once he turned and identified himself the challenger would back off.

Sebastian turned slowly, every muscle tense. A young man stood in the doorway, a pistol aimed straight at Sebastian's heart.

Carmen turned at the same time, staring, white as a ghost. "Oh, no, it can't be," Carmen breathed, swaying.

"Put your gun down, *Señor*," Sebastian suggested calmly. "We have no quarrel."

The young man was tall and muscular, with tawny skin and clear, blue eyes. His brown hair fell over his forehead in a way that emphasized his boyish good looks, but there was a strength there also, and more than enough bravado to back up his impulses. Sebastian had never seen him before, but the young man seemed to have a grudge. There was abject hatred in his eyes.

"I never quarrel with villainous bastards," he spit out. "I just kill them wherever I find them." He cocked the pistol. "Prepare to die."

"Mother of God," Carmen sighed, crumbling as though there were no more strength left to hold her upright.

Sebastian didn't look at her. His entire attention was focused entirely on the young man, and on just how far he would have to move his hand to find the butt of his own gun. Did he have enough time?

Marina stared vacantly at the tiny whitecaps as they lapped against the side of the ship. Her mind was dull, devoid of all thought or emotion. She was living on a plane of pure existence, waiting for the tide and the winds that would speed them on their way out of the harbor and into the Pacific, away from her homeland forever.

"Marina, how are you feeling?"

She looked up to see Alex hovering over her worriedly.

"I'm just fine, Alex," she managed to get out, trying to smile. "Just fine."

He patted her shoulder awkwardly and went on

about his duties, and she sighed, slumping against the railing. It was unfair to him to be so morose, so distant, but the mood hung on her like a sticky fog and she was powerless to shake it off. Whenever the ship gave an especially heavy lurch, her gaze shot to the shore, clinging to the sand, the hills, the distant mountains, as though she couldn't drink it all in. Soon, they would all be out of sight. Would she ever see them again?

They were planning to set sail that afternoon rather than wait for the next morning. Though Alex claimed it was a business decision, as there was no further need of any contact with the California shore with the holds full and all hands aboard, they both knew he had decided to leave early mainly to avoid possible pursuit. For this reason they would also pass San Diego without a pause. Quietly and thoughtfully, the captain was attempting to make this break as painless for Marina as he could.

He had done all he could for her ever since they had left the Diaz *rancho*. She was grateful for his care, but she felt a bit resentful nonetheless. The easier he made things for her, the less she did for herself and the more dependent she became on him. She knew what was happening but she didn't seem to be able to gather the will to resist.

They had ridden through the night into San Feliz from the *rancho* and had stopped by the Crafts house, where she had gathered a few clothes and other belongings to take along. She had been unable to compose her thoughts sufficiently to leave a message for her family, so they had gone on without a word.

Once aboard the *Prospect,* Captain Alex had insisted she take the bed in his cabin. Where he was sleeping, she wasn't sure. She had fallen asleep immediately, exhausted by the day and her ride, but she had awakened when the movement of the ship had told her that the anchor had been weighed and San Feliz was sinking into the distance. She had lain for hours, unable to rise to say good-bye to her old life, unable to clearly think about what she was doing and where she was going. Finally, she had dressed and gone out on deck to greet the new day, the first day of her new existence.

The day had seemed to stretch into forever. Were they all going to be endless like this? Was she sinking into a giant slough of eternal nothingness? She felt sure that her whole life would be this way.

She knew she was going to have to get hold of herself and function as a woman was supposed to eventually, if only for the captain's sake. But deep inside a void would remain, a charred black hole where once her heart had been. She had no hope of ever losing that.

They had reached San Pedro late in the evening and now were preparing to set sail once more. Looking up, she realized that the captain was beside her again, leaning against the railing and looking at her anxiously.

She tried to read his eyes. "Is there something wrong? Are you regretting all this?" she asked him.

"Oh, no," he answered quickly, though his eyes weren't entirely convincing. "But I am concerned about something." He shuffled uneasily, staring at the whitecaps on the sea.

"Yes?" she coaxed. "Tell me what it is."

He turned to look at her, set himself, and then let it all out in a rush.

"If we are going to do it, I think we had better go ahead and do it. We can't really . . . well, it just isn't right, you sleeping aboard and all, unless we do. You know how people talk, and I don't ever want them to say those things about you. So, I'm sending a man ashore to get a preacher out here. I just wanted to let you know." He looked about to run away.

"Now?" Marina asked, aghast. "You want to get married now?"

A feeling of panic was rising in her. Marrying Alex had been only a vague part of this scheme, and when it came right down to it, she wasn't sure it was such a good idea after all.

"But I thought we would wait until . . . until Boston. If we find Jonathan, he could be with us. It would mean so much more to me."

Alex looked very worried. "Well, I'd like that too, but I don't see how we can wait that long. And if we're going to do it anyway, why not just go ahead and get it over with? That way, there won't be so much talk and fault finding afterward."

She knew he was right, but still she desperately searched her mind for an excuse to postpone the ceremony.

"But a priest won't come out here to do it, surely."

"I know one who will." He hesitated. "I'm sorry that this can't be more traditional, with flower girls and decorated horses and all that . . ."

"My dear Captain." She stopped him with a smile.

Despite her present reservations, she owed him so much. "That is certainly my fault, not yours. Please, think nothing of it." She hesitated. Marrying Alex seemed so strange. But what else could she do? She had come with him for her father's sake. She would do anything to help her father. If marrying a stable man would help, so be it. She was determined to do that, and to find Jonathan. That was what she had come for. And Alex was probably right. She couldn't travel with him unless they did marry.

She sighed. "Send for your priest. As you say, we might as well go ahead and get it over with."

He shuffled uneasily. "Well, that's what I thought. All right. Listen, I think it would be a good idea for you to write your family now and explain it all. Then the priest can see that your letter is delivered. Don't you agree?"

She nodded miserably. Yes, she knew she had to do it. She had known for hours that she should have done it. But how would she begin? How would she explain that it was partly for them that she was doing all this? Still, she had to. Putting her father's mind at ease was the whole point, and if he didn't know about what she was doing, the point was lost.

As Alex went to send for the priest, Marina went down to the cabin and sat herself down at the mahogany desk. She took out paper, pen, and ink and stared glumly into space.

Self-pity washed over her. Just a few weeks before, she'd been a happy, carefree California girl, ready and eager to taste life's fruits. Now she seemed to have bitten off more than she could chew and her whole life had been poisoned as a result. Soon she would be married to Alex Brandene. She glanced at the bed where she'd spent the last night. Tonight she would lie there by his side.

By his side. She would have to do with him what she had done by the stream with Sebastian. But there was a big difference here. She loved Sebastian. The thought of doing that with Alex made her skin crawl.

Horror rose in her throat until she thought she would vomit. Rising, she began to pace. No, no, every part of her rebelled at what she was about to do. Alex was a good man who deserved a good wife, but how could she be that wife? It wasn't fair to either one of them.

She thought of Sebastian again, of his intense eyes, the way he had looked as his body lowered over hers, and she felt again his hands on her skin, his mouth hot against hers, his hard, virile body.

The memory made her gasp, her stomach contracting. She remembered how she had felt with him, how her soul had blossomed under his touch, how her body had cried out to have him. That was the way one felt when one was in love. That was the way she should feel toward her husband. And she knew she would never feel like that with Alex.

How could she lie beside him and pretend, when all the while she knew she would be longing for Sebastian? How could she live, knowing she would never feel Sebastian's presence envelop hers again?

Her hands rose and covered her face and she sobbed as though her heart were broken.

Sebastian's mouth went dry as he recognized the passion in the young man's eyes. This was serious. A man his age in this kind of incomprehensible rage was liable to do things he'd later regret. Sebastian knew that from personal experience.

There was no time to talk him out of it. He'd glanced down at where Carmen had fallen to the floor, and his mouth had hardened. When he looked back, his hatred for Sebastian was stronger than ever.

"What have you done to her?" he snarled.

"To Carmen?" Sebastian glanced down at where she was swooning. "Nothing." He looked back up. "Who are you and what business is it of yours, anyway?"

"I'm the only man who has a right to touch Carmen, bastard. It's time for you to die for your sins."

His finger began to squeeze down on the trigger.

Sebastian didn't stop to think. His instincts were keen for survival. There would be no firing into the air this time. Bobbing quickly to the right, he fumbled for his own firearm and jerked it into place, firing only a split second after the report from the young man's gun spit through the air. But in that second he felt the ball slice through his shoulder, and he groaned as he staggered back.

He'd been hit. Leaning against a chair, he reached around to examine the wound. It was in the other shoulder this time, and it burned like fire, but all in all it wasn't too bad. The ball had merely cut through the fleshy upper arm and gone on. The bleeding would stop once he'd tied it up.

Catching his breath, he looked down at where the young man lay on the ground. He'd hit him, maybe through the heart. The way he had crumpled, it was hard to tell, but there definitely was blood.

The curious thing was, Carmen had run to the stranger, crying and screaming out something unfathomable, and now she was cradling his head in her lap and sobbing.

Sebastian blinked, just a little groggy from shock. Rita was back, and she was screaming also, and shouting out things about jail cells and firing squads.

He shook his head to clear it. He didn't have time for this. He had to get to Marina. Not giving Carmen another glance, he stepped around her and the body of the young man and went down the back steps, hurrying toward where the horses were tied. The horse he'd ridden all day was tired, but he would have to go another few miles. There was no choice.

Marina stared hard at the small boat as it began the long pull from the shore. Yes, she was sure of it, there was a priest aboard. He was on his way out to marry her, marry her to Captain Alex Brandene in a ceremony at sea.

Her mind reeled and she put her hand to her head. She couldn't do it. Even for the sake of her own honor, even for the sake of her family, she couldn't do it. Even to contemplate such a thing now seemed ugly and sinful. It was contrary to every ideal, every moral, every conviction she held. To pledge herself, her life, and her love, before God, to this man, would be a sacrilege. She couldn't do it.

Where had her mind been? Totally blown to tatters by the experiences of the other night, that was certain. Being betrothed to Felipe, then making love with Sebastian and realizing she was in love with him, then finding that her father was dying, all at once, had been too much for her brain to take in.

She'd gone temporarily mad. That was it. That must have been what had made her think she had to run off with Alex.

She couldn't stop her father from dying, but she could help allay his fears, either by marrying Felipe, an option that was destroyed when Felipe backed out, or marrying someone else her father trusted. That someone was Alex.

But there were other ways to help her father, surely. Finding Jonathan would be one. That had been her main goal in leaving with Alex. She wanted to get to the Caribbean, where she could search for her brother. But if she was married to Alex, he would never let her do that. What had she been thinking of?

No; it was settled, then. She couldn't marry Alex.

She began to run along the deck, stumbling clumsily. She had to find Alex and explain, beg his forgiveness. What she would do then, she didn't know. She knew only that she couldn't go through with this wedding.

Alex came around a corner and caught hold of her as she almost went spinning past.

"Marina, what is it?"

"Oh, Alex." She clung to his coat sleeve. "I'm so sorry. I've been such a fool. This is all so unfair to you, but to go ahead would be even more unfair."

A troubled frown twisted his heavy brow and he spoke a bit stiffly. "There isn't much point in going

311

on this way, Marina. We have to do what we have to do."

She tried to catch her breath. "No, Alex—listen. It really isn't necessary for us to marry." Her huge eyes were earnest. "If you could just allow me to ride with you until we get to the Caribbean. What I really *must* do is look for Jonathan. Perhaps you know of an island family I could stay with . . ."

"Marina, this is out of the question. We're getting married." His face had a stubborn look she'd never seen him use before.

"No, really, Alex." If only he would listen, he would understand how impossible this was. "We can't. It isn't right. I don't love you and you don't really love me."

His brow furled as he looked at her. "Marina, calm yourself. People marry every day without love. It's really much better that way. No emotions involved."

She was beginning to worry about this. He refused to listen to reason. "But Alex, emotions *are* involved. How could they not be?" She looked at him anxiously. Surely he understood. "I don't love you, Alex, I could never love you, because . . . because I love somebody else."

Alex sighed with annoyance. "So now you have changed your mind again and want to marry Felipe. I have to warn you, my dear, Felipe being the sort of man he is, he's not going to marry you after you've gone and run off with me. His pride won't let him. Besides, he'd figure you were dishonored by now, and he could never . . ."

"No, Alex. It's not Felipe I love." She hesitated.

312

She couldn't tell him about Sebastian. There was really no point to it. Sebastian was the one man she could never have.

But he wasn't listening to any more of this anyway. Taking her by the shoulders, he gave her a firm shake that startled her.

"That's enough, Marina. You eloped with me. You've spent the night on my ship. We have to marry. We have no choice. The priest is here. Let's have no more of these histrionics."

He strode off to welcome the rowboat and Marina slumped against the rail, surprised at his vehemence. Alex was a gentle, considerate man, but he also had some firm ideas about how things should be, and he obviously wasn't prepared to abandon them easily. What on earth had she let herself in for? He was making it very clear that he wasn't about to let her go. There didn't seem to be an inch of give to him.

That didn't mean things were hopeless, of course. There was always the priest. If she explained to him how she felt, surely he would refuse to go on with the wedding. Yes, that was what she would do. She sighed and rubbed her shoulders where he had shaken her, frowning slightly. Alex at sea was a very different man from Alex as a guest in her house.

She looked across the water. A moist gray fog was rolling in off the sea, a cloud as bleak as her emotions. What a fitting atmosphere for this ill-fated day.

Chapter Twenty-three

Tears were streaming down Carmen's face as she worked frantically to find the wound made by Sebastian's shot.

"There's too much blood. I can't tell if the ball went into his heart," she said, her voice high with restrained tension. "His heart is still beating. At least, I think . . ."

"Is he breathing? Go down near his mouth. Is he breathing? Oh, Carmen, I could slit my own wrists for telling him you were here with a lover. I didn't know he would . . ."

"Never mind that now," Carmen ordered. "Just get that doctor here." She looked down at the pale, handsome face and a sob shook her. "Oh, Jonathan—to have you so near, and to lose you again!"

Rita ran down the stairs to look out for the doctor and Carmen raised the man's hand to her lips and kissed it tenderly.

"Jonathan, Jonathan," she said softly, new tears quivering in her eyes. "What were you doing?"

"The question is," he said through drawn lips, though his eyes still seemed to be closed, "my beloved cousin who promised to wait for me if it took forever—the question is, what were you doing?"

"Jonathan!" She pounced on him. "You spoke!

Are you really alive? Are you going to be all right?"

"I'm really alive," he said, opening his eyes and wincing as she hugged him. "It's only a little pain."

"I'm going to bind up your wound to stop the bleeding, and Rita has gone for a doctor. Lie still. Don't move. Oh, Jonathan, you're alive!"

"Alive," he muttered, grimacing. "But hardly well, I'm afraid. He did get me, the son of a bitch." He frowned. "But not in the chest, *querida*. Look a little lower and I think you'll find the source of all this blood."

Sure enough, the ball had gone into his thigh. Carmen worked quickly, tearing away the cloth to get to the wound.

"Don't talk." She touched his cheek. "Oh, Jonathan, how I love you."

He still lay on the floor as he gazed at her coolly, completely disregarding her orders. "But my question stands, *querida*. Who was that man? Rita said he had kidnapped you."

"Oh." Carmen closed her eyes and sighed. "That was my fault. I told her that tale as a joke. He's not interested in me at all. He's after Marina."

His eyebrow lifted. "Come on, Carmen. You can do better than that. If he wants Marina, why did he look so comfortable with his arms around you?"

She shook her head. "No, Jonathan, it wasn't like that. I asked him to cool my neck with a damp cloth, and he was doing it — impatiently, I might add. Without a lot of interest in how I was enjoying it."

He almost smiled. "I will still have to kill him

315

for having touched you." His arm shot out and his hand closed on hers. "And how many others, Carmen? How many will I have to kill?"

She stared back into his deep eyes for a long moment, then threw back her head and laughed. "Two years in New England and you're still a rough Californio *vaquero* at heart, aren't you?" she said. "I'll tell you this, *querido*. I have danced with half the men in San Feliz, not to mention a few in Santa Barbara. I have even kissed a few. And I have certainly contemplated running away with one or two, just to get out of this provincial place and set myself free into the great big world." She shrugged, sighing.

"I couldn't stand it, Jonathan. The loneliness, the boredom, the restlessness. I nearly went mad trying to be good for your sake and for the sake of your family."

She closed her eyes for a moment, steadying herself. "But Jonathan, I'm not good. I'm not steadfast. I'm selfish and headstrong and impulsive. I can't be what you want me to be. I can only be what I am." Her eyes darkened as she stared into his. "But I have never loved another man like I love you. And I never will."

He stared back for a moment, searching the hidden places in her eyes, and finally he tugged on her arm, pulling her down to lean against him, kissing her mouth with his own as though he was starving for the taste of her. It was enough.

Alex returned with the priest, a tall, gray-haired

man with whom he seemed to be close.

"Father Francisco, this is Marina Crafts, my wife-to-be as soon as you say the right words."

The *padre* smiled at her benignly and took her hands in his.

"Come, my dear, let us have a time of prayer and preparation for this, one of the most important steps in your life. Captain? Where may the *señorita* and I go to be alone?"

Alex showed them down to his cabin, and soon Marina and the priest were left alone. Before she had a chance to explain her problem, Father Francisco motioned her to her knees and began a long series of prayers which he said standing above her. Marina closed her eyes and relaxed, letting the familiar Latin phrases wash over her, comforting and soothing her soul. Soon she would confess everything to him and he would help her escape this nightmare.

When the prayers ended, the priest put out his hand and helped her to her feet.

"And now, my child, have you any problems with which I might help you?"

She nodded, smiling at him gratefully. "Yes, Father. A horrible problem. I can't marry the captain at all."

"What?" He stared at her, plainly surprised.

"Yes. It's impossible. I don't love him and I don't want to marry him. Please, help me get away. Can you take me back to shore with you?" She gazed at him hopefully.

He frowned, puzzled. "But has he brought you here against your will? What did he do to you?"

"Oh, no, it was nothing like that. Actually, it was all my fault. I thought I could go through with it. As you know, Captain Alex is all that is good and kind. He offered to marry me to help me escape a bad situation. Because I respect him and have a friendly affection for him, I agreed. But now that it comes down to it, I realize it is a terrible mistake. I don't love him. I love someone else. It wouldn't be right to marry him, feeling as I do."

She got it all out in a rush and relaxed. There, it was over. He knew now, and he would take care of it. Anticipating help, she smiled at him.

He was shaking his head, but he was smiling too. "Come, come my dear," he said. "Everyone has these little doubts, especially young girls such as yourself. Alex is a good man. I'm sure he knows what's best for you."

Marina stared at the man. Hadn't he heard her? "No, you see, I don't love him. How can I marry him when I love another?"

He sighed and patted her shoulder. "You're so young, dear, how could you possibly understand? These feelings are very shallow and short-lived, and usually the worst basis on which to found a marriage. Union with a fine, strong man like Captain Brandene can do you nothing but good, as long as you are a modest, dutiful wife to him. These other feelings you have for some romantic image of your girlhood, well, someday you'll laugh and be amazed that you could have ever been so foolish."

She wanted to yell and stamp her foot as she might have as a little girl. Why didn't anybody listen?

"You don't understand," she said evenly, holding back her temper as best she could. "I can't do it. It's impossible. I won't marry him."

He was beginning to lose patience. "As I understand the situation, it is impossible that you do anything else. You are only lucky that the captain is the virtuous sort of man he is. You have stayed overnight on his boat. No decent young man would marry you now. You have no choice. Now please, kneel again. We shall ask forgiveness for your attitude and pray that you may acquire a bit of appreciation and a little peace of mind."

Jonathan was sitting up in a chair now, with Carmen and Rita fussing about him. The doctor had come, dug out the ball, and pronounced him wounded but reparable. The bandages had been placed about his leg, and it would be some time before he would be able to run or even ride with any strength, but he felt fit and well enough again.

"But you were unconscious for so long," Carmen insisted. "I'm sure the wound is worse than the doctor thinks it is."

"The only reason I was out is that I hit my head when I fell back," Jonathan retorted. "Here, feel the lump."

She felt the lump and gave little cries of sympathy. She was ready to touch any part of him, look at every inch of him, devour him before the world, she was so happy to have him back.

"We thought you were dead," she told him over and over. "When my uncle sees you, I know he will revive immediately."

Jonathan had been told about James's seizure and he was eager to hurry home to see his father. But he still didn't understand what was going on with Marina.

"She was supposed to marry Don Felipe," Carmen told him.

He nodded. "A good match."

"Not in her opinion. At the last moment, she decided not to marry him."

"Why not? He's a great fellow."

Carmen's eyebrow arched. "Yes, but not the right fellow."

He nodded wisely. "Ah, she's in love with another. Who?"

Carmen hesitated, then gave him a quick smile. "A new lieutenant at the Presidio. Sebastian de la Cruz. The man . . . the man who shot you this afternoon."

"That man?" His face darkened dangerously. "What does she want with a scoundrel like that?"

"She's in love, Jonathan. You know very well that logic flies out the window when one is in love."

"Well, she had better fall out of love quickly," he said coldly. "Because I'm going to kill him."

"Never mind that. He's on his way to try to catch her before Alex marries her . . ."

Jonathan looked thunderstruck. "The captain? Why would Marina be marrying Alex?"

She frowned, trying to think of a way to explain it to him quickly, then shook her head. "It's a long story. She thinks your father will be happier if she's married, and now Felipe won't have her, and Alex offered . . . so she ran away with him."

It was all going too fast for Jonathan. "Wait a minute—why won't Felipe have her?"

"Because of Sebastian. Don't you see?"

His eyes narrowed shrewdly. He supposed he did. But he didn't quite believe it. "All right. And this Sebastian is trying to stop her from marrying Alex. Am I right?"

"Yes."

"Does the blackguard mean to marry her himself?"

Carmen bit her lip. "Not necessarily."

"That's just as I thought." He scowled. "Maybe killing's too good for him." He looked up. "But tell me." His eyes hardened again. "Why are you along? Can't the man find his own way to the sea?"

She hesitated, and suddenly she couldn't meet his gaze. "I tried to explain to you. I just couldn't stand it any longer. I had to get away. I came along with Sebastian because I . . . I was going to take Marina's place."

"What? And marry Alex?" Jonathan threw back his head and gave a laugh much too hearty for a man who had just been shot. "What a picture that would make."

"No, you fool." She pretended to frown at him. "I would be able to handle Alex. Besides, he doesn't want me. But I could have gotten to South America, or to Europe, or even to Boston. Anywhere but here."

He stared at her, his eyes deep as mountain

lakes. "Anywhere but here, waiting for me," he murmured.

She shook her head, looking miserable. "I've already tried to explain that."

Reaching out, he took her hand. "Never mind; I understand. It's dangerous to leave you alone. I guess I won't be making that mistake again."

Carmen looked up at him, tears quivering in her eyes once more. "Oh Jonathan, I love you so," she said, and then she was in the curve of his arm, her lips parted for his and for the moment, everything was going to be all right.

The clammy fog encircled the ship now, cutting it off from the shore. Marina felt it only a part of the conspiracy to cut her off from reality, from any hope of assistance. As she stared out the small porthole in the captain's cabin, she looked into a vast, gray nothingness. There was no help for someone like her, nor did she feel she really deserved any.

She had put herself in this position of her own free will. It was her responsibility to extricate herself.

Suddenly the realization caused her hope to soar. Of course. There was no need to wait and beg and plead. It was up to her to take hold of her destiny, to make a move, to take a chance.

The awareness was tremendously freeing. Her soul felt light again and her mind seemed suddenly released to evaluate and explore.

What could she do? Father Francisco had left

her here to quiet her mind in preparation for the ceremony. It wouldn't be long before they would be back to get her. She would have to move quickly.

She must get away from the ship. Swimming for shore was out of the question, she knew she would never make it. The rowboat the priest had brought in was still tied in the water, waiting to take him back. It was that or nothing.

She opened the door and peered out. A sailor brushed past, but then nothing. No one was in sight. Slipping out, in a moment she was at the ship's rail, then over and climbing down as agilely as a seasoned sailor. The boat tipped crazily as she sank into it, but she kept her balance and concentrated on untying the rope that held it to its mother ship. That proved to be a more difficult job, but with determination she managed it. Then she was drifting and she waited to get a bit away from the ship before dipping her noisy oars into the water.

In moments the misty gray world had sucked her in. She couldn't see the ship any more. She couldn't see land. She couldn't really hear anything but the water gently lapping against the sides of her tiny craft. She was all alone—and suddenly terrified.

As a child, she had often gone rowing with Carmen and Jonathan, and though that had been years ago, she felt sure she could perform well enough with a pair of oars to get herself to the beach. If only she knew where the beach was! With no reference point, how was she to know which way to aim the boat?

Her panic started to grow. She had already lost direction and couldn't even tell which way she had come from. She might row and row and end up in the deep ocean. What was to stop it from happening?

Holding her breath, she made herself focus for a moment, closing her eyes and quieting herself. And as she sat, she became aware of a steady, repetitive sound off through the fog.

The surf! Of course. All she had to do was follow the sound of the breakers on the beach. What could be more simple?

Actually, it turned out to be a bit harder than she had at first supposed, for the heavy blanket of fog tended to obscure the accuracy of her judgment, causing the noise to seem to echo from side to side. But she felt she was making progress. Three or four pulls with the oars and she stopped to judge her direction. This process was repeated over and over again, until suddenly a pause revealed a new sound upon the sea.

She stopped, frozen, listening carefully. It was the other boat, of course, the second boat that was kept upon the *Prospect* deck. They were coming after her.

Her first impulse was to pull furiously on the oars and try to outrun them, but that was absurd. She could never beat men used to this work. Her best chance was to keep still and hope they would miss her in the fog.

She sat in the boat without moving, trying to still her hammering heart, her chattering teeth, wishing she could somehow become momentarily invisible. They were almost on top of her, so near she could hear their voices over the water. She held her breath and prayed, but the voices came closer. Alex's voice was the first she could understand.

". . . find her way in this fog? If anything happens to that girl, I'll never forgive myself."

"Now, now, Captain, we'll find her. Young girls often take these fancies into their heads. I'm sure when we come upon her she will be wholly repentant . . ."

And there it was. They had a lantern on board and she could see the glow of it through the grayness. They were so near, she could almost reach out and touch them. For one wild moment, she stared into the water. Should she try to swim? Could she make it? Would she drown? But what if she did? Better the icy water than Alex Brandene's bed.

Sebastian sat wearily aback his horse. He was in San Pedro, but with the weather in this condition, the journey seemed hardly worth the effort. How was he going to find her in this fog?

He'd run into the first wisps of it a few miles out, and by the time he had come to what should have been sight of the ocean, the fog was so thick he could hardly make out his horse's head before him. Darkness would fall soon. And then it would be truly hopeless.

He swung down off his horse and tied him outside a small cantina, the only sign of life he had found along the waterfront. There were voices inside, and laughter. At least he could make inquiries.

The inside of the building was crudely furnished with primitive tables and chairs. All of five customers were seated about the room, each one obviously a man of the sea. Sebastian looked the room over, then stepped up to the bar to talk to the bar keep.

The man was a grizzled fellow with bleary eyes, and when he heard that Sebastian wanted to hire a boat out to the Prospect, he laughed.

"You won't get anyone to take you out now," he said. "Pea soup, matey — didn't you notice?"

"Is she still here?" he asked, ignoring the jibe.

"The *Prospect?* Aye, she's here. From what they say, she sails tomorrow at dawn. Maybe the fog will lift by then." He shrugged and grinned. "Maybe not."

A nearby sailor, a tough looking Peruvian with a strange smashed-in face, spoke up. "It's too dangerous, *amigo*. You could pass the ship and just keep going out to sea. Wait until it lifts."

Sebastian moved impatiently. "I can't wait. I have important business aboard the *Prospect*."

Another sailor, a young, heavy-set Hawaiian, laughed aloud. "Too much important business today on that ship, eh? First the wedding . . ."

Sebastian spun on him. "What wedding? What happened?"

The man looked up apprehensively, swallowing his laughter at Sebastian's deadly tone. "I just heard some things, that's all."

Sebastian restrained himself and nodded as

326

calmly as he could. "Go ahead. Tell me what you heard."

The Hawaiian shrugged and his natural good humor came back slowly. "Early today, a boat was sent in from the ship to fetch a priest. Word was the captain and his lady were so hot to tie the knot, they couldn't wait any longer. It'll be long over by now." He chuckled, not noticing that Sebastian's eyes had gone hard and cold as flint. "The honeymoon should be in full swing. Lucky man, eh?"

Sebastian had to hold back the impulse to go for the man's throat. "I have to get out to that ship," he said harshly. "If no one will take me, at least give me a boat. I'll take myself."

He looked around at the others, who muttered among themselves, shaking their heads.

"No one is going to risk giving you a boat, *amigo*," the Peruvian advised. "They know they would never see it again."

"Then sell me a boat. Anyone. Any sort of boat. As long as it can make it out to the *Prospect*."

Sebastian looked around the room and knew he still had no takers. That settled it. He would have to steal a boat. Without another word, he stormed out of the cantina, untied his horse and mounted, riding toward the beach.

Marina and Alex—married. The shock still stung like fire, and he felt slightly sick to his stomach. But it didn't really matter. He was taking her anyway.

Chapter Twenty-four

Marina closed her eyes. It was over. They'd caught her. And she didn't quite have the nerve to jump into the water and swim for it. She sat very still, waiting for Alex to shout out, waiting to feel their hands on her, dragging her out of this boat and into theirs.

But it didn't happen. The voices began to sound further away. Opening her eyes, she realized the lantern light was fading. Soon all she could hear was the splashing of their oars.

They hadn't seen her. She let out a long sigh of relief. At least they hadn't caught her yet. Starting slowly and as quietly as she could, she began to row again, pausing often to judge her direction and listen for the other boat.

The swells began to form near her and she knew she was close to shore. A large swell picked up her boat and carried her in, thrilling her as it broke into a white, foamy wave all around her. The boat crunched into the sand and she was up and out of it, wetting her shoes and a good six inches of her hem, and running up the beach, running away as fast as she could from anywhere Alex might think to look for her.

A structure loomed in the mist ahead of her. A storage shed, she decided quickly. Just the sort of place Alex would think she might be hiding. She had better avoid it at all costs.

Veering off to the right, she ran quickly up a path of pebbles leading, she hoped, to the main road. If she could just find someplace to hide away for the night, in the morning she would walk to el Pueblo de los Angeles and find the *cantina* where her old nurse, Rita, now lived. Then she would think about what she would do next.

Her wet skirt slapped against her ankles and suddenly she realized she was tired enough to drop. And hungry. How long had it been since she'd eaten? It seemed like days.

What a nightmare. The problem was, she hadn't stopped to think things through. Too many bad decisions had been made too quickly. She needed some peace and quiet and time to think her life over.

There never seemed to be enough time for that lately. Ever since Sebastian de la Cruz had come sailing into their town, events had come thick and fast until her life seemed to be spinning by like a top, too fast for her to see any details clearly. Only one thing stood out. Only one thing stood like a rock to cling to. She loved Sebastian. She yearned for him.

Then why was she running away from him? She had to remind herself of a few home truths. Things like—he doesn't love you, you fool. For all his claims, everyone knows he is a ladies' man who will never be true to one woman. He hates California. He is just waiting to get back to Spain. For all you know, he may be married there. Or in Mexico City.

But none of those things could dampen her love for him. They might mean she had no future to look forward to, but they didn't mean she loved him any less. To her surprise, love seemed to be something she had no control over at all. It just was.

She was breathing like an overworked horse but she couldn't stop running. The prospect of Alex finding her was driving her on. She would do anything to keep from falling into his hands again — *anything*.

There were lights ahead. She slowed, gazing intently through the mist. It was a small *cantina* and there were men coming out of it. Should she go in and ask for help? No; much too risky. For all she knew, Alex might be in there himself. She would have to go on.

The pebble path had given way to a hard dirt track. She ran along the side of it, listening for horses from behind, ready to dash into the brush along the side of the road if anyone came.

She was so tired. She was going to have to stop to rest. Slowing she walked off the track and tried to see what manner of field she was in. Sand dunes surrounded her. The sand was cold, but it was soft. Finding a tuft of beach grass, she sat down behind it, and then lay down her head, just for a moment. She had to rest.

She didn't mean to fall asleep, but she must have, for when she next opened her eyes, the fog had thinned, but darkness had fallen, and a lantern was coming toward her through the dunes. And then voices . . . and shouts.

She leapt up, but it was too late. Lanterns were coming from all around. There was no place left to run. She felt like a trapped animal, her heart in her throat.

330

"Marina!"

Alex was running toward her. She had to get away. She whirled, looking desperately for an escape. The road. Stumbling in the sand, she dashed toward it, but her feet had barely reached hard ground again when she was surrounded and Alex had almost caught her.

"Marina, my dear, thank God you're all right."

They were all around her, their eyes bright and beady in the lantern light, like ferrets, like weasels. She looked from one pair to another, a scream starting up her throat.

"Marina."

His hands were coming toward her. It was all over. She began to shake.

And then a sound seemed to stop everyone in his tracks. Hoofbeats. A horseman was coming, riding fast.

Shouts again. Men were scrambling out of the way. Alex reached for her, but she turned out of his grasp. She would rather be trampled by horses than go with him.

The hoofbeats were so loud they blotted out the shouts of the men, and then there was a whirl of light, a swirl of red, and she felt herself being lifted.

"Hold on, *querida*. I have you now."

She blinked, dazed, and he thrust her before him in the saddle. She reached out, clinging to him, and they were off, leaving the shouts behind, racing through the tattered shreds of mist. They rode hard, and she closed her eyes, holding onto his warmth. The voice had been Sebastian's, but she wouldn't have been surprised to find it was the devil who had snatched her from the crowd.

331

On and on they rode, and she melted against him, floating in a dream, not letting herself think. She only wanted to feel.

When at last he let the horse slow to a walk, she still clung to him. She didn't want to wake up from the dream.

"*Querida,* look at me," he said at last, gently pulling her back so that she could look into his face.

She stared up, her lips tilted in a faint smile. "Is it really you?" she whispered.

He looked at her face as though he meant to devour her features. "Thank God I found you," he breathed at last. "Marina, don't ever run from me like that again."

She shook her head. "I wasn't running from you. Not from you."

He kissed her then, soft and gentle, his mouth hot on hers, his hands caressing her face. She returned his kiss as though she'd found something she'd been dreaming of for a long, long time and meant to savor it.

Here, in his arms, she knew she'd done the right thing. She could never have made love to Alex. Or to Felipe. Or to anyone else, ever. Only to Sebastian. Only him.

"Do you think they will find us?" she asked him softly, her lips still touching his.

"Never. They had no horses, and by the time they'd have found any, we were well away. I left them going east, but I doubled back and we're heading up the coast now."

She drew back and looked around her, though there wasn't much to see in the darkness. "Where are we going?"

"It's not much farther. There's a *hacienda* on the beach. It belongs to a brother of a friend of mine from Mexico City. I visited there on the way up to San Feliz all those weeks ago. I'm sure they will take us in."

Marina nodded. Of course they would, Californio hospitality being what it was. And she wouldn't let herself dwell on what these nice people would think of an unmarried woman traveling with Sebastian this way. He would think of something to say. She wasn't going to let herself worry. That would ruin this downy dream she was floating through. And it was so delicious.

They rode through a small settlement. The fog had thinned and Marina could see lights on inside the houses, and people at supper around tables.

"Here we are," Sebastian said at last. He stopped his horse. "But there are no lights."

That wasn't quite true. There were no lights in the main house, but a small adobe hut near the top of the drive showed flickering candlelight.

"You stay here," Sebastian said, sliding down off the horse and catching her in his arms as she descended. "I'll check with whoever is in that hut."

He flinched as he caught her, and she noticed immediately.

"What is it?" she cried, reaching for him.

"Nothing. I . . . just a slight wound."

"In your shoulder?" Yes, even in the moonlight she could see the blood. Wrenching it must have started the bleeding again. "What happened to you?"

"A slight wound. The ball barely touched me, really."

She was shocked. "Did Felipe . . . ?"

333

"No, not this time." His grin was crooked. "This was a total stranger. Forget about it. It means nothing."

It meant everything. He might have been killed. Her heart felt like a stone as she thought of it. Finally she was beginning to understand why they said that love was as much pain as pleasure. Every wound inflicted on him would hurt her so much more.

He walked away, his boots crunching in the dirt, and she wanted to call out to him, to make sure he was coming back. She bit her lip to keep from doing it. She couldn't count on him, not ever. And she had to remember that.

But he was back in moments.

"They're traveling to San Diego," he told her. "The whole family. The hut belongs to the caretaker. He remembers me from my last visit and he invited us to use the *hacienda* for as long as we like."

She nodded. That was the way it was in California. She'd never had a doubt. Wearily, they trudged to the door of the large house. It opened easily. There might be locks on the bedrooms of all daughters in Californio houses, but the front door was seldom barred. Sebastian found a lantern and lit it, and the warm, luxurious comfort of the room sprang into focus.

"This is very nice," Marina said, looking around at the opulent furniture and the paintings on the wall.

"Yes. The Sosas are very wealthy. They own two large *ranchos* back in Mexico as well as this place." He reached for her, looking down at her large, trusting eyes, and for the first time he let himself think about what he was doing.

For the last two days he had been hell-bent on getting her back. He had her now. What on earth was he going to do with her? His fingers tightened on her shoulders.

"You married Alex?" he asked, his face hard and expressionless, but his eyes tortured.

She shook her head and smiled. "No. He brought a priest on board and I couldn't bear to think of marrying him. So I ran off with the boat. They were only just catching me again when you came to my rescue."

Relief flooded him and he pulled her to him, holding her closely, stroking her hair.

"But how did you find me?" she asked, her face pressed to his chest.

"I've been searching for you since the morning after you left the Diaz *rancho*. I was trying to get a boat out to the *Prospect,* but I couldn't even find one to steal. So I was riding down to the next harbor, hoping to find something there, and purely by luck, I came upon you being waylaid by ruffians."

She giggled, so tired she had to lean against him to hold herself up. "Alex makes a strange ruffian," she murmured. "Poor man. I didn't treat him very well. But he became so domineering and self-righteous once we were on his ship."

"Never mind him." He looked down at her. She seemed smaller, more vulnerable than ever. He wanted to take her in the cup of his hand and hold her safe from all harm, forever. "You don't have to think about him again."

She nodded, feeling sleepy, feeling hungry. "Do you suppose they've left any food behind?" she hinted gently.

"No doubt. But first . . ." He grinned at her.

"Would you like a bath?"

She gazed at him with her mouth slightly ajar. "A bath? What do you mean?"

He held out his hand to her. "Come. I'll show you."

He led her to a little room off the kitchen that held something she had never seen before. It looked like a huge open kettle over a laid fire.

"A bathtub," Sebastian told her. "I saw this when I was here before. Ever seen anything like it?"

She shook her head, fascinated. He showed her how to start the water pumping in from the cistern outside.

"Then you light the fire, like this." He demonstrated, using a flint and steel lighter kept there for just that purpose. "And in a little while, you have nice warm bathwater."

Marina danced around the contraption, rejuvenated and as excited as a child with a new toy. Sebastian watched her and his heart ached. He wanted her as he had never wanted any other woman. But for the first time in his life, that wasn't all that mattered to him. He knew he had to act responsibly with her. She was something precious, something that had to be protected. What had happened the other night by the stream must not be allowed to happen again, no matter how irresistible the temptation.

He was going to take her home. That was the only thing to do. And for once in his life he was going to do the honorable thing and keep his hands off her. It wouldn't be easy, but it was necessary. She deserved it.

"This is lovely," she said, smiling up at him. "I'd love to try it."

336

Instead of smiling back, as she expected him to, he frowned and looked away. "All right," he said gruffly. "After all the riding I've been doing, I'd like a bath, too. You can go first."

He lit the fire and, while the water was heating, set up the stepladder for her to use to climb down inside. The ladder wouldn't go in straight at first, and he had to adjust it.

"Take off your damp clothes," he called back as he worked. "I'll put them by the fireplace in the parlor to dry."

Her fingers hesitated on the laces of her bodice, but then she tugged them free and began to disrobe, her heart beating wildly. As her petticoats fell to the floor, and then her skirt, she stole glances at him periodically, sure that he would turn any moment and come and take her in his arms, and then . . .

"That ought to take care of it," he said, turning away from the bathtub and wiping his hands without a glance in her direction. "Hand me your clothes."

She stood shivering without a stitch on, and just her driest petticoat held in front of herself in an attempt at a semblance of modesty. But as she handed her skirt and bodice to the hand he stretched out toward her, she fully expected to have that scant covering yanked away in one quick move, and when it didn't happen, she was dumbfounded.

"I'll get this dry," he muttered, never looking at her at all. "Go ahead. I'll go out and take care of the horse, and after that I'll be out in the parlor, if you need me."

And then he was gone.

She stared after where he had disappeared and blinked. Was she dreaming? Where was the rake she knew so well? This didn't seem like him at all.

Slightly disappointed, she climbed the rickety ladder, sure she was taking her life in her hands, and lowered herself into the warm water.

It was heaven. Leaning back, she closed her eyes and let every muscle relax, even her mind. She didn't want to think at all. Thinking was going to involve choices and regrets, and she could put that off until tomorrow.

There were so many things to think over. She had to deal with what had happened with her father, and the break-up with Felipe, and poor Captain Alex. But it was too late to do anything about any of those things tonight.

Tonight she just wanted to enjoy, to be with Sebastian and drift. Tomorrow reality would slap her in the face like a cold wind. Time enough for that.

Her eyes snapped open. She'd been dozing. It felt as though she'd been in the water for an awfully long time. And Sebastian hadn't come back for a visit. She'd been so sure he would.

She frowned. He was acting strangely. When he had first snatched her up out of the midst of the crowd, he had seemed as happy to see her as she was to see him. But now something had changed in him. He was acting almost as though he wished he had never found her at all.

But how could that be? From the first moment she had met him, even when he had hated her, there had always been a fervor to their dealings with one another. And lately, that fervor had most decidedly taken on a tone of ardor that couldn't be denied. So for him to act like this so suddenly was very strange. Unless . . . she winced. Unless his chase down the coast after her had more to do with guilt than passion. Unless he had decided he really didn't want her.

There was a chill to the water now. She shivered and climbed out, pulling on a long white robe embroidered with rosebuds that hung on a peg nearby. Padding out into the house, she found Sebastian sitting before a roaring fire, staring broodingly into the flames, a glass of *aguardiente* in his hand.

"Sebastian?"

He looked up and saw her and something flickered through his eyes, but he quickly looked away.

"All finished?" he said, rising. "Good. I'll take my turn." He looked back over his shoulder as he left the room. "I won't be long." And then he was gone.

She stood where she was, frozen to the spot. He hated her. What else could it be? He'd thought it over and decided she wasn't really worth the trouble. Now he could hardly wait to be rid of her.

She didn't know whether to laugh or cry. She was such a fool, such a stupid, ignorant fool.

Swallowing the sting of his rejection, she turned toward the kitchen. There were dried fruits, some dried vegetables, and beef jerky. Drawing some water, she put together a makeshift soup and carried it into the parlor to cook over the fire. Then she sat where Sebastian had been sitting and stared into the flames, just as he had.

She heard him coming out when he was finished, and she thought she was prepared. If this was the way he wanted to treat their relationship, coolly, distantly, she would do the same. After all, it was what she should have done from the beginning.

When he stepped into the room, she lifted her chin in a frosty manner and turned slowly to greet him.

But when she caught sight of him, she stared and something inside her curled into a tight knot, almost choking her.

He was the most beautiful man she'd ever seen. Wearing a soft white shirt with full sleeves, and snug black trousers that fit him like a glove, he presented a picture that stopped the breath in her throat. His hair was mussed, a lock falling down over his forehead, and his green eyes looked black in the firelight. She wanted to throw herself into his arms and hold on forever.

But that wasn't the way they were doing things any longer. She tore her gaze away without a word to him and rose, going to check how the soup was doing. It was still weak, but she was too hungry to wait any longer. Taking up a cloth to protect her hand, she swung the heavy kettle down and almost dropped it.

"Oh!" she cried, starting to lose her balance.

Sebastian sprang forward and took the kettle from her, holding her steady with a hand on her arm.

"Here," he said. "I'll take care of that."

She looked up at him and he stared down into her eyes for a long moment. Then he shook his head and turned away, carrying the kettle to the table where she had laid out the bowls and spoons.

They sat across from each other at the table, eating in silence, with only the crackling of the nearby fire and the distant pounding of the surf to provide background to their meal. Finally, Marina couldn't take any more.

Putting down her spoon, she confronted him, her gray eyes level.

"Thank you very much for rescuing me, Lieutenant," she said formally. "May I ask what you

340

plan to do next?"

"Next?" He stared at her.

"Tomorrow. With me. Or am I free to chart my own course?"

He frowned. "That depends upon what you want to do. I intend to take you back to your father, where you belong."

Her father. Just thinking about him and wondering what might have happened by now brought a wave of sadness. She forced it back into the far reaches of her mind and looked at him coolly.

"I'm not sure that's where I belong at all," she said.

He arched an eyebrow. "Oh, really? Does that mean you have actually made up your mind at this point? It seems to me your idea of where you belong changes with the wind. First it's with Felipe, then Alex Brandene, now, who knows where?"

Her eyes flashed. "So that's it. You're afraid I may have decided I belong with you. And that wouldn't fit in with your plans at all." She pushed back her chair and rose majestically to her feet. "Don't worry, Lieutenant. I won't burden you with the responsibility of my welfare any longer. Tomorrow we will go our separate ways."

She would have swept out of the room, but he was too fast for her. Jumping up, he stopped her at the doorway, his hands grasping her upper arms.

"You're going home with me," he ordered.

Her nose tilted. "I might just have someplace else to go," she said impudently.

His hands tightened. "Where?"

Her gaze shifted and she pulled a thought out of the air, remembering Rita. "I know someone who

341

runs a *cantina* in Los Angeles. She'll give me a job."

His eyes burned. He'd seen that cantina. "So sailors and *vaqueros* can leer at you and put their dirty hands up your clothes? Never."

She was furious. He was just as domineering as Alex. Did all men get this way? What was the use of it all?

She glanced pointedly down at where his hands held her. "I suppose you think you are the only man who should have free reign in touching me?" she snapped. "Just because of what happened the other night doesn't give you any special rights."

His face twisted as though in pain, and his hands loosened and slipped away from her arms. That night which had seemed so glorious at the time was beginning to be his nightmare. He'd taken her innocence as casually as he might break in a new horse. What had he been thinking of? How could he have been so uncaring, so callous? He looked at her, so lovely in all her shining purity and candor, and he hated what he had done to her.

"I didn't mean to imply any such thing," he said abruptly.

But she didn't want to listen. Whirling, she pulled the white robe more tightly about her and began to stamp off toward where she assumed the bedrooms must be. He came right behind her.

"You can sleep in this room," he said, pointing out a small bedroom decorated in blue colors. "I'll take this one."

She stood very still, staring in at the tiny bed he was assigning to her, not wanting him to see her face. A memory washed over her, a recollection of the night she had spent cradled in his arms, as he gently

342

comforted her after she had learned of Jonathan's disappearance. The memory was so strong she could taste his lips and feel how his body had crushed hers, and tears threatened to spring into her eyes.

Angrily she blinked them back. He was rejecting her so blatantly, she wouldn't give him the satisfaction of seeing how much he hurt her.

"This will do fine," she said evenly. "It will be nice to have some solitude—and some room on the bed."

Her gray eyes challenged him and he remembered the night in his quarters as well. His mouth went dry, remembering.

What was wrong with him, anyway? She was just another woman. He'd had so many women. Why should she be different? What was it about her that caught at his heart like this? Why did he care so much?

She was angry. He didn't quite understand why. But he supposed he might as well try to explain. "This isn't easy, Marina," he said defensively. "Do you think I don't want to share a bed with you?"

Her eyes widened, baffled. "You don't hate me?" she asked softly, completely bewildered.

"Marina . . ." He started to reach for her, then stopped himself, his eyes as dark as midnight. "I could never hate you. But don't you understand? We can't . . . what we did the other night was wrong. We should never have done it."

Her face was stricken now. "You regret it?" she whispered.

He stared at her, shaking his head. "I just want to take you back to your father unharmed, Marina. I think I owe him that much."

"Unharmed?" She frowned, not sure what he was

saying, but touched by the emotion she saw in his eyes. Reaching out, she put a hand on his arm. "How could you harm me, Sebastian?"

He stared at her, his turmoil too deep to hide. "I have already harmed you, *querida,*" he said in a voice as harsh as hail on gravel. "I've stolen from you. I took your virginity, and I had no right to it."

He turned away, and she gasped, wanting to follow him. "No," she said softly, tears pooling in her eyes. "You stole nothing from me. What . . . what you have I gave of my own free will."

If he heard, he didn't answer. The bedroom door shut firmly, leaving her alone in the hallway. As though in a trance, she turned and went to her own bed.

Chapter Twenty-five

But, tired as she was, sleep didn't come. She lay staring into the moonlight that slanted in through the barred window, making a silver trail across the room. It seemed she wasn't going to get her one night of happiness after all. The worries were already crowding in.

He was right about her going home, much as she hated to admit it. She had to go home, of course, to see how her father was. Now that she wasn't going to be able to set herself up in any sort of relationship that would put his mind at ease, she would at least be with him to do all she could for him. Carmen and Josefa were most likely doing as good a job as could be done of caring for him, but he needed his daughter with him as well, and she wanted to be by his side.

Tomorrow Sebastian would obtain a horse for her and they would ride north, up the coast, not stopping for any length of time until they reached San Feliz. And once she was back home, Josefa would watch her like a hawk. No doubt she would lock her in her room at night. For the rest of her life she would be a prisoner. Was that all her future was destined to hold?

Time crawled by as she lay trying to sleep. She wondered if Sebastian was awake. She could imagine him lying in the bed in the next room. She ached to lie with him.

But he didn't want her. He could hardly wait to deposit her at her father's house and wash his hands of her. He'd said as much, hadn't he?

No, if she were honest, she'd have to admit that wasn't exactly what he'd said. But he did say that he regretted that they had made love. Regretted it. It made her sick to think of it.

Sick, and angry.

She didn't regret it. She would never regret it. It was the most beautiful and thrilling thing she had ever done in her life. She would do it again in a minute. Didn't he see that? Couldn't he tell?

Sitting up, she looked out the barred window. She could see the ocean in the distance. The moon had lit it up like a pool of silver. The *Prospect* was bobbing in that same ocean, somewhere to the south. Alex was either asleep on board, or still wandering in the night, looking for her. She was going to have to do something to make this up to him.

And here she was, bouncing from one prison to another, at the whim of the decisions of others. For just a moment, she had thought she was going to have one night to be free. One night.

Slowly she rose from the bed.

One night. That was all she had left. If she didn't reach out and try to get what she wanted, she was never going to have it. She wanted Sebastian. Why wasn't she doing something to get him?

She started toward the door, her heart in her throat. If he rejected her this time, she wasn't sure she could bear it. But she had to try.

Walking softly down the hall, she stopped at his door.

She hesitated for a moment, holding her breath, then shook her head and pulled on the latch. With a small creak, the door swung open.

He was lying very still. It somehow outraged her to think he could be asleep when she was so very much awake. She walked softly to the edge of the bed and looked down. The moonlight filled the room with such brightness it was almost like daylight. His long lashes lay against his cheeks and his chest was moving slowly. He was sound asleep.

He was also beautiful, his hair curling in an unruly cap, his naked shoulders wide and golden, one of them newly bandaged. She wanted to touch his perfect ear, kiss his cheek, but she held herself back and took in every feature, cherishing the moment.

She would never see him this way again. She would be locked in her room from now on, and he would be leaving soon, for Spain. She had to soak up every detail, loving everything about him. He was as magnificent as a statue and yet as warm and desirable as any man could ever be.

Perhaps this was all she needed. She could turn around now and walk quietly back to bed and he would never know . . .

But there was little chance of that. None at all, in fact. Now that she was here, she knew more than ever how much she loved him. Her heart was full with it. This was her last chance. She had to do something about it, something to show him . . .

Slowly she untied the sash of her robe and let it slip from her shoulders and crumple into a pile on the floor. For just a moment she stood, straight and tall and naked in the moonlight, savoring the cool air on her tender breasts, her legs, her skin. Then, as softly as she could, she slid into the bed, gliding inbetween the blankets, reaching for his naked body with her own.

Sebastian was deep in sleep. At first he thought he was dreaming. He was aroused before he was awake, and when he realized that the warm hand gliding across his belly was real, he grabbed it and swung around to face her.

"Marina. What in God's name . . . ?"

She used her kiss as an answer, rising over him and coming down on his mouth as though she meant to conquer it. He kissed her back for a moment, then broke away.

"Marina, no, we can't. I don't want to hurt you again."

"You've never hurt me," she whispered very near his ear, her breath tickling his skin, her fingertips barely touching his temples, her eyes liquid with the love she felt. "The only way you could hurt me would be to send me away again."

He groaned, reaching to pull her hands away, trying to draw back, but she clung to him, pressing her naked body to his, and his resistance went up in smoke.

He took in the feel of her firm breasts, her slender legs, her caressing fingers, and his mind went blank with desire. He couldn't think any longer. Logic and caution were foreign concepts, things he had never heard of. Guilt didn't exist. He was strong and hard and male and he needed her as though having her was the only thing that could possibly keep him alive.

When he reached for her, she seemed to melt under his hands, her breasts, her hips, her satiny stomach, everything about her soft and pliant and drawing him in, so that he felt he could reach inside her, plunge in with his tongue, his hands, his need, and drown in her, become one with her, take her in and devour her, and that was all he ever wanted to do, on and on, spinning in space.

She was saying his name and it was driving him crazy. He kissed her hard, pulling her on top of him, glorying in the feel of her, knowing he was going to have to stop this plunge over the cliff before it was too late, determined not to hurt her. But when she moaned, he felt a wildness building in him, and he wasn't sure how long he could keep it leashed.

She wasn't going to stop him. This time she had more of an idea of what to expect and she wanted it all. His body was hard and rigid beneath her, delighting her, making her breathe in quick little pants of pleasure. She slipped her hand down until she caught hold of him, amazed at how smooth and warm he was, amazed at how her body could tingle with such longing.

And then he reversed their positions, placing her on her back, stroking and rubbing to ready her, kissing her breasts, murmuring sweet words between tugging at her nipples with his lips and tongue.

Her moans were coming more quickly now, and her eyes were open, staring at him as though she didn't quite know who he was.

"Please," she whispered huskily. "Oh, please, please . . ."

His body trembled with need for her, but he held back for another moment, making sure . . .

"Now!" she ordered, spiking her fingers down into his hair and grabbing tightly.

He did as she demanded, arching like a bow, driving in and then holding on as she went racing ahead, her hands, her mouth, her hips forcing him faster, until he caught up and they both took the last dive over the edge, sailing into the headwinds, crashing through clouds, and exploding into a sea of stars and light.

Tears were pouring from her eyes as she lay back. He saw them before he'd regained his breath. Shock flashed through him.

"Did I hurt you?" he asked, appalled.

She shook her head, her smile shining through the rain. "You were s-s-so wonderful," she managed to get out. "Sebastian . . ." She sobbed and he frowned, pulling her delicious body close for comfort, rocking her gently, stroking her hair.

"What is it?" he asked anxiously. "Tell me what's wrong."

"Nothing's wrong," she murmured, her face buried against him. She wanted to stay this way forever. "Sebastian . . . I love you."

He went very still and she pulled her head back so that she could look into his face.

"Oh, don't worry," she said quickly. "I know you don't love me. It's all right. But I can't bear to think that we're never going to do this again." She swallowed and managed a smile. "Please forget that I said that. I'm resigned to my future, believe me. I'll go back to my father's house and I'll probably never marry. But, could you please do one thing for me? After you go back to Spain, do you think you might write me a letter once in a while? Just a short note, nothing fancy. To let me know how you are. Please?"

He didn't answer. He stared at her for a long time, and then he crushed her to his chest, burying his face in her hair, rocking her, but unable to say a word.

And she lay against him, luxuriating in the feel of him, until his hands began to move on her skin and she found out that they were going to do it again after all.

There wasn't a hint of fog in the morning and they lay in bed, talking and giggling while the sun played on their faces. After a leisurely breakfast of dried fruit and chocolate, they walked on the beach and chased the waves and ran into each other's arms.

It was almost as though they were both in love, Marina thought as she raced him toward a large piece of driftwood. It was almost as though he really loved her as much as she loved him. If only the day could last forever.

He let her win the race, and they both flopped down in the sand and leaned against one another, looking out at the rippling reflection of the sun in the water.

"We'll have to start getting ready to ride for home," he said at last, his voice sounding as reluctant as she felt.

She smiled up at him. "Will the Sosas lend us a horse?" she asked.

"Of course," he replied. "We can choose one when we get back to the house. I'll tell the caretaker."

"We'll probably be home before midnight," she mused, losing her smile. "I hope Carmen isn't worn out from taking care of my father."

"Carmen?" He moved uncomfortably. "She's not there."

Marina looked up in surprise. "Not there? What do you mean?"

He realized he should have told her about this from the beginning. It was only now that he knew he had held back because he wanted to put off the time when her mind would go to other people and other things. He wanted her all to himself for as long as possible. But the time had come when that was going to have to end. He sighed and smiled at her ruefully.

"She's the one who told me where you'd gone."

Marina nodded, still puzzled. "I knew that. She was the only one who knew. I didn't really tell her what I was doing, but I did talk to her about taking care of my father and that I meant to do something to set his mind at ease. And she saw me leave with Alex, so I'm sure she put two and two together."

He nodded. "She did that, all right. They locked her in a room at the Diaz *hacienda* and browbeat her, but she refused to divulge what she knew, even to Josefa." He shrugged. "Until I broke in and persuaded her."

"Persuaded her?" she repeated with an arch look. "And pray, how did you do that?"

He hesitated. This was the touchy part. "I promised to take her with me when I went looking for you," he admitted at last.

"You *what?*" Her face went white. "But then, where is she?"

He shook his head. "I'm not sure."

She turned on him, grabbing his shirt with both hands, her eyes wild. "Sebastian! Tell me. What route did you take? Where did you last see her?"

"We rode down the coast together and stayed at a house of a family called Hernandez."

"Yes," she nodded impatiently. "I know them. Go on."

"Then we rode on into Los Angeles. Carmen wanted to stop and see a woman named Rita who she said used to be nanny to you two."

"Yes, yes. That was where I was headed, too."

He tried a faint smile. "Well . . . the last time I saw Carmen, she was still there."

Marina frowned, her hands loosening on his shirt. "Why did she stay with Rita instead of coming on to find me with you?"

His face was pensive. He had a feeling the rest of this story just might cause a problem. "Well, you see . . ." He grimaced, looking like a man about to face a firing squad. "I shot a man, and she knew him, so she stayed to take care of the body . . ."

352

"What?" Her hands went to her face in horror.

He reached for her. "Now, calm down. I don't know who he was, but he drew on me first . . ."

"And Carmen knew him?" Her bright eyes looked into the distance as she thought that over.

He frowned. He had a feeling he knew what she was thinking, because he had been thinking the same thing himself lately. When he went over in his mind just what had happened in that room in Los Angeles, one inescapable fact was clear: Carmen knew the young man with the gun — and cared about him. Sebastian had a sinking feeling he might know who that young man was himself.

"She seemed to know him very well. She was certainly upset when I shot him."

She winced when he said the word, but her face was impassive as she frowned again. "But what did she say? What did she call him?"

"I can't remember her calling him by name. But she fainted when she saw him first. And then she ran to *him* when the both of us were shot, which I thought was a bit crusty of her."

Marina's eyes were bright with hope and fear, but her face was set. "What did he look like?"

Sebastian shrugged. "More New England than San Feliz, if you ask me. He was tall, with brown hair and light eyes."

Marina stood and stared down at him. Her mind was working very fast, but she wasn't telling him a thing about what she was thinking. "What did he say to you?"

Sebastian shrugged. "He had it in his head that I had been with Carmen, and he wanted to kill me. He shot at me. So I shot back."

Her eyes widened as she realized the full implica-

353

tions. "You hit him?" she demanded.

He nodded, his eyes hooded. "He was out on the floor when I left."

"Dead?" She could hardly force the word out.

He hesitated. "I don't know," he said, telling the truth. "He wasn't moving."

Whirling, Marina started back for the house. Sebastian sprang to his feet and followed her.

"Where are you going?" he asked, as it was clear she had something in mind.

"I have to go to Rita's," she said quickly, avoiding his eyes. "I must see if Carmen is all right."

But they both knew what she really was going for.

Chapter Twenty-six

Marina's face was set but the emotion boiling beneath her reserve was all too evident. He could see it in the tremor of her fingers as she pulled her cloak about her, in the nervous way she tossed her hair back again and again. He knew what she was afraid of. He was just as afraid of it himself.

Had he killed her brother? The man had drawn on him. He'd had no choice. But deep inside him, a dark dread was building. If he'd killed her brother, would she ever be able to forgive him?

Still, neither one of them said anything about it as they prepared to leave quickly. They rode off toward the small, dirty town of Los Angeles at a good clip. Within two hours they drew up alongside the crumbling building where Rita lived.

They tied the horses outside and went up the back stairs to the room where Sebastian had spent a few moments the day before. The room was empty, but there was still a splash of blood on the floor. They both looked at it, but neither said a word.

"Come," Marina said stiffly, her face a mask of control. "Let's go down around to the front."

She raced down the stairs and Sebastian followed her at a slower pace. Just as she disappeared around the corner of the building, a voice called out to him, low and menacing, and he turned, hand on the butt of his pistol.

"So, you came back, Lieutenant. That will save me the trouble of going out to look for you."

The young man stepped out of the shadows holding a gun on him again. Sebastian's feelings were mixed. He wasn't dead, but he was still a threat. Whoever he was, he was getting to be a real annoyance.

He looked him over quickly. The man's thigh was wrapped tightly in a large bandage, but for the rest, he looked hale and hearty.

"I thought I might have killed you," Sebastian said softly, his green eyes glittering in the sunlight.

"No such luck. I've got more lives than a cat." The young man grinned. "Though walking is not what it once was. They do say I will get back to normal someday, however. So I suppose I'm grateful."

Sebastian nodded, his face reflecting the irony of that statement. "But not to me."

"No. Not to you." The muzzle of the gun steadied its aim at his heart. "What are you doing here, Spaniard? If you've come back for Carmen, I'm going to have to kill you after all."

"Sebastian." Marina's voice came around the corner before she did. When she appeared, she saw only her companion and she blinked at him, annoyed. "Are you coming, or . . ."

She caught sight of the stranger and gasped, hands to her mouth. But her shock lasted only a moment. Joy filled her face and she started toward him.

"I knew it," she said decisively. "Jonathan, put that gun down and let me see if it is really you."

"Marina." He looked a bit disconcerted. "I'm in the middle of something here. Better stand back."

But she was having none of that. She advanced on him like a small typhoon, pushing away the gun and throwing her arms around her brother, holding him as tightly as she possibly could.

"I knew you were alive! Do you know how sick with worry we were?"

"Carmen has given me some idea." He clung to the gun, glancing at Sebastian as though he were still afraid he might be up to something. "I want to get back and see Papa as soon as I can ride."

She glanced down at his leg. "Is that where Sebastian shot you? He told me he killed you."

She looked back at the Spaniard mockingly. "It takes a long time to die from a thigh wound, Lieutenant. Don't they teach you that in soldier school?"

Sebastian shook his head, too relieved to take offense at her taunts. "I thought I'd hit him higher," he said dryly. "His shot must have thrown me off."

"Yes, you did hit him too, you know," she told her brother reassuringly. "So now you're both even."

Jonathan disentangled himself from her embrace, readjusting his aim. "Not quite, Marina. We haven't settled scores."

Sebastian stood easily, facing him, his green eyes glacial. "I told you before that we have no quarrel, and I meant it. I've never done anything to Carmen. I'm sure she has told you the same."

"Don't be silly, Jonathan," Marina chimed in, looking at the two of them uneasily. "Sebastian has never pursued Carmen."

Jonathan's gun didn't waver. "And how do you know that with such certainty?"

She stepped across the tiles and curled herself into Sebastian's arms. "Because he has been much too busy pursuing me, brother." Her chin rose defiantly. "If you

357

shoot him, you'll have to put the shot through me as well."

Sebastian looked down into the mass of curling brown hair against his shoulder, and he smiled. Under ordinary circumstances, he would never have let a woman shield him like this. But the circumstances were anything but ordinary. And she felt so good standing beside him. He never wanted to let her go.

Jonathan lowered his pistol, frowning. "Marina, how could you choose a man like this when I hear Don Felipe wanted to marry you?"

"I don't love Don Felipe," she said very clearly, staring at her brother.

His gaze went from her eyes to Sebastian's and he understood what she was trying to tell him. For a moment he looked stunned.

Marina took advantage of the situation and stepped forward, taking the gun from his unresisting fingers. "And let's have no more of this." She dropped the heavy thing into a handy box and turned back to hold her brother again, tears trembling in her eyes.

"Jonathan, Jonathan, don't ever scare us like that again. We missed you so. Now that you're back, everything will be all right."

He pulled back and took her face between his hands, smiling down into her eyes. "I don't know if everything will be all right, Marina, but if Papa is still alive when we get home, I promise you, I'll do all I can to put his fears to rest."

She held him again, her eyes closed, tears squeezing out between the lids. Then a thought came to her.

"Where's Carmen?" she asked, drawing away and looking about the room.

"Right here." Carmen herself appeared, looking them all over with a jaundiced eye. "Have the boys finished playing soldier?" she asked Marina.

"Yes, for the time being," she told her friend. "But we'll have to keep an eye on them." Without hesitating another moment, she threw her arms around her cousin as well. "Carmen, he's alive. And he's back. Can we be friends again?"

Carmen hugged her back, holding tightly, the emotions of weeks of anguish finally spilling out, and when at last she looked at her again, tears sparkled in her own eyes. "If you can accept that Jonathan and I love each other," she said softly, "We'll have no problems at all."

Marina nodded. She'd had a long time to think about the relationship among the three of them. They weren't children any longer. What Jonathan and Carmen felt for each other should have no bearing on what she felt for either one of them. It might be awkward at first, but they would work it out. She had no doubt about it.

She leaned back and looked into Carmen's face. "You really do love him?" she asked softly.

Carmen nodded, wiping her eyes dry with an impatient gesture. "I really do. I always have."

Marina frowned. "Then why did you act so . . . ?"

Carmen glanced at Jonathan and shrugged. "Because I never had him, not really. I had only a part of him, and it was a part he seemed ready to ignore. Going to Boston to study law was what consumed him." She made a face at him. "And then, all I heard about were the lovely, cultured New England ladies who invited him to tea and to call on social evenings."

Jonathan chuckled at that, and she cast him a reproving glance.

"I couldn't imagine why he would come back for me after all that." A smile wreathed her face. "But he did."

"Of course I did," Jonathan said gruffly. He was still eyeing Sebastian with distrust. "Why don't we go up to the room? People are beginning to stare."

It was true. Two little boys and an old man had stopped to watch what was going on. The four of them left the onlookers to find new entertainment and settled in the room, where Carmen cut up fruit for a light meal, placing pears and oranges on a plate in the middle of the table.

"So, tell me quickly, brother — where have you been all these weeks?"

He grinned and teased her. "Oh, so you really did miss me, then?"

She made a face. "We missed knowing where you were, that was all. Alex said you had abandoned your room in Boston. It did seem strange."

He nodded. "Alex was right."

"Well, where did you go?"

"I'll tell you why I left, first." He glanced at Carmen. "I was studying and getting along quite nicely, except for periodic visits from people who had been through San Feliz. And from every one of them I heard the same story. Carmen was the toast of the town. Carmen was seen with every handsome man within a radius of ten miles. Carmen was dancing with strangers at every *baile*."

Carmen sighed. "People sometimes tend to exaggerate, you know."

"You were flirting. You've already admitted it."

Carmen shrugged. "It meant nothing, and still means nothing, so go on with your story."

"These reports, combined with letters from Carmen saying that she was about to stow away on the next ship sailing for China . . ."

"Hawaii," she corrected, wagging a finger at him. "I

360

said I would go to Hawaii."

"Hawaii," Jonathan agreed. "Well, I couldn't have her going to Hawaii without me, could I? So when a friend told me there was a place available on a ship heading for the Caribbean, a ship that would connect with another destined round the Horn, I jumped at the chance, leaving with only a few hours' notice. We made good time, but we had barely sailed into the warm waters of the Caribbean when we were waylaid by vicious pirates. Most on board were killed. I managed to escape, and then I swam for what seemed like days before washing ashore on a small island."

"Where a dusky Caribbean princess nursed him back to health," Carmen interjected. "Or so he told me."

Jonathan laughed. "I said that only to make you jealous, and you know it. Actually, my rescuers were three grizzled pirates only one of whom had both his legs, and they saved me only because they thought I might lead them back to where the ship was sunk so they could plunder any treasure left. I wasn't able to help them there, but we did travel from island to island, and in one unlikely spot, we found an old sea chest that must have washed in from a Spanish galleon sunk two hundred years ago."

Marina's eyes were wide. "And what was inside?"

Jonathan laughed and touched her cheek affectionately. "Not all the wealth in the world, unfortunately, but enough to be of some help." He pulled out a pouch and let the contents spill out on the table. Cut emeralds and rubies jumbled against huge gold nuggets. Marina cried out.

"Oh, Jonathan, we must tell Papa immediately!"

He nodded. "This ought to be enough to let him get back to running his own affairs instead of the Alcalde's. And there just might be enough left over for a trip." He smiled at Carmen, who glowed back at him.

"Europe," Carmen said decisively, her eyes sparkling. "We'll go as soon as everything is cleared up at home."

"And I've completed my studies in Boston."

Marina looked from one to the other and smiled. "Beware, brother. Once you get this one to Paris, you may never get her to leave again."

"I'll take my chances. I've always wanted to see the Continent myself."

They chatted for only a few moments more. Marina was anxious to get back to her father, and Sebastian was just as happy to get her off to himself again. He was glad he hadn't killed her brother, but he knew his position with the family was a tenuous one. And what was his future? He still couldn't say with any certainty.

"We must go," Marina said at last. "I've got to get home to Papa as soon as I can. I . . . I only hope . . ." She looked at Jonathan's face, then Carmen's, not daring to say the words aloud.

"He's still alive, Marina," Jonathan said firmly, covering her hand with his own as Carmen said a quick prayer. "I can feel it. But you're right to rush home. I'll be coming right behind you, though it might take me a bit longer with this leg." He threw a glance at Sebastian. "But how are you to get home, sister? You can't go with this scoundrel. I won't allow it."

Marina leaned over and kissed her brother on the cheek. "I've just spent the night with him, Jonathan," she said boldly. "If you think I'll be in more danger during daylight on a long ride home, I don't know what I can say to convince you." She stood and put a hand on Sebastian's shoulder. "I'm going with him. He rescued me from Alex last night. I trust him with my life."

"I don't know why. He seems pretty free with other people's lives," Jonathan said with a sneer on his handsome face.

Marina smiled and murmured. "Not unlike yourself."

Jonathan gave her a look, but when she hugged him good-bye, his affection was just as warm as it had always been.

"Watch out for him," he whispered to her, glancing at Sebastian. "I know you think you're in love, but Marina . . ."

"Hush." She put her finger to his lips. "I'll see you at home."

"Marina." He grabbed hold of her hand. "I see you still wear the unicorn ring I gave you. Has it given you good luck?"

Marina looked over his shoulder and met Sebastian's eyes. "Oh yes," she breathed, laughing softly. "Oh yes."

It was almost noon before they could get away, riding their horses up through San Fernando and then back out to the sea shore. They rode hard. Marina was very eager to get back to her father with the news. They rode on through twilight, and then into darkness, determined to make it all the way home in one trip.

As they crested the hills overlooking San Feliz, Sebastian reined in his horse and gestured for Marina to stop. They dismounted and stood together, looking over the valley.

"We're almost home," he said. "Soon you'll be back with your family, and I won't be welcome in your house."

She turned to search his eyes. "What do you mean?"

"They'll be so happy to have you back, they will forgive your having left. But as for me . . ." He shook his

363

head, his smile crooked. "They won't forgive me, *querida*. You know that."

She stared at him confused. "But you didn't do anything."

He touched her cheek. "Marina, I ruined everyone's plans. You know I did."

"Yes, but . . ."

"You said yourself that they would probably lock you up from now on. We won't have many chances to see each other any longer."

She felt chilled, not sure where he was going with this. "I'll find a way," she vowed ardently. "Believe me, I will."

He shrugged. "You'll sneak out in the night to meet me? I don't think so, Marina. I can't put you through that."

Her heart was aching. What did he mean? Why was he saying this?

"I think I'd better go."

"Go?"

"Away from San Feliz."

She clutched his arm. This was exactly what she had dreaded would happen. "No. Oh Sebastian, please, no."

He dropped a soft kiss on her lips. "I have things to take care of, Marina. Matters to settle."

He still wanted to go back to Spain. If ever she could hate a country, she hated that one right now. She hid her face against his chest, tears welling in her eyes.

"Sebastian, please don't leave me."

His large hand stroked her hair, and he buried his face into her fragrance. "I don't want to leave you, *querida*. I don't ever want to leave you."

"Then stay." She looked up at him. "We can find some way to be together."

He kissed her again, longer this time, his mouth warm, his emotions revealed in a way she didn't remember him revealing them before. His hands held her as though she were precious to him. But it couldn't last, and finally he drew back.

"We'd better go."

She turned, doing as he said. She was too tired, too upset, to think clearly. He mustn't go. She would talk to him again. She would find a way to persuade him. But for now, she had to concentrate on her father.

They rode down out of the hills and clattered down the sleepy streets of San Feliz and came to a halt before the Crafts home. Marina slid down off her horse and ran in through the big front doorway.

"Papa!" she called. "Tía! Where is everyone?"

Josefa came out of the hallway looking as though she'd seen a ghost. "You! *Hija.*" She grasped her to her ample breast. "Where have you been? We have been worried sick . . ."

"I'm fine, Carmen's fine . . . and Tía . . . Jonathan is fine, too."

Josefa's face registered bewilderment. "What? What are you saying?"

Marina hugged her again. "I'll tell you all about it later. But first, how is Papa?"

"Marina." Josefa took her hand. "He is still very bad. We are nursing him around the clock. But go to him, quickly. He will be better once he knows you are here. Go."

She ran down the hallway and eased open the door to his bedroom. Her father was lying very still on his bed. He was pale, gaunt, hardly the robust man she knew. She crept up to his bedside, determined not to excite him, but when he saw her, he cried out and reached for her with his bony hand.

"Marina," he said in a whispery voice. "Have I been dreaming these last two days? Where have you been?"

"Looking for Jonathan, Papa." Her smile lit up the room. "And we found him."

His watery eyes stared at her as though he were trying to take in the full import of her words and couldn't quite do it. "What? Where?"

"In Los Angeles. He is on his way home. Papa, he is wounded in the leg, but it is nothing serious, and he will be home in the next two days, I'm sure." She kissed his hand. "Now I want you to lie very still. You need to get your strength back to welcome him."

She leaned over and kissed his cool cheek. "I love you, Papa," she said, her voice choked. "Everything is going to be all right. I swear it."

His hand squeezed hers tightly, but he couldn't speak. Tears were rolling down his cheeks. She kissed him again and rose, wiping her own eyes. She was so happy. Everything was going to be all right, just as she had promised him.

Well, almost everything. She glanced out into the hallway and saw Sebastian standing there, watching. She stared at him, but his face didn't change. Her first impulse was to go to him, quickly, to pull him into her life, into her family. But before she could move, her father called to her from the bed. She looked at him.

"Just a minute, Papa," she said, then turned back to go to Sebastian. But she was too late. He was walking away, leaving. Her heart broke as she watched him go.

No, everything wouldn't be all right. Quietly, she shut the door and turned back to her father.

Chapter Twenty-seven

"I don't know why we're bothering to do this. I'm sure I'll burn every dress I own once I get to Boston."

Carmen looked up from the trunk she was packing, her hands hovering over a velvet skirt, her eyes taking in her distant future, filled, no doubt, with silks. "I'll have five new dresses made as soon as I get there."

"And I suppose you'll burn those once you get to Paris," Marina teased as she folded a camisole and placed it inside the case. It had been a month since they had come back from Los Angeles, and Carmen was preparing to leave again.

"Of course. One must stay in fashion, you know." Carmen struck a pose. "I want to have ton." Her elegant affectation deserted her as she added anxiously, "Do you think it's possible? I mean, can I carry it off?"

Marina laughed. "I have no doubt you can do whatever you set your mind to," she said, looking at her cousin with affection tinged only slightly by an underlying sadness. "If it takes changing your wardrobe every six months, so be it."

Carmen's nose went back into the air. "Life is a learning experience, you know," she counseled wisely. "You must take the stairs one step at a time."

"Or one complete set of evening wear at a time, as

367

the case may be," Marina chimed in. "My, Carmen, what a philosopher you have become."

"I've got to grow, don't you think?" Carmen grinned at her. "Soon I'll be meeting with such educated people. Jonathan's friends."

Marina laughed. "What makes you think our mischievous boy will have educated friends?"

Carmen shrugged. "Isn't everyone in Boston educated?"

"I doubt it." Marina sat down on Carmen's bed with a sigh. "And what will you do all day while Jonathan is studying?"

"I'll be learning to give teas and pay social calls, like a proper New England lady."

Marina shook her head. "Carmen Ortega as a proper New England lady — I wish I could see this."

Carmen flopped down on the bed beside her and sighed dramatically. "I wish you could too. I'm going to do such a good job of it, I may end up giving lessons when I get back."

Marina smiled and put an arm around her shoulders. "Why not? And in Paris? What will you do there?"

Carmen didn't have to think about her answer. "I'll be so busy soaking up culture, I won't even have time to write you a letter."

"Well, well!"

They laughed together, hugging one another as though Carmen's departure were coming up in hours rather than another two weeks away. Marina clung to her cousin, sobering.

"Meanwhile, what will I do back here all alone?" she said at last as she drew back.

Carmen frowned. "Marina, you won't be alone."

"Oh? And who, pray tell, will be with me?"

That was a puzzle. It seemed that she had lost just about everyone who was dear to her. Except Papa, of course, and Tía Josefa. Don Felipe's family didn't speak to her. The town as a whole had been very disapproving. No one knew the full story of what she had done and where she had gone, but everyone had his own version to pass on to the next person. She wasn't about to tell them the truth, so each story got more outlandish and her reputation had taken a severe beating. When she went out, people who had once been her friends looked at her as though she were some sort of creature that had just crawled up out of the sea.

Sebastian was gone. It had been four weeks since her mad race down the coast. And it had been four weeks since she'd seen the man she loved.

Jonathan had returned and had a wonderful reunion with her father. It did truly seem that their financial worries were over for good. Jonathan and Carmen were about to get married. But that meant they were also leaving. And that was a sadness for everyone to bear.

For the first few days after her return, Marina had been completely engrossed in nursing her father back to health. And he was fairly healthy now—shaky and weak, but no longer at death's door.

She'd thought about Sebastian every moment, but she hadn't been able to go to him, and to her disappointment, he hadn't tried to contact her. Finally, once her father was able to sit up and eat on his own, she took a few minutes off and stole away in the night, her cloak wrapped tightly around her, into the Presidio. She'd knocked on his door but there was no answer. Asking around, she finally got hold of Tomas Bata,

Sebastian's friend, and asked where he was.

"Didn't you know, *Señorita?* Sebastian de la Cruz has left."

"Left?" Her heart had gone cold as a stone in her chest. "What do you mean, left? Where did he go?"

"I'm not sure. Maybe back to Mexico City. He was determined to give up his commission. Perhaps he went to plead his case in person to the general."

It was as though her world had fallen away, leaving her standing on the brink of a precipice, looking down into a swirl of dark nothingness. Sebastian was gone.

She hurried back to take care of her father and she spent the next few days immersed in those duties. But the pain never left her. She felt as though she'd been beaten with a stick: sore and aching. It was only after lying in bed for two nights, unable to sleep, that she realized that the pain wasn't really physical. It was all in her heart.

The worst times came at night, when she didn't have anything else to take up her thoughts. She went back in her mind over every detail of their relationship, every-time they had spoken, every touch, every kiss. But she didn't cry. She couldn't cry. It was as though all her tears had been used up in the emotions of the last few weeks. She thought about Sebastian all the time, ached for him, longed for him, but she couldn't cry at all.

And she was much better now. The first week had been hard, but now she knew she was going to live. A broken heart wouldn't kill her. It would just wound her for the rest of time, making it impossible for her ever to feel true joy again. But she would go on.

It was a bright, cheerful day, just three days before

the wedding, and she was helping her father walk slowly out to take a seat in the courtyard, in the sun.

"Is that warm enough for you?" she asked as she bundled him into the chair set by the fountain.

"More than enough, daughter," James told her lovingly. "Where is Josefa?"

"Gone to market. There are so many things to do to prepare for this wedding." She patted his shoulder. "And that's where I'm going, too. I forgot to tell her to get more eggs. I'm going to have to go out and get them myself."

She started off. "I'll be back in no time," she called to him as she hurried away.

"Don't rush," he called after her. "I'll be fine here in the sun."

She stopped at the edge of the courtyard, looking back. A moment's queasiness came over her and she reached out to lean against the wall, holding a hand over her stomach. These waves of nausea were coming more often, and she knew what they meant. She glanced quickly to make sure her father hadn't seen. But what was the use of that? He would know soon enough. The whole town would know.

She closed her eyes for a moment, and then the feeling passed and she smiled. Sebastian's baby. She refused to regret it. If this was all she was to have of him, she would cherish this child as no other child had ever been cherished. She was only sorry that the shame would hurt her family. It would never hurt her, because she would refuse to accept it. She loved Sebastian. She would love his child. And that was all there was to it.

Taking a deep breath, she hurried off.

James Crafts sat back with his eyes half closed, listening to the birds chattering in the pomegranate tree. It was a lovely summer day, and he was thankful that he had it. He was a lucky man. He had so much, and that included the new life his children were making possible for him. If there was anything he had learned in his sojourn through this world, it was to be grateful for every day, for every good thing, and to dismiss the bad.

There was a clanking behind him. He turned, knowing it was the courtyard gate opening. Someone had neglected to lock it. He hoped it wasn't some back-alley hooligans bent on making trouble. There had been some reports lately, someone throwing eggs at the neighbors . . .

But no, this was no hooligan. It was merely that Spanish scoundrel Sebastian de la Cruz.

James stared at him coolly. "If you've come to see Marina, she's not here."

Sebastian nodded. "I know. I saw her leaving. I've been waiting for her to leave. It's you I want to talk to." He came close, but James didn't invite him to sit down. "We haven't spoken since the *rodeo*."

James nodded, still watching him without warmth.

"In fact, we haven't really talked since the day you found Marina's scarf in my quarters and thought the worst."

James stared at Sebastian, then gestured for him to sit down. "That is true," he said hoarsely. "I . . . I was shocked to see the evidence . . ."

"I'm afraid you may have misinterpreted the evidence," Sebastian broke in as he lowered himself to the bench facing James's chair. "She came to me the night you got the report that Jonathan was dead. She was distraught and needed comforting. And that was all

372

she got while she was with me that night."

James searched his gaze, nodding slowly. "I see," he said. "You must understand, Lieutenant, that I trust my daughter. I know she's not a foolish, flighty little thing." He shook his head. "Still, when one falls in love . . ."

Sebastian's eyebrow lifted. "Did Marina tell you that she is in love?" he asked as though it were some sort of distant philosophical point.

James shook his head. "She doesn't have to tell me a thing. I can see it on her face."

Sebastian nodded. "Do you find me an unsuitable prospect?" he asked simply.

James thought for a moment. "I find you an unwilling prospect," he said. "I haven't seen any indication at all that you want to marry."

Sebastian nodded, accepting that. "I've been in Yerba Buena for the last few weeks," he said. "I went to visit the governor."

"Ah."

"I asked that he help intercede with the general. I want to buy out my commission and be free of the Mexican Army as soon as possible."

"I see. And was he helpful?"

"Yes. He assured me it would be taken care of immediately."

"Congratulations."

Sebastian nodded, then went on. "Unfortunately, I had a second request which he was unable to fulfill."

"And what was that?"

Sebastian looked James full in the face. "I want a land grant. I want to take up ranching, and in order to do that, I need property."

"I see."

"But since I haven't done anything particularly note-worthy in my short stay in California, the governor couldn't see any reason to grant my wish."

James nodded slowly. "I have to say I agree with him."

"Oh yes. I really didn't expect to be handed a parcel of land outright. I was hoping I could bargain with the man. But it seemed there were no more grants available in this area."

James nodded. "I know we're pretty full up." His gaze sharpened. "And what will you do now?"

Sebastian smiled. "I know exactly the piece of land I want," he said slowly.

James blinked, hardly believing his ears. "You want my land . . . you want me to give you my land." He stared at the younger man, appalled.

Sebastian shook his head. "Not *give,* Señor. I will pay you for your land. It will take me time, but I will pay for every stone on the property."

James almost laughed, so astounded was he by the man's arrogance. "What makes you think I would be interested in such a bargain? I'm keeping that land for my children."

Sebastian nodded. "You have two children. You have two land grants. You're working neither one of them. The one I want is the smaller of the two. I respectfully suggest that you save the larger for Jonathan and sell the smaller to me."

James shook his head, frowning. "Why would I do that?"

Sebastian's head went back, his eyes hard as steel. "Because, *Señor,* I'm going to marry your daughter."

James opened his mouth and then closed it again without saying a word. The man was incredible. Finally he laughed, shaking his head in admiration. "So you want my land after all, just as they've been warning me. I heard you were already riding the borders, making plans, scheming to take over."

"No, *Señor.* I will admit, I was measuring your land. I was surveying it. I was planning every inch of it." He frowned, shaking his head. "I can't believe you have left it fallow for this long, when it has so much potential. But believe me, I wasn't interested in wresting the land from you by ensnaring your daughter in marriage."

James's mouth turned down at the corners. "Then explain to me just what you were doing."

"It began, *Señor,* purely as an intellectual exercise, I assure you. I found papers in your library regarding the history of San Feliz, and of your land. The papers followed the trail of ownership from the tribe of Indians who first used it as a resting spot when traveling north, to the mission *padres* who claimed it for Spain, to the governor when the mission lands were taken away, to when the acres were presented to you in recognition of services rendered to the Mexican government. It was a fascinating example of the history of this whole area. So, to amuse myself, I went to take a look."

James nodded. "They told me as much."

"I had no other interest in that land until I realized that I was going to have to marry Marina."

James cocked an eyebrow. *"Have* to marry her?"

He shrugged. "I love her. I want her with me. I no longer have any choice in the matter."

James hid a smile. "Does this mean you've given up on going back to Spain?"

Sebastian frowned thoughtfully. "Not altogether. I

must go back some day, just to settle affairs. But if the alternatives are Spain or Marina, I don't think you would be surprised to learn my choice." His eyes darkened. "I would do anything to keep Marina in my life. Anything."

James sighed and sat back, suddenly feeling more relaxed than he had in weeks. It would be hard to explain to anyone else why this match pleased him. After all, the Spaniard had revealed himself to be something less than honorable on some occasions. And his arrogance was beyond belief. Still, there was a strength to the man. That, combined with the sharp intelligence and love of learning he exhibited, made him rather more attractive than the average suitor for Marina's hand. And when you added to that the fact that Marina was crazy in love with the fellow, it all began to make a peculiar sort of sense.

"You do understand that the land runs along the Diaz property? I'm afraid there is going to be bad blood between the two of you for a long, long time if you do this."

"I understand that, and I think I can deal with it."

Yes, James was sure he could. He smiled. "You seem determined," he murmured.

Sebastian nodded. "Please understand me. I will take Marina, with or without the land. But I am sure you would rather have your daughter nearby than in some other part of California."

James shook his head, studying the Spaniard. "You've certainly got this whole thing worked out," he said, eyes glinting in admiration for the man his daughter was going to marry.

"Here." He stuck out his hand. "Let's shake on it."

When Marina returned from the market and checked on her father, he was dozing in the sun, looking remarkably relaxed and happy, she thought. She didn't have the heart to wake him.

Instead, she went to her bedroom and took off her bonnet, and then she saw the note lying on her bed. It was a piece of white paper, folded in half.

She stared at it for a moment, and her heart began to beat a rapid rhythm. Slowly, she picked it up and unfolded it.

"Marina — meet me at your father's land grant by the dry river."

There was no signature, and she didn't recognize the handwriting. A spark of hope flared in her chest, but she damped it down. This was no time to let herself anticipate things that could never be.

Perhaps it was someone with ideas for developing the land. Her father and brother had been talking about exactly that lately, making plans, drawing up projections. Maybe she should run out and see what this was about.

Checking to see that Josefa was back to take care of her father, she slipped out the back way and saddled her horse. All her predictions that they would lock her in by the hour had come to nought. No one had even suggested such a thing. In fact, they now seemed to look at her as more of an adult than they ever had before, deferring to her in certain aspects, asking her advice, seeking her opinion. That had never happened before. She rather liked it.

She rode slowly, enjoying the sunshine, the wind in her hair. It felt good to be out riding again. She'd spent too much time indoors lately.

She rode by the Delgado rancho, and then the Ortiz place. A row of children waved, and she waved back. And there in the distance was the land the government had given her father years ago.

The parcel was fronted by a stand of cottonwoods. She let her horse walk through them, and on the far side they found a big gelding tethered, munching on grass. There was no human in sight.

Marina got down off her horse, tied him up, and shaded her eyes, looking against the afternoon sun to try to see who had called her here.

"Hello," she called out, but there was no answer.

Then she looked up and noticed something moving on the crest of the hill that sat in the center of the land. She squinted, shading her eyes. There was a man doing something up there, but she couldn't make out his identity because of the sun behind him.

Her heart was beating a little harder. She started up the hill, going faster and faster. The way was rocky and she had to watch her step. There was no path. When she got to the top, she was panting and out of breath, and she shaded her eyes quickly to see who the man was.

It was Sebastian. Her heart stood still.

It was Sebastian, just as she had secretly hoped it would be. But he was paying no attention to her. He was busy dragging back the heel of his boot, making markings in the dirt.

She watched him for a few minutes, her heart full. It was enough just to fill her gaze with him, just to have him near, after she had been so afraid she had lost him forever. She feasted her eyes on his handsome face, his beautiful body. He was just the same.

And yet, somehow different. The scar was fading.

378

And he wasn't in uniform. Instead, he wore a white shirt with a deerskin vest and velveteen trousers with silver buttons up the seams.

"Sebastian," she called out at last.

But he still didn't answer. Putting up a hand as though to stay her while he finished his chore, he went on making the marks in the ground, and she frowned, trying to puzzle out what he was doing. It seemed to be some sort of plan.

"What are you doing?" she asked, unable to wait any longer.

He looked up, his hair falling over his forehead, and his eyes were brimming with humor as he came toward her. Taking her shoulders, he kissed her firmly, then drew back and took her hand.

"Come with me," he said, leading her to his dirt maze. "We'll go in the front door."

"What front door?" she asked, looking about with her brows knit together.

"Come into the parlor," he said, ignoring her question. "Here. What do you think of the view?"

She stood where he put her and looked out. The valley swept before her. She could see everything, out to the sea.

"It's beautiful," she said. "I never realized. . . ."

But he was already leading her off to another part of the maze. "The dining room," he said. "I want it big enough to seat huge family reunions."

"What?" She frowned at him, beginning to wonder if he had been drinking too much *aguardiente*.

"And the kitchen. I want an indoor kitchen. With two stoves."

She nodded blankly. "Very nice."

"Would you like a bathtub like the one we used

at the Sosa's?"

"I . . ." She remembered that night and slipped her hand back into his. "Of course."

He smiled, holding her hand to his heart. Then he was off again, leading her through the plan.

"The library will sit here. Although it will probably be years before we can afford to order any books."

She shook her head. "Sebastian, what. . . . ?"

"And this. . . ." He pulled her a few feet to the right. "This will be the bedroom for the first boy. The first girl will have this room." He pulled her further down the way. "And here. . . ." He spread his arms grandly, looking at her, then pulled her close and kissed her soundly. "This is the room where we will make all those little children," he said huskily. "What do you think?"

She stared up at him, too wary to let herself be happy just yet. "Sebastian, what does this mean?"

His kiss was warm and loving. "This means, my darling, that I am asking you to marry me. Will you?"

She shook her head. She'd never expected this. And she still didn't trust it. It was too much, too suddenly. "But what about Spain?"

His arms came around her and he held her tightly. "Spain can wait. We can go together some day." He kissed her again, lingering at her lips. "You haven't answered my question."

She pulled away from him, stepping back. Her gray eyes were huge, staring at him. "You want to marry me," she said softly, her face unconvinced.

He watched her, not smiling. "Yes, Marina, I want to marry you."

She blinked rapidly, then forced out the word, her voice shaking. "Why?"

380

"Why?" He frowned. "Why do you think?"

He started toward her, but she shook her head and took another step back, holding out her hand to stop him.

"Tell me . . . tell me why."

He was at a loss, palms open. Then he swallowed hard and looked down at the ground, his hands curling into fists. "I want to marry you, Marina Crafts, because. . . ." He took a deep breath and raised his gaze to hers. "Because I love you," he said, his voice cracking.

Tears welled in her eyes. Giving a cry, she rushed to him, throwing herself into his arms.

"Sebastian de la Cruz," she cried, tears streaming down her cheeks. "I will marry you. I love you more than life itself."

He held her close, as though his own life depended on it. "Marina," he said, his voice choked, "I never thought I would want to marry. But you've changed my life. I can't imagine going on without you."

"Good," she murmured, kissing his neck and snuggling against him. "Because my life would be over without you."

He kissed her again and again, and she began to wish the walls of his imaginary house were really in place.

"But Sebastian," she said, her hand to his face. "Why are you planning a house on my father's land?"

"Because I am buying the land from him," he said simply. "We need a place to put our family, don't we?"

She nodded. "You've talked to Papa?"

"Yes. We've worked it out."

She drew her head back and looked at him. "But Sebastian, tell me . . . how soon will this house be ready?"

He shrugged. "As soon as I can hire men to work. Why, *querida?*"

"Because. . . ." She smiled through her tears. "I think we are going to need that bedroom for our first son very soon."

He stared at her for a moment, uncomprehending. Then realization broke across his face like the sun coming from behind a cloud. "A baby?" he whispered. He glanced down at her stomach. "Already?"

She nodded, putting her hand there. "It's early to tell, but I think so."

"Marina." He crushed her to him, his joy overwhelming him. "I will love you forever."

"Sebastian," she murmured back, her eyes closed, loving him. "Forever won't be long enough."

DANA RANSOM'S RED-HOT HEARTFIRES!

ALEXANDRA'S ECSTASY (2773, $3.75)

Alexandra had known Tucker for all her seventeen years, but all at once she realized her childhood friend was the man capable of tempting her to leave innocence behind!

LIAR'S PROMISE (2881, $4.25)

Kathryn Mallory's sincere questions about her father's ship to the disreputable Captain Brady Rogan were met with mocking indifference. Then he noticed her trim waist, angelic face and Kathryn won the wrong kind of attention!

LOVE'S GLORIOUS GAMBLE (2497, $3.75)

Nothing could match the true thrill that coursed through Gloria Daniels when she first spotted the gambler, Sterling Caulder. Experiencing his embrace, feeling his lips against hers would be a risk, but she was willing to chance it all!

WILD, SAVAGE LOVE (3055, $4.25)

Evangeline, set free from Indians, discovered liberty had its price to pay when her uncle sold her into marriage to Royce Tanner. Dreaming of her return to the people she loved, she vowed never to submit to her husband's caress.

WILD WYOMING LOVE (3427, $4.25)

Lucille Blessing had no time for the new marshal Sam Zachary. His mocking and arrogant manner grated her nerves, yet she longed to ease the tension she knew he held inside. She knew that if he wanted her, she could never say no!

Available wherever paperbacks are sold, or order direct from the Publisher. Send cover price plus 50¢ per copy for mailing and handling to Zebra Books, Dept. 3864, 475 Park Avenue South, New York, N.Y. 10016. Residents of New York and Tennessee must include sales tax. DO NOT SEND CASH. For a free Zebra/ Pinnacle catalog please write to the above address.